# BREAKING FAITH
## By
## Joy Eileen

To Van's wife Dayna, you are amazing and I love you sooo much! I appreciate everything you have done to help me publish.

Smooshy kisses & Big Hugs

Published: Joy Eileen 2015:

Cover Design: Kristen Hope Mazzola
Cover Images:
File ID: 67255319 © Anna Ismagilova/ Dollar Photo Club
File ID: 68128919 © Kserina/ Dollar Photo Club
Formatting by: Kristen Hope Mazzola

Editing by:
Tracie Roe: Traciroe89@Yahoo.com
Kira Will: Kirawill68005@gmail.com

# DEDICATION:

To anyone who was strong enough to survive, and the ones who haven't realized their strength.

Table of Contents

# CHAPTER 1

"Oww, shit!" I cried as I pulled my oozing finger back and stuck it in my mouth.

Glaring at the offending messenger bag, or more specifically the felonious paper sticking out of it, I fought back the tears and expelled a bitter laugh.

My eyes stayed glued to the awful document that signified escape. How dare it hurt me! It was a paper replica of the person it was protecting me from, a façade of security, but in reality, nothing but pain.

I glanced back at my injured finger to see if any more blood had come trickling out. A thin red line appeared, nothing more. No rivulets of crimson, no summoning of vampires for an all-you-can-suck buffet, just a small droplet of blood, nothing major. I grabbed a tissue to wipe it away. Crisis averted. Life continued.

I snuggled further into my hoodie as the interior of my lime-green 67' Mustang cooled in the night air. My body begged me to turn on the heater. I refused, afraid of getting too comfortable.

I was parked in front of a typical biker bar. The wood exterior was stained with matter that would horrify even the most seasoned forensic team.

A large neon sign on the top of the bar announced its name, Ray's. It ignited the parking lot, bathing the closer cars in red. A marquee in the front boasted that Ray's was the home of the JackholeS, a popular Portland band.

Taking a deep breath, I tried to fill myself with fake confidence, hoping this time to succeed. I didn't.

I gave myself permission to dwell on Jason for five minutes. After that, I would file him away in the dark recesses of my mind, just like the paperwork for the restraining order buried in the county clerk's office.

Leaning back in the driver's seat, I welcomed the images of my past as they flashed through my mind. I watched my own personal horror movie. Significant moments were

5

highlighted, giving insight on how I ended up sitting in my car, outside a bar, broken and bruised.

When I received a scholarship out of state, excitement and heartbreak coursed through me. Oregon State University offered me an escape. The payment they required? I had to leave my dad.

My dad is a retired police chief, and my biggest supporter. My mom was the complete opposite, and couldn't handle motherhood. She was stuck in her high school mentality. On my fourth birthday she left, taking the amber-tinted bottles lining her bathroom sink with her.

After cleaning up my ruined party, my dad held me in a soul-crushing embrace, and told me it was us against the world. The older I became, the more responsibilities I shouldered, taking his statement to heart.

I could never be the typical teenager; my mommy-issues ran too deep. Parties, dances, and other rites of passage, which shepherd a teen into adulthood, were not high on my list of priorities.

Keeping busy with my school work, I avoided the pity-filled stares from my peers. I owned my pariah status with pride, never letting them know how self-conscious they made me.

My scholarship was awarded before graduation, mocking my life of teenage solitude. When I received the acceptance letter, panic sliced through me and I flat out refused to leave. After much coaxing and bribing, of the Mustang variety, I reluctantly agreed to go.

My freshman year was uneventful. Throughout the year I could be found in my dorm room studying. I wanted to make sure the university knew they weren't wasting their time and money on me.

During summer break, I got a job at the local coffee shop, Cool Beans. The extra money assisted in my one non-school related obsession: shoes.

I had a savings account my dad had set up for me as soon as the flake showed him the positive pregnancy test, but I was *paranoid to use it. Worried if I spent it on something frivolous, the universe would enact punishment. Guilt was not an emotion I wanted to surface when purchasing a new pair of heels; that would be tragic.*

*During my first shift at Cool Beans, I met Jason.*

*He had dark brown eyes that sparkled when he laughed, and sandy blonde hair chopped close to his head, reminiscent of newly sworn in police cadets.*

*I couldn't ogle the fine specimen in front of me since there was an irate middle-aged customer, with a raging case of short man syndrome, screaming at me. I accidentally put one shot of espresso in his coffee instead of the two he had ordered.*

*Gazing at the bulging veins popping out of the angry customer's neck, I remained patient, waiting for them to explode from the extreme strain they were under. His hair had successfully emulated a cul-de-sac, and the buttons around his enlarged middle, strained to stay together.*

*I apologized and remade his order when Jason came to my rescue. Jason spun Mr. One-Shot-Down around as if he weighed nothing. The guy spewed an anger-filled rant until he saw the size of Jason and reserved the rest of his words. His cowardliness caused me to stare at the floor to hide a smirk.*

*"Apologize to her," Jason commanded through clenched teeth.*

*The man turned bright red, refusing to do as Jason demanded. Using the most convincing smile I could muster, I sputtered, "No, no it's ok. I messed up his order."*

*"No," Jason declared, giving me a stern look, before turning his gaze back to the man he still had by the shoulders. "A missing shot is no reason to yell at a beautiful girl. Hell, she did your poor heart a favor."*

*The firm look Jason gave his prisoner made him turn an even brighter shade of red. Jason's hostage then noticed he held the attention of everyone in the coffee shop and struggled to get away. Jason just gripped him tighter.*

*I blushed after hearing this perfect specimen call me, of all people, beautiful. The captured customer muttered his apology, and only then did Jason release him. As soon as the apology left his mouth, my first angry customer turned around* and fled, not bothering to take the cup containing his now correct order.

"Thank you," I said to my hero, trying to stand up straight and exude fake confidence.

He smiled and I swear I heard angels sing, or orgasm, whatever fit. "You're welcome, but I don't think your 'thank you' will be enough for what I just did."

"Of course, your drink's on the house."

I moved to make his drink, the one he hadn't ordered yet. This made him throw back his head and laugh. The muscles in his neck bulged from his amusement, resembling the man he just released.

I gave him a puzzled look, confused by his laughter. He then asked me a question that threw my whole axis off balance. "What time do you get off..." He looked at my name tag and added, "Faith?"

"Uhmm, in four hours," I replied, looking at the clock behind the espresso machine, still baffled as to what type of thanks he thought he was entitled to receive.

He nodded and walked away. Right before he stepped out of the shop, he glanced at me with a wicked grin. "I'll pick you up in four hours. My name's Jason, by the way." He then winked and vanished.

My boss, Ginger, who had been watching with the rest of the customers, reached around to close my open mouth with her index finger.

"Did that just happen?" I whispered, ignoring everyone else, still looking at the empty doorway.

"Yep," Ginger responded, laughing and telling me to take a break.

In the bathroom I splashed cold water on my face, obsessing over every detail of our encounter.

Why me? I studied my face, yearning to find something, anything to validate Jason's interest. I shook my head, assured the answer would continue to elude me.

My dark brown hair was pulled up in a ponytail, giving an unobstructed view of my face. Thanks to Portland's fantastic weather, my skin had a pale hue to it, making my green eyes stand out, large and uncertain. The smattering of freckles on my nose were prominent under the fluorescent lighting.

I shook my head in disgust. Hell, if my own mother couldn't stand to be near me, there was no reason for someone like Jason to spend any time with me.

I left the bathroom frustrated. As the minutes ticked away, I found myself getting anxious. When my shift ended, I glanced around the coffee shop to check if he was there. I knew he wasn't, because I had scanned the room every time someone entered.

Of course he wouldn't show up. Someone as gorgeous as he was had no reason to go on a date with me. He was probably trying to get me to stop staring at him like some slack-jawed lackey.

I left the coffee shop feeling dejected and stupid for believing he meant what he said. As I headed to my car, I heard his deep voice behind me.

"Hey, you aren't ditching me, are you?"

Stunned, I turned to see my knight in coffee justice, leaning by the back entrance of the shop, his muscles doing that delicious bulgy thing. "Uhmm, no," I replied, while I face-palmed myself in my head.

I had a full scholarship, earned straight A's with a full load in my double major of Biology and Literature, but around him I became a bumbling idiot.

He hooked his arm around my shoulders and steered me toward his car, a silver Honda Civic. I'll admit it made me sad when I saw his car; it felt somewhat anticlimactic.

We went to dinner and talked, well, he talked the majority of the time. He acted interested when asking me questions to see if I fit in with his life, which I was desperate to do.

I convinced myself I didn't mind his hostile takeover of our dinner conversation. I'd never received attention from someone like Jason before. It was exhilarating and bewildering.

After dinner, we walked around. He became more interested in my life, allowing me to fill the rest of the walk with my interests. Driving back to the coffee shop, Jason's true personality surfaced. The moment I should have known I needed to end all contact with him.

A car cut him off and his face morphed into an angry red orb, the exact color of the guy he had berated that afternoon. He followed the wrongdoer, honking his horn, and screaming. The veins in his neck popped out so far I could almost trace the blood pumping through them.

The offender was an older gentleman. I knew this because when Jason drove on to the side walk, I got a good look at his terrified face. I was unsure which one I should have been more afraid for; they both looked as if they were on the verge of having a heart attack.

Once Jason had scolded the poor man, he calmed. He threw me a quick smile while turning the car around to head back to Cool Beans, which we had passed in the pursuit.

I had my hand poised on the door handle so I could get out as soon as we stopped. In the parking lot, I jumped out of his car and ran to mine, throwing the door open. My only thought was of escaping.

"Hey, wait!" He was quicker than I gave him credit for because he grabbed onto the door as soon as I had opened it, sandwiching me in between him and the car.

"I'm sorry. I overreacted. It just scared me; he could have hurt you." He ran a finger down my cheek, and I leaned into his touch.

"Don't do it again," I tried to scold him. The fact that I leaned into him with a goofy smile on my face somewhat undermined the severity of the reprimand.

"Promise." He leaned in and kissed me on the cheek. "Can I see you tomorrow?" His brown eyes were making me weak in the knees, and hot everywhere else.

"Yeah, I get off at five."

He leaned in closer, brushing his lips across mine. "I will see you at five tomorrow, Faith."

I nodded, not wanting to contemplate what I was getting into, telling myself he had a reasonable reaction.

Once he pulled out of the parking lot, I sat in my car breathing in through my nose and out of my mouth. I had a hard time pushing down the dread flowing through me. I allowed the explanation he was worried for my safety keep my apprehension at bay. Even though in the back of my mind, I knew this was a *bad sign.*

*Jason picked me up the next day, and the next several days after that. By the end of the week we were inseparable, and he had everyone in the coffee shop enamored.*

*I became swept up in the romance, and soon found myself unable to catch my breath from the whirlwind that was Jason. I pushed the road rage incident out of my head, convincing myself I overreacted.*

*The summer rushed by and I allowed myself to fall head over beautiful heels in love with Jason. It seemed we were together every waking moment.*

*When Jason's temper flared, I let him convince me it was because he thought I was in danger. I unplugged every bell and whistle going off in my head, blissful in their silence.*

*When summer ended, we were happy and in love. My mind refused to notice any other emotion.*

*We were registering for our classes when, I was on the receiving end of Jason's temper for the first time. Jason noticed the huge course load I signed up for, and he was furious. He screamed that I would never have time for him.*

*School, being important to me, made me stand my ground against Jason's demands. I refused to let him sway me to take on a lighter load, not wanting to stray from the path I had methodically laid out.*

*Jason stopped showing up at the coffee shop. Upset he wanted me to give up my schooling for him, I refused to be sad about his absence, or so I told myself. His tantrum irritated me, and I allowed my anger to burn away the pain.*

*Jason showed up the day before school started, carrying a bouquet of red roses. He fell to his knees, telling me how much he missed me and couldn't be separated from me a second longer.*

*Every woman's panties in the coffee shop became wet when he strolled in carting the obscenely expensive roses.*

*I flipped the breaker to stop the warnings from shrieking. Running into his arms, I kissed him and told him how much I loved and missed him.*

*Watching the women swooning for Jason in the middle of the shop made me realize how lucky I was he picked me. That night, I apologized and explained my actions were for our future.*

*During the semester I allowed myself to get swept up in the Jason vortex. His charm and good looks had my head in the clouds most of the day.*

*My next encounter with Jason's temper happened one slow afternoon at Cool Beans. While waiting on the only customer in the store, a handsome college boy, Jason came in.*

*The grin on his face was quickly replaced. Icy dread ran through my veins from the look his face transformed in to. I gave him an encouraging smile, wanting to convey I saw nobody else but him, but Jason was beyond my assurances.*

*Jason forced his body between the customer and the counter. I caught a glimpse of the patron's stunned expression just before Jason grabbed my face.*

*His fingers ground the sensitive flesh of my cheeks into my teeth, until I tasted the hot metallic tang of blood. Not releasing his grip, he pulled me forward, until I leaned over the counter, and he kissed me fiercely. "Hey baby, see if you can get off early. Then we can go to my place, and I'll get you off again."*

*Ginger chose that moment to walk in, oblivious to Jason's temper. She looked at the clock. "Go on, sweetie. We aren't busy."*

*Jason moved and smiled at Ginger, releasing my face at the same time. Glancing around, I noticed the accosted customer had vanished. The adoration on Ginger's face kept me silent. I felt like I was plunged into another reality, one where I was in the wrong instead of Jason.*

*Untying my apron, I decided I was done with this nonsense. Once outside, I was ready to unleash a fury-filled rant. Before I could expel my well thought out speech, Jason surprised me by asking me to move in with him.*

*Run! My brain screamed, but my heart screamed louder.*

*"I love you, Faith. Seeing that guy flirt with you made me crazy. Please move in with me, so I can take care of you."*

*My rant faded away as his eyes filled with tears. He chose the awkward girl with the crazy mother and over protective father. He chose me.*

I refused to move unless he flew home with me to meet my dad during winter break. We boarded the plane as soon as I finished my last class, three weeks later.

Jason was perfect. My dad was smitten with him, just like everyone else. As I snuggled in with my charmer on Christmas Eve, I wondered why I was so reluctant in our relationship.

Once home, we went straight to my dorm to pack. We both wanted to start the new chapter of our lives together as soon as possible. Being so enamored with love, I didn't comprehend the situation I had put myself into, until it was too late.

Our apartment quickly became a prison, and I would constantly try to fly under his anger radar. Luckily I was a quick study on what would make him go off on his tangents, and after a while, I mastered keeping his temper in check.

Soon, the next semester started, and once again I had a massive course load. Thankfully, so did Jason. I avoided him, as the pressure he was under made his temper simmer closer to the surface.

Jason snapped at the slightest provocation, and the master status I thought I earned was put to shame. The days blended together. My life consisted of school, work, and trying to figure out Jason's mood.

The semester ended, and it was time for Jason to graduate. I hoped with the stress of school removed, Jason's temper would mellow. I crossed my fingers as the thought went through my head for the hundredth time.

When I slid into the dress I had painstakingly picked out for the occasion, they were still crossed. The dress was black; the top was a halter style with a red belt across the high waist, the skirt flared out-ending just short of my knees. I put on a pair of fishnet stockings and matched it with bright red pumps.

*My hair and makeup were in perfect pin-up style. I thought I looked pretty good; a rare occurrence with my self-esteem.*

*In the room where Jason was tying his tie; I ran my hands up his back, settling them around his neck.*

*"Damn it, Faith! I'm trying to get ready." He shrugged my arms off, and I stepped away as humiliation, hot and prickly, crawled up my neck. His eyes softened when he turned. "You look amazing. I'm sorry for snapping at you, I'm just nervous." He grabbed me and kissed me hard, halting only when a knock sounded on the door.*

*My dad opted to stay in a hotel, and I was grateful he wasn't around to see Jason's temper flare. "You're breathtaking," he said, and swept me up in a hug, lifting me off the floor.*

*Jason emerged, a grin on his face. "Isn't she beautiful?" he asked my dad.*

*Blushing from the attention, I rushed them out of our apartment so I could watch my man graduate.*

*After the ceremony, where I came close to screaming myself mute, we went to dinner at an upscale restaurant. Unfortunately, Jason's parents joined us. This wasn't the first time I'd met them, and my impression still hadn't changed.*

*They were very stuffy people.*

*Jason's dad, Mr. Hutchingson, owned a large advertising agency. Now that Jason had graduated, he held the title of Junior Executive in the company. His dad had a harsh look on his face, and I imagined he would feel physical pain if he laughed.*

*Jason's mom was a slight woman and wore a face that looked as though she was having a constant affair with a lemon.*

*After dinner, I excused myself to escape Jason's rigid parents, and upon returning someone called my name. A boy in one of my classes sat at a nearby table, waving at me. Going over to greet him, I shot Jason a nervous glance.*

*He got up and gave me a hug, making me nauseous with Jason watching. I stepped back as fast as I could, my stomach threatening an upheaval.*

*"Hey, what are you doing here?"*

*Jason's smiled as he talked to my dad, but his attention never wavered from me. I pointed over to him and blew him a* kiss hoping it would placate his temper.

"My boyfriend just graduated," I answered, still smiling at Jason.

"Congratulations. I'm here with my family." He indicated the people sitting at the table next to him. I introduced myself with lightning speed before heading back to Jason.

When I reached the table, Jason clamped down on my hand, making me whimper. My dad nodded at Jason and he proceeded to kneel on one knee.

I went numb as Jason started his proposal.

Everything slowed. Jason's voice sounded distorted, and I had to concentrate to understand what he was saying. "Faith, I'm so happy you came into my life. Please make me the happiest man in the world and marry me."

He squeezed my hand so hard I ended up on my knees trying to lessen the pressure. Yanking my hand out of his, I flung my arms around his neck, kissing him as I whispered yes in his ear.

He put a large ring on my finger. My mind gave one last-ditch effort and screamed at me to run; I ignored it. Just when I thought I couldn't be more pathetic, I had sunk even lower.

My dad hugged me after we rose from the ground, tears shining in his eyes. "Now, he promised me he would wait until after your graduation before he takes you away," he sniffled in my hair.

"Oh, Daddy," I said, sobbing, letting my tears melt into his shirt.

Dinner was a blur as everyone extended their congratulations. His mom even managed to smile around her lemon.

Jason then made the comment, "We're going home to celebrate," putting extra emphasis on the word celebrate. My dad turned as red as the wine he just gulped down.

Later, while leaning against the kitchen counter at home, I surveyed the giant diamond gracing my finger. Jason strutted toward me, loosening his tie.

"You'll never take that off. That way everyone will know you're taken. Even when you dress like a whore, and I'm not around, that ring on your finger will let them know you're a taken whore."

My head snapped up, staring at him in horror.

"What? Don't act innocent. You were falling out of your dress, and don't think I didn't see you fawning all over that guy to make me jealous." He leaned into me until my back dug into the counter. "You're mine; don't ever forget that."

His fingers encircled my arms, digging into the soft flesh. I cried out in pain as he squeezed them. Blood rushed past my ears, deafening me. All I could hear was the roar of fear circulating through me.

He carried me to the bedroom, throwing me on the bed. I cried silently as he yanked my dress up and ripped my fishnets until they hung limp and ruined down my legs.

He pulled on a condom before shoving himself into me. I whimpered at the burning sensation the dry friction caused. He whispered I belonged to him and nobody else, over and over again in my ear.

My fear intensified the pain. I bit my lip to keep the cry of agony within, but it escaped, only to be muffled by the slapping of our skin violently colliding.

When finished, he rolled over and fell asleep, still clinging to me.

Tears tracked down my cheeks, soaking my pillow, before I passed out from exhaustion and humiliation.

The next morning, I woke up alone, as the events of the night bombarded me. Jason whistled in the kitchen, and the smell of bacon wafted through the air.

I hurt all over, my heart included. In the bathroom, I surveyed myself, acknowledging the nasty bruises marring my upper arms, and everywhere else.

I convinced myself nobody would believe Jason was capable of this type of violence. Who would believe me if I tried to shatter the illusion I helped create?

Throwing away the tattered fishnets, I pushed them to the bottom of the waste basket and added toilet paper to hide the evidence, not able to stomach the sight.

While showering I avoided the garish ring. I became nauseous every time I caught sight of it. Jason yelled at me to hurry up and get ready so we could eat before taking my dad to *the airport.*

*I put on more makeup than normal, hiding the puffiness of my eyes from my all night crying session. Dressed in a tank top and skinny jeans, I put on a pair of black pumps. I also snagged my fitted leather jacket out of the closet so I could wear it to hide the offending bruises.*

*"Hey, sleepy head," he said, coming up and hugging me, causing my body to scream in pain while my face didn't register a wince. He pulled back and examined the bruises on my arms. "You need to be more careful, clumsy. I hate seeing my girl's skin bruised, and I'm afraid when we tell your dad you fell, he'll think you're some battered woman."*

*He laughed at the audacity, while he ran his fingers through my hair and kissed me.*

*I put this on myself. Jason had manipulated everyone, myself included, to consider him the perfect guy.*

*"I will," I replied in a shaky voice, walking over to the chair with a plate of food in front of it.*

*"That's my girl," he said from behind me, squeezing my arms in the exact spot the bruises were.*

*My plate had a waffle in the shape of a heart, with bacon arrows shooting through it. I forced myself to take several bites, not wanting to anger him.*

*"Ready to go?" he asked after cleaning up, and helping me put on my jacket. "Don't be sad, we'll see your dad again soon."*

*I nodded, unable to form words as my heart squeezed with the pain of my circumstances.*

# CHAPTER 2

I blinked back to reality. The clock showed the five minutes I allotted myself had expanded into half an hour. My phone alerted me of the many missed calls and text messages I had, but I just ignored them.

I shoved the restraining order further into my bag, and the rest of our relationship back in a dark corner of my mind. Adjusting my hoodie, I felt secure with the fabric draped around me, as I stepped out into the night.

The laid back atmosphere of Ray's surprised me. From the outside, it looked like a rough and tumble biker bar, but the inside was inviting.

The dark wood of the bar wore its scars with pride. Every stool was occupied with drooling men attempting to get the bartender's attention. High tables and tall chairs decorated the main floor. They were full of women in tight fitting clothes, leaving little to the imagination.

In front of the dance floor, the stage was set for a show. The JackholeS played here on Fridays and Saturdays, as the marquee outside had stated.

The other side of the room had the typical bar sports: pool tables, dart boards, and a pinball machine I needed to claim high score on soon.

At a table near the side of the stage, my friends waved me over. As I approached them, I noticed the table behind them full of four perfect specimens of the male gender. Each one exemplified different traits that would make any female's panties catch fire, just to have it doused from the dampness to follow.

My hibernating vagina shrugged off sleep to get a look at them before retreating back into her cave. I hadn't been attracted to anyone since I started dating Jason, and seeing how well our relationship had gone, she no longer got excited. I refused to trust myself when it came to the male species.

Jason's jealousy had put my vagina into submission. An

orgasm? That's a mythical creature, right?

The first guy was body-builder huge. He had a shaved head and wore a tight fitting shirt, with the sleeves cut off, molded to his chiseled abdomen. I wondered if he could wear sleeves with the anaconda-like limbs hanging from his shoulders.

Tattoos ran up both of his arms. His presence made me timid. If Jason were his size, I would have never lasted through one of his tirades. His warm hazel eyes radiated sincerity. Even with all the piercings, tattoos and muscles he couldn't conceal his warm nature.

Thinking only of the pain he could inflict, I was ashamed with myself for the snap judgment I made on Mr. Snuggles.

Mr. Snuggles talked to a guy with a mop of curly brown hair. When he pushed the disheveled mop back, I caught sight of his face. A big smile lit up his honey colored eyes as they exuded mischief.

His caramel-colored arms were covered in more tattoos than Mr. Snuggles. The theme on his arms could be described as boobs, and then bigger boobs. He wasn't as muscular as Mr. Snuggles, and I could tell he used his charm to get his way.

The guy next to the curly haired Mr. Mischief, had long dark hair hanging past his shoulders. He kept running a hand through it as he studied a notebook in front of him.

His hunched back did nothing to diminish his athletic build. I couldn't see any visible tattoos, or his eyes for that matter, as they were preoccupied with whatever he was reading, securing his nickname as The Professor.

The last of the foursome left me breathless; he was gorgeous. This time my vagina not only woke up to get a look, but ran to her closet to find her sluttiest outfit.

My nipples, not wanting to be outdone, pressed against my bra and aimed for his mouth. Dark sunglasses covered his eyes, but from what I saw, he was every girl's wet dream.

He had a natural tan, not an easy task in Portland, where most of the residents are many shades of pasty. His full brooding lips made me want to pull them into my mouth before they roamed over my body, the facial hair surrounding his perfect lips was too scruffy to be called a five o'clock shadow. He was sin.

His messy dark brown hair looked as if a woman ran her hands through it, tugging at it in the throes of an orgasm. A black shirt hugged his body, making a pang of lust shoot through me. His body reminded me of a predator, long and sleek. The definition etched through his shirt had my tongue darting past my lips without permission from my vacated brain.

After my blatant perusal of his body, I looked up to see his lips quirked. I didn't know if it was toward me or something else, as his glasses made it impossible to tell.

My vagina was wide awake now; the electric current I felt upon seeing him resuscitated her more efficiently than crash paddles.

My brain made a valiant effort of escape as an apology for its abandonment as I stared at Mr. Sex-in-a-bar. Shaking my head, I walked over to Jessie, Amy, and Trent; my three best friends.

He must have thought I was coming toward him because he straightened in his chair. My steps faltered, not having enough brain power to walk and be in his presence at the same time.

His stare made me hot in my hoodie, and for the first time since putting it on, I didn't feel sufficiently shielded. My eyes traveled back to my friends. The sight of them put my emotions at war. Tonight, I would confess the dark secret I had kept from them.

Thoughts drifted to our first meeting. The reminder of the fateful night they came into my life quieted my nerves. I was positive they wouldn't abandon me.

*We met almost two years ago, after I was assigned to a study group in one of my more grueling classes. I pleaded with the professor to excuse me, but he refused to budge. Terrified, I went home to face Jason's wrath. Astonishingly, he understood.*

When I had to miss one of his work functions for our first group meeting, I received my punishment.

Jason yanked me by the hair, making me tell him I was his and nobody else's. He forced me to my knees, thrusting himself between my lips. Jason rode my mouth until satisfied I was marked for the night.

"I can't lose you, Faith. I love you so much." He pulled me to his chest, hugging me tight. My heart, which I thought had been obliterated, shattered.

"I know you love me, Jason. I'm not going anywhere."

I was late to our first meeting because of my discussion with Jason. Amy was the first to see me that night at the coffee shop. She swung her licorice at me, pointed to the seat next to her and ordered me to sit, which I did. For someone so petite, she packed a punch.

Amy was a tiny Chinese girl with dark hair that hung at an angle around her heart shaped face. Her bob was in constant motion due to her endless supply of energy.

She was eating candy non-stop; red licorice and Skittles were her drugs of choice. Her crude statements shocked me every time they came out of her sugar-lined mouth, and she burrowed her way into my heart in seconds.

Amy introduced me to Jessie, the next in our group. Jessie had the face and body of a supermodel. I wanted to hate her on principle, but couldn't because she was a sweetheart. I knew we would be friends forever.

Trent was the last of our group. He was handsome, in a boy-next-door way. With his sandy blonde hair sticking up around his head, the black-framed glasses he wore magnified his intense brown eyes.

Instead of studying, we ended up talking.

Amy was on an academic scholarship and majoring in Biology. She grew up in New York. I surmised this from her accent that became more pronounced when she got excited, which with her constant candy buzz, was often.

Jessie was an only child who grew up in Texas. Her parents owned a bar that had been in her family since her great-grandpa had established it. Jessie admitted when she moved to Portland, she sought out a position at a bar, explaining it made *her less homesick.*

*Her eyes filled with tears as she confessed she spoke to her parents weekly. She struggled being so far away, and often considered moving back home to finish school. I empathized with her, telling her this was the first time I'd been away from my father as well.*

*Trent grew up in Portland, and his parents had attended Oregon State. They actually met in one of their mutual classes. He was enrolled in the university before the ink was dry on his birth certificate.*

*Trent had two brothers, one older who had finished college at Oregon State, and a younger one being prepped to enter his college career there in four years.*

*By the time I finished telling them about my romance with Jason, I'm sure they had a crush on him. Enjoying the adult interaction, which didn't include Jason, I lost track of time. Looking up when someone approached the table, I saw Jason standing in front of us.*

*I jumped up to kiss him, getting a head start on easing his temper. Jason was his charming self and had them eating out of the palm of his hand. All except Jessie. She kept shooting Jason a suspicious look.*

I must have slowed considerably as I reminisced of our first fateful meeting all those months ago, making Amy impatient. She ran over and gave me a quick hug before stuffing a licorice stick in my mouth. Dragging me toward the table, she was oblivious to my discomfort from the bruises covering my body.

Mr. Sex-in-a-bar was still staring at me, his lips turned into a frown, making me change his name to Mr. Moody. The way he looked at me, I was positive he saw through my shield. My vagina, not caring about my comfort, begged me to go suck on his turned down lips.

"Where have you been? We've been waiting for you. We ordered you a drink, but the ice melted, so you need to drink it quick so we can order you another one." In true Amy fashion, she didn't stop to take a breath.

When we reached the table, I laughed at what had to be Amy's drink. It was the only one with a licorice stick for a straw, the real straw on the table looking dejected.

"Sorry I'm late," I said.

Jessie gazed at me, and it was time to come clean. Right before I opened my mouth, a drunken lady, eyeing the perfection of the table behind us, walked into me and spilled her drink all over my hoodie.

"Oh, sorry," she slurred. Her friends were in hysterics. She shrugged, retreating back over to them, her mission abandoned.

I was in shock as the icy liquid seeped into the material surrounding me. The insane impulse to run to my car and drive flashed through my mind. I thought I wanted to explain everything, but the longer I stood there-the more I wanted to run.

Jessie got up and grabbed my hand. "Come on. I have an extra Ray's shirt in my locker," she said, while pulling me to the back of the bar toward the breakroom.

I followed Jessie, refusing to cry, if I started, I would never stop. She handed me a form-fitting black shirt with Ray's embroidered across the bust. Backing away from the revealing garment, I spotted a man's t-shirt draped across a chair. It had Bouncer written across it, and I reached for it, frantic for a new shield.

"I'll take this one," I said, and headed toward the bathroom.

I rushed inside the nearest stall, pushing past several intoxicated women. Not wanting to see my damaged arms, I threw on the shirt. The shirt was a men's 3X, and the sleeves went past my elbows, effectively hiding the bruising on my arms.

Jason knew where to leave a bruise so they could be hidden with little effort, or at least he did until last night. That's when I noticed dark finger-shaped imprints circling both wrists, mocking my plight.

How could I have missed those? So much for Jason being discreet.

I tucked both of my arms inside the sleeves. Pushing the door open with my back, I looked like I was doing a poor imitation of a T-rex.

Drunken women shouted their orders at me, mistaking my ridiculous outfit for a waitress uniform. Not one to have trouble keeping orders straight, I tucked them into my head to help out the frantic waitress.

I felt Mr. Moody's eyes watching me as I approached the table. His lips quirked, in amusement and curiosity at my state of dress.

As his gaze burned through my body, I focused on my friends staring at me as if I'd lost my mind. Seeing as how I was wearing an enormous t-shirt, with my arms tucked into it so only my hands were visible, I figured I was close.

Jessie opened her mouth, and I chickened out, wanting to prolong my admission a little longer.

"What's the bartender's name?" I blurted out.

Jessie glared at me, and I was afraid she was going to push it. Shaking her head, she answered, "Ryan."

Ryan had dark brown eyes that stood out from the black eyeliner surrounding them. Her hair was cut so the front was shorter than the back, with stripes of hot pink running through it. Her eyebrows were plucked with precision, a ring flashing in one of them. At that moment, she was trying to calm the distressed waitress.

Figuring yelling would be the lesser of two evils, I shouted, "Hey, Ryan!"

Her eyes widened in amusement as she took in my appearance. I glanced at our table, spying a number on the edge of it. Checking out the guys' table behind us I saw how the numerical system worked.

Ryan walked off. A customer at the other end of the bar flagged her down while drooling at her butt, dismissing me.

"Table sixteen needs another pitcher of beer; they didn't know what kind, but said you would know, a Cadillac margarita, and an order of french fries. Table eighteen needs another round of apple martinis and wanted to know if you could do an order of cheese sticks for six instead of four. Table twenty wants another two pitchers and a round of Jaeger shots, and...." I glanced around at the tables and noticed Mr. Mischief finishing his beer, while staring at me in all my crazy glory. "Table thirteen needs another round."

"Are you fucking with me?" Ryan asked, eyeing me to see if my ability to remember the orders shouted at me was real.

The poor waitress wailed. She whipped off her apron, threw it on the bar and screamed, "I quit," as she made a hasty exit.

Ryan went to call her back, but shook her head and began filling the orders I shouted out to her.

One of the tables I just ordered for whistled and hooted like they had witnessed me perform a miracle, and exclaimed I was *the man*!

I smiled, but it disappeared when I remembered what I was here to do.

Amy bounced on her seat, smiling so wide her eyes were almost gone. "That was awesome," she stated, and dove into her purse to pull out a handful of Skittles and shoved them in her mouth.

Trent had a look of awe on his face, making me uncomfortable.

Jessie let the questions in her eyes go for a minute. How long the reprieve would last? I didn't know, but I planned on exhausting it.

"Well, are you going to deliver all of those drinks?" Jessie asked.

I balked at the pointed look she gave my hidden arms. I hadn't thought of that, and searched the bar hoping to be saved by another waitress. Hell, even Jessie worked here; maybe she would take pity on me. Seeing the question in my eyes she shook her head.

"Oh, heck no, I'm not working tonight. I took today off."

The table behind us harassed her, except for Mr. Moody, who stared at me through his darkened buffer.

"Come on, Jessie, serve us. You know you're our favorite waitress," Mr. Mischief said. "I might have to change my mind though." He gave me a wink.

The Professor, not looking up from his notebook, hit

him on the back of the head to break his heated stare. "Hey!" Mr. Mischief cried, pushing him with his shoulder.

Not fazed in the slightest, The Professor continued to study his notebook. "That hurt," Mr. Mischief grumbled, rubbing the back of his head.

Jessie leaned over and smacked him, telling him to behave. That got Mr. Moody to chuckle, and the low rumble made my whole body smolder. His straight white teeth made a cameo appearance and my panties dampened from the sight. My vagina, now in full slutty attire, pleaded with me to go grind on him like a cat in heat.

Watching his tongue as it traced his top lip caused my mouth to go dry, and other places to become soaked. I sucked in a sharp breath, knowing the cause for spontaneous combustion was Mr. Moody's tongue. He chuckled, and I realized I was staring again.

Jessie turned me away. She touched a sensitive part of my arm, causing me to jump from the unexpected contact. I knocked into an older waitress who had two shots on her tray. The first one toppled over, emptying its contents on the corkboard lining while the other rocked before steadying.

"I'm so sorry." I was horrified at how the night had progressed.

"What's going on?" Jessie demanded.

I closed my eyes, still facing the waitress. My reprieve from Jessie's questioning was over.

"I'll give you fifty dollars for the shot I spilled, and the other, if you let me drink it while you go get another round and deliver the drinks I just ordered," I begged the waitress.

Her skin had a leathery quality to it, and her blond hair was pulled back in a low ponytail, her dark roots visible, but her eyes were soft and kind. "Ok hon, don't worry about paying for the shot, but how are you going to take it without your arms?"

Already humiliated, I decided I might as well make my quota for the month.

Bending over, I wrapped my lips around the top of the glass. Once secured, I threw my head back, letting the liquid burn a path to my stomach. The guys at the table behind us clapped at my performance. I dropped the shot glass on the tray, not making eye contact with the waitress, afraid to see pity reflected in her knowing eyes. She patted me on the head before turning away.

Jessie spun me around and glared. "You're going to talk to us."

Each of my friends wore matching expressions of worry. I could feel a heated stare focused on me from the table behind us.

"Ok," I sighed. "I have to tell you something. I need you to promise you won't say a word. If you start in, I'll leave and cut off contact with all of you." Tears threatened to spill, and I blinked rapidly until they were no longer blurring my vision.

Amy was the most subdued I had ever seen her. The energy normally humming through her was restrained as she nodded her head in agreement. "Promise," she said, gnawing on her licorice.

Trent conceded after a silent stare down. I dragged my gaze to Jessie. Her cooperation was the one I was concerned with, and sure enough my eyes were met with a defiant stare. I quirked an eyebrow at her, knowing the gesture annoyed her because she couldn't do it.

Amy bounced in her chair with less enthusiasm while Trent nursed his beer. "Oh come on, Jessie, just agree so we can start having fun," Amy said in an exasperated tone, slapping her in the arm with a licorice stick before popping it into her mouth.

"Fine," Jessie agreed, an angry stare stuck on her face.

"Not a word," I reiterated, as I lifted my multicolored arms out of my shirt.

Amy stopped her incessant buzzing, her eyes narrowing into slits. Trent's eyes went wide with questions, then denial, then anger. He clenched his beer before pounding it back, gazing at the table, unable to meet my eyes or arms, or any other part of me.

"Shit! I knew it," Jessie exclaimed, showing how upset she was. Being the consummate southern belle, we had never heard her swear. She opened her mouth, and I gathered my wet hoodie ready to leave.

It was hard to admit what I had lived with, but I couldn't have them judging me. That was my job, and I was up for employee of the year.

"Wait, I'm sorry. Don't leave," Jessie cried, getting out of her chair to block my escape. "I knew," she admitted, her eyes filling up with tears. "I tried so many times to get you to confide in me. You're my best friend."

"I can't believe I fell for his charming bullshit; I'm going to kill him," Amy stated. Her New York accent became thick with the threat as her tiny frame vibrated with anger.

"NO!" I shouted. I softly added, "Stay away from him. He's dangerous. If he knows you know, he no longer has to hold up his good guy pretext."

My face paled as I realized what I said was the truth. By telling them, I had put my friends in jeopardy. I was being selfish, wanting their support, not thinking of the consequences.

"I have to go," I said, putting my hand across my stomach, as it clenched in pain. "I put you guys in danger. Oh My God, what have I done?" I stumbled backwards in horror.

"Stop." Amy's voice was low but full of authority. "We love you. Don't worry about us, and DO. NOT. Try to skip out on us. We'll find you. We'll get through this together."

She gave me a firm look before putting her licorice straw in her mouth and taking a drink. Trent stared at his beer.

"We will get through this. I just can't believe you didn't tell me." Jessie's eyes brimmed with tears, and I hated myself even more. My friends were putting themselves in danger for me, not caring about the repercussions.

"I had to do it by myself to make sure I was strong enough," I rambled, not wanting Jessie to feel bad.

"You don't have to do this alone. Ugh, your pride's going to kill you." When those words slipped from her mouth, any trace of color leached from her face.

"Don't," I commanded, reaching out to her, refusing to be coddled. "I took out a restraining order on him today. Everything's packed in my car. I ran out the door as soon as he left the parking lot. I'm done with him. Well sort of," I confessed, biting the inside of my bottom lip.

"What do you mean, sort of?" Jessie growled, throwing her arms up in exasperation.

"Well, in order for the restraining order to become legal, he needs to be served, which I cannot do." I bit on the inside of my lip again.

"I'll do it," the three of them said in unison.

"NO!" I cried, not caring if the whole bar became engrossed in my drama. I needed to protect them. Jason's rage-filled eyes flashed through my mind, making me even more determined to keep them safe.

"Please, promise me you'll stay away from him. I'll hire a big tough guy to serve him when he comes back. Stay away from him." I was on the verge of hysteria, my arms flailing around as I made my point.

Jessie's eyes widened. She pushed up my sleeves, revealing the extent of my injured arms. Someone sucked in a breath, and I was fairly certain some profanities were thrown out around me. Revealing my bruised arms secured my future without Jason; there was no turning back now.

I was about to receive one of Jessie's long winded lectures, but she held it back. "Where's the papers?" she asked.

I nodded toward my bag.

"Ok, good," she replied as if she was approaching a frightened animal. "When will he get back?"

I shrugged, trying to remember if he told me. She shot me an aggravated look at my lack of response.

"I don't know. I haven't answered my phone all day," I admitted.

"What?" she hissed, putting her fingers on my chin so I looked her in the eyes. "He'll know something's happening. He always calls you before he boards."

"Oh My God," I whispered, realizing my crucial mistake.

I never missed one of his calls, not wanting his temper to get too elevated, and of all days, I ignored him on the day I made my escape.

I raced toward my messenger bag, trying to think of an excuse. Before I reached it, the door of the bar banged open, hitting the wall from the force pushed on it.

"Faith," Jason called from across the bar. His smile was

at full watt tonight. Dread enveloped me.

I ruined my chance. The only escape I would be granted now would be when he ended my life.

"Hey, are you ok, honey?" He held a bouquet of red roses in his hand, moving toward me as I began to sway.

Before I blacked out, I was bumped in the shoulder, jarring me into taking a breath and providing my body with the oxygen it craved.

The four guys from the table behind us were now standing in front of me like a beautiful testosterone-wall of protection. Even with the turmoil I was in, my vagina couldn't help but make me appreciate their finer *assets*.

"Jessie, why don't you go introduce Ray to his newest waitress. I just text him to let him know you were headed back to his office. From her performance with the orders, and since he just lost a waitress, I don't think he'll have any trouble getting her on the schedule. We have some stuff to take care of before we go onstage," Mr. Moody said.

His voice was low and menacing. My vagina tossed off her outfit for easier access.

"Ok, Kill," she replied.

I jerked to look at Jessie, who had just commanded Mr. Moody to murder my ex.

"Don't kill him, I'm not worth it," I whispered to his back, touching the hard muscles underneath.

His body tensed at my touch. I then noticed all four of them were chuckling. Was my drama really that amusing? His laugh was the easiest to pick out, the sound of it caused my inner thighs to catch fire and my knees to go weak.

Jessie gave me a sad smile, but humor sparkled in her eyes. "No, Faith. That's his name. Well, it's Killian, but everyone calls him Kill, and yes, you are worth it. It's him," Jessie said, pointing her head toward Jason, "that's not worth it."

"Oh," was all my numb mind could come up with as she dragged me away.

We passed the kitchen, and I hardly registered the delicious aromas wafting from it while my mind tried to catch up.

What was going to happen to Jason?

Was I still free?

We entered a small office where an older gentleman pored over a schedule. His silver hair reflected the light above him.

"Hey, Ray, I found a solution to your waitress shortage. Well... it was Kill's idea. Her name's Faith."

Ray looked up, his eyes a light shade of blue. They sparkled when he smiled. He had a kind, weathered face.

"Hi, I'm Ray. Kill just text me and gave you a glowing recommendation. He told me what you did out there with the orders young lady; I'm impressed. Welcome, Faith. And thank you. Ryan was about to resort to elderly abuse if I didn't find a competent waitress soon."

# CHAPTER 3

As we finished up the hiring process, I tried to express my gratitude to Ray; getting out of my old job was a necessary step to my independence.

I was puzzled, but grateful Kill vouched for me. I couldn't help wondering what happened outside with Jason, but Ray and Jessie kept distracting me, making it hard to concentrate. This could all be in vain if Jason charmed his way out of the trouble I put him in.

Ray received a text and frowned. Panic shot through me, afraid he had heard about the drama I brought with me and would snatch the job back. I was prepared to beg to keep my new position, but his frown disappeared.

"Hold on, Faith. Kill isn't quite done."

My heart skipped a beat as I wondered how Kill was handling Jason. Ray's phone dinged again, and his shoulders relaxed.

"You're all clear to go and party it up tonight. Party hard, because you're now the possessor of a grueling job as of tomorrow night. I hear the boss is a tyrant."

It may have seemed silly a waitressing job gave me such relief, but I knew I needed this. It brought me one step closer to becoming whole.

I felt safe here, at least until I remembered what was waiting for me. I hoped Kill and the rest of the testosterone wall were able to handle Jason without too much grief.

Jessie gave me a reassuring smile as she put her arm around my waist. "It's all good now, Faith."

I wanted to ask her how she could possibly know, but my ears were assaulted with wild screams.

My four saviors were onstage; the dance floor was now inundated with alcohol-infused women screaming and writhing for the band's attention. The music temporarily made me forget about Jason as I thought back to what I had heard about the JackholeS.

I should have guessed the boys at the table were the band who had all of Portland's panties damp from the mere mention of their name.

Mr. Snuggles was the drummer. His tattooed arms moved as if they had a life of their own. With a smile on his face, he looked content to be exactly where he was.

The guitar player was none other than Mr. Mischief. His face lit up with humor and you could tell he loved the attention being thrown at him; literally thrown at him, as one of the drunk women tossed her panties toward him.

The panties hit his guitar, and he plucked them off, burying his nose in them. This created a maelstrom of noise as the rowdy women went crazy. I rolled my eyes at his theatrics, laughing at his energy.

The bassist was The Professor. With his face no longer buried in a notebook, I could finally see his hazel eyes. Every time he looked up, women screamed at him in an attempt to keep his beautiful face directed forward. It didn't sway him, and no matter how loud they were, he always returned to his instrument.

Then there was Mr. Moody. He looked bigger than life onstage as he cradled the microphone. He moved with panther-like grace, and the crowd, which I thought was already rambunctious, went riotous.

A dimple appeared on his cheek, cinching his beauty to perfection. His dark glasses had been removed, revealing his light green eyes; they exuded sexual energy and confidence, causing goose bumps to break out over my body.

Just one look from those hypnotic eyes, and you knew he could fulfill your every desire, and some you didn't even know you had.

"Thank you all for coming out tonight," Mr. Moody said into the microphone, a half-smile in place.

The crowd went silent to hear what he had to say, but then erupted back into a cacophony of noise.

The deep timbre of his voice bee-lined straight to my vagina, making her pant and search for chocolate. I had to hold back a groan as his words caressed my skin. The microphone amplified his words, hitting every one of my erogenous zones.

We were still behind the bar staring at the magnificent foursome when Jessie interrupted. I was embarrassed when she broke into my inappropriate thoughts.

Instead of wondering what had happened with Jason, my thoughts were centered on the gorgeous rock god in front of me. What the hell was wrong with me?

"The bassist's Daniel Copper. Everyone calls him D." She nodded her head to the man I had dubbed The Professor.

"The guitarist's Jet Stone."

I gave her an incredulous look, making her smile.

"His real name's Jetson. Don't ever mention it, or he'll make your life a living hell. He made a waitress run out of here in tears when she called him by his real name by accident. The drummer's Donovan Gilmore, Van for short."

Her eyes went soft when she mentioned Van, and I wondered if she didn't have a thing for him. It made me laugh to think of the southern belle who refused to curse, falling for a tattooed bad boy.

"And you've already met Killian Taylor."

We stood and listened as they sang a song I'd never heard, but from the crowd's participation, I must have been the only one. I was amazed at how good they were. They complemented each other perfectly, and Kill's rich voice provided my ears with a mythical creature called an orgasm.

While performing a fast rock song, the whole bar pulsed with energy, making the performance extraordinary.

"They're really good." I couldn't hide the surprise in my voice. I wasn't expecting to hear such an amazing band in a tiny bar, and I now understood the hype. Seeing the fans scream and sing along as they segued into their next song, I didn't expect them to have gigs at Ray's much longer.

"Yep," Jessie replied, popping the P at the end. "They're getting offers for bigger venues. It won't be long before those boys are plastered everywhere," Jessie said, reiterating what I had just been thinking.

The pang of jealousy that shot up my spine was unexpected, and certainly unwanted.

Kill strutted across the stage, making the women in the

34

crowd who had clamored and fought to get up front feel vindicated. He looked down at them and gave them a half-smile while he sang, making them swoon from his attention.

He was born to be a frontman, and he would be packing arenas soon. As Kill belted out the last vocal of the song, the cheers increased along with his voice, until it hit the apex and fell away; the band, not missing a beat, followed his voice faultlessly.

Kill waited for Van to go into the next song and frowned when the drummer didn't start the intro.

"What the fuck, Van? Let's go; these people want to see us play, not diddle ourselves." He looked at the crowd with a panty-melting smirk. "The diddling's for later."

The women in the crowd went wild and more undergarments were thrown onstage.

Kill laughed and picked up one particularly skimpy hot pink thong. He put his hand over his face to shield his eyes searching the crowd for the owner. Kill held the panties up in the air. "You come find me after the performance."

The women in the crowd once again erupted, making me roll my eyes. My stomach plummeted when I saw what a jerk Kill was. It figures I would be attracted to him. My taste in men was abysmal.

D walked over to his microphone on center stage. Kill gave him the death glare. I upped my opinion of him from jerk, to jerk with a temper, and promised to stay away from him. My vagina be damned.

"Hey everyone," D addressed the crowd shyly.

Women expressed their love for him, making his cheeks turn beet red. Wondering what was happening, I stood up, looking over the sea of silicone and spandex.

When D looked straight at me, I had the same instinct as before; to jump in my car and drive as far away as I could. D's face became an even darker shade of red as the attention became focused on him, but his eyes stayed fixed on me.

"We have a new waitress as of tomorrow," he stated, and I considered crawling under the table.

"And she's fucking hot," Jet added, causing some snickers in the crowd.

35

I turned to leave. Ray would understand when I didn't show up to work the next day. Jessie halted my retreat by placing a shot in my hand, which I immediately slugged back, coughing as the harsh liquid slid down my throat.

Van got up from behind the drums and pushed Jet away from the microphone, muttering something.

"What these two dumbasses are trying to ineloquently say is we have a new waitress. I'm sure most of you witnessed what happened earlier, and how upset the douchebag was when we handed him the restraining order."

Jessie took the shot glass from my hand, and replaced it with another, which I gulped down, breathing through the burn.

"He knows not to fuck with her, or he'll be messing with us." Van looked pointedly at me, his eyes softening, as the crowd went insane. "I have sisters, and would want someone to help them if I wasn't around."

Jessie replaced my shot, and this time the fire was easier to deal with.

"We all have things going on in our life, and having people there makes it easier. We want you to feel safe here..."

He looked at me, and Jessie filled in the blank. "Faith."

Van smiled. "Faith, you're a part of Ray's family, and we protect family."

The crowd let out a collective sigh. Some of the faces looked at me with support, while others were etched in pity, with a sprinkling of jealousy.

I told myself I didn't care that the whole time his band was initiating me into Ray's, Kill looked like he could live up to his name. His jaw was clenched so tight his dimple was visible, and fuck me if he wasn't even more gorgeous.

I blew a kiss to the band. The crowd was so loud they wouldn't have been able to hear a verbal response. Van winked at me, and Jet made a crude gesture with his hips, while D just nodded his head.

I sat down, the alcohol making my limbs feel fluid. Jessie kissed my cheek, sighing that Van was so sweet, as she went to her chair.

Trent smiled at me and winked when we made eye

contact. I looked away just in time to see Amy bound out of her chair and kiss me on the opposite cheek. "See? Everyone loves you, Faith."

Trent nodded at Amy's statement. I tried to remember why I should be worried when it came to him, but the alcohol flowing through me caused it to keep slipping by me.

I took a drink of the margarita that magically appeared in front of me.

Amy, unable to sit any longer, pulled me to the dance floor. I followed, grinning; the alcohol made it easy to forget everything for the moment. It had been so long since I could just let go.

The thought of Jason made my stomach roll as reality tried to push into my drunken fog. I ran back to the table, slamming the rest of my margarita, before turning to go back to Amy.

Jessie looked over at me and smiled. Trent put his hand on my shoulder before I could walk away. "Maybe you should slow down, Faith. You don't normally drink, and you've been putting them away."

Jessie removed Trent's hand. "Let her have tonight. You know if she doesn't get hammered she's going to think about Jason."

His face was not convinced as he chugged his beer and asked me if I wanted to dance.

The JackholeS were incredible, making me crave the dance floor. Jessie stopped Trent, and I shrugged as I made my way toward Amy who bounced around the dance floor like a pinball on crack.

Once I caught up to her, I was laughing so hard my knees were giving out, and I had to grab a hold of my amped up friend to stay upright.

Amy threw her head back, laughing along with me as we swayed together in a drunken rhythm.

Just then, the JackholeS switched to a slower song. Amy and I danced like seventh graders, giggling and leaning into each other more for stability than anything else.

Trent came over in the middle of the song, shaking his head.

"Dance with us," Amy said, slinging her arm around Trent.

I followed her lead, and all three of us swayed to the emotional melody. Jessie joined us and got in between me and Trent.

The song ended, and we were still swaying in the middle of the dance floor, not changing when a faster song started. After a moment, Amy couldn't resist the beat and started jumping around clumsily.

Trent closed the gap Amy had made. I couldn't stop laughing, and this time my knees did go out from under me. Trent and Jessie kept me upright, making me laugh even harder.

They maneuvered me off the dance floor and back to our table, with no help from me. I caught Trent giving me a worried look, and a hot surge of anger shot through me.

"Don't look at me like that. I had someone try to rule me by giving me those faces, and see where that got me."

Trent's face went slack. He placed me in my chair and waited for me to stabilize before moving away.

"I'm sorry," I said, kissing him on the cheek. I hoped he understood the gesture as an apology, and nothing more.

"No problem."

I was grateful when Jessie interrupted our stare down, afraid Trent took my action as something more.

"Come on, let's go find Amy. It's time to put little Miss Margarita on a time out." She grabbed Trent's hand, but before he turned to leave on their reconnaissance operation to retrieve Amy, he said, "I would treat you like a princess."

Jessie yanked Trent away while whispering in his ear. She kept looking back and forth between us as they walked.

My mind felt fuzzy, but seeing him on the receiving end of one of Jessie's rants instead of me, made me laugh, causing me to almost fall over.

Right before I toppled off the chair, I was surrounded by a pair of strong arms. I looked up at the muscular appendages cradling me, and right into a pair of angry green eyes.

My sluggish mind realized I was wrong. Mr. Moody's

eyes weren't just green; they had flecks of blue scattered throughout them. I thought of changing his nickname to Mr. Asshole. Every time he looked at me he seemed to be angry.

"You got it there, Slick?" he asked, with no hint of amusement in his voice.

He retracted his arms slowly, allowing the heat radiating off him to sink into me. His warmth lingered everywhere he had touched. I resisted the urge to take his arms and thread them back around me, just to feel the electrical current his touch caused.

His stare felt just as potent as his touch. Wherever his eyes roamed, it felt like they were penetrating me. I couldn't help but think I wanted something else of his to penetrate me as well. I blinked, needing to break away from his heated stare before I did something stupid, like pledge to be his sex slave.

Breaking our trance, he looked past my shoulder, no longer studying me. My body ached for him to bring his gaze back; sex slave didn't sound so bad.

"Yep, I'm fine. Thanks for the rescue there, Killer."

He scowled, bringing his eyes back, making me giddy for garnering his attention again. His scowl may have been hotter than his half-smirk. I conjured up different scenarios to keep it on his face.

The alcohol in my system convinced me if I stuck my tongue out, the scowl would stay. Not wanting to miss out on an opportunity, I did just that, making me erupt into uncontrollable giggles as he cocked his eyebrow at me. Damn it to hell, that move made him even sexier.

"Alright, you're cut off."

"Alright, you're cut off," I mimicked, causing the rest of the band, which I hadn't realized were behind me, to crack up.

"Faith, come hang out with us before we have to go back up onstage," Mr. Snuggles extended an invitation.

I stuck my tongue out at Kill again, and got up to walk over to them. I use the term 'walk' loosely, being more of a stumble.

Kill guided me to an empty chair.

Right before he released me, he whispered in my ear, "You better be careful about sticking that tongue out, Slick.

Next time I see it, I'm going to suck on it until you moan."

My lower abdomen churned molten lava, as my blood flowed triple its normal speed. The blood rushing through my ears, made it impossible to understand what Van asked me.

"What did you say, Mr. Snuggles?" I asked, causing the whole band to laugh. Even Kill chuckled.

"What'd you call him?" Jet asked.

"Mr. Snuggles," I mumbled, my cheeks flaming red. Even with copious amounts of alcohol flowing through me, it did nothing to numb my embarrassment.

"Ahh, wittle Mr. Snuggles," Jet cooed, throwing his arms around Van, as he tried to kiss him on the cheek.

"Get the hell off me," Van grunted, pushing Jet away.

"Thanks, Faith," Van sighed, pushing Jet away at another attempt to cuddle.

"Sorry, I kind of gave you guys nicknames when I first saw you. I didn't know you were the band, and I was trying to get my mind off of..." I paused, reality bitch-slapping me in the face again.

Van reached out and put his hand on mine, giving it a gentle squeeze before releasing it.

"What's my name?" D asked, changing the subject.

"The Professor," I said brightly.

"Yeah, that's about right. So I guess I would be The Sex God?" Jet said, making me laugh as I shook my head.

"Well, what else could it be?" he asked.

I truly believe he couldn't think of an alternative.

"Dickhead, dumbass, fucktard," Kill ticked off names, and from the look on his face he could have kept going.

"Mr. Mischief," I responded.

Jet seemed upset it didn't mention his prowess. I hurried to explain myself.

"When I saw you, you just seemed to have trouble written all over you, and you were very comfortable with its presence."

Jet smiled and took a drink of his beer. "Ok, I'll go with it, but I still think you should reconsider Sex God."

I snorted and clamped my hand over my mouth, mortified.

"That's bullshit. How come I get Mr. Snuggles?" Van pouted, and even though he tried to look tough, his sincerity shined through him, verifying his nickname.

"Because even though you look scary with your tattoos and bulging muscles, I could tell you have an amazing heart. So suck it up buttercup, you're Mr. Snuggles."

"What's Kill's nickname? Please let it be worse than mine."

I glanced over at Kill, and his eyebrow cocked up, waiting for me to answer. Thankfully, I was saved when I saw Jessie herding a still-dancing-Amy toward me as Trent trudged behind.

Jessie held Amy around the waist, trying to get her to stop bouncing. Her face wore a worried expression, and she avoided making eye contact.

"What is it?" I asked, not letting her cop out.

"Umm, I went outside to switch shoes, and I saw Jason sitting in his car."

I took Kill's beer bottle out of his hand and finished it, not caring about him cutting me off. Before the band could take a step toward the door, Ryan yelled at them that they were up. They overlooked her order, but I stepped in.

"Go finish your set. He isn't going to come back in here. I'm sure he's just waiting for me to run out and beg him to forgive me, and that sure as hell isn't going to happen."

Kill shot me a lethal glare.

"Go, play. You guys are amazing; I want to hear the rest of your set. You shouldn't let your night get ruined by some drama from a girl you just met."

They waited for Kill to decide, giving him final say in whatever action they took.

"Stay here. No more alcohol," Kill ordered, shooting me another cold glare. He stared at me for another second before turning on his heels, and stomped toward the stage. The band followed, except for Van.

"You're family now, Faith. Your drama is our drama," he said. "I'm a hugger. Is it ok if I give you a hug?" he asked.

Nodding my head yes, he gently hugged me. I was embarrassed to feel tears pricking the back of my eyes when he released me.

"I'm a big girl, Mr. Snuggles. I can take care of myself."

"I know you can, but you don't have to."

Once everyone was situated onstage, the noise decibels reached an extreme level as the now well-rested women had their eye candy back. Jessie handed me another shot.

Kill's voice melted every woman's panties, but his eyes were on the shot in my hand. His face dared me to defy his order.

None of the women seemed to notice where his attention actually was, because they were too busy trying garner the attention I currently had.

I stuck my tongue out at him, and tossed the shot back, not caring about the consequences I would have to endure the next day. I was unsure if the punishment would be doled out from the alcohol, Kill, or both.

The band switched to another song, causing the crowd to jump around, fists pumping. Kill ran all over the stage, making them even crazier as they sang along.

The alcohol was doing its job. After a couple more songs, I struggled to keep my eyes open. The JackholeS ended their set and stepped offstage into their screaming fans.

Trent stared at me, his eyes heavy from intoxication. Jessie had her head propped on her hands as she dreamily tracked Van's movement. Amy was eating a licorice stick, her eyelids bobbing up and down as she tried to stay awake.

I felt an arm snake around my waist, pulling me off the chair. I went willingly, allowing someone else to make decisions for the moment. I knew it was Kill just from the electrical current his touch caused. What little feeling I had left in my body headed straight toward my vagina.

Van put his arm around Jessie's shoulders as he guided her out of the bar. Jet grabbed Amy's licorice out of her hand, sticking it in his mouth. She wobbled toward him, her eyes shining with trouble. D grabbed our bags and assisted Trent as he weaved through the bar.

"Which one's yours, Slick?" Kill whispered in my ear, making heat pool between my legs.

I pointed to my Mustang, patiently waiting like a good

girl.

"Fuck. You would drive a Mustang. Give me your keys," he mumbled.

I shook my head, refusing to let him drive my car before he drove me.

"Where are your keys?" He ran his hands over my body. Heat flared everywhere he touched, and I let out an actual purr, causing his face to go tight.

"I don't have them. They're in my bag," I replied, my voice husky. I secretly wished he would go back to searching me again.

He leaned me on my car. "Take this," he said, handing me a bottle of water and three Advil.

I hit myself as I tried to salute him. "Ouch!" I cried, rubbing my forehead.

Kill laughed and jogged back to D, grabbing my bag. When he found my keys, he situated me into the passenger seat.

"I have nowhere to go," I said dismally, leaning my head back in defeat. "I'm going to have to drop my scholarship, move out of state, and somehow convince my dad nothing's wrong, so I don't kill him from stress."

Kill didn't respond, and I was uncertain if he was ignoring me or my dialogue was silent.

"Sounds like it would be easier if you just went back to him."

Huh. So I had spoken out loud.

"Never going to happen. I escaped, and I'll never go back to him," I responded, with as much conviction my drunk ass could muster.

"We'll see. I've heard that before," he replied, his voice tight with anger.

Before I could ask him why he was so mad, I passed out.

# CHAPTER 4

My alcohol-riddled mind played out the events of my past, not allowing me to escape Jason, even in my sleep. I wanted to scream at myself for being so stupid, and not running from him.

The semester after Jason proposed, I threw myself into school and work. I no longer wore my high heels, trading them in for a pair of chucks. My skinny jeans now hung off me and a black hoodie became my new uniform, or shield, depending on how you looked at it.

Jason traveled more, trying to drum up business. I kept myself quarantined in our apartment, leaving only for school and work.

After the night of the proposal, the menial tasks of everyday living were exhausting. Jason's mood was determined by how things went with his clients, and I was thankful he was a smooth talker.

Jason took my melancholy attitude as me missing him; I never corrected his assumption.

The semester went by, and our group meetings happened more than we needed them. For the most part, I could relax around my best friends and let go of my reality.

The beginning of summer was amazing. Jason's temper stayed in check most of the time. He was caring and romantic, making the goofy smile appear on my face more often. When my friends would call, he would become attentive and I would blow them off.

One day, Jessie showed up at our place. "You, go get dressed," she commanded. "I'm stealing you. Sorry, Jason, but I miss my best friend and I'm going to take her for the day."

*He knew he was stuck, and had to play his role. He smiled at Jessie and chuckled. "I understand. It's just so hard to give up my time with her, but I guess I should share. Go get ready. I'll be here when you get back."*

*Fear coursed through me, afraid of which Jason would be at the apartment when I returned. I skipped to the bedroom, trying to play my part.*

*I dressed in a pair of yoga pants, and my uniform black hoodie.*

*Jessie took one look at me and shook her head. "Oh heck, no."*

*Her face had a look of disgust as she took in my appearance. "Nope, go change. It's actually warm outside. Go put something cute on or I'll pick it out myself. Besides, you have a big rock on your finger; don't you want everyone to know Jason's marrying a beautiful girl, and not a slob?" Jessie's eyes glinted evilly.*

*Jason agreed with her, his public image had to be as pristine as his life. So I had his assent to look amazing, and would probably get in trouble if I didn't do him proud.*

*Leery to leave the two of them alone, I hurried along. Between Jessie's inquisitive stares, and Jason admitting he didn't like Jessie, it was a recipe for disaster.*

*I put on a cute summer dress I had stowed in the back of my closet, thankful Jason required me to shave before I got into bed. He felt hair on a woman was unnatural. I had to search for my makeup bag because it had been awhile since I took time on my appearance.*

*Both Jessie and Jason's eyes lit up when they saw me, so I knew I had passed their test.*

*Outside, Jessie pulled me to her dark blue Saturn and pushed me into the passenger seat. I was surprised she didn't buckle my seatbelt. She jumped in, and we sped out of the parking lot.*

*"Are we running from the law?" I asked, nervous from her weird behavior.*

*"I was worried about you. We never see you anymore. Are you ok?"*

*My stomached flopped around. I questioned what I had*

done to give it away. Had I not covered the bruises as well as I thought?

"I'm fine."

"You know you can tell me anything, right?"

"I know, and I love you for that, Jessie."

Her shoulders slunk down, and I had the distinct feeling I had disappointed her.

I frowned when I saw both Amy and Trent's cars at our favorite hangout. I suddenly found myself paranoid this was an intervention and they figured out my secret.

Amy flitted around the table, while Trent tried to talk to her in her ever-changing positions. She threw her tiny body at me, squealing the whole way.

"I missed you so much. Where have you been?" she asked in one breath and stuck a Skittle in my mouth.

I walked over to greet Trent after I detached myself from Amy. I excused my absence by telling them I wanted to hang out with Jason, because next semester would be intense.

We walked to Pizza Schmizza, drank beer, and indulged in way too much pizza. Stuffed and content, I said goodbye to Amy and Trent, promising them I wouldn't be such a stranger.

Jessie drove me home, looking at me every so often. I ignored her, too preoccupied with which Jason would be waiting for me to worry about Jessie's behavior.

"Do you want me to come up? We could watch a movie."

"No, I'm tired. I'll see you soon, I promise."

"I'm here if you need me. I love you, Faith."

The apartment was draped in utter darkness when I walked in. My hope rose I would wake up to happy Jason in the morning, as I had for the past couple weeks. Trying to be as quiet as possible, I shrugged into a t-shirt and the yoga pants I had been denied wearing earlier.

Later, I woke up to Jason whispering in my ear, "Did you have fun?" He sat on my side of the bed, his body was rigid with anger.

"I did, but I would rather have been here with you." I tried to snuggle up to him, but he pushed off the bed.

"You called her, didn't you? You didn't want to spend time with me. I love you so much, why do you hurt me? I do

46

everything for you." He snagged my shirt by the collar and pulled me out of bed, the shirt gave way across my neck, leaving a trail of fire in its path.

"No, Jason," I pleaded. "I didn't call her. I wanted to spend time with you, and only you. I love you." I refused to cry, afraid of what the moisture would ignite.

"Liar," he whispered as he shoved me.

Pain lanced through my back as the corner of the nightstand dug into it. Terror kept rearing up, but I tamped it down, knowing it wouldn't do me any good.

"See what you make me do?" he whispered.

My head snapped back and forth as he shook me.

"No, Jason, I love you," I cried.

When my neck swung forward he kissed me ruthlessly.

He threw me on the bed, and the sound of a condom wrapper tearing echoed through the room. I prepared myself for what would happen next, and refused to cry.

After ripping my clothes off, he pushed into me, whispering, "You are mine," repeatedly. His face clenched as he released. I stroked his face, reiterating, "I'm yours. I love you."

When I woke up, Jason was making his special breakfast. My stomach recoiled, at the thought of eating.

My neck sported a long, hickey-like mark from the T-shirt ripping across it, and with every step my back would twinge from where the nightstand had dug into it.

In the shower, I willed the hot water to wash away my pain. Tears were no longer an option. I was beyond shedding them to ease my pain. I needed to leave Jason. My ravaged body was too much, and he would kill me if I stayed.

My dad would help me. I would try to transfer my scholarship, but if not, I would use my savings to finish. Leaving my friends was the only reason I allowed myself to shed any tears. I guess I wasn't as beyond them as I had thought.

Jason sat on the kitchen chair with his head in his hands, his elbows resting on his knees. His eyes brimmed with unshed tears. "Faith."

He tried to put his arms around me, but I stepped back.

"Honey, your dad had a stroke. I just bought our plane tickets, we leave in two hours. Come on, I'll help you pack. You should put

47

some medicine on that curling iron burn."

Not my dad. My foundation. It was us against the world. How was I going to get away from Jason without him?

"Is he ok?" I asked, my voice barely audible, afraid if I spoke too loudly the universe would put more attention on him.

"He's stable. I just spoke to your aunt. She couldn't give me details because the doctor just walked in." He held me, kissing me on the head, telling me everything would be ok, and he loved me. I hugged him back, sick to my stomach as I took solace from him.

At the hospital, I ran to my dad's room and threw myself on his bed, sobbing into his strong shoulder. He patted my back, murmuring to me everything was ok. His left side sagged, but didn't seem to be noticeable unless you were looking for it, which I was.

"Hey baby girl, I'm fine. Don't cry. Thanks for getting her here, and taking care of our girl, son."

My breath caught at my dad's term of endearment toward Jason.

"I'll always take good care of her, Mr. Annabelle; she's my heart," he responded.

I swallowed all the emotion trying to escape, choking on them.

My dad fell asleep, and the doctor took us outside so we could talk. He explained my dad was strong and the stroke was minor. He could go home in a couple of days because of the vast improvement he'd been showing, but we would need to keep him calm and stress-free during his recovery.

The weight of the world, or at least of Jason's muscle-bound body, settled on my shoulders. I would have to pull up my big girl panties and live the life I chose, no longer having a partner to help me.

When my dad came home from the hospital, Jason arranged for in-home care. We did it under the guise they were there to keep the house in order as he recovered.

The first two were young and didn't understand what I was asking of them. I started to lose hope I would find someone competent, when Martha walked in.

She was a couple of years younger than my dad, and

extremely bored. Her husband had left her for their older male car mechanic when their kids were teenagers. She dedicated her life to her children and now that they were grown, she had nothing to do except for the once-a-year cruise she went on with her ex-husband and his mechanic life partner.

During the interview her eyes drifted past me. When I realized I'd lost her attention, I glanced back to see what had stolen it. My dad was in the kitchen with a handful of Oreos he'd just grabbed out of the cabinet.

Martha got up and snatched the cookies right out of my stunned father's grasp. She took an apple from the bowl of fruit sitting on the kitchen counter, and put it in his hand, which was frozen in the same position it had been in when the cookies occupied it.

"Eat that, and when you're done, we'll go grocery shopping."

"Who are you?" my dad asked, looking at me and then back to the woman standing in front of him.

"I'm your new housekeeper. Go get dressed, you can buy me lunch while we talk about my salary."

My dad stared at her, dumbfounded, and I put my hand over my mouth to stop the giggle. "Fine, but I want a milkshake." He turned around and went to his bedroom to get ready for his lunch date.

"I think I just fell in love," my aunt Julie said from the other side of the dining room. "I haven't seen anyone order my big brother around like that in...well, ever."

Martha waved off my thanks, telling me she was going to enjoy bossing my father around, saying he should take care of himself because handsome men were scarce at their age.

Martha promised to keep us updated, and our tearful goodbye ended when Jason pulled me through airport security. Jason had been the perfect doting fiancé, making my dad and aunt fall even more in love with him.

Fall semester finished up. Jason was once again the Jason whom I loved, and I tried to stay positive.

Christmas break came and went. My dad was getting stronger every day, and my worry for him diminished after seeing him so spry. Martha kept him in line, and as much as he complained, I could tell he adored her.

Spring semester started, and Jason traveled constantly. He hated leaving me, and called me at all hours to check up on me.

When finals were over, our group decided to meet the next night to celebrate.

Jason was gone, and I was excited to get out. I told Jason I was invited, but I wanted to surprise him and rearrange the kitchen instead. He freaked out, afraid I would ruin his kitchen, and told me to go and have fun. Luck, with a little bit of manipulation, was on my side.

Relaxing after my long day of finals, I was lounging on the couch listening to music. I sang along to Nonpoint when keys rattled in the door. I sat up just in time to see Jason enter.

"Hey, honey, I didn't expect you to be home so soon," I sputtered, taking my feet off the couch.

"Why, am I interrupting something?" he sneered.

I smiled and tried to play off his comment. My skin crawled from the look in his eyes; the pure unadulterated fury emanating from him made me realize today would be my last day on this earth. Jason was past the point of the controlled anger he always lived in.

"Nope, but you're welcome to come join me on the couch." I had a small sliver of fight still left in me, and I wanted to see if I could maneuver him back to his controlled fury; where he would toy with me, hurting me, but in the end releasing me.

I longed for the smell of heart-shaped waffles and roses in the morning.

The vehemence in his eyes melted away. I foolishly thought he'd put the monster back in its cage, and Jason was back in control. He kneeled down on his knees in front of me, pulling me off of the couch so we were facing each other.

"I missed you, Faith," he said into my lips, pulling me into a false sense of security. He laid back, pulling me with him until I straddled him. I ran my hands up his chest.

"I missed you too."

He stroked my hair as he inquired, "So how about a celebratory dinner tomorrow?"

He wanted to ruin my plan. Seeing the kindness in his eyes I took a chance, and furrowed my brows, feigning confused innocence.

"An early dinner? I'm meeting the gang at Ray's tomorrow, remember? We talked about it this morning, and you told me to go."

I laid my head down on his chest, running my hand over his body. His hand in my hair clenched painfully.

"I figured with me being here," he said through clenched teeth, "you would want to hang out with me."

"I do. It's just I promised everyone I would meet them. We have all summer to hang out."

I tried to stay calm, but his hand still hadn't relaxed and my scalp ached from the consistent pull. He sat up, and twisted around, causing me to land on my back. Pain shot through me.

"You don't care about me." His voice was low. I was relieved at his quiet tone, knowing he had some control.

"I do. It's just one night, Jason." I flashed him my ring. "You have me forever. Hell, I'm sure you'll be sick of me, we'll be together so much."

He ripped off my ring and chucked it across the room. I put my hand up to my mouth and stifled the scream wanting to rip from me. My throat clenched, not allowing any sound to escape as he sneered at me. Drenched in terror, I couldn't stop the tremors racking through my body.

"You're a whore. You don't care about me. How many guys did you fuck while I was gone?"

I shook my head, willing the words to come. With strength I didn't know I possessed, I squeaked out, "None, only you. It has always been just you. I'm yours."

"Liar!" he snarled, backhanding me across the face, forcing my head to snap to the side.

Blood rushed into my mouth so fast I almost choked on it. He pushed me down, climbing on top of me, his hands digging into my arms.

"I love you, only you," I pleaded.

Jason was so far gone, he didn't hear a word I said. It was

51

useless, and I stayed silent as he brutalized my body.

His eyes never left mine as he undid his belt buckle, pulling himself out of his jeans, his erection purple from the strain of his arousal. Donning a condom he had in his pocket, he shoved into me without warning.

Once he finished, he kissed me while he carried me to our room, for the first time leaving a mess on the floor.

I woke up to the sounds of Jason preparing his makeup breakfast. I put on a pair of jeans and a t-shirt, as I carried my hoodie out with me. A bouquet of red roses was perched on the table.

"I missed you. I love you so much," Jason said, concentrating on the food he was preparing.

"I know, Jason, I love you too," I said to his back, trying to avoid inhaling the stench the roses were giving off.

"I'm sorry about last night."

My head shot up. This was the first time he acknowledged something, other than me being exceptionally clumsy, caused the bruising on my skin.

"I was so worried when you called and said you fell down the stairs. Thinking of you in pain made me insane; I wanted to make sure you were all right."

Ah, there was my story. It terrified me when Jason gave me these stories, once he created them they became his reality. He held onto them with such conviction, there were times I would falter between my reality and his.

I held back the hysterical giggle bubbling up inside of me. How stupid of me to think he would admit he was at fault when he could digress into his reality where he lived guilt-free.

"Thanks for coming home to take care of me," I said, digging into the waffle he just set in front of me. I tried to put the bite into my mouth, but a sharp pain stabbed my stomach and I was sure if I swallowed, it would come back up.

"Anything for you, Faith," he replied, sitting down, and digging into his breakfast with the vigor of a starving man. "Don't be upset," he said between bites, his mouth wide enough to see the food being masticated inside of it. "They called me this morning and I need to fly back today."

I pouted and went to sit on his lap, allowing me to get

52

away from my full plate. The smell of food mingling with the roses had me swallowing multiple times to keep the bile at bay. Jason's plate being cleared of every morsel seemed the best bet to keep my stomach under control.

"I'm going to miss you," I said, hugging him while burying my face in his neck, not trusting my facial expressions.

"I know how hard it is for you to be without me. I'll be back in a day or two, and I promise I'll spend the summer making it up to you. You'll have so much of me your clingy heart will be satisfied."

"Ok," I responded, kissing him lightly.

I cleaned up while Jason got ready. He kissed me goodbye, murmuring he loved me, and left.

I waited ten minutes and then walked down to the parking lot to guarantee he was gone. When I didn't see his Honda, I ran up the stairs, not allowing my sore muscles to slow me down.

I packed everything I could, shoving it into my car. Whatever I left behind would be lost forever. Once I had what I needed, I rushed to the courthouse.

They took a report, and I was granted a restraining order. I didn't want to press charges, afraid Jason's dad would pay for it to be swept under the rug. All I requested was the restraining order.

# CHAPTER 5

I woke up to a pounding in my ear drums and a torture device squeezing my head. I cracked open one eye to see Jessie passed out next to me, drool oozing out of her mouth. Amy was curled up like a cat on the end of the bed.

Opening the other eye I surveyed my surroundings, and realized I had no idea where I was.

The room had minimal furniture, the California King being the focal point, with one nightstand on the right side and a matching dresser pushed against the wall. A small flat screen T.V. sat on the dresser, with a DVD player and cable box on the side. Nothing decorated the white walls, and a lone mirror hung on the door.

I got up with slow measured movements. My head argued as my stomach pleaded with me to stay still. Taking deep breaths, I tried to calm my body.

The door across from us was ajar, revealing the bathroom. My stomach took this as the permission it needed to kick everything out. Rushing to the bathroom, I heaved until I was spent.

Each time my stomach revolted, my head wanted to explode. Once I could trust myself to move, I stripped out of my clothes. It felt odd taking a shower in a strange house, but I couldn't resist the siren's call of hot water.

As the grime washed away, I felt some semblance of being human again. With the help of the hot water, my head was now a low thud compared to the pounding had been.

Finding a bottle of mouth wash, I swished it around before redressing. My body protested when I put on my stolen t-shirt. I was sore everywhere.

Feeling grubby in my dirty clothes, I vowed to change as soon as possible. Spotting a hamper overflowing with men's clothing, I got my first clue to my whereabouts.

The sink had nothing on it except for hand soap, a

razor, and hair gel- no female presence anywhere. I checked to see if Jessie or Amy were awake before investigating further. Both of them were still out, Amy was now sprawled out with her arms and legs spread wide.

There were pictures on the wall throughout the stairwell. They consisted of different bands and candid black and whites of the JackholeS at different venues. I ventured out to see who else was awake.

The living room at the bottom of the stairs sported a huge brown sectional couch. A thick black rug covered the hardwood floors with a dark wooden table in the center.

The entertainment center sported a ginormous T.V., with every type of gaming system scattered around it. Through the living room, I went into the formal dining room. Instead of a dining table, it contained a plethora of different instruments. On the walls were poster boards with lyrics and musical notes handwritten on them.

I walked through the archway which led to the kitchen; Kill sat at the table. He appeared freshly showered and disgustingly handsome. His face registered surprise when he saw me.

"Coffee?" he asked, a dimple flickering on his cheek.

I nodded, not trusting myself to speak in front of him. He motioned his head toward the coffee maker.

"The mugs are in the cabinet above it, sugar's in the little blue canister, and creamer's in the fridge." His attention went back to his glass, filled with a frothy green liquid. I nodded my head again, unaware if he saw it.

I hoped the liquid caffeine would take the ache out of my head. When my coffee lightened to the perfect caramel color, I sat across from Kill. We sipped our drinks in silence.

"How's your head?" Kill asked, startling me.

I hadn't expected him to break the silence between us. "Better," I replied. "Where am I?" I asked, taking advantage of the broken silence.

"My house. The band lives here too." He didn't explain anymore, and I realized I would have to drag every bit of information out of him.

"Whose room were we in?"

"That's the guest room. It's empty. The guys thought it would be safer if you all stayed with us last night, being that none of you could move." He smiled at his comment, before wiping it off of his face.

"Your boyfriend saw me taking you home, but he didn't follow us. I'm sure he isn't giving up on you that easily. He's just biding his time, unless you go back to him before he figures something out." His voice was laced with anger.

I didn't understand what I did to him to make him so mad at me. The way he seemed convinced I would run back to Jason pissed me off. "I'm not going back to him, ever. I don't know what crawled up your ass, but I got away from him by myself. I'm sure you think I'm weak for staying for so long, and damn it if you aren't right, but I guarantee, I will not be going back."

He remained silent, so I continued.

"And you don't need to remind me how pathetic I am, because I berate myself enough. It took every bit of strength I had to get away, but it will take nothing to stay away."

I didn't mean to rant like I did. He looked stunned from my outburst. I just yelled at someone named Kill; what the hell was I thinking?

"I hope you're right; you deserve better than him. Also, I don't think you're weak for staying. I just wonder if you can stay away."

My mouth hung open, not expecting to hear the compassion in his voice. Before I could reply, Jet and Van walked downstairs.

"Please tell me you made the coffee, Faith," Jet said, getting a mug.

"Sorry, it was already made when I came in."

"Ugh, Kill always makes it too strong," Jet replied, putting a generous amount of sugar in the offending coffee. "I don't know why the fuck you bother making it, you don't even drink it."

"How are you doing?" Van asked. He gave me a questioning look, and I nodded my head giving him permission to hug me. After a quick hug he poured his coffee, also adding tons of sugar into it.

"The coffee's good," I said, defending Kill for reasons unknown to me. I punctuated my statement by taking a sip.

"With as much sugar and cream you added, I'm surprised you can taste the coffee at all."

There he was. I knew he couldn't stay civil without the jerk resurfacing. I stuck my tongue out at him before taking another caffeine laced drink. Kill quirked his eyebrow, not replying as he sipped his own drink while the other two took a seat.

"So?" Van looked at me, waiting for me to answer his question.

"I'm doing ok," I answered. "I have a lot to do today. My boss and coworkers love Jason, and I'm afraid they'll want to talk me into a reconciliation. So, I definitely need to quit. Finding a place to live is my top priority. Jessie and Amy don't have any room for me, and I don't want to ask Trent." I was babbling. I couldn't stop the words when they started to flow.

"Well, we have a proposition for you," D said, startling me with his appearance. "Who made the coffee?"

"It's not that bad!" I exclaimed, not understanding why they were such babies when it came to strong coffee.

They laughed, except for Kill, who gave me a curious look. I started to stick my tongue out until I remembered what he told me last night. The memory was hazy, but clear enough to make me keep my tongue tucked inside my mouth. Kill chuckled, and I was pretty sure he knew exactly what I was thinking.

D leaned against the kitchen counter as he surveyed us while sipping on his sugar-enriched coffee.

"What type of proposition?" I asked, having no idea what these crazy boys had in mind.

"Well, we have an extra room here nobody's using, and your crazy ex won't bother you," D started.

"Not if you're surrounded by a bunch of sexy, scary rockers," Jet added, leaning over the table for a high five. He gave me puppy dog eyes until I gave in and slapped his hand.

"I can't move in with you guys!" I was floored by their offer. "I'll figure something out. I don't want to impose," I finished, feeling breathless.

"Why not? You can't live by yourself. We talked to that guy, and you could see the crazy in him. You're working at the bar we play at, so we could keep an eye on you. It's a perfect solution," Van said, getting up and standing next to me.

"You guys don't even know me," I argued, unable to think of another reason.

"Shut up, you're moving in with us. You walk around the house naked, right?" Jet asked, and I couldn't help but laugh.

"Are you sure?" I asked Kill, who had been quiet during the conversation.

Van gave me a light squeeze on my shoulder, taking the long way back to his chair so he could punch Kill in the arm.

"Yeah, Slick. You can stay here until Romeo romances you back to his love cave, but if I catch that douche box near my property, I'll make good on my threat."

"Why the hell do you keep insisting I'm going back to him? And did you just refer to him as a douche box?"

The guys laughed at my statement. I waited for one of them to answer me.

"He's a douche box because he's lower than a douchebag. He couldn't get near even the skankiest pussy," Jet explained, making my face turn bright red because I had let Jason become well acquainted with my, uhm, skanky girly part.

"No offense," Jet said, back peddling.

I tried to look offended, wanting my fake outrage to eclipse my burning face. It must have worked because Jet started stammering. "I wasn't saying you have a skanky pussy. Hell, I would do you right now..."

Before he could dig himself a bigger hole, I let him off the hook by laughing, unable to fake anger anymore.

"Are you sure?" I asked one more time.

They nodded their heads yes.

"I promise I won't bother you guys. You won't even know I'm here. Hell, I'll even cook."

"You cook?" Van asked, leaning his bulging muscles on the table.

"Don't attack her," Jet said. "I called first dibs."

"Whatever you want. Well, until I start school, then you

may have to fend for yourself some nights," I said smiling, ignoring Jet.

"Lasagna," Van and D said at the same time.

Laughing, I got up and kissed Van on the cheek. I tried to give Jet a kiss on the cheek, but he had other ideas and tried to stick his tongue down my throat. Slapping him on the back of the head, I walked over to give D a hug. He seemed embarrassed, but let me hug him anyway.

"No problem, Faith. Like I said, I have sisters, and you remind me of them," Van explained, as I let go of D.

"Fuck that," Jet replied, wiggling his eyebrows. "I definitely do not see you as a sister. And if you don't want a ride, your hot little friend is invited."

Just then, Amy and Jessie walked into the kitchen, both of them looking worse for wear. Although, Amy had a licorice stick in her mouth and was getting more energy by the second.

"Hey, Candy," Jet said, getting out of his seat and heading straight toward Amy.

She looked outraged and pushed him when he reached her. "My name's not Candy," she pouted, pointing her licorice stick at him.

Jet took the candy out of her hand and popped it in his mouth. "I know, but you taste like it."

Amy had a smug smile on her face. "And you better not forget it." She threw her arms around his neck and kissed him like she was trying to retrieve her stolen candy.

"Ewww, it's way too early to see that stuff," Jessie squealed, taking Jet's abandoned seat, avoiding Van.

Jessie swiped my coffee and took a drink. "Jeez, did you put a whole cup of sugar in this?" She put my mug back in front of me, making a face. "Did you guys tell her?" Jessie asked, still avoiding Van.

"She's right, it is too early for anyone to see this," Jet said, grabbing Amy. He lifted her over his shoulder, bounding toward the stairs. Amy waved at us before she was out of sight.

Van slid his coffee in front of Jessie, she still refused to look at him. She mumbled a thank you and took a sip.

"Much better," she replied.

I smiled into my mug; he had dumped just as much

sugar into his as I did. I guess I missed a lot in my drunken stupor.

"And to answer your question, yes, they did, and I agreed. I'm going to the store to get stuff for dinner, anyone need anything?" I asked, feeling claustrophobic in Kill's presence. He'd been staring at me the whole time, and my body couldn't take much more before I caught on fire or grabbed his face and stuck my tongue down his gorgeous throat.

"I'm good," D answered, before going into the living room and slouching on the couch to watch T.V.

"Are you cooking?" Jessie asked excitedly. "Can I stay? We work the same shift tonight. We could ride together, or you could follow me so you have your car."

Van answered before I could, which I was thankful for, being they just allowed me to move in and I didn't want to start inviting people over. "Of course you can stay. This is Faith's house now, too."

Jessie gave me a worried look. "The boys told me last night they were going to ask you to move in. Are you ok with that?"

"Yeah, I am. Jason will never bother me while I'm here. What about money?" I asked, realizing I had just agreed to stay somewhere without asking about rent. If I needed to dip into my savings, so be it.

"We split the utilities. Kill owns the house, so between the four of us it's not much. If you cook, I'm sure Kill will overlook your share altogether," Van replied, while shooting glances at Jessie.

"No, I'm not a charity case. You've already done so much; I want this to be fair." I refused to accept Kill's pity. I felt empowered leaving Jason, and I wanted the feeling to stay.

This opportunity would confirm I was capable of making it on my own. I wanted to put myself together and be a normal person. Coming to that conclusion made me more determined to pave my own way.

"Shut the hell up," Van said, giving me a stern look.

"What?" I whispered, embarrassed at how weak my voice sounded. Sickness rolled in my stomach as I shrunk back into the chair. When Van saw my reaction, his face fell.

"I didn't mean to yell at you. We don't think you're a charity case, and we decided it would be nice to have someone around to keep us in line. Now that we know you cook, we aren't letting you out of our sight. So just say thank you," he explained.

Jessie smiled at him, causing him to give her big googly eyes.

Whispering a thank you, my watery eyes remained focused on the table, unable to make eye contact with anyone.

"There you go. Now go to the store so you can make us a kick ass dinner," Van joked.

I heard the smile in his voice, but I couldn't look up. Walking to the archway, I realized I needed to get my things out of my car. "Uhm.... can I get my keys, so I can get my stuff?" I asked the floor.

When nobody answered, I looked up to see Kill, Van, Jessie, and even D looking everywhere but me. "What?" I asked.

Kill finally made eye contact, his half-smile causing that damn dimple to appear. The sight of it made me want to go over and lick that beautiful indent.

"We kind of moved your stuff into the room when we decided you were going to stay with us," he replied, giving me a sheepish grin, making him even more adorable.

"Ok," I responded, stunned at his revelation. "Well, I guess I'll go get dressed. Where is everything?" I asked, knowing I looked all over the room before getting sick, and I didn't see any of my stuff.

"We stashed it in the closet. There wasn't much. For a girl, you pack light," Kill responded, cocking his eyebrow. "Unless you just grabbed the essentials, knowing you would go back to him soon."

"I. Am. Not. Going. Back. To. Him," I growled, feeling my temper rise. "I just took the important things, my life being of the most value; everything else is replaceable."

Shock registered in his eyes, and it made me happy I caught him off guard again. I needed to get to the bottom of why he kept insisting I would run back to Jason.

"Come on, I'll go shopping with you so I can pick up dessert," Jessie said, trying to ease the tension in the room.

**61**

Breaking eye contact first, I walked to my new room, not waiting for Jessie.

I threw the closet doors open, and sure enough my clothes, and everything else I had hastily packed, waited for me. Going through a disorganized garbage bag full of clothes, I pulled out a pair of black skinny jeans and a dark blue t-shirt.

Doing a quick inventory of my stuff, I searched for my hoodie, but I couldn't locate it. I hoped it wasn't lost forever.

Someone entered the room, and thinking it was Jessie, I threw off my grungy t-shirt and replaced it with a clean one. I began to shuck off my jeans when I heard a very non-Jessie grunt.

Twirling around, I tripped on my jeans, now wrapped around my ankles. Right before I hit the ground, Kill caught me, holding me against his well-defined abs.

"Sorry, Slick. I wanted to tell you I would be accompanying you to the store, as Van and Jessie are occupied." He wiggled his eyebrows, making me giggle.

Realizing I was half naked and pressed against him, I slowly backed away. The immediate sadness from the removal of his electricity was staggering.

His grin disappeared, and the laughter in his eyes was replaced with desire. I could see why girls all over Portland were infatuated with him. Just one fierce look, and I wanted to wrap myself around him until you couldn't tell where he stopped and I began.

I took the step I had just taken away from him back toward him. We both inhaled sharply when our bodies collided.

He pulled in his bottom lip, raking his teeth over it until it popped out. My attention became rapt on his bottom lip and I wanted to bite it like he had just done.

The wet heat between my legs was on fire, and the only way I could think of getting rid of the burning ache was to have him buried deep within me. The look in his eyes, before my attention went to his lips, showed he was thinking the same thing.

My tongue darted out, and he groaned, making his chest rumble. The sound caused my nipples to pebble, aching along with the rest of my body for his attention.

He lowered his face to mine until our foreheads touched, our lips a breath away. Both of us were panting, the dull pain between my legs caused me to press my thighs together, trying to gain friction to help with the need building inside of me.

When I was about to break and press my lips to his, Kill turned around and stormed away, leaving me confused and unsatisfyingly hot.

"Get ready, Slick, I'll meet you in the kitchen." He closed the door with an audible click. I sunk to the floor, my pulse pounding. My lips were swollen with need, frustrating me even more being he hadn't done anything before he cruelly left me. Asshole.

I yanked up my pants and grabbed my makeup bag to cover up the bags under my eyes, adding eyeliner to make me look less haggard. My reflection showed proof of how turned on I was just minutes before. I let out an irritated huff and headed downstairs, vowing I wouldn't let him get to me again.

Kill stared at the kitchen table, deep in thought. Trying to show him how unaffected I was with whatever happened up in my room, I slapped on my perfected fake smile.

"You ready to go, Killer?"

He scowled at me and heat shot through me, causing my thighs to tighten, but I refused to let myself go down that road. Stupid, fucking, adorable scowl.

He walked by me without saying a word. I rolled my eyes at his back, realizing he was going to be the epitome of the moody artist everyone talked about in books and movies.

My Mustang was parked on the side of the road looking as pretty as ever. She always knew how to put a smile on my face.

"Are you going to moon over your car all day?" Kill broke into my happy mood, so I took his cue and scowled back at him. This caused him to smile his panty-dropping grin. Fucker.

We walked to a huge monstrous black truck. He opened the door and got in, not waiting for me. The engine roared to life, causing me to jump from the unexpected sound as I

63

walked to the passenger side and practically had to pole vault into the cab.

"Nice truck. Overcompensating?" I asked, glancing at the juncture between his legs.

Kill's laugh was amazing. The rumbling in his chest made my traitorous nipples harden. I wrapped my arms around myself, trying to keep the vow I made minutes ago.

"It's Jet's," he said, when he got his laughter under control. "I'll let him know you're curious about his Sex God status in contrast to his truck size."

This time I laughed along with him as he pulled on the road.

"So, Slick, what do you do for fun besides fantasize about how big my cock is?"

I sputtered, unable to keep my face from turning an impressive shade of crimson. "I do not fantasize about your..." I didn't finish my sentence verbally. Instead I nodded my head in the general direction of his lap.

"You don't have to lie. You were very concerned when you thought this was my truck." He had a grin on his face, and I was at odds, not sure if I should slap the look off his face, or grab him and molest him with my tongue.

"Shut up. I'm sure if I was fascinated with anything near your crotchel area, all I would have to do is ask any semi good looking girl, and she would be able to give me a detailed explanation."

His smile dimmed, but after a second of faltering it came back in full force. "Did you just refer to my manly package as my crotchel area?"

"Did you just refer to your crotchel area as your manly package?" I shot back. He laughed at my remark. "Why are you driving Jet's truck?" I asked when we were close to the store.

"I park my car in the garage, and it's a pain in the ass to get Jet to move his truck. The other day I walked in on him asleep, naked on his bed with no covers. I decided to start taking his truck instead of having to see that again."

I laughed at the horror on Kill's face. "So is he overcompensating?" I asked, causing Kill to swerve.

He glanced over at me with his damn half-smile. "Well,

if you want to compare it to mine, then he needs to raise this truck a couple more feet."

He looked back at the road, his smirk turning into a full blown smile. I glanced at his crotch before turning to stare out the window. Kill pulled into the parking lot and turned off the truck. Instead of getting out, he unbuckled and turned to me.

"Well, I would tell you the real size of my manly parts, but I would have to kill you or fuck you senseless. Which would you prefer, Slick?"

My mouth dropped open, and I was appalled by how fast I answered in my head.

He laughed, hopping out of the truck. When I opened the door, he was there waiting for me. Kill latched onto my waist and helped me out, letting my body slide down his. When my feet hit the ground, he held on. I was thankful, not sure my legs would hold me up.

Even with my height, he towered over me and it made me feel feminine and safe. My breath hitched when I saw the lust burning in his eyes. It brought me back to earlier. That thought, like a dose of cold water, pulled me out of my stupor.

I heaved out of his embrace, forcing my heartbeat to go back to a normal beat. He let me go without resistance, and the pang of sadness engulfing me frustrated me.

We walked into the store, both of us lost in our own thoughts, mine revolving around the moody man next to me. Stupid man, I thought. Instead of calling him Mr. Moody I would start calling him Stupid Ass Man, or Sam for short.

I grabbed a cart while I put together a mental list of everything I needed for dinner.

Kill took the cart from me and wheeled away, not waiting for me. I had the childish impulse to get my own and leave him to do whatever the hell he wanted. In the end, I surrendered and followed him. I reminded myself he was letting me stay in his house, just as I caught up to him.

"Where to?"

"Follow me, Killer, and keep up," I responded, trying to look sassy, but probably looked like a drunken crackhead.

"Lead the way," he replied, smacking me on the ass.

I tried to give him his scowl back, but he just smiled.

While shopping, Kill reverted back to a little boy, running down the aisle and putting his feet up, leaning on the cart, and almost smashing into a couple who gave him dirty looks.

He made it almost impossible to get produce. Every time I picked something up to check the freshness, Kill moaned in my ear whispering *"Oh yeah, squeeze it just like that,"* and, *"I have something you could check for hardness,"* or, *"You could squeeze me like that anytime."*

By the time I was putting things on the conveyer belt, I was flushed and throbbing in places a girl should not be throbbing while in a grocery store, or any public place for that matter.

When we stowed everything away in the truck, I was unsure if I should just smile and laugh, or rip off his clothes and let him know how badly I wanted him.

"You all right over there, Slick?" he asked, looking smug.

"I'm fine," I said, smiling brightly at him while repeating over and over again in my head, *I will not let this guy get to me.*

We made it to the house without killing each other, or ripping our clothes off and going at it, so I filed it under the successful outing category.

Kill surprised me by helping put everything away. We went back and forth throwing insults at each other, and my cheeks were sore from laughing.

Jet and Amy came in while we were just finishing. Jet had his arm around Amy's shoulder and she had a content smile on her face.

I gave her a questioning look, which just made her giggle into Jet's side. I was caught off guard when Jet kissed her on the top of her head, showing tenderness I didn't think he was capable of.

"We're going to drive around. When's dinner going to be ready?"

"You have to be at work at six-thirty, and we go on at ten-thirty," Kill responded.

"Ok," I said, trying to get my bearings. How stupid was I

that him knowing my schedule got me weepy?

"Five?" I asked, uncertain of everyone's schedule.

"Five works for me, Slick," Kill said, going into the living room and reclining on the couch.

"Fuck yeah," Jet said, putting his hand out for a high five, which I reciprocated.

"Alright, Candy, let's get the hell out of here." Amy followed Jet, waving goodbye with the licorice in her hand.

"Where's Jessie?" I asked the retreating couple.

"Van took her to the movies," Amy answered, walking toward the door.

I called out to her, "I'll text her. Have a good time."

I guess I could ask Amy if the truck compensated for anything. I laughed, and Kill turned around to look at me questioningly.

"As happy as Amy seems, maybe Jet isn't compensating for anything."

Kill laughed, and the rich sound followed me upstairs as I went to get my charger. While shopping, I found my phone buried at the bottom of my messenger bag, dead. I ran back downstairs to get it.

"You can plug it in over here," Kill said, lounging on the couch, watching a movie with way too many explosions in it.

I found a surge protector under the side table by the couch and plugged it in. I pressed the power button and waited for my phone to turn on. By the time it was up, I was sitting on the couch with Kill, taking apart every detail of the movie.

"Really, she's wearing that in the middle of the city during a crisis?" I asked when one of the main characters ran out wearing skin tight cutoff shorts and a tank top.

"And look at those nipples, I wonder if the explosions turn her on?" Kill replied, joining in on being a movie critic.

My phone beeped indicating I had missed a call. When I picked it up, it showed I had forty missed calls from a private number. My stomach turned to stone, and my hands shook. By using a private number, I couldn't prove Jason was violating the restraining order.

"You ok, Slick?" Kill asked, pausing the movie. I tried to give him my most convincing smile, but he didn't buy it. He took the phone from my hand and swore.

"He did it from a private number, so I couldn't turn him in," I explained, there was no reason to lie to him now.

"Let's go report it." Kill stood up, his face simmered with anger.

"Why? I can't prove it was from him. Sit back down."

He stood over me, as he ran his hands through his hair. His anger was palpable. "You're just going to let him get away with harassing you? Is this so he'll forgive you, when you go running back to him?"

His question hit a nerve. I was tired, still a little hungover, and sore. I stood up, so I was inches away from him and held up my bruised arms. At the store, he pretended the discoloration on my arms wasn't there, but now I threw the evidence in his face.

"If Jason calling from a private number keeps him away from me, then yes, I am going to let him get away with it. I don't want to be near him again. Look what he did to me."

Kill tried to wrap his arms around me, but I was beyond comfort.

"Yes, I know it's stupid and stubborn to stay here instead of getting away. But he has ruled my life for so long, I don't want him to make my decisions anymore. I have friends, and now thanks to your dumbass, a job and a place to live. I want to finish what I worked so hard for. It will make me feel like I'm beating him this time around."

I punctuated my retort by poking Kill in the chest, and he did nothing to stop my assault. So, I went on, "I'm never going back to him. I'm mortified I stayed with him as long as I did. So get that stupid idea out of your dumbass head, do you hear me?"

My head was tilted back, with my finger planted in his chest. I was heaving from my outburst.

"I get you, Slick," Kill said, removing my finger from his chest. He had an indent where it had been drilled into him. I took my hand away, smoothing the crease.

"Sorry," I said, leaving my hand on his hard pec.

"No problem," he replied, giving me a half-smile, his dimple showing on his cheek.

I sat back down, feeling exhausted from my rant. Putting my head on the back of the couch, I closed my eyes. The headache I had been trying to stave off was fighting back.

I was rubbing my temples when the couch dipped down. Kill removed my hands and pushed my shoulder until my head was on his lap. My eyes snapped open, and he just smiled his panty-dropping smile.

"Relax," he whispered, as he worked magic on my head.

I must admit, his whispered voice was sexier than his singing one. Soon my eyes were closing of their own volition, and my headache receded.

"I need to start dinner soon." My voice sounded disembodied.

"I'll wake you up. When do you need to start it?" His hand ran through my hair. It was nirvana.

"I need to be up by three-thirty," I responded right before a huge yawn split my face in two.

Kill chuckled, and the rumble was soothing and sexy at the same time. As exhausted as I was my body was still hyper-aware of his proximity.

"You have an hour and half; sleep. I'll wake you up."

I tried to argue with him that it wouldn't be fair for him to sit there while I slept, but he shushed my protest, telling me it was fine.

My body quickly lost the battle, and I dropped into a deep sleep with the comfort of Kill's legs underneath me, and his hand running through my hair.

# CHAPTER 6

"Hey, Slick, it's time to wake up," a rough voice whispered in my ear.

I didn't want to move, I snuggled further into whatever was keeping me warm.

Kill's chuckle caused the warm wall my face was planted on to move, reminding me where I was. Embarrassed, I sat up swiftly and hit my head on his face.

"Shit, that hurt," Kill said, rubbing his chin where the back of my head had connected. "Hey, are you ok?" Kill asked in his sexy whisper.

I opened one eye, not ready for him to turn into asshole Kill. This was a stupid wish though. I needed asshole Kill to be around to help keep my emotions in check.

"Yeah, I can't believe you let me sleep on you. Don't laugh, but I haven't slept that well in a long time." Heat bloomed on my face, wishing for a filter on my mouth for these moments.

"Anytime, Slick. Now, come on woman, you owe me dinner for my comfort, and making me endure your snoring." Pulling me off of the couch, he walked us toward the kitchen.

"I don't snore." Oh god, please tell me I didn't snore.

He chuckled and hauled his arm around my waist, bringing my back to his chest. Leaning down, he pushed my hair off my neck, causing my pulse to skyrocket. "We'll have to do it again, to verify if you snore or not."

He let go of me and headed toward the refrigerator, pulling everything out and putting it on the marble countertop.

Taking a deep breath, I hoped my shirt hid my nipples that were standing at attention and waiting for orders.

"What do we do first?" Kill asked, staring at me with a knowing grin.

Trying to repair my dignity by not melting at his feet and begging him to take me caveman style up to his room, I arched an eyebrow, "We?"

I planned on using my cooking time to get my overactive libido in check, at least where a certain sexy rocker was concerned, I was afraid I wouldn't be able to control myself being in the kitchen with Kill.

It wasn't fair he was talented and sexy. Maybe he had a deformity that would ruin his perfection. I eyed his feet, concentrating on counting his toes. Of course his damn feet were sexy too.

"See something you like?" he asked.

"Not a damn thing, Killer," I replied, bending over to rummage through the assortment of pots and pans, Kill stood behind me.

His body pressed against mine with his mouth next to my ear. Shivering at his closeness, I made the decision, I couldn't stay here.

I couldn't contain myself when I was near him, certain he would hurt me more than Jason's fists ever did. I needed to feel whole again, and Kill was a band-aid. I wanted more than just a superficial fix.

"You shouldn't tease me by wiggling that damn thing at me. You have the greatest ass," he told me, as he unfolded his body and stretched.

When his arms reached over his head, his shirt rode up, giving me a view of his sculpted abs and blood rushed to my most sensitive areas.

"Do you think you can handle the salad?" I asked as I squatted, to get the pots and pans I needed.

"Oh, I can handle a lot."

My whole body ignited from just that simple statement, confirming this man was dangerous to my body, and heart. "Just the salad," I mumbled.

He chuckled while chopping vegetables. When slipping the lasagna into the oven, I remembered I needed to text Jessie. I jerked up and burnt my hand on the rack. Searing pain shot up my arm before I could pull it away.

"Shit!" I closed the oven door and jumped around, trying to jump the pain away. Kill pulled me toward the sink, turning on the cold water and shoved my blazing hand under it.

"I think I'm good, Annie Wilkes," I said, taking my hand out from under the water when it went numb.

Kill's hand was still around my wrist. He gently ran his thumb over the burn marring my skin. "You need to be more careful, Mr. Sheldon. I might have to hobble you if you keep this up."

I laughed, appreciating he got my reference to Stephen King's, *Misery*. "Nice pull there, Killer."

"That's what she said."

This time I laughed so hard I had to hold onto the counter for support. "You did not just do a 'that's what she said' joke."

"What can I say, Slick, I aim to please."

I let out a very unladylike snort, which had me laughing all over again.

"What had you so startled you tried to burn your hand off?"

"Oh shit. I forgot to text Jessie to let her know when dinner would be ready. She'll be pissed if she misses my lasagna."

"I already did," Kill said, as I started my trek to the living room.

I spun around, to find his half-smile I craved on his face.

"When?" I already knew the answer, but I had nothing else to say.

"Between your snoring and trying to crawl into my stomach like a ton-ton."

"You're a nerd!" I said, doing a happy dance. "Mr. Moody, Broody, all hot and sexy, who has every girl in Portland's panties wet, is a Star Wars nerd." I jumped around the kitchen.

"The fact that you knew it was a Star Wars reference, makes you just as nerdy as I am."

I stopped jumping so I could look at him, a smile still plastered on my face. "Yeah, but everyone knows I'm a nerd. Hell, I have never had a grade lower than an A. But you, it's unexpected, and in all honesty it makes you less intimidating."

"You think I'm intimidating?" he asked, taking a step toward me, then another, stalking me.

He stopped when he was a foot away. I swallowed, remembering we were the only ones in the house, and the oven wasn't the only thing making it hot.

"Yes," I whispered, not breaking eye contact. My brain yelled at me to run far away, while my vagina put out the welcome mat and baked cookies.

"Why?" he asked, reaching out and running his finger down my cheek.

My body short circuited from his simple touch. "Huh?" I asked, not thinking clearly, except for how fast I could have him on the floor, naked.

He chuckled and removed his finger. I instantly missed his touch. Knowing him less than twenty-four hours, and I was addicted. I was so fucked.

"I asked why you're intimidated by me."

"Well, look at you."

As soon as the words left my mouth, I wanted to take them back. He didn't respond, and I assumed he wanted me to spell it out for him, so I did.

I moved my arms in a sweeping motion so he knew I was talking about his whole body. "You're gorgeous, you're talented, and from what I have seen of your body, you have no deformities to bring you to the level of us common people. It's not fair you have no flaws, well.... you have no comprehension of personal space, and you can switch from hot to cold in an instant. I'm not saying being a Star Wars nerd is a flaw, but I have to reach far with you. So I'm taking Star Wars and running with it, and you can't have it."

"You think I'm gorgeous?" His smile made him look like a kid on Christmas, and I couldn't help but snort again.

"Everyone in Portland thinks you're gorgeous."

"I'm not asking about Portland, I'm asking about you."

His eyes were burning with something I couldn't describe, and I had the impulse to run.

"I'm not blind," I said, turning around to check on dinner, needing a break from his intense stare.

"Neither am I."

"So does that mean you stare at yourself in the mirror to see how perfect you are?" I asked, trying to get the intensity of the room back to our playful bantering.

"You have no idea, do you?" he said, stalking toward me again.

I backed up until I was against the kitchen counter. He smiled that damn sexy half-smile, and kept moving toward me with a predatory gleam in his eyes.

"Honey, we're home," Van yelled out from the front door saving me from answering.

Kill backed away from me and I let out a shaky breath.

Van's arm was draped around Jessie's shoulders and she beamed from ear to ear.

Why was it so easy for them? I thought, giving myself a brief pity party before I pushed it out of my mind. Jessie was my best friend, and I wanted her to be happy.

She walked out of Van's embrace and pulled me into a hug. "It smells delicious. What was on the playlist tonight?" Jessie asked when she let me go, opening the oven door to get a peek.

"Playlist?" Kill asked, as I blushed.

"Yeah," Jessie responded, oblivious to my humiliation. "She picks music to match the food, and I know it sounds silly, but she can do it. Then she dances around, singing at the top of her lungs while she cooks. It's utterly adorable. If you guys ever need a girl singer, your new roommate's amazing."

"I was gypped!" Kill cried out in mock outrage.

"Shut up."

"No! Not one lyric, not one song, not even humming. This dinner was not properly made, and you will need to rectify this tomorrow, rightfully christening the kitchen."

"Jackass," I said, getting out the garlic bread.

Jet and Amy came in later, with tootsie pops in their mouths. I laughed at the sight of my friend sugarcoating her new man.

"Dinner ready?" Jet asked, sitting down. He hooked Amy around the waist and pulled her down, wrapping his arms around her to secure her.

Another stab of jealousy hit me, but I pushed it away,

wanting my friends to be happy. I was a hopeless case, broken when it came to working relationships. I needed to become secure in myself before I pursued anything.

"Almost. You boys want to set the table while I get everything ready?"

"Hell no, I helped cook. Let these lazy asses do it."

"You cooked?" Van and Jet asked at the same time.

"Fuck yeah, I did," Kill answered, looking at me, daring me to correct him.

"You made a salad," I replied, taking his dare.

"That's something."

Amy jumped up when there was a knock at the door. "I invited Trent," she explained. "He should be here to celebrate your escape from that douche box, Jason."

Wincing at the mention of Jason's name, I turned around trying to compose myself. My stomach knotted up, my appetite vanished. I wondered how much longer Jason would affect my life. My shoulders sagged and I willed back the tears, feeling pathetic and defeated. Kill came over and put his arm around me.

"You ok?"

We were alone in the kitchen; everyone else was prepping the living room. I gave myself a moment of weakness, and leaned into Kill, breathing him in. He smelled like body wash and something that was pure Kill.

"Are you worried your food's going to be awful? Because it sure does smell like it."

The tears threatening to spill over were gone, a real smile replacing them. "Thanks," I whispered, knowing he understood.

"Anytime, Slick. Now let's eat your nasty ass food. I'm starving." He smacked me on the ass, donning oven mitts, before taking the lasagna.

Trent leaned in the archway, glaring at us. I put on the best fake smile I could muster. "Hey you, I'm glad you made it. You remember Kill, don't you, Trent?" I asked, nervousness overwhelming me.

Trent nodded at Kill before coming over and taking the salad from my hand. Surprising me when he kissed me on the cheek.

"Hey, Faith, everything smells great. Can I talk to you?" His face had a look of desperation to it, making me uneasy.

"Uhm, yeah, can we eat first?"

He sighed, but nodded his head going into the living room. Kill stood next to me, and gave me a questioning look. I shrugged my shoulders.

The living room table contained everything I had cooked, and of course Kill's salad. D emerged from wherever he'd been.

"This smells awesome," he said, with the first genuine smile I had ever seen from him.

I had a hard time reading D; I was unsure how to break down his walls. "Thank you. Where have you been all day?"

D looked pleased with whatever it was. "Kill wrote an awesome song, and I worked on the instrumentals. I also made a bunch of calls, trying to get the band more gigs."

"D's our manager, so not only does he get to play awesome music, he gets to pick where we play it," Van explained, giving D a huge smile.

"Yeah, double the work to keep these assholes in line. It's a dream job," D replied dryly.

"You know you love us," Jet said, giving D a wet kiss on his cheek.

"Eat your food, dumbass," D replied, laughing.

"You write the songs?" I asked Kill. I wasn't surprised.

"Fuck yeah. Our boy's going to make us rich and famous. We'll be wading in pussy," Jet responded, while receiving a shot in the arm from Amy.

He had the decency to look ashamed. Amy shot him a dirty look, in which he responded to by kissing her on the forehead. "Well, they will be wading in it, I've got my own now," he said, making Amy kiss him hard on the lips.

During dinner the guys told stories of the horrible things their fans had done, making dinner go by quickly.

Noticing the time, I jumped up. "I have to get ready for work. I don't want to be late!"

"I better get going too. I'll come back so we can drive together," Jessie said.

"Don't worry, I'll meet you there so you don't have to make an extra trip."

"Ok, thanks for dinner. See you at work." Van followed Jessie into the kitchen, and then outside.

We had everything put away in a matter of minutes. I didn't hear Van come back in when Jessie left, so I assumed he must have gone with her to *help her* get dressed for work.

Trent called my name before I could make it upstairs. I took a deep breath, slapping on a fake smile before turning around. He gazed at the floor, standing at the bottom of the stairs. He looked nervous, making me even more uncomfortable.

"Are you sure you want to stay here? You know you could always crash at my place." His voice had a pleading edge to it, and I was afraid he would confess something that would change our friendship forever.

"It makes sense for me to stay here. You have a little one bedroom apartment. I wouldn't fit there." I was lying. I'd decided I couldn't stay under the same roof as Kill, but staying with Trent seemed like an even worse idea.

"My lease is up soon, we could get a bigger place." His face was distressed, and my stomach tightened.

"I couldn't ask you to do that. You're an awesome friend, and I love you for being there for me, Trent." I walked down the couple of stairs separating us and gave him a hug. "Now, I have to get ready. I don't want to be late for my first day. I'll call you later."

I dashed upstairs as fast as my cowardly ass could take me. Running into the bedroom that had been mine for less than twenty-four hours, I felt a pang of sadness that I wouldn't be staying here.

I put hair it into a high ponytail. My makeup was darker than normal, realizing tips would be essential in assisting me in getting my own place. I didn't want to dip too far into my savings, afraid it would alert my dad.

Pulling on my dark skinny jeans and a pair of zebra pumps, I shrugged into a t-shirt.

In the living room I snatched my charged phone and shoved it into my bag.

Kill sat on the couch watching T.V. "Your feet are going to be killing you by the time your shift's done tonight," he said, eyeing my shoes with pure male adoration.

"Nope. I've been wearing heels since I was a little girl. I love them." I turned my ankle around to appreciate my beautiful footwear.

"Whatever you say, Slick. Don't come crying to me when your feet are throbbing."

"I won't," I said, sticking my tongue out at him.

"You need to stop waving that damn thing around," he growled.

"I have no idea what you're talking about," I said, walking out the door.

I rummaged through my bag looking for my keys, I frowned when I reached the bottom, just before they jingled next to my ear. I looked up to see Kill holding them.

"Thanks," I said, trying to swipe them.

He held them out of my reach, an impressive feat since I was in heels. "What, no kiss?" he asked, his panty-dropping grin plastered on his face, making my mouth want to become plastered to his face as well.

I was thrumming with heat, all of which was centered in between my thighs. Knowing I was playing with fire, I decided to play this round. I put on my most seductive face, hoping I didn't look like I was having a stroke.

I saw his throat move as he swallowed, and I stopped myself from licking it. His pupils dilated, and I felt empowered I could make him want me, at least a fraction of how much he made me want him.

I sucked in my bottom lip and let my teeth scrape it as I pulled it out, tasting the Dr. Pepper ChapStick. His breath went ragged and his eyes darkened, not moving from my lips.

I locked my knees to keep myself upright. Slowly, I inched closer, his eyes pinned on mine. He licked his bottom lip, and it took all my willpower not to take him into the house, or hell, right there on the lawn.

I brushed past his lips, not allowing myself to graze them, afraid even the slightest hint of Kill would be devastating. I planted a big juicy kiss on his cheek.

"Thanks, Killer," I whispered into his ear, our ragged breaths coming out in pants.

I bit his earlobe, making him hiss through his teeth, as I held back the moan building in my throat since I started this. Running my hand down his arm, I pulled my keys out of his clenched fists.

I walked to the driver's side of my car, putting more movement into my step than necessary. Kill let out a deep breath, and I couldn't help the smile that surfaced.

He was still standing where I had left him. His gaze burning into me, and I was terrified I may have bitten off more than I could chew.

Kill's eyes were fierce with desire, and I was drowning in their penetrating green depths, proving I was in way over my head. Shit, I needed to get away from him before I did something I would regret.

I winked at him in the rear view mirror and started my car, trying to look composed.

My knuckles were white as the gripped the steering wheel, and I refused to look back. I felt his gaze on me until my car was out of sight.

I took my time driving to Ray's, I would be confronted with Kill's powerful eyes soon enough. His intensity, combined with his singing voice, confirmed I was going to be in hell trying to resist him.

I tried to remind myself he was an asshole, but every time I had myself convinced, my double-crossing thoughts went back to him running his fingers through my hair while I slept.

# CHAPTER 7

Fuck, I had it bad. Why did I want him? He was a total man slut, and even though last night was the first time I heard them play, I knew of the JackholeS notorious whore of a lead singer.

Just thinking about watching Kill onstage, as he looked into the crowd of horny women, certain most of them knew exactly what he was like in bed, made my insides crawl.

I needed a lobotomy. My choices in men were appalling. Since that would never change, I elected to make a different decision: to finish school and abstain from men altogether. Feeling powerful from my affirmation, I got out of my car and walked to the back entrance where Jessie waited for me.

I smiled at her, trying my hardest to stop myself from picturing Kill's gorgeous face as he ran his hands through my hair.

Damn him.

"Hey sexy, you ready for your first day?"

"Yeah, I think I am."

"Have you called Ginger to let her know you aren't coming back in?" Jessie asked as we walked to the breakroom. She handed me my new uniform, which was a tight black T-shirt with Ray's written across it in a deep red, and a black apron.

I knew Ginger deserved a two week notice, but she adored Jason and I didn't want to explain anything to her. So if that meant leaving her high and dry by leaving her a message tomorrow during the shop's peak hours, that's exactly what I would do.

"No, I had three days off. I should start back tomorrow. I'm going to take the coward's way out and leave her a message."

Jessie came over and touched my arms, careful not to place her hands on my bruises. "You're not a coward, Faith. You did something very brave by getting away from Jason. I know how Ginger loves him, and I understand your need to get away. Don't let him take your power away from you. It's your life and you're going to live it by making your own decisions; if anyone doesn't like it they can answer to me."

Jessie's eyes were on fire, and I had no doubt she would hurt anyone who decided to question me.

"You're hot when you're on your soap box."

Jessie smacked me, but laughed, making me feel like I might get through this. "Hurry up, and get dressed," she said, pointing to my locker. "This is your locker number." She handed me a slip of paper with the combination on it. I ran into the bathroom, throwing on my new uniform.

The crowd was sparse, as Jessie introduced me to the other two waitresses. The older waitress I took the shot from the other night was Denise. She gave me a big hug, telling me if I needed anything to let her know.

The other waitress was around our age, with a huge chip on her shoulder, and if she didn't get it removed soon, it would leave her buried in chiropractic bills. Her name was Bambi. Yes, Bambi. I had to ask if I'd heard it right when Jessie introduced her.

Bambi was beautiful in a bitchy sort of way. She was thin with huge aftermarket boobs, making her look even tinier. Her blond hair fell down past her bra line, and her face was done up like she was going clubbing.

As we walked away from Bambi, Jessie whispered in my ear, "She's a witch, watch out for her."

I nodded at her, letting her know I had already figured that out.

"Ryan, this is our new waitress, Faith," Jessie announced when we reached the bar.

Ryan put her hand out so I could shake it, and I noticed just how incredibly beautiful she was. "You were awesome last night. I'm so glad Ray hired you. If I had to deal with one more pathetically incompetent girl, I was going to lose my shit. Now if Ray would get rid of Bambi, my life would be peachy fucking keen."

I laughed, we were going to get along fine. Jessie walked me around the bar, showing me the tables and introducing me to the regulars.

There were a lot of women waiting to see if they would be the lucky one a Jackhole would pick to warm their beds. A sea of push up bras were scattered throughout the bar; some of the poor things were trying to perform resurrections.

My stomach turned thinking about one of them going home with Kill, but I didn't let myself dwell on it. Instead, I put my attention into learning the ropes of Ray's.

With the exception of a couple of creepers, everyone seemed nice. After an hour of getting familiar with the regulars and making sure everyone had their drinks, a bell rang. Everyone turned toward the commotion.

I hadn't noticed the big brass bell the night before, but with Jet clanging it, everyone knew of its existence.

"We have arrived; you're fucking welcome." Jet made his way toward the table they were at last night. Van walked in next, shaking his head at Jet. D was staring down at his phone, tapping away on it. He was oblivious to the sighs that escaped some of the women's lips upon seeing him.

Kill came in last and scanned the bar when he entered. When he landed on me, he stopped. Everything faded away as our eyes stayed locked on each other.

Nobody noticed our exchange as they were all too busy trying to pose themselves in the best position to get his attention. When he turned and followed the band, I had a small smile playing on my lips. I'd I received the attention most of the women in the bar were dying for.

Spinning around in a daze, I ran into one of the creepers I had been avoiding.

"Hey sweetheart, you look lost." He leaned in, and I could smell the stale beer on his hot breath.

I tried to push him away, but he had a firm grasp on both of my upper arms, where he reached out to stabilize me when I stumbled into him. I winced as he pressed into the bruises on my arms.

It figured the jerk would have the same size hands as Jason. It must be the universal dickhead size assigned when an asshole received his personality.

"Yep, you can let go now," I said, trying again to get

away.

This time he moved easily away from me. I blinked, wondering if I had one of those adrenaline bursts, you hear about when a woman has the ability to lift a car off her child. I saw it wasn't my super strength, but Kill standing in all of his angry glory, holding the creeper by his shirt collar.

"Don't touch her again," he growled. Everyone in the bar watched and waited to see what would happen next.

"Hey man, she threw herself at me. I'm sure you know how it is when they can't stay away from your cock," the creeper said, now demoting himself to dumbass.

He obviously didn't care about the bodily harm promised in Kill's eyes. A huge bald man wearing a Ray's t-shirt with the word bouncer printed on it, came over and took the dumbass out of Kill's hands, saving him from the beating of his life.

"I've got him from here, Kill," the bouncer announced.

Kill transferred his fury-filled gaze toward me.

"I had it!" I said, upset he was acting like I did it on purpose.

"Catcher, this is Faith, the new waitress. I'm sure you will get to know her soon; she has the ability to attract trouble," he seethed.

Catcher smiled as he shifted the dumbass over, so he was holding him in one hand, and he held out the other for me to shake. I was amazed to see my hand become engulfed by his ginormous paw.

"Nice to meet you, Faith. I heard about your ex last night. I was at the other side of bar, stopping a fight. I promise to keep a better eye out for him. Sorry about that." He gave me a wink, his face filled with sincerity, before picking up the dumbass and heading toward the door.

I turned to give Kill a piece of my mind, and was faced with his muscular back walking away, and damn if his ass wasn't edible, just like the rest of him. "Dick," I muttered under my breath, and went to the bar.

"Hey, sexy bitch, how are you holding up?" Ryan asked.

"Good," I replied as I gave her my orders. I had embarked on my own. Jessie excused my shadowing her earlier, deeming me ready to venture out with the customers.

My eyes swept over to Kill. His face was tight with irritation. D was talking to him, but he just stared at the table.

"You're a liar," Ryan replied, as I turned back around to see her scrutinizing me.

"Well, it's better now that the creeper has been escorted out." My fake smile was itching to bloom.

"I thought Kill was going to beat that idiot. I've never seen him get so angry before."

"Hey, sugar, are you ok?" Denise asked as Jessie put her arm around my waist.

"I'm fine. Believe me, I've dealt with bigger assholes."

Denise's eyes skimmed my bruised arms, before looking away.

"Catcher will take care of you. I should've introduced you to him first. Sorry, Faith, I wasn't thinking," Jessie said with her head on my shoulder.

"Enough! I'm fine. Kill had him off me before I had a chance to worry."

"That was kind of hot," Denise sighed, and Ryan nodded her head in agreement.

"And what's this thing between you and Van?" Ryan asked Jessie, causing her to blush.

"I don't know what you're talking about."

"All I can say is, it's about damn time. I was getting sick of you two eye-fucking each other across the room every night," Denise replied, leaving before any of us could respond.

Jessie sputtered, staring at her retreating back. I laughed so hard I had to lean on the bar for support. "Shut up," Jessie grumbled.

I went to grab my drink orders for the gaming area, but Jessie stopped me. "Why don't you go give the boys their drinks? I'll deliver these for you," she said, taking my full tray.

"I don't need you to baby me, Jessie. I'm fine."

"Shut the fuck up," she said with a straight face and sauntered off.

My mouth hung open from hearing my little southern belle tell me to *shut the fuck up*, without even flinching, and damned if it didn't make me proud.

"Shit, we're corrupting her. They grow up so fast," Ryan said, wiping a pretend tear off of her cheek.

Jet saw me first, giving me a huge smile. "Hey, sexy, you want to come home to my house tonight?" he said, wiggling his eyebrow.

Kill glowered at me, causing me to roll my eyes at him. "Are you always so damn pissy?" I asked him when I sat the last beer in front of him.

The Kill who had ran his fingers through my hair had vanished.

"Actually no, my attitude only comes out when you're near."

The pain that shot through me from his harsh words caused me to inhale sharply. I shook my head, embarrassed at my reaction.

"Don't worry, Killer, I promise to stay away from you while I work here. I will come get my stuff tomorrow. You're welcome. I just fixed your attitude," I whispered in his ear.

Someone called me from across the bar, and I hurried away. Kill tried to stop me, but in an expert move, I dodged him.

I questioned if all his flirting and touching was just a way to scare me off, so I wouldn't stay at their house. How stupid was I?

Instead of letting his overly sexual touches scare me off, it did the opposite, turning me on to the point where I foresaw my fingers getting a vigorous work out later.

But why he was so sweet to me on the couch? Maybe he thought I would be afraid of him and his invasion in my personal space, being I just got out of an abusive relationship.

Like any normal person in my situation, I should have been shying away from males instead of throwing myself at them. So much for being on the right track and piecing myself together.

In a fog, I obsessed over every minute detail that had happened today. I jumped when the band started their set; I hadn't even heard them get onstage.

The whole bar was screaming, competing over who loved the band more. Kill talked to the crowd, getting them even more revved up, while the rest of the band got situated.

They started with a song they had sung last night. I stopped for a moment; he really was amazing. The way he commanded the stage, making each person feel as though he had some intimate connection with them, was inspiring. I recoiled, thinking he probably did have an intimate connection with most of the females in the crowd.

They seamlessly merged into the next song. It must have been a fan favorite, being the whole bar sang along. Ugh, did he have to be so good? I thought, singing the song in my head with everyone else.

The charisma Kill had onstage was going to take them far, yet another reason I needed to stay away. When they took a break, some of the braver women attempted to talk to them. The band flirted right back. A couple women tried to sit on their laps, but they turned them down so smoothly they didn't even know it happened.

Kill caught me staring and came toward me. I busied myself with my tables, not ready to talk to him. My traitorous body tingled at his proximity. I put on a bland face and turned toward him. His face was ignited with annoyance, and it made me even hotter. Yeah, I know I'm all kinds of fucked up.

"We need to talk," he said through gritted teeth.

The couple I was serving seemed surprised to see Kill at their table. I took a shot at fleeing. I didn't get very far before his fingers encircled my wrist, and electricity zipped up my arm settling deep in my lower abdomen.

He walked me toward the breakroom, and all I could do was try to keep up with him. Once we made it to our destination, he let go of my wrist and twirled me around.

"What the hell, Kill? You don't get to just manhandle me," I yelled, matching his anger. My emotions had run the gambit these past couple of days. I was exhausted and done with everything.

"You can't just say you're going to come get your stuff without explaining why."

We were now toe to toe, fuming at each other. "What, did you talk to that dickhead? Did you forgive him already? I was sure you would last a week before caving in."

I rubbed my temples, as my headache roared back to life. I finally got it; he saw me as some pathetic girl who would go back to her abuser in time. He had no respect for me, which I understood. I had no respect for myself. I lowered my hands, as the effort proved to be useless, my headache was now in full force.

Pulling together all the pride I feasibly could, I told myself I could cry later tonight. Knowing there was nothing I could tell him to get him to change his opinion, I turned on my beautiful heels and walked away. I thought I heard him whisper my name, but I was sure it was just my imagination.

The band finished their second set, doing an amazing job, and I thought to myself again, they wouldn't be playing this small bar much longer.

After last call, Jessie and Denise taught me how to shut down the bar. Every time my eyes wandered over to the boys' table, on their own accord, Kill was staring at me with his fathomless green eyes burning with emotion.

Ray called me into his office and asked me how my first day went. With the look he shot me, I knew he heard about the creeper incident. I explained, between Kill and Catcher, I couldn't have been safer. Ray cautioned me to be careful and to let Catcher know if anyone else bothered me. Jessie was waiting for me by our lockers when I was dismissed.

"Are you going to stay with Van tonight?" I asked.

Her face flushed. "He's coming over to my place tonight," she squealed, "I just wish he wasn't a drummer. He went home, to change. I know he won't be around long, but I'm just living in the moment. By the way, Kill asked me if you wanted them to wait so one of them could ride with you, but I told him you were fine."

I was grateful Kill didn't mention my moving out. I didn't want Jessie to worry, especially when she seemed so happy.

"Yep, I'm headed there now. Love you, 'night." We hugged goodnight and I climbed in my car. I circled around the block, before pulling back into the Ray's parking lot.

Yanking on my hoodie, I loved it could make me feel snug and secure. I was surprised when I found it clean and folded, on my passenger seat. Thankfully, my laptop was hidden under my seat. While my computer booted up, I leaned my head on the seat.

Guilt clawed at me for lying to Jessie, and I was sure I would catch hell when she found out. I must have drifted off because I was jolted awake to a banging on my window. Looking up through sleepy eyes, I caught Kill glaring at me. His jaw ticked, and his dimple kept appearing and vanishing from his cheek.

I sighed, no longer able to avoid him, yet longing for a couple more hours of sleep before I had to deal with him. Leaning over, I unlocked the passenger door, nodding with my head for him to get in if he wanted to talk. I moved my computer to the backseat while he got situated.

He stared straight ahead, and I was at a loss on how to start. He finally looked at me. "Ray called. He has cameras back here and was worried when he saw you."

My stupid heart dropped. He wasn't worried about me; he was helping a friend get rid of unwanted loiterers.

"Sorry, I was looking for a hotel room. I must have fallen asleep," I said, wanting to get this over with, and him out of my car as soon as possible. The tiny space was allowing his scent to drift over me, warming me even more than my hoodie. He smelled clean, and his hair was wet from the shower he must have taken.

"You weren't going back to him?"

"No, asshole. I already told you I wasn't. I figured I'd give it another week," I retorted, throwing his words back in his face.

"Come home." His eyes pleaded with me to comply, and I was close to agreeing.

"No, I know you think I'm this pathetic girl, but I don't need you or your charity. I left him, and I'll make it by myself." The tears threatening to fall, broke free, and I was too tired to stop them.

He brushed a tear from my cheeks. The gentle brush of his finger caused my heart to break for what could never be. "I don't think you're pathetic," he replied, leaning back on the seat. "I had a friend, Melissa." The way he said her name, made my throat clog up.

"She was in a relationship like yours. With my help she left him. Two weeks later she was gone; just packed up without telling me. She went back to him."

The anguish in his voice caused more tears to fall from my eyes.

"She fell down the stairs and broke her neck, killing her instantly. Her boyfriend swore he wasn't around when it happened. His dad was high up on the police force, and the questioning never went any further than his first statement. She told me the night she left him he threatened to kill her by throwing her down the stairs."

His fists were so tight his knuckles were white. I reached over and wrapped my hand around his hand. We stared out the windshield, lost in our own thoughts.

After a while, it got cold, my hoodie no longer kept me warm. Our hands were intertwined, and I didn't know which one of us linked them together.

"Well, I hate to admit it, but you were right," I said breaking the silence.

His face blanched, and he removed his hand from mine. The ticking in his jaw started again. *His dentist must have a field day*.

"My feet are killing me," I replied, lifting up my shoes I pried off of my feet earlier.

Kill chuckled as he tossed them in the back seat.

"Hey, Killer, those cost a lot of money. You shouldn't treat them like that."

I went to apologize to them, but Kill caught my chin between his fingers, and in just one look, I was no longer cold; that boy's eyes could do more for me than a dozen blankets.

"Let's go home." His face was firm, and I knew he wasn't going to relent.

"We want you there, Faith. We're trying to get our karma points up so we'll hit it big soon."

I closed my eyes to block his gaze, keeping a clear mind when those powerful orbs were staring at me was impossible. "I don't want to be a charity case, Kill. Besides, the JackholeS are going to make it with or without karma. You guys are amazing. I'm surprised you haven't already hit it big already." I opened my eyes, and his were blazing with passion.

"You think I'm amazing?" he said in a sing-song voice, causing me to roll my eyes.

He so didn't need a bigger ego. "No, Killer. I said you guys are amazing - as in all of you."

"Yeah, but I'm a part of the *'guys'*, therefore I'm, according to you, amazing."

I laughed at his logic. "Ok, you know you're pretty awesome, so you have to know your big break will happen soon." His face reddened from my praise.

"No, we're just like any other band. I would like to make it for the boys though. They have been through so much. I don't really care about the fame."

"But you're so good. Hell, every woman in the crowd thinks you're singing to her, and everyone of them wants you. Every man either hates you because their woman is lusting after you, or they want to thank you for getting them hot so all they have to do is quirk their finger."

Kill gave me his damn half-smile, while his eyebrow raised. "Do you want me, Slick?"

His voice was low and rough, almost as if he growled his question. My stomach flip flopped, and heat flooded my body, centering in my most intimate spot.

"Sorry, Killer. I don't find you attractive, you're too arrogant for my taste."

His half-smile turned into a full blown smile, causing his dimple to become present and accounted for, and fuck if he didn't look adorable with that naughty expression.

"Liar," he taunted, as he got out of my car, his smile still plastered on his face. "Follow me home, and don't get any ideas. We want you there; you're stuck with us now."

With that, he walked over to Jet's truck. He drove toward the exit, not pulling out until he was satisfied I was following him. I stayed close behind him, and pulled into the exact spot I was parked in before.

In front of me was a black Toyota Highlander, which I assumed was D's. Earlier today, next to Jet's truck, was an orange El Camino. It was missing, so I was guessing it was

Van's.

I slid around to get my shoes, apologizing to them for Kill's rough behavior. He came over to see what the hold up was, and snatched my shoes from my hands.

"Hey, jackass, be careful with those," I shrieked, lunging for him.

When my feet hit the ground, I jumped back into my car. The asphalt was freezing, and my feet cramped on contact. Kill chuckled, throwing me over his shoulder, getting my laptop and bag in one swoop.

"What the hell are you doing?" I asked his perfectly shaped ass.

"I'm carrying you into the house you're now living at, so you don't have to put those hot as hell torture devices back on. Well, at least until your next shift, because watching you prance around in those damn things tonight was sexy as fuck."

I didn't know how to respond. My blood was centered around the fire his words caused, short circuiting my brain from any logical thought.

In the house, the guys were playing video games. "Uhm, hey, Faith?" I heard D say, unable to see him as I was still looking at the sexiest ass ever.

"Put me down, asshole." I tried to sound outraged.

Once again I slid over his body. I couldn't stop from gasping when his jeans scraped across my stomach. Passion reflected on his face. Remembering we weren't alone I spun around. The guys were on the couch watching us. Van was absent, already over at Jessie's.

"What the hell, Faith. Why are you trying to deny us your cooking?" Jet whined. He looked wounded, and I couldn't help but laugh before sobering.

"Look, I appreciate you guys trying to help me, but I feel like a charity case."

Kill whirled me around. His nostrils flaring. "Go upstairs to your room. Enough of this shit, and if you ever try to run again I will find you. Don't worry about finding a damn place, you're staying here, at least until you're done with school. This isn't charity, so get your ass to bed. We want you here. We'll protect you, so you get to live the life you deserve, without worrying about your ex."

"Fine," I relented, but decided to use my newly discovered independence. "But, I'm paying rent."

He wanted to argue, but seeing the determination in my eyes, he nodded. "Alright, Slick," he spun me around to face the guys again.

They gazed at me with support in their eyes, and I felt myself start to mend.

"Thank you," I said, and shyly went upstairs.

In the room that would be mine for the remainder of my schooling, I dug through my clothes. I found my Nikes before pulling out a pair of yoga pants, sports bra, socks, and tank top. Deciding to go for a run in the morning.

I used to run every day with my dad. Jason hated it, saying I was just looking for attention. With him out of the picture, there was nothing to stop me.

In the bathroom, a fresh pink towel hung on the towel rack, making my heart swell. After a quick shower, the day finally caught up with me. I dressed in my running clothes, figuring it would be an incentive to get out of bed in the morning.

Setting the alarm on my phone, I noticed it was half charged. I went through my bag looking for my charger, before remembering I left it in the living room.

My thighs clenched as I recalled Kill's long, smooth fingers running through my hair. I cleared my head of those thoughts, and went downstairs.

D and Jet were arguing about their game while Kill sat on the couch. Kill, being less engrossed, saw me first.

"Going somewhere?" he asked with fire in his eyes, ready for a fight.

"Nope," I replied, putting extra emphasis on the p. I unplugged my charger and turned to walk back to my room, but Kill stopped me.

"Why are you dressed? You aren't going to sneak out in the middle of the night are you?" he asked, causing Jet to pause the game.

Jet looked at me with puppy dog eyes. "Faith, you can't deny the Sex God of home-cooked meals."

"Relax," I said, talking to Jet instead of Kill. "I'm going to go for a run later. I wanted my phone charged, that's all. Geez, you guys are worse than mother hens."

"That's because we love you, doll-face," Jet replied, making me smile on my way upstairs.

With everything that went on today, I hoped sleep find me fast, but it must have lost my new address, because it was nowhere to be found.

Plugging in my iPod, I put my ear buds in. I turned on my sleep music, which to anyone else would be the least bit soothing. I listened to hard rock when I couldn't sleep.

If I turned it on loud enough, it would drown out my worries, letting my mind shut down and lull me to sleep. When Halestorm's *'Freak Like Me'* started, sleep finally GPS'd my new bedroom and claimed me.

# CHAPTER 8

I became discombobulated as my alarm went off, trying to figure out where I was. Then, like a harping aunt, the reality of the last couple of days hit me.

I contemplated if I should call Ginger before or after my run. Undecided, I went into the bathroom to get ready. I tried to be quiet, not wanting to wake anyone as I left my room.

I stopped mid-stride when I saw Kill sitting on the couch, a glass of green froth in his hands. He was wearing black gym shorts and a matching tank. His defined arms and abs were showcased by his tight shirt. The black tennis shoes laced on his feet made him look like the quintessential badass.

"Like what you see?" he asked, bringing me back from perusing his body.

I snapped my mouth shut. "Nope, just wondering why you're dressed up," I said, as I walked into the kitchen to get a bottle of water.

Kill followed me. I leaned against the counter, putting space between us. His eyes lit up with laughter, and that adorable half-smile was back. "Well, I was hoping you'd let me run with you."

"No," I said, flat out rejecting him, knowing with him anywhere near me, I would most likely trip and fall. Being near Kill had a way of making me feel off balance.

"Why?" he asked, surprised by my answer.

It made me smile to think his offers weren't denied often, or ever, and I just did. "Because I haven't run in a while, and I don't know how far I'll get."

"All the more reason for me to go; to make sure you don't pass out."

"I'm not going to pass out," I retorted, putting my hands on my hips.

"Good," he replied, rinsing out his cup.

"What the hell is that?" I asked, pointing to his now

clean glass.

"A protein shake, much better for you than coffee." He snatched a bottle of water out of the fridge, before leaving the kitchen. I stood there and fumed as he opened the door. It didn't close as he waited for me on the other side.

"Don't be scared, Slick." His taunt was all the motivation I needed.

As I pried my eyes from his ass while he stretched, I hoped he didn't see me. The smile on his face was a dead giveaway I was caught.

After a block, Kill slapped my ass and ran ahead of me. "Come on, show me what you got."

Letting the rhythm of my feet on the pavement, and the music in my ears take over, I tried to ignore him. Anytime I slowed my pace, Kill slapped me on my ass, laughing as I glared at him.

After a while, my body was exhausted from being pushed so hard, so soon. I slowed, evading Kill's hand when he reached for me. My legs were shaking when we reached the house. While taking a drink of water, a tremor from my spent muscles caused me to spill.

I swiped the water off of my chin, missing the rest as it trekked down my neck. Kill traced the rivulets of water with his eyes as they trailed down my throat, soaking into my tank top.

When his eyes flicked to mine, desire was smoldering in them. He took a step toward me, and I froze, caught in his gaze. He ran his thumb over my bottom lip, before dropping his hand to the side.

My tongue traced the path his thumb just made. I could taste the salt from both of us, and the fire inside of me burned hotter.

He tracked my tongue during its journey, causing my body to become a bundle of sensations. Closing his eyes, he rubbed the back of his neck, cursing under his breath.

When he opened his eyes, the need swimming in them had vanished, replaced by an impenetrable wall of aloofness. The sudden change was shocking.

He walked into the house, leaving me standing in the

yard, trying to catch the breath he knocked out of me. The inside of my thighs tingled with want. I shook my head at my stupidity. When would I learn to stay away from men, especially dark, broody, sexy-as-hell musicians?

I climbed into the shower, letting it wash away the grime and confusion. After dressing in a purple Five Finger Death Punch t-shirt, button-fly Levi's, and a pair of red sparkly sandals, my sexual frustration was at a manageable simmer.

I put on a small amount of makeup and curled my hair in big ringlets, certain it would be in a ponytail before nightfall.

"Where are you headed?" Jet asked, watching T.V. on the couch when I made it downstairs.

"I need to go grocery shopping, There's a brood of boys holding me hostage and making me feed them."

"Damn skippy, woman. What's for dinner tonight?" His eyes were as bright as a kid with a brand new toy, a brand new toy that cooked.

"I don't know, what do you want?"

"Pancakes!"

"Done."

"You're awesome. Marry me?"

"What about Amy?"

"She'll be wife number two, and we can share one big bed."

"Pig," I retorted.

If his eyes were shining from the thought of pancakes, they were nothing compared to the thought of the three of us in his bed. "But you love me, and don't knock my idea until you've had a chance to think about it."

Closing the door at his final request, I considered forgetting pancake mix.

At the store, I spotted a silver Honda parked at the edge of the lot. Squinting, I tried to see if it was Jason's. My heart beat rapidly, and my body grew clammy.

I realized at some point I would have to face Jason; I just wasn't prepared to do it so soon. Getting out of the car, I walked quickly into the store, my phone clenched in my hand. The whole trip my nerves were on overload, jumping at the slightest noise.

The car was gone when I came back out. In my car my phone's alarm went off, scaring the hell out of me. I reached for my birth control, and I noticed I was on the sugar pills, making me wonder if my paranoid state was due to my hormones.

Really, how many silver Honda Civics were driving around Portland? Jason wasn't stupid enough to violate the restraining order. Mentally inventorying the groceries in my trunk, I realized they consisted mostly of sugar, solidifying my conclusion I needed to get a grip.

At Walgreen's, I stocked up for the impending red tide, purchasing yet another bottle of Tums, a staple in my diet the past couple of years.

There was a sporting store next door, and I ran in and bought mace that attached to my key chain. I was in a hurry, not wanting my gallon of chocolate milk and carton of pralines and cream to get warm.

I pulled up into my spot, and popped the trunk, getting as many bags as I could so I wouldn't have to make numerous trips. They dug into my forearm as I strained to open the door.

Kill opened it as I fumbled with the knob. Without a word he took the bags from me. I protested, telling him I had everything under control, but he wouldn't listen. As I was loading up my arms for my next trip, Kill came up behind me.

"Did you leave any food for the rest of Portland?"

Ahhh, the playful Kill had returned during my absence. "Shut up, Killer," I muttered, pushing past him.

He laughed, taking the rest of the bags and closing the trunk. "What has your panties in a knot?"

Assuming some of my annoyance was from my upcoming visit from Aunt Flo, and the Honda, I decided to mess with him, to lift my mood. "Nothing has my panties in a knot, Killer, because that would require me to wear them."

He sucked in deep breath, and a smile cemented on my face.

I unpacked the groceries by myself, Kill quickly abandoned me after my remark. That done, I snatched an apple, telling Jet and Van I would start dinner soon.

Upstairs, Kill's bedroom door was closed. I smirked at it, hoping he was stewing in sexual frustration like I had been since meeting him.

In my room, my stomach pitched forward. I put off my call to Ginger long enough. Finishing my apple, I got up to throw it away. Realizing it was a stall tactic, I sat back down.

I dialed Cool Beans, hoping she wouldn't answer. But the universe gave me a big middle finger as Ginger answered after the second ring.

"Where have you been, honey? Jason's been frantic."

I pinched the bridge of my nose, annoyed Jason was playing the distressed boyfriend. "Ginger," I cut in, wanting to stop her rant.

Figuring it would entail how great Jason was, and how I shouldn't play games with a boy like that, because he will be snatched up in seconds by some girl who will treat him right, blah, blah, blah.

"I'm not going back to Jason, and I'm not coming back to Cool Beans," I expelled in a rush, pushing the words out as fast as I could.

Ginger was quiet for so long, I checked the screen on my phone to see if the call dropped. "Listen, Faith. Jason's worried about you. He said you were having a mental breakdown from the pressures of school and worrying over your dad. I get that kid, but you need to go back to him. He loves you. How about I take you off the schedule until you can get your life together? You will always have a job with us, but please call him. He's sick with worry."

"I'm sorry Ginger, but I can't." I pressed the end button, letting my phone drop to the floor before she could try to persuade me.

Pushing the heels of my palms into my eyes, I tried to stop the tears, but they escaped through the fissures they found. I pressed so hard I saw flashes of light. Removing my hands, I stared at the wall.

There was a light knock on my door before Jessie came in. She walked over and wrapped her arms around me. Her entrance sparked something, and grief hit me, hard. A loud cry escaped my lips. I turned my head into her shoulder and sobbed.

I let my heartbreak flow through me, not able to, and

not wanting to, hold it back. Needing to purge all the useless years spent with Jason from my system.

Once the tears had stopped, my eyes were swollen from the emotion that had flowed out of them. Jessie told me she would take care of dinner. Too emotionally drained to talk, I just snuggled into bed.

I heard her murmuring to someone in the hallway. The door opened, and without opening my eyes, I knew it was Kill. The bed dipped next to me, and a cold washcloth was placed across my eyes.

He got up, and I placed a hand on his arm, not fully understanding what I was doing. With everything that had happened, I wanted to feel secure, and Kill had a way of soothing me.

"Stay," I pleaded.

He stopped, and I didn't know if he would comply with my request. Knowing how pathetic it was going to sound, the word pushed through my lips. "Please."

He groaned, sounding defeated and crawled into the bed. "Roll over," he ordered, and I hurried to obey him, not wanting him to change his mind.

When I was on my side facing away from him, he wrapped his arm around my waist, hauling me to his chest. I breathed in his scent, feeling protected in his arms.

"Hey, sleepyhead, you need to get up, you have work soon," Kill's deep voice whispered in my ear.

I leaned further into his hard body, relishing the heat radiating off of him. Being rested and emotionally exorcised, my body was fully aware of how close he was, on my bed no less. He chuckled as I pressed myself into him, feeling his delectable hardness pressed against me.

"Are you awake, Slick?" he whispered in my ear, causing goosebumps to flare over my body.

My vagina was on fire, begging me to press myself into him again.

He let out a husky laugh when I shook my head no. I needed to stop. I was on an emotional roller coaster, and making any decision involving Kill would be bad.

Removing my body from him, I shivered from the loss

of his body heat. I turned so I faced him, his eyes were still behind the wall he built after our run, banning me from his thoughts.

"Thank you." My face heated up as I remembered begging him to stay.

"No problem. Although I'm worried I've lost my touch, being every time you're near me, you start snoring like a damn chainsaw."

"I don't snore," I retorted, rolling over so I could get off the other side of the bed instead of crawling over him, like my vagina was screaming at me to do.

"Come on, Slick. Let's get you fed so you can go to work."

I groaned, afraid to look at my reflection as I tried to run my hands through my knotted hair.

"You look beautiful. Come on, I'm starving. Watching you sleep while you roar in my ear would cause any guy to need sustenance."

"Go without me, Killer, I need to get ready for work," I said, and headed to the bathroom.

My hair was a disaster. I brushed my teeth vigorously, and put on makeup to hide the puffiness. I put my hair in a loose french braid, letting it fall to the side of my face.

I checked my shirt to make sure I didn't have any residual snot stains. Satisfied I was snot-free, I headed downstairs.

The boys were in the dining room looking over one of D's many notebooks. I felt shy, positive they heard my breakdown and were regretting letting an emotional female move in.

Amy and Jessie were at the kitchen table. Jessie warmed up a stack of pancakes she had saved for me. Amy had a handful of pixie sticks in front of her and handed me one. I tore it open and let the sour powder coat my mouth. Satisfied she had fixed my problems she went back to her sugar stash.

I walked over to the pantry and took out the peanut butter, syrup, and poured a glass of chocolate milk from the almost empty gallon jug. Slathering my pancakes with peanut butter and syrup, I cut a big bite and savored it. Amy looked at me with disgust on her face. "That's nasty," she said, her little face scrunched up as she looked at my plate.

"Really? This from the girl who gets her sugar fix from dyed powder?" I retorted, defending my pancakes.

I took another bite and chewed, closing my eyes and moaning, as if I had the answer to multiple orgasms in my mouth. Kill cleared his throat, and my eyes flew open to see him leaning on the wall, staring at me. My cheeks flooded red.

"We are so having pancakes every night." He perused my assortment of condiments on the table. "Is that peanut butter?" he asked, coming over to stare at my plate.

"Yes, she ruined a perfectly good stack of pancakes," Amy said in her little high and mighty voice.

I wanted to stick my tongue out at her, but Kill was too close, and I wasn't sure if his threat was for me sticking it out at him, or it coming out in general. Being it had made multiple appearances, I didn't want to push my luck.

"Shut up. Leave my pancakes alone," I said, pulling my plate closer to me.

Kill grabbed my fork and cut off a piece.

"Hey!" I yelled, as he put the bite into his mouth. I stopped, speechless, when he closed his eyes and moaned deep in his throat. Watching him swallow, I wanted Kill to eat me for dinner.

He went for my plate again. I tried to snatch my fork back, but I wasn't fast enough, and he had another bite in his mouth. He went in for another bite, but this time I got my fork away from him.

"Stop eating my dinner," I said, proud my voice didn't sound as breathless as I felt while watching him make love to my fork.

He shot me his delicious half-grin before taking a drink of my chocolate milk. Once again I was hypnotized, wanting to run my tongue over his neck, and if I'm being honest, everywhere else.

"That was good," he said. His eyes held a hint of desire, and I pictured myself spreading pancakes and peanut butter all over me to get him to look at me like that.

"We're going to practice. Let me know when you guys

are leaving." He glanced at Jessie, but his eyes traveled back to me.

I stayed quiet, my brain useless. Jessie got her brainpower back before me, and told him his dinner was in the microwave. He winked at me, before walking toward the garage.

"Holy poop, that was sexy," Jessie said, while fanning herself with her hand.

Amy had a pixie stick halfway to her mouth the entire time Kill tasted my pancakes. She placed it on the table, her mouth still open. Kill must be some sort of sexy if he could get Amy to put down her candy.

"Did you seriously say 'holy poop'?"

"Shut up," Jessie snapped, before the three of us dissolved into hysterics.

"Ready?" Jessie asked, looking at her phone to check the time.

"Yep, let me get my stuff," I said putting my dishes away.

Since the boys didn't play on Sundays, Jessie and I decided to ride together.

With a pair of bright red heels with a black bow on the back, I checked my makeup one last time.

Jessie met me at the bottom of the stairs. We heard the growl of a large engine start in the vicinity of the garage. I opened the door just in time to see Kill backing up a newer model Mustang. It was all black, and sexy as hell. *He couldn't drive a fucking Prius?*

"Fuck, that's hot," Amy whispered next to me.

He looked every part of the bad boy rocker getting out of his car, and I wanted a piece of it. Hell, I wanted the whole thing. He looked over at me with confusion, and I realized I was scowling.

"What, you don't like her?" he questioned.

"She's beautiful. I was just wondering what you're compensating for?" I replied, causing the girls to gasp and the guys to bust out laughing.

"Any time you want to find out, Slick," he smirked. "Where are your tennis shoes?" he asked, stalking over toward me and my beautiful shoes.

"They're in my closet ready for tomorrow's run."

"You're going to break your neck in those damn things."

Jessie laughed. "Don't even try, Kill. You can't get between Faith and her shoes. It's a losing battle."

"I think they're fucking sexy as hell," Jet interceded, helping D set up.

"Thanks, Sex God," I said, causing him to preen like a rooster.

Amy ran over and threw her arms around him. "That's my Sex God," she exclaimed, pulling him down for a kiss.

"Damn straight," he replied. His hands were planted on her ass. I rolled my eyes and looked back at Kill who was glaring at my shoes and shaking his head.

"Ok, bye," I said, wanting to leave.

Jessie launched herself at Van, kissing him on the lips leaving me to stand by Kill. Kill quirked his eyebrow at me.

"What, no kiss?"

My thoughts went to yesterday, and I reminded myself I needed to keep my distance. I sashayed by him and grabbed D's face, giving him a loud kiss on the lips. D's face turned bright red.

I caught Jessie's hand, dragging her out of the garage, refusing to look at Kill. On the way to work Jessie kept glancing at me. After the fourth worried look, I got frustrated.

"What?"

"Do you have the hots for Kill?"

"I'm so not thinking about boys right now," I said, purposely being vague.

"Good. I don't want to see you get hurt again, and Kill isn't the relationship kind of guy."

"Besides, he's gorgeous, Jessie. There's no way he would want some broken girl, when he has beautiful women with far less baggage, readily available to him."

Jessie voice was thick with anger, "You're not broken, Faith. You're the strongest person I know, and any man you choose should thank their lucky stars. It's just, I know how Kill is, and I just don't think he's right for you." She smiled as we pulled into Ray's back-lot, and parked.

I got out the car without answering her, not ready to admit to her or myself I wanted Kill.

The Sunday crowd was more subdued. Music was being piped through the sound system, trying to liven up the atmosphere. The band's table was empty, taking some of the energy out of the bar. More people ordered food tonight than the other nights, and I became well acquainted with the menu.

Ryan was in her usual spot, yelling at Dax, the cook, as he yelled back at her. The banter made me laugh every time I went to pick up an order.

Trent came in later and went straight toward the boys' table. I steered him to another table, and his face registered surprise, and then pure joy. My stomach sunk, hoping I wouldn't have to hurt one of my best friends.

"Hey, this is a surprise. What are you doing here?"

"I wanted to check on you and ask if you have thought any more about my offer."

"I'm going to stay with the boys. They have an extra room, and Jason won't bother me with them around."

His face fell immediately. "He'll leave you alone. You would be safe with me. Besides, the only reason Kill wants you there is to get in your pants. I've seen the way he looks at you."

My heart dropped to my stomach. Trent refused to understand how dangerous Jason was. Jason was just biding his time, waiting to pounce when he had the least possible chance of getting caught.

"I'm sorry, Trent. I love you, but I'm going to stay with the boys. And don't worry about Kill. He thinks I'm going back to Jason. Believe me, he wants nothing to do with me. Besides, you don't want me hanging around cramping your style with the girls." I wiggled my eyebrows, but he didn't smile back.

"There are no girls," he replied, looking directly at me.

Instead of telling him he had no chance with me, I chickened out and played dumb. "There will be soon. You'll find the girl for you," I responded, with my fake smile firmly in place.

"I've already found her," he mumbled under his breath, and I chose to ignore that comment.

"What do you want to eat? My treat."

104

Trent acted like he wanted to say more, but decided against it. "I will have a Cadillac margarita and an order of cheese sticks."

I rushed off to put his order in, feeling like a coward. It was official; men and I did not mix well. Maybe I should just join a convent, but knowing my luck I would get hit on by a creepy priest.

Trent was pulling on his chin, a sign he was thinking hard about something when I returned. "Here you go," I interrupted as I sat his order down.

"Thanks, Faith."

"No problem. Let me know if you need anything else. I have to go deliver my other orders. Enjoy." I walked away swiftly, but not before I heard him mutter, *I need you.*

I leaned on the bar while Ryan made my drinks for a group of businessmen. "You ok?"

"Yeah," I said, rubbing my temples.

"Are you sure?"

"Yes. No, hell no," I answered, making Ryan laugh.

"Been there. Here's your drinks. My advice, stay busy."

"Thanks." I took my tray, heeding her advice.

I managed to avoid Trent by having Jessie wait on him. After delivering his latest round, she walked over to me.

"Faith, be careful around Trent. He said some things the other night, and well, I'm convinced he thinks he has feelings for you."

"He keeps hinting along those lines," I admitted, wanting her opinion.

Jessie scowled over at him. "Idiot. I told him to leave you alone, and not put any more stress on your shoulders. He promised me he would not bring it up."

"He asked me to move in with him," I confessed.

"I'll talk to him, Faith."

I latched onto her hand before she could stomp over to him. "No, don't. I told him I was going to stay with the boys. I'm sure he'll get over it. As soon as he realizes I'm only interested in a friendship, he'll move on."

"I don't think that's a good idea, Faith. You need to tell him to back off, or he'll never get over you. The other night he watched you with intense possessiveness. Maybe we don't know him as well as we thought."

"Please, don't say anything," I begged.

We both jumped when the bell above the door clanged, ending our conversation.

Jet had his arm draped over Amy; the other was out like he was expecting people to run toward him. "Yes, I'm here. You people are so fucking lucky."

The bar chanted for the JackholeS as the boys entered. Van pushed past Jet, and he smiled when he saw Jessie.

"We'll talk later," she said, before walking over to Van.

D went straight to the band's table. I tried to stop my heart from speeding up, but the fucker wasn't paying attention to my orders. It was beating in time with the chanting crowd.

Kill walked in with a pair of worn blue jeans and a black thermal that hugged his beautiful body. He looked around the bar smiling at the people he recognized. When his eyes landed on mine, I held my breath.

He had his half-smile on his face and his eyes darkened when we connected. I couldn't pull my eyes off of him. He raised an eyebrow at me and I rolled my eyes at him. When the band settled in their seats, I picked up their drinks from Ryan.

She already set up four beer bottles on a tray, and a margarita for Amy. Trent grabbed my arm on my way to the boys. His eyes were unfocused, and he had a sloppy smile on his face. Maneuvering out of his grip, I was putting the drinks down in front of the boys, when an arm draped over my shoulder.

"Faith, I'm all out. I need a refill." His voice was slurred, and I could feel his breath wash over my cheek. I shrugged out from under the weight of him. His arm fell off my shoulder, catching him off guard. Thankfully, D and Van caught him before he fell.

"I don't think you need any more, Trent," I chided.

"You don't know what I need." His finger was wagging in front of my face, but his depth perception was so skewed he ended up bumping my nose.

"I try to tell you what I need, but you keep ignoring me, Faith. Why do you ignore me?"

**106**

Kill's jaw was clenched, and his hands were white as he gripped the table.

"Trent, you need to stop now," Jessie told him, coming up behind us.

"She has to know," Trent pleaded, setting his blurry eyes toward Jessie and Amy.

"Stop, Trent. You're drunk," Jessie replied, looking over at Ryan who gave her the thumbs up. "Trent, there's a cab outside waiting for you. You need to go home before you say something you'll regret."

Trent eyes locked with mine, and they were swimming with pain. He reached out and tried to stroke my cheek but missed and ended up petting air.

While D and Van helped him outside, I told Jessie I was going to take my break, and headed straight to the back entrance.

I took deep breaths when the night air hit me trying to get my emotions under control. The door opened, and I was surrounded by strong arms. I buried my face in his chest, breathing him in.

"What's wrong with me?" My question was muffled in his chest. "Why can't I have a normal relationship with a man?" I decided to clarify, so he would know which imperfection I was asking about.

"There's nothing wrong with you, Slick. It isn't your fault. You're just the type of girl that makes men lose their minds when they're around you." His voice reverberated in his chest. I closed my eyes, letting his essence flood me.

"So it's my fault?" I pouted, knowing I sounded like a petulant child, but unable to stop it.

He chuckled, and I relished the sound. "No, it's the man's fault for not being able to keep his sanity around you."

"That doesn't even make sense," I cried, still buried in his chest, never wanting to move.

"That right there. You argue with everything, pushing people away even though you bring out the protector in us. Then you refuse to accept help and get upset."

This time I pushed off of his chest. My circumstances making anger surge through me. I was premenstrual, pretty sure I saw my ex's car, and completely fucked when it came to the sexy man in front of me.

"I don't argue with everything, only when people say stupid things. It's not my fault most of the things that leave your mouth piss me off."

He laughed, firing me up even more. I walked past him, not wanting to be in the presence of his stupid beautiful face.

"Faith, wait." He tried to get me to stop, but I was already through the back door. My anger at the world fueled me through the rest of my shift.

Jessie finally caught up with me in the breakroom. "Are you, ok?"

In that moment, I realized just how much I hated that question. "I'm fine," I snapped.

I sighed, unsure if my attitude was from the impending red tide, or everything combined. "I'm sorry Jess, I didn't mean to be a bitch. Yes, I'm ok. I just want my life to be normal. When will I feel whole again?"

Jessie hugged me. "Soon, I promise. Van and I are going back to my house, since Candice is out of town. You're going to catch a ride home with the boys."

I wiggled my eyebrows, and she swatted my shoulder turning bright red. cheering me up. "Hey, Jess, don't do anything I wouldn't do, and if you do, name it after me."

Outside, the Highlander I parked behind at home was idling, confirming it was D's ride.

"Nice car," I commented, crawling in the back. I ignored Kill, and turned on the heated seats.

"Thanks. Someone had to be sensible and get a car that fits all of us."

I let the heat lull me to sleep, and by the time we were at the house, I was out.

"Hey, you're snoring again," Kill whispered in my ear.

I sat up, noticing it was just the two of us in the cooling car. After my second failed attempt to unlatch my seatbelt, Kill helped me.

The light mist in the air caused me to shiver when we stepped out of the car. Kill wrapped his arm around me. When we made it inside, I started upstairs.

108

"Where are you going, Slick?" Kill asked, putting his hand on my shoulder, stopping me from any further advancement.

"Bed," I mumbled, unable to keep my eyes open any longer.

"Aren't you hungry?"

I looked over at him, my eyes at half mast, and shook my head. "Sleep." I replied, making him release his grip.

When I got to my room, I put on a tank top and a pair of shorts, and climbed into bed. I plugged in my phone, deleting another missed call from a private number, and I was asleep before my head hit the pillow.

# CHAPTER 9

I woke up groggy as my alarm screeched at me to get up. My body was sore from yesterday's workout and I groaned when I stretched.

Searching through my garbage bags I pulled out a pair of tight workout pants. I rummaged around for another pair, but they eluded me. I felt self-conscious as they clung to my body when I put them on.

Jason hated when I wore tight clothing, telling me I looked like whore. My hoodie being so familiar, made me feel vulnerable in the revealing clothing.

Refusing to think about it I grabbed a load of laundry, mixing my stuff in with everyone's, and stuffed it in the washer in the garage.

I flipped Kill's car off, before walking out, pissed that in some cosmic prank, we both drove the same car. Mine old and out of fashion, while his was sleek and new, making them incomparable, just like the two of us.

Kill was dressed in workout clothes, and he looked fresh and ready to go as he waited for me in the kitchen. "Afternoon, Sleeping Beauty."

He smirked as his eyes traveled down my body, all of my curves on display. Flipping him off, I walked over to the coffee maker.

His eyes were on me, and it caused heat to pool in my lower abdomen. I came to the realization that as long as I lived with Kill, I was going to be in a constant state of arousal.

"Are you really a morning person? Because I absolutely hate morning people." I cupped my coffee in my hands so I wouldn't throw it at him.

"Technically, it's afternoon."

"Ugh, it is too early for specifics. Planning on going with me again?"

"Well, someone has to keep you motivated." He smiled

that half-smile and the heat between my legs slowly simmered, approaching a boil.

"Eat," he ordered me.

"After," I said, bristling at his order.

"You didn't eat last night after your shift, and I don't want to haul your ass home when you pass out, so eat."

"Then don't come. I don't remember inviting you."

His eyes flashed with hurt, and then understanding. "Will you please eat something?"

He took a different approach, figuring out I would refuse any order, even if it was for my own good.

"Fine," I relented, grabbing a bowl and spoon. Pulling out the box of Frosted Flakes. I drowned the flakes with milk and placed a dollop of peanut butter on the edge.

Sitting down across from Kill, I took a big bite and stared at him while I chewed. When I swallowed, I gave him an *are you happy now* look before taking another bite.

He smiled and watched me finish my cereal. A sharp pain cleaved through my stomach when the first bite hit it. I kept going until the bowl was empty and my abdomen was screaming in pain.

As I finished, I was clutching the table. Afraid to breathe in fear that my stomach would protest. Kill came up behind me, caging me in with his body. He leaned in until his face was close to my ear. "What's wrong?"

I didn't want to scare him so I took a shaky breath when the pain was less, and then another.

"Faith?" he asked again, panic lacing his voice.

"I'm fine," I gasped out.

He bent down and picked me up, depositing me on the couch, looming over me with his hands crossed over his chest, his biceps bulging. "What the fuck?"

I decided to embarrass myself, hoping he would accept my response so I wouldn't have to tell him there was something wrong with me. I'd been ignoring the sharp pains in my stomach for over a year. My daily staple of Tums was turning into a necessity.

"Cramp," I answered.

He quirked his eyebrow at me, silently telling me my

111

answer wasn't good enough.

"I'm about to start, and I get horrible cramps. I have since I was a kid."

His face reddened at my explanation. "Do you need anything?" he asked, sitting next to me.

He put his arm around me and pulled me close. I leaned on him, relieved he bought my excuse.

"No, let me digest my food, and we can go running."

His cheek was pressed against my hair, and I could feel the smile form on his face. "Are you inviting me to go running with you?"

I smiled back as he tunneled further under my skin. "Four days a week sound ok?"

"Yeah, that'll work."

We leaned on each other in silence until the rest of the house began to stir, and only then did we separate.

My stomach twinged, but I kept my face calm, not wanting to give anything away as he scrutinized my every facial movement.

"Ready?"

When he opened his mouth to protest, I put my hand out to stop him.

"Come on Killer, let's go. I bet you don't get to slap my ass at all today." I threw out the challenge, certain it would get him off the couch more than any reassurance.

He came out while I bent over to stretch. Coming over, he cracked my ass hard with his hand. I yelped, catching myself before I tumbled over.

"Challenge accepted."

My body was still sore from our last run, and now my ass was stinging. We started off jogging, until my muscles let go, moving more fluidly.

Kill reached over and smacked my ass. Thank goodness it was the other cheek. He increased his speed, and I had no choice but to follow him.

I was thankful when I saw we had circled back home. Seeing the house caused my legs to give up, and I slowed my pace. Kill took my cue, slowing until we were walking.

"You did good, Slick." He smiled, and I was proud I

pushed myself further.

"What are your plans today?" he asked.

"I don't know." Spotting Jessie and Amy's cars I had my answer. "I guess I'm hanging out with my girls," I told him, skipping up to the house.

"Umm, I don't think they're here for you," Kill said, rubbing the back of his neck, looking at the ground.

"Well, shit," I responded, dumbfounded. I finally got rid of Jason, and had time for them, and they up and found guys.

"You should watch us practice?"

He was still staring at the ground, and if I wasn't sure his ego had its own zip code, I would have thought he was nervous.

"Sure, let me go take a shower. What time?"

The smile that lit up his face made me wonder if I would ever be able to tell him no again. "In a couple of hours, and then I'll help you make dinner."

In my room I pulled out a light summer dress from my many garbage bags. It was dark blue and cinched at the waist with tiny pink flowers at the bottom. I dug out my blue flip flops since it was almost warm outside-those days are few and far between in Portland-and put them by the door.

After a quick shower, I blew my hair dry, putting it up in the wonder that was the messy bun.

I assumed the girls were with their respective boys when I didn't see any sign of them. Leaving my door open in case one of them decided to visit, I took out everything stashed in the closet.

I ran downstairs to switch the clothes, noticing Kill's Mustang was gone.

Singing along with my iPod, I unpacked my stuff. Inspecting my heels to make sure none of them sustained any damage in my rushed exit. Satisfied they were fine, I fired up my laptop.

The Wi-Fi was locked, so I ended up shutting it down. I surveyed the room, feeling relieved I'd decided to stay here.

Chomping down on a handful of Tums I went to switch out another load of laundry. Not knowing what belonged to whom, I put the stack of unknowns on the bottom step, and

113

took my stuff to my room.

Kill was on the couch flipping through channels when I came back down.

"Hey, Slick. Come sit down." His panty-dropping smile made me nervous when I sat down next to him.

"Stay here, I'll be right back."

He jogged upstairs and came back with a satisfied smile.

"What was that about?"

He shrugged his reply and sat down on the far end of the couch. I tried not to let it bother me he'd moved so far away. I mean, why would we be sitting right next to each other?

"Give me a foot," he said patting his lap.

When I didn't move, he leaned over and grabbed my ankle, hauling my foot on his thigh. I tried to take it away, but when he sunk his thumb in my arch, all thoughts vanished.

I leaned on the back of the couch, and watched his fingers do their magic. When he pressed his thumb into the pad of my foot, I moaned, loud. It took me a moment to notice he went still.

His eyes were shut tight, and there was a pained look on his face. I nudged him with my foot to get his attention. His face relaxed and the half-smile I love appeared.

"Only one foot, Killer?"

He smiled even wider, and I put my other foot on his lap. He dug into my arch, and I moaned again as my eyes rolled back.

"Alright. You need to stop making those noises if you want me to finish."

My cheeks flushed red from embarrassment. "Sorry," I said, staring at my foot still encircled in his strong hands.

He chuckled, and continued his ministrations. I bit my bottom lip to keep myself from moaning like a sex starved nympho.

"That isn't any better, Slick."

"Huh?" I asked, still dazed from his magic fingers.

"You biting your fucking lip. It's making me jealous your teeth get to taste your mouth and I can't."

The fire burning in his eyes heated up my lower belly and spread between my legs causing my already damp panties to become soaked.

"Sorry," I replied breathlessly.

He put one of foot down on the floor; the other was shoved to the back of the couch. Leaning over me, he covered my body with his. When he moved over my breasts, my nipples puckered to the point of pain. They throbbed for any attention he was willing to give them.

Our breaths were coming out in short pants. When he placed his leg right in the apex of my desire, I inhaled sharply finally receiving friction I craved. I unabashedly writhed under him trying to get more pressure to alleviate the fire he had started, certain if I sought it out I would obtain it.

My tongue darted out, almost brushing his lips as his eyes went molten. Kill groaned, pushing harder with his leg, grinding it deliciously into me, bringing me closer to the edge.

My inner voice warned me, if I went over, I would never be the same, shattering me in more ways than one. He let me brazenly rub my drenched heat on his leg.

I'd lost all sanity, only wanting to ease the fire roaring through me. His erection dug into my stomach as it strained against his jeans. His lips were mere millimeters from mine, and his pupils were dilated; a minute green ring surrounded them.

When he lowered his lips mine parted to grant immediate access. A door upstairs slammed shut, causing Kill to jump off of me, swearing under his breath.

Jet yelled downstairs. "Faith, I need sustenance. Your friend's insatiable, and I don't think I can go any more without food, and now I have to practice for Kill the tyrant, even though you can't fix perfection."

Kill stood up and adjusted his erection, shocking me when I saw the outline through his jeans, knowing there was no way that....thing would fit in me.

My vagina, being the team player she is, started doing yoga exercises in an effort to accommodate him.

I sat up on the couch and got my ragged breathing settled. Jet emerged with Amy on his back; both of them had candy in their mouths.

"There's the diabetic couple," Kill said sharply, his eyes crackling with annoyance.

"Dude, chill the fuck out. You need to get laid. You've been an asshole the past couple of days."

"Shut the fuck up and go get Van and D. Tell them we're starting practice in five. I'm going to move my car." Kill stormed in to the garage, slamming the door.

Jet flipped him off after he walked out, shrugging Amy off his back. He swallowed his candy and kissed her on the cheek. "Sorry, baby, I guess we'll have to rain check the next round. The dictator has spoken."

Amy bounced over and sat next to me, tucking one leg under her. "So, what have you been up to?"

"Nothing, just watching T.V." I pretended to watch the T.V. intently and hoped I was not as transparent as I felt.

"Are you going to watch the boys practice?" she asked.

I was relieved she seemed oblivious to what had almost transpired between me and Kill.

Jet, determined walking upstairs would require too much energy, yelled instead. "Douche bags, get your fucking asses down here. The tyrant wants to punish us for having pussy while he's going through a dry spell."

Jet went through the folded clothes on the bottom of the steps. He pulled out what was his and put it on another step for later.

I contemplated what Jet had mentioned twice now and of course my mouth, having a mind of its own blurted out, "Does Kill have dry spells often?"

Jet let out a shocked laugh. "Fuck no! That boy has a different girl on his cock every night. Hell, sometimes more than one. He's just been such an asshole the past couple of days, nobody wants to be around him. I hope he finds whatever crawled up his ass and pulls it the fuck out. I can't handle another brutal practice." He shook his head and yelled back upstairs. "If you don't get down here now, I'm coming up there and ripping your dicks out of whatever it's in."

Two doors slammed shut, and moments later Van emerged, punching Jet in the stomach. D walked down with a handful of notebooks, tapping on his phone and not paying attention to his surroundings.

When they opened the garage door, Kill yelled at them for taking their sweet ass time. The rest of his rant was cut off when Van awkwardly closed the door behind him.

Amy bounced up and down on the couch watching the door, to see if anymore drama would unfold.

Jessie appeared at the bottom of the stairs. Her hair was messy, and her lips were swollen. "Well, what have you been up to, young lady?"

She flipped me off, and I stared at her in shock. "You're being corrupted by a gorgeous rock star. I'm so proud of you," I said, getting up and hugging her.

"Well, I would have been doing a lot more if Jet hadn't interrupted us," Jessie pouted, sticking her already puffy bottom lip out more.

"Don't blame Jet. We were just coming up for food. It was Kill who called the early practice," Amy explained, bounding over to us and putting her arm around Jessie.

Jet walked through the door and saw us hugging each other and smiled widely. "Please tell me you three are about to kiss." He put his hands together like he was praying.

Amy let go of us and slapped him on the shoulder. "Please, you can't handle any more than me."

He rubbed his arm and kissed her hard on the mouth. "Who said I want to be a part of it? I just want to watch."

"Jet, get your ass in here now," Kill yelled through the open door.

"Alright," Jet yelled back, walking into the dining room to get his guitar. "Fucker needs to get laid. I wonder if he would get the hint if I put my big bottle of lotion on his pillow."

He bit Amy's shoulder causing her to squeal. "Please come out and watch us practice. Maybe he won't be such a dick if we have an audience of beautiful women," Jet begged, putting on his sad puppy dog face, making it impossible to say no. He opened the door wider, bending down low with his arm outstretched.

"Ladies," he said in a dry tone, kissing Amy on the neck as she walked through the door.

We situated ourselves on the chairs D put out for us. My mind drifted to Jet's comments, while the boys got ready. I wondered if I was the cause of Kill's dry spell.

The fire always simmering when I was near Kill flared at the sight of him. His voice in the microphone was like being doused in gasoline. He exuded confidence, and whether in front of his band practicing or in a stadium full of people, it was where he belonged.

When they were discovered, and I was confident they would be, they were going to be huge. All four of them were gorgeous, with generous hearts, giving them the bad boy appeal without the bad attitude.

Kill, being the heart of the band, would be the most sought after of them all. I was entranced as they went through their set. The four of them were the epitome of professionalism-well, as professional as a rock band could be, pouring their hearts into the music they were creating.

A desperate energy surged through me, wanting them to succeed, knowing in my heart they deserved it. They took me in without question, bringing me into their little family and making me feel more at home here in forty-eight hours than I had in the years I lived with Jason.

My heart filled up from the love I felt for this band of gorgeous misfits, and I vowed I would do whatever I could to help them reach their dreams.

"They're amazing," Jessie whispered in my ear. She had a sad smile on her face. Her eyes plastered on Van even as she spoke. Her face was in awe as she watched Van execute a drum solo. Amy watched Jet in the same manner Jessie was watching Van.

My eyes sought Kill. He was holding the microphone with his eyes closed, lost in the emotion of the song. When he reached the crescendo of the verse, his eyes locked on mine as he sang about finding someone who helped piece together the broken fragments of a soul.

The song ended, and we continued our stare down until Van started the intro to the next song. Kill broke the eye contact first, yelling at Jet to stop air humping, causing Amy to giggle. Jet looked over at her and winked, causing another fit of giggles to burst out from her.

I rolled my eyes at their antics, happy my friend had found someone who matched her boundless energy. We listened to them go over a couple new songs, stopping every so often to tweak something here or there until it was seamless.

After a while, Jet pretended to swoon by putting the back of his hand on his forehead, dramatically falling to the ground. "I can't do it anymore," he said in an exaggerated southern accent.

Van and D smiled at him still positioned on the ground, his guitar resting on his chest.

Amy scrambled to him throwing herself on her knees, glaring at Kill. "If you exhausted his energy, and he's too tired to get me off tonight, I promise retribution will be served, and you will not like it."

Jet grabbed Amy by the back of the neck, kissing her until she moaned. "Don't worry, Candy, if I'm too tired, you can ride me. I'll get you off one way or another."

"Practice is over," D exclaimed, blushing deep burgundy, and exiting the garage quickly.

Jessie let out a squeal and ran to Van as he maneuvered from behind his drums. She jumped into his arms, wrapping her legs around him and kissing him deeply.

They walked out of the garage, not saying a word, which was impossible with his tongue down her throat. I looked down at Jet and Amy just in time to see Jet's hand working on unsnapping Amy's bra.

Kill's eyes burned with lust as he stared at me, causing my mouth to go dry while my vagina started a strip tease.

I needed to put up barriers with him soon before I did something I would regret, or at least my brain and heart would. The hooker now living in my vagina was begging me to get down and dirty with Kill.

Amy let out a loud moan, and I heard a zipper slide down, breaking the mesmerizing stare. I hurried out of the garage with Kill behind me, both of us wanting to get out before witnessing anymore.

Kill went upstairs and I was left alone, not wanting to go to my room, afraid of what I would hear from Van's room.

Knowing what one friend sounded like when they were about to have sex met my quota for the day.

In the kitchen I plunged myself into cooking, hoping it would keep me busy. I contemplated going upstairs to get my iPod so I could get my cooking music on, but remembering Amy's moans, I quickly rejected the idea. Unfortunately, cooking didn't seem to need as much concentration as I thought it would, so my mind drifted to Kill.

It was obvious he wanted me, and I couldn't deny I wanted him just as bad, if not more. I also knew he wasn't a one-woman-man, and I wasn't the type of girl to have sex and not have feelings involved, especially if I was going to be living with him for the next year.

Kill was freaking hot, and I worried I was letting his looks muddle my morals. Although, if I was being honest with myself, which I'd been trying to do lately, it wasn't just his looks that had me hooked.

He had a sweet, vulnerable side to him he kept hidden. It was because of that side, I needed to avoid him. I already determined he would break my heart if I didn't stay away. The moment I saw him I felt an instant attraction, and the more I was around him the more secure I felt.

I need to explain to him we were only going to be friends, and I didn't want anything more. Panic coursed through me at the thought of him not accepting my friend stipulations.

In the few days I had known him, he had cemented himself in my heart, and I didn't want to lose his friendship. I wasn't sure why I felt I could trust him as much as I did, but I couldn't deny the soothing affect he had on me.

He didn't treat me like something fragile. He treated me like a regular person, and I felt less broken when he was near.

The chicken finished, and I moved it to the back burner while I methodically grated a block of cheese, still thinking of my predicament.

Without looking over my shoulder, I knew Kill had walked in. He carried an electrical current that had a direct link to my nervous system.

His hair was wet and pushed back off his face. He was

wearing a white t-shirt and a pair of jeans; his feet were bare, and he was mouthwatering.

I debated tossing out my whole let's-be-friends idea, but reminded myself how he could crush me if I let him. I would survive Jason; I wasn't so sure I would survive Kill.

"Need any help?" he asked.

I pushed the cheese grater and the bowl over to him. Kill helped me assemble the enchiladas. Our hands brushed together, sending licking flames through me at each minute contact.

Once the food was in the oven, I finally made eye contact.

"Got something on your mind, Slick?" Amusement was evident in his voice. His eyes were full of challenge, and I figured this was as good a time as any to set the boundaries.

"I can't sleep with you," I blurted out, face palming my forehead. "I mean, I'm not the type of girl that just sleeps with a guy."

This was coming out all wrong. Kill took my hand off of my face and lifted my chin with his index finger. "What the hell's going on in that brain of yours?"

He was trying to stop from smiling, but failed miserably.

"Never mind, I'm going to go crawl under a rock."

He tightened his hold. "Where's this coming from? You can tell me. We're friends, right?"

"Well, that's the thing. Even though I've only known you for a couple of days, I feel like we've become friends. I don't want to ruin it by giving into my attraction. I don't think I could take losing any more friends. They seem to be dropping like flies lately."

"Alright, Slick, I won't let you get into my pants, even when you're begging for it."

I punched him in the arm, amazed he could make me feel so normal. "I'll do my best to keep my begging to a minimum, Killer."

He tried to hug me, but I pulled back.

"I don't think it's fair to let you keep touching me. I don't want you to think I'm a tease," I admitted.

"Since you won't let me get you naked, I'll settle for a casual feel up. Come here, friend."

It wasn't fair to Kill, but I couldn't resist the comfort he gave me and as weak as it sounded, I wasn't going to push him away.

"Now with that over, what else do we need to do to finish dinner for these heathens we live with?"

And just like that, some of my reservations disappeared, and I knew it was the right thing to keep him away from my vagina, because with him, it would have a direct line to my heart.

I put the food on the living room table when Kill, D, Van, and Jessie walked downstairs.

"Where's Amy and Jet?" I asked, craning my neck to see if they were behind everyone.

Kill smiled and nodded his head to the garage door. My eyes widened as he went and banged on it.

"Hold the fuck on." Jet's screams were muffled, and I couldn't help but laugh with everyone.

"Dinner's ready," Kill said to the door.

Seconds later, Jet came out, his hair was in disarray and missing a shirt. His chest was now sporting fresh scratches. Amy looked similar to Jet, except she had all of her clothes on. Jet grabbed Amy's hand and led her toward the food. Kill put his arm over my shoulder, and we walked to the living room with everyone.

We watched *National Lampoon's European Vacation*, laughing as we recited the lines verbatim. After dinner was cleaned up, we were sprawled out, full and sleepy. Van put on *Christmas Vacation*.

My abs were sore from laughing. Jet and Amy were kicked out in the middle of the movie when they started moaning. Jessie fell asleep on Van, and he carried her upstairs. D left later when he got a text with a lead on the Tryptophan Torture Fest.

Kill patted the seat next to him. "Come over here, friend."

I wasted no time, crawling over to him and curling up into his side. Whenever he laughed, the fire caused by Kill, and

Kill only, turned up a notch.

By the time the credits rolled, I was focused on not breaking our friend pact. It was fucked up to push him away and pull him closer at the same time, but I couldn't help it.

I ran my hand across his stomach, stroking his heated skin through the fabric of his shirt, trying to push my unfair treatment to the back of my mind.

"Ready for bed, Slick?" he questioned, stilling my hand. His tone was pure sex, and it caused my lower muscles to clench, wanting to take his question in a very non-friendly manner. If I opened my mouth, I would give him a naughty version of my answer, so I stuck with the nod.

My vagina kept flipping me off, wanting me to do more than nod. We stayed together until the movie returned to the main menu. He turned everything off, and we sat there in silence, not ready to part ways.

"Come on, let's get you to bed," he said when I nodded off.

I wasn't ready to end the night, even though I was fighting a losing battle against sleep. He put his arm around me, and I snuggled into his side. As he led me upstairs, I saw most of the clothes I had folded were gone.

"I need to get the clothes out of the dryer." I moved out from under his arm, but he held me tightly.

"Get it tomorrow. We'll just turn it on again to get the wrinkles out. Old rock band secret."

I smiled, pushing my nose into his side, breathing him in. When we reached my room I moved out from under him, wanting nothing more than to pull him into my bedroom and use him as my own personal pillow.

He chuckled at my pouting face and leaned down, kissing my forehead before going to his room. Before he closed the door, he glanced back at me still standing where he left me. "Night, friend. I'll see you later."

He winked and closed his door. After convincing myself running into his room and stripping both of us naked was a bad idea I went into my room.

When changing into my jammies, I noticed a brownie on my pillow wrapped in colored cellophane. A note was folded underneath it.

**Slick,**
**Bite this instead of biting**
**our heads off from your**
**impending visit from Flo-ida.**
**Killer**

I put the brownie on my dresser and once again I had to persuade my vagina that I should not go and play naked Slip-N-Slide with Kill.

He was my friend and nothing more, I lied to myself, as I put everything on their chargers and slipped in my ear buds.

My thoughts wandered back to Kill, as usual. I wondered if he was as sexually frustrated as I was. I felt a twinge of guilt, and hoped not, for a second.

My breath finally evened out, and I fell asleep to Slip Knot serenading me. I woke up hours later with searing pain scorching through me, alerting me Aunt Flo had arrived.

# CHAPTER 10

From the time I first got my period in seventh grade I've had horrible cramps. When it got bad enough I was vomiting and blacking out, my dad took me to the doctor.

The doctor prescribed me birth control pills. My dad refused to put his seventh grader on them. He dragged me to herbalists and every other natural doctor in the area. By the summer of my freshman year, he relented and filled the prescription.

I'd been taking them consistently since I got my first pack. They seemed to help, not alleviating the pain, but I was able to make it through my day without throwing up everywhere.

Jason was more habitual about me taking my pills than I was. He would watch me and make me lift my tongue to verify I had swallowed it. Although we were exclusive, Jason would insist on wearing a condom. Even during his down-swings, he never forgot to put one on.

When we would have sex during his up-swings before he would come, he would make me promise I wouldn't get pregnant. Even with my assurance, he would pull out and finish in the condom.

Anytime I was out longer than expected, he accused me of cheating. The only cure Jason could think of to get rid of unwanted offspring from his cheating whore of a girlfriend was to punch me in the stomach, making sure nothing viable would survive.

After a couple of times of being in this predicament, I avoided leaving the apartment. My periods became progressively worse, and Jason used a punch in the lower abdomen as punishment for many other occurrences of disobedience.

One month, my flow was exceedingly heavy, and my uterus felt like it was trying to escape my body Alien style. I made an appointment and went to my OB/GYN when my flow lasted two weeks.

When the doctor came in, I must have been as white as the crinkly paper on the exam table. When the ultrasound technician started the initial exam, her face furrowed before she left to get the doctor. The technician pointed to the thick tissue angrily crisscrossing my uterus when they came back in.

"What is that?" she asked.

It was alarming to have a trained technician unable to identify what was in my body.

The doctor gave an apprehensive look before answering me directly. "That's scar tissue. Lots of scar tissue."

They finished the exam, and when the technician left, the doctor pulled up a chair.

"Faith, you have a lot of scar tissue. I want you to know if there's anything you would like to tell me, I would help you."

I swallowed the tears before taking a page out of Jason's book and making up a new reality. "I was in really bad car accident, and the lap belt dug deep into my abdomen. Most likely that's where it came from."

I plastered on my well-rehearsed smile. Giving me a disappointed look, she pursed her lips, trying to decide if it was worth pursuing. She must have thought I was a lost cause, because she didn't.

After writing a prescription to stop the bleeding she wanted me to make another appointment for further testing when my flow was over. I still had my smile on my face, not letting it fall until I was dressed and out of the office.

At home I explained to Jason I would be out of commission for a little while longer. He was convinced I was doing it on purpose.

That night, he grabbed me by the back of the head and forced himself in my mouth. He pounded into me with no concern for the gagging sounds coming from the back of my throat. After he spent himself in me, he kicked me in the stomach and walked away. He repeated this little performance every night until we could have sex again.

That night, he drilled into me, trying to cause as much pain as he could, pulling out at the last minute to rip off the condom and jerk himself off on my stomach, staring at me with disgust the whole time.

The next day, I went back to the doctor to get the rest of my examination done. She inserted a dildo-looking thing with a condom on it to get a better look. She frowned at the grainy black and white screen. Even I could see the scar tissue overtaking my uterus.

Her eyes begged me to tell her something, but I shut down. "Your uterus looks inflamed. Has there been any recent trauma?"

"I was walking into the bedroom with a laundry basket and it caught the door."

She was waiting for me to break, but what she didn't know was, if I hadn't broken from Jason's physical assaults, a severe look from a doctor wasn't going to cause me to crack.

After the exam, she told me to meet her in her office. I thought about bolting, before pausing to knock on the open door.

"Faith, please shut the door and have a seat."

When the door clicked into place, my heart rate skyrocketed. I walked over to the chair and sat up straight.

She had the audacity to open the file in front of her. I wanted to scream at her. She knew damn well what was in it without having to go through it again.

"Faith, from your test results, and the ultrasound preformed today, I'm sorry but I have to tell you, your chances of conceiving a child are very slim."

The air in my body left in an audible rush. I had never thought of children, but the knowledge I couldn't have them was devastating. When I didn't respond, she continued.

"I know you're young, and the thought of children is probably not even on your mind yet, but with the extensive damage you have sustained, your uterus is uninhabitable. And if by chance a viable egg attached, you wouldn't be able to sustain a healthy pregnancy and would most likely miscarry before you reached your second term."

I still hadn't recovered from the initial shock, and with every new word flung out of her mouth, it felt like another punch was being thrown into my abdomen.

"I suggest you keep using your birth control for now, but I would like to put you on a higher dosage. Use the pills I prescribed when your flow becomes heavy like it has this month and contact me if it doesn't stop after a couple of days. When you're older, we can discuss your options."

She got up and leaned on her desk, looking at me with a mixture of pity and sadness. "Do you have any questions, or would you like to tell me anything?"

I shook my head knowing my tears weren't going to stay back much longer. "I'm fine, thank you."

I was shrouded in numbness. Once in my car, I turned on the heat, not wanting to idle too long. Afraid she would remember something horrible she forgot to mention and come out to tell me.

I text Jason telling him I was getting my new prescription filled, and I would bring dinner home. He text back immediately, with his order, not bothering to ask me about my doctors visit. What a gentleman.

When I pulled my car into my parking spot, I grabbed Jason's dinner and my bag, containing a year supply of pills. I let out a bitter laugh, realizing I was a walking, talking birth control pill now. Did the pills make me a cannibal?

Jason greeted me at the door, snatching the bag of food, oblivious my world had just been altered.

Jason didn't wait for me before digging in. I wasn't hungry, but one of Jason's triggers was me eating without him. I nibbled on my food as it churned in my stomach. Jason smiled at my portion control while telling me about his day.

I excused myself from the table when he finished his food. In the shower I let the tears of what could never be, mingle with the warm water. I climbed into bed with my headphones jammed in my ears the music as loud as I could get it, and went numb.

# CHAPTER 11

Pain shot through my abdomen, bringing me back to reality and away from Jason and his punishments. My stomach made the universal sign for "you're going to heave." In a clumsy run I made it to the bathroom, dry heaving into the toilet until I was shaking on the floor.

Peeling my clothes from my sweat covered body, I crawled into the shower. When the tremors subsided, I washed off, feeling weak from the pain and memories.

Making sure I wasn't leaving a trail of blood like a slasher version of Hansel and Gretel, I stumbled back into my room. Swallowing the pills my doctor prescribed for the pain, and I begged them to hurry.

Wrapped in my towel, I crawled into bed and waited for the pills to take mercy on me. I was curled into a tight ball when Kill came in, filling up the room with his presence.

"Hey lazy, what are you still doing in bed?" He walked over and sat on the edge.

"Dying," I replied, wishing those damn pills would hurry the fuck up.

Kill cocked an eyebrow, baffled.

"I'm recreating the battle of Gettysburg in between my legs." I was disgusted at how whiney I sounded.

Kill laughed, and if I wasn't curled into such a tight ball, I would have kicked him. "Can I get you anything?"

I shook my head as a vicious cramp stabbed through me, causing me to wince. Kill's face transformed from amusement to worried.

"I have extra pain pills somewhere from when I sprained my ankle. I could go find them." His face was frantic as he tried to remember where they were. I grasped his hand before he could make it off of the bed, pulling him back.

"I took some. Just talk to me until they kick in."

He nudged off his running shoes and got in bed behind

**129**

me, running his hands through my wet hair. "Does this happen every month?"

"It only gets bad if I'm stressed."

Wanting to get my mind off of my pain, I asked, "How did you sprain your ankle?" The cramps began to fade away, and I unfurled from the fetal position.

Kill chuckled behind me, and I pressed my back deeper into his chest. "A very determined fan."

I waited for him to give me more details, but finally prompted him to continue. "Ok, you have to explain."

"Pushy little thing aren't you?" he quipped back. "One night at Ray's, when we finished our set, I umm, kind of made a comment about the one that made it to me first, would be the one that would get to finish first."

My cheeks burned, embarrassed when I thought I would have been pushing bitches out of my way. "Ok, I'm still not clear on the details."

"Well, there was sort of a stampede, and I was focused on some very eager uhm, bouncy friends. Because my attention was elsewhere, I didn't see the damn ninja running at me from the side until she had jumped on me. Her ambush caught me off guard, and I stumbled, spraining my ankle while trying to keep us upright so we weren't trampled by the approaching herd."

I laughed so hard I had to hold my stomach. When I turned onto my back he had a smile on his face.

He started to say something else, but lust filled his eyes, causing my heart to trip as it tried to catch up with the new rhythm it was pacing at. "Slick," he said, his voice was husky, and he was not looking at my face. "Are you naked?"

His voice was raw, and downright sexy. Following his eyes, I saw one of my breasts had went rogue and escaped the confines of the towel and blanket. I flushed red, as my erect nipple looked for attention. I pulled my blanket up to my chin, refusing to look Kill in the eyes.

"I'm not naked, I'm in a towel. I just haven't gotten dressed yet."

He still hadn't said anything, and I peeked at him in curiosity. His eyes were shut tight, creasing at the sides. His jaw was doing that twitchy thing again, causing his dimple to flicker in and out like bad reception on an old T.V.

"I'm sorry, Kill," I apologized, not really sure what for. This was the man-whore of Portland after all. He'd probably seen more nipples than I have, and I see mine at least once a day.

He reached over, and pushed up so my jaw was shut and nothing more could come out. Removing his hand he put his finger on my mouth in the universal sign of shut the hell up.

I wanted to flick my tongue out and taste his finger, but I resisted, not wanting him to freak out anymore. After a while, he relaxed, before springing off the bed. "I think we should take a break from running today," he said, as he made a hasty retreat.

When I got out of bed, I tripped over his shoes still on the floor. Shaking my head at his fluctuating attitude, I went to my closet. Dressing in jeans and one of my favorite Halestorm tank tops, relieved the pills were doing their job.

The boys played at another bar on Tuesday's, meaning I would have the whole house to myself. I figured this would be a good time to work on my nearly completed thesis. I was comparing the women of Pride and Prejudice to the seven deadly sins.

Chomping on Tums, I hoped it would curb the ache the boulder in my stomach was causing. The living room was deserted when I went downstairs, but the clothes from the dryer were folded on the bottom step.

Van sat at the kitchen table drinking coffee. His eyes lit up when he saw me. I loved that my best friend had found him. "Hey Faith, whatcha up to?"

"I wanted some breakfast, or lunch," I corrected myself when I noticed the time. "Then I was going to go work on a paper for school. By the way, what's the Wi-Fi password?" I asked, as I peeled a banana and poured a glass of juice.

"JackholeS rule. One word."

I should have guessed. "Thanks," I said, rinsing out my now empty glass.

"Is that all you're going to eat?"

Not wanting to explain my stomach felt like lit matches

were burning a hole through it, I changed the subject. "Where's Jessie?"

I wiggled my eyebrow at him and smiled when the huge tattooed pierced rockstar turned red.

"She went home to talk to her parents. It's been a couple of days and they threatened to come and take her home." His forehead creased with worry.

"Ahh, the family phone calls. She would have to leave our study groups when they called to reassure them she wasn't being corrupted."

I patted his shoulder for support. Jessie's family was very intimidating. "They're going to love you, Van. Don't let them scare you off if you want to be with her. They're overbearing, but they only want the best for Jessie. I understand it's early to think about the future, but don't give up."

He squeezed my hand. "Thanks. Are you coming to the show tonight? I don't like the idea of you being here all alone."

My heart filled from his brotherly concern. "I'll be fine, I'm going to sit in my room all night and write, and I promise I'll call you if anything happens."

I let go of his shoulder to start dinner, wanting get it out of the way.

"All of our numbers are on the table by the door. Call if you need us. I'm going to take a nap before we have to go."

Giving him a hug before he left the kitchen, I smiled when he flopped down on the couch. He turned on the T.V. for background noise, as I pulled out the crockpot.

When I was back upstairs, and my laptop was connected with the WiFi, I pulled out my notes. I was so absorbed in my paper, I screamed when my phone buzzed under my leg.

Annoyed at the interruption, I glowered as Trent's name flashed on the screen. Already out of the zone, I answered it.

"Hey Faith." His voice was hesitant. I wanted to feel sorry for him, but it was his fault for being in this position.

"Hi Trent, how are you feeling?" I asked, uncertain of how this conversation would unfold.

"Faith, I'm so sorry. I didn't mean to drink that much, and truthfully I don't remember most of the night. I wanted to apologize if I got out of line."

He paused, and I was at a loss at what to do. On one hand, I could let him off of the hook, and I could avoid the awkward conversation. But on the other, I was positive it would happen again if I didn't address it now. So I plunged ahead.

"I understand you were drunk, but, well, you said some things that made me weary. You're a really good friend, and I don't want to lose you."

His heavy breathing on the other end was all I could hear. My heart squeezed, hoping he understood what I was going to tell him.

"I can't be anything more to you than just a friend, and I hope you can accept that."

I waited for him to respond, but when he didn't, I called out his name. He let out a frustrated breath.

"Faith, I'm sorry I put all of that on you. I've had feelings for you for a long time, and I hated you being with Jason."

I was shocked at his confession, not the one where he had feelings for me, because he had made that clear, but he acted like Jason was a hero. "I always thought you liked Jason."

"No, I was envious because he had you, and I just wanted you to be happy. As long as I thought he was making you happy, I tolerated him."

I took the phone away from my ear, my mind was whirling. When I returned the phone back, he was still talking.

"Now that I know you weren't happy, I'm upset I didn't try to steal you away sooner. I can make you happy. Please give me a chance. You can live with those guys until you feel comfortable enough to move in. We'll be an awesome couple."

The way he said *those guys* made it sound as if the words left a bad taste in his mouth. My temper rose, upset he would talk shit about the boys who had showed me nothing but kindness. I tried to harness it in before I spoke, reminding myself Trent was my friend.

"Trent, I'm sorry, but I'm not going to date you. Ever. I

don't want to lose you, but if you can't just be friends, then I don't think we can continue talking to each other." My head ached, and I wished I hadn't answered the phone.

"What the fuck? Are you just going to be some house-whore to be passed around when nobody else is willing to warm their bed?"

No longer trying to keep my temper in check, I yelled into the phone. "Yes, I am, but instead of being passed around, we do it together at once. It saves time."

I was seething he would say something like that, and I realized I never really knew Trent, and again, I had terrible intuition when it came to people.

"I'm sorry," he said, desperately trying to repair the damage he just caused, making him sound eerily like Jason. "Fuck!" he yelled. "I'm sorry, you just make me so crazy, and I've been in love with you for so long that not being able to have a chance with you makes me insane. Please, Faith."

"Trent, never call me again. I can't be your friend anymore. Goodbye."

As I hung up on him he screamed my name. Pouring out a handful of Tums, I chewed on them forcefully, reminding me of Amy and her ever-present candy.

I stared at the blinking curser, as it waited for me to type something brilliant on the keyboard so it could copy it to the screen. Unable to get my groove back, I gave up.

Snatching the brownie off my nightstand I ripped off the cellophane, taking a huge bite. It was a chocolate orgasm. I swallowed and took another bite, savoring it.

My phone rang, Trent's name flashing on the screen. I hit ignore and took another bite. My phone rang again, and I was frustrated. He not only took me out of my writing zone, but now he was ruining my perfect brownie moment.

I snatched up my phone, "Stop calling me, I don't want to talk to you ever again!"

"Faith?" My dad's voice was cautious.

Fuck, why didn't check my caller ID?

"Hi Dad," I replied, guilt evident in my voice. "Sorry, I've been getting harassed by a telemarketer, and I was trying to finish my paper. I'm kind of frazzled right now." I crossed my fingers I had convinced him.

"Assholes. I hate when they call. So, how have you been little girl?" he asked, and I let a couple more lies mingle with the truth.

"Good, I got a new job, and I've been busy trying to finish everything I wanted to do during summer."

"You work too hard. Make sure Jason takes you somewhere nice."

My stomach seized when he mentioned Jason, causing me to reach for my handy dandy bottle of Tums.

"What happened to your old job?"

"Jessie got me a job at the bar she works at so I could get better tips. You know, for better shoes. Besides, I get to work with my best friend, which makes it fun."

"You work at a bar?" I heard the condemnation in his voice, and my heart sunk realizing I was disappointing yet another person in my life.

"Yes dad, and I'm watched out for by a huge guy name Catcher, and Jessie and I work the same schedule." I purposely left out the detail about my four new roommate/bodyguards.

"How does Jason feel about this?"

The frustration at how much I allowed Jason to rule my life simmered in my veins. "He has been traveling a lot for work, so I think he likes I'm not alone all of the time."

I wanted to tell my dad I didn't give a flying fuck through a doughnut hole what Jason thought, but I was not ready for that talk. Afraid of what the stress would do to him if he knew the truth.

"Well, as long as you're safe. Anything else new and exciting?"

Well, I left my crazy abusive boyfriend and filed a restraining order against him; I left the job I had for years because my boss wanted me to live with the fucker; I got a job at a bar; I moved into a house with four boys, one of which causes my whole body to go haywire anytime he's near me; I was just screamed at by a guy I thought was my friend; and I have the best brownie in the world in front of me begging me to eat it. All of that went through my head as I tried to find some truth I could relay to him.

"Nope, nothing much. Although, I did have the most amazing brownie today."

He chuckled, confirming I did the right thing by not telling him.

"How have you been, Dad? I see Martha hasn't killed you yet."

"No, I'm too clever for that woman to get me."

I heard Martha snort in the background and perked up. "Is she there?"

My dad cleared his throat nervously. "I called you because I wanted to tell you Martha's moving in with me."

"What?" I yelled into the phone, doing a happy dance.

My dad got the wrong impression from my outburst and tried to backpedal. "Well, she's here most of the time, and it just seemed more economical."

"Dad, I love Martha. I knew something was going on when the two of you disappeared at Christmas and came back flushed. I want you to be happy, and I'm so glad you found someone."

He let out the pent-up breath he'd been holding, and I heard Martha in the background. "I told you she would be fine with it. I'm going to get ready for lunch."

"Do you love her?" I asked, desperately wanting him to say yes. The thought of my dad being happy and loved made me feel at peace with some of my choices.

"Yes, I do. Are you sure you're ok with this?" I could tell he was just as desperate for me to say yes to him.

"Yes, dad, I'm happy for you. I always worried you were putting off finding someone because you were too busy dealing with me."

"You were never a chore, and although I wished you had a mom to help you for certain things, I wouldn't have changed anything."

I felt those damn stupid tears prickle my eyes again, but I pushed them back. Assholes. "I wouldn't have changed it either. You're my rock, and now we can add Martha to the *it's us against the world*. It will be nice to have someone else to depend on."

"The four of us make a pretty damn good team, don't

136

we kiddo?"

My stomach turned as he referred to Jason as the fourth in our group. "We're a good team," I said, referring to the three of us.

"Now, take that woman to eat, and I'll talk to you later."

"Ok, call me soon, alright? I love you."

A sad smile played on my face, knowing my dad would be taken care of by someone else. Even though Martha had been doing it for a while now, the passing of the torch was still painful.

"I love you too. Tell Martha I love her, and I'm happy for you guys."

No longer in the mood to write, I wrapped the rest of my brownie up and went downstairs.

When I made my way to the kitchen, all four boys were huddled together staring at the counter.

Van had a confused look on his face, while D attempted to touch whatever had their attention. Jet stood behind D like he would pull him away if something went wrong. Kill's face was blank. They were so engrossed in whatever was on the counter they didn't hear me walk in.

"Whatcha guys doing?" I asked, causing them to jump.

They had guilty looks on their faces, making the scene even more curious. "Why are all of you bunched together staring at dinner?"

"What the fuck is it?" Jet cried, pointing at the crockpot. "Don't get me wrong, it smells awesome, but I've never seen anything but a pot roast inside one of these things, and that definitely is not a pot roast."

I couldn't stop laughing when they shook their heads in agreement, rallying behind Jet. "You guys are jackasses, and for your information it's a crockpot. You can make more than just pot roast in it. What you will be eating for dinner tonight is spaghetti."

They glared at the offending appliance, like it had somehow betrayed them by not telling them it could be versatile in its cooking ability.

"Chickens," I said, nudging past Jet to get the salad.

Taking a diet Pepsi along with my meal, I didn't

acknowledge them as I went to the living room. I sat on the floor, and turned on the T.V. There was silence for a minute or two, before the boys started filling their plates.

Van was the first one to walk out of the kitchen. He gave me an awkward look before sitting down. I quirked my eyebrow as he stared at his full plate. D came in, sitting on the floor further away from us. Kill strode in next and sat by me. He didn't leave much room between us, causing my body to ignite.

Jet swore in the kitchen. "Shit, this is fucking awesome. Holy shit, I'll never doubt you again, Faith."

I grinned into my soda. With the jester's endorsement, the others dug in, making grunts of satisfaction.

Jet walked in with spaghetti sauce on his face and a plateful of food. We watched a show where people commented on various clips of idiots performing random acts of stupidity.

The door opened, and Jessie yelled out in her southern accent. "Is anybody here?"

"We're in here, babe. Get a plate, and get your sexy ass over here," Van replied, chuckling as some nimrod got a bar to the nuts.

Jessie walked in with a smaller plate, snuggling next to Van.

"Why are you all sexed up?" I asked.

She turned a light shade of red, and I was impressed by how well she kept her blush in check. "I'm going to watch the boys play tonight. Do you want to go?"

She sounded hopeful, and since I felt better, I agreed.

Kill nudged me with his knee. "Are you sure you're up for it, Slick?"

"Yep, I'm much better."

I got up, putting the small amount of leftovers away. Jessie tried to take Van's plate, but he shoo'd her away, taking hers instead. Seeing my chance to get Jessie alone, I caught her eye. "Jess, why don't you come upstairs with me while I get ready."

"I want to watch, please, I promise to be good," Jet pleaded puppy dog eyes in place. D smacked him on the back of the head.

138

Jessie gave a longing look toward the kitchen where Van had disappeared. Feeling like I was about to get the brush off, I looked pointedly at her. "Trent called me today."

Her eyes snapped back to mine. She tried to read my face to find out what transpired. Kill's attention was focused on me. I didn't pay attention to him.

"What did he want?" he asked, refusing to be overlooked.

I kept my eyes on Jessie when he asked. Jessie gave me a questioning look, and I nodded my head toward the stairs. She nodded back, walking past me to tell Van where she was going.

When I reached my door, I heard heavy footsteps behind me. I stopped and waited for Kill. When he reached the top his face was hard, and his eyes burned holes through me.

"What did he say?" He brushed his finger down my cheek causing me to shiver. The gentle touch of his finger, and the burning emotions in his eyes turned my body into a hectic myriad of feelings.

I glanced over at the stairs, knowing Jessie would be up soon. He followed my gaze but focused back on me.

"Friends tell each other stuff like this, and didn't you want to be friends?" Challenge was written all over his face, waiting to see if I would push him away from the role I had forced him into.

"He wanted me to give him a chance to fill Jason's vacated spot."

His jaw went tight and the ticking started. "What did you tell him?"

"I told him I would never see him as anything but a friend."

His tick quickened when I mention the word friend. He had to know my reasons for friending him were incomparable to the reason I had put Trent in the friend status.

"He didn't like the idea of being friends and tried to convince me he was in love with me, and we would be amazing together. After turning him down, he called me some ugly names, and after enduring his abuse, then apologies, followed by more abuse, I hung up."

The anger pulsing in his eyes made him look deadly. Just then Jessie walked upstairs, her lips plump from her encounter with Van. She took my hand, and pulled me into my room, shutting the door in Kill's face. We flopped down on my bed.

"So, that was intense," she said, turning on her side to face me.

Kill made me feel off-kilter, and I didn't know how I felt when it came to anything related to him. He made me so hot I short circuited when he was around, unable to get a true reading on my emotions.

"It looked like you two were about to have angry sex right there in the hallway."

"I told him I didn't want to have sex with him," I explained, deciding if I couldn't get my mind to help me out, maybe my best friend could. I hoped she could shed some light on what I was getting myself into, or should I say, keeping myself out of.

"Did you say it like that? Because if you did and he's still looking at you like you're a prime piece of meat, you may not have gotten through to him."

The damn girl was Texas through and through, always using meat as her way of putting value on things.

"I kind of did tell him like that. He was teasing me like normal, and I just blurted out I couldn't sleep with him. Then I told him I just wanted to be friends."

"You asked a boy that oozes sex from every pore in his body to be friends?" Her voice raised, and I shushed her.

"How long did he laugh at you?"

My cheeks flooded red at her assumption he would scoff at my request. "Actually, he agreed." I picked at the blanket on my bed.

She exhaled sharply at my confession. "Wow, I didn't expect someone like him to agree to something like that."

"Well, look at who you're dating, he's bald with tattoos all over his arms, which are bigger than most people's thighs," I responded, wanting to defend Kill's agreement.

"I didn't mean it like that. I'm the last person to judge anyone. It's just Kill goes through women like most people go

140

through water, and it surprised me. He probably agreed because he doesn't want to make you uncomfortable, and I shouldn't be surprised, you're awesome. Any relationship you give someone is a blessing."

"You aren't so bad yourself."

"So did you explain why you weren't going to have sex with him?" she asked, her eyes greedy for the low down.

"I told him I couldn't be some girl that warms his sheets for the night, and he is becoming someone I depend on as a friend and I didn't want to jeopardize our relationship."

She nodded her head, listening intently. I let her think for awhile, hoping she would have some clarity on the enigma that was Kill. I got antsy when she didn't answer right away.

"Well?" I asked, exasperated.

"We've all heard about the JackholeS, and the notorious man-whore lead singer. He does seem different with you, and that worries me. I'm afraid since he has never had to chase a woman before, he sees you as a challenge. You need to heal before you put yourself out there, and you'll know when it's time, but I don't think Kill's the right one for you. I'm proud you held your ground against his charm. Ok, now spill on Trent. I know I just blew your mind with my wisdom, and I don't want you to hurt yourself by trying to wrap your mind around my astuteness."

I snorted, before giving her the details of the conversation I had with Trent. She was livid, and I had to wrestle her phone away so she wouldn't call him and rip him a new one. Once I got her calmed down, I made the mistake of sticking up for him.

Explaining he felt like I was breaking his heart, and he was just lashing out at me. After saying this, I received one of her famous lectures on how I didn't make him lash out at me with hurtful words, it was his decision to do so, and I needed to stop giving people a way out by taking blame that was rightfully theirs.

Van knocked on the door and came in after we called out it was safe. "Hey, baby, we have to leave soon."

Jessie threw her arms around his neck, kissing him soundly. I looked away as they played with the back of each other's throats.

Hearing a throat clear I looked up to see Kill. His anger had receded, and he had a playful smile tugging at his lips.

I wondered briefly what he would do if I walked over to him and kissed him like Jessie was doing with Van. My cheeks flamed red and his smile turned up, wiggling his eyebrow, as if he read my mind.

"Alright, get out of my room so I can get ready and get your woman to the show," I announced, making Van smile as they finally broke apart.

"Get her there soon, ok?" Van walked by Kill and smiled widely. "Come on man, we're going to have a kick ass show tonight, because three of the hottest girls in Portland will be there cheering us on."

Jessie giggled and I looked at her, surprised at her reaction. She flipped me off, causing me to laugh. I loved that my best friend was coming out of her shell, and thankful Van was helping.

"Hottest in Portland, huh?" Kill asked, as he slowly perused my body from top to bottom, causing little flames to lick over my skin.

Van looked over at Jessie; his eyes bright with happiness and lust. "You're right, these girls are the hottest in the world."

Jessie blew him a kiss, and he pretended to catch it and put it in his pocket. I couldn't help but roll my eyes at the two of them; they were so fucking romantic.

Kill shrugged off of the door jamb and followed Van out of the room. Jessie went over to my closet to find something suitable for me to wear to her man's show.

"Is Amy going to be there?"

"Yeah, Jet told her I would be there tonight, and it isn't fair Van's chick gets to see him in all of his glory when he's so much better."

I shook my head and smiled. Those two being together would never get boring, nor would they ever have a sugar shortage.

Jessie pulled something out and examined it. When she turned around, she was holding the dress I had worn the night of my engagement. Blood rushed to my head.

"How about this one?" I read Jessie's lips more than heard her. She saw my face and walked over to me, concerned, putting the dress on my bed before she reached me.

"What's wrong?"

"I wore that dress the night Jason proposed to me," I whispered, looking at it. The memories tried to surface, but I pushed them back.

"Ok, then this is the dress you're wearing tonight."

Her face was determined, and I knew there was no arguing with her when she wore that face. "You can't let him run your life anymore. You escaped him, and I'm so proud of you. That dress is going to look amazing on you, and you need to put a new memory with it. Let's replace all the bad memories with great ones."

My legs felt stilted with every step toward the bed. When I reached it, I touched the material letting my fingers glide over it.

Jessie had a smile on her face, and I was warming up to the idea of purging the bad memories and replacing them with something better, somehow redeeming the dress and maybe some of myself in the process.

I put the dress on and fished out a pair of red heels with little black skulls and crossbones across them. Jessie did my hair in big curls, piling them on top of my head, making them look artfully messy.

She did my makeup, giving my eyes a dramatic edge, and topped it all off with bright red lipstick I would never have been able to put on without coating all of my teeth.

Jessie talked the whole drive, telling me how perfect Van was as we pulled in to the parking lot of The Note, the bar the boys were playing at. And if I didn't know any better, I would think she was trying to convince herself.

# CHAPTER 12

The Note's atmosphere was different from Ray's. A line wrapped around the building and a smaller version of Catcher guarded the front door.

"Wow, I wasn't expecting this," I told Jessie, taking in the massive crowd.

"This place has been around forever. Tons of bands have been discovered here. When D got this gig a month ago, the boys were at a restaurant, and Jet went around kissing everybody, and I mean everybody. Van had to haul him out before he got in a fight with a bunch of frat boys that didn't take his affections kindly."

I could picture Jet running around kissing people with the excitement of getting one step closer to his dream.

We were ushered in when we gave the bouncer our names. Some people yelled at us for cutting, while others stared at us curiously trying to figure out who we were.

Once inside, I was even more impressed. The stage was raised just enough to keep the boys separated from the crowd, but not too high to make them inaccessible.

The walls were littered with posters and candid pictures of various bands that had played there; all signed with their appreciation for letting them have the stage.

I was in awe by the caliber of talent this place had held. There were two bars flanking both sides of the dance floor. The bars were a deep cherry wood that gleamed even in the dim light. The high chairs lining the bar were filled to capacity.

There were several tables and booths plastered against the wall. The chairs were upholstered in a dark red material, with brass tacks lining the seams.

As expected, the JackholeS brought in a huge crowd. Unlike Ray's where the audience consisted of women in tight, skimpy clothing, The Note had a more diverse crowd.

People seemed genuinely sincere to hear the band, not just throw their panties at the stage hoping to be the lucky bed warmer. Not that the place was skank free. There were many women, that if they bent over, I would have the same view as their gynecologist.

We walked to the bar to get our drinks. Jessie ordered a Jack and coke, and I got whatever diet drink they had on tap, telling her I would drive home.

Scoping out an empty table near the stage we waded through the increasing crowd to nab it. We high fived and toasted our accomplishment. A group of catty women walked by, giving us dirty looks as they went by. I smiled and waved as if they were long lost friends. They flipped their hair and stormed off. Jessie and I dissolved in a fit of laughter.

A tall guy wearing a pair of tight jeans and long sleeves rolled up to his elbows walked toward us. He was cute, but he was trying too hard. His dark blonde hair was styled to make it look messy, but it didn't have the effortless quality like Kill's did.

He smiled, acting like he was going to bestow a great gift by coming over. Tattoos covered his forearms, and even those weren't imaginative. They looked like he walked into a tattoo parlor and randomly picked a bunch of pictures right off the wall.

Jessie rolled her eyes, making me smile. He mistook my smile as encouragement and tried to look alluring, but instead he looked like a lockjaw victim.

"Hi, I'm Robert." Confidence exuded from him, and it boggled my mind at how clueless he was. I was about to tell him Jessie and I were a couple, but Van ran up and threw his arm around her attaching his face to hers.

"Hi, I'm Faith, and the girl with the two tongues is Jessie, and her boyfriend, Van." I glared at them as they ignored me. He glanced at the two lovebirds, but set his sights back on me.

"So, Faith, what does someone as pretty as you do?"

I was going to answer I taught castration school, but Amy caught my attention. She was carrying an enormous drink. It was in a fishbowl type glass with music notes scattered across it.

The drink was a shocking blue with maraschino cherries floating near the bottom. It had slices of orange, pineapple, with a pink umbrella floating on the top, the red straws bobbed as she walked.

"What the hell is that?" Van asked as she set her drink down.

"It's called the blue note," she said proudly.

"It looks like Smurf pee," he responded, still looking at the drink.

Amy scoffed and took a sip. "Faith, you should get a job here, the drinks are way sweeter than at Ray's. I could totally see you waitressing here."

Robert mumbled Ray's under his breath, catching his answer from Amy. I mentally cussed her out.

"Who are you?" Amy asked over her drink, eyeing Robert suspiciously.

"I'm Robert."

Van, no longer having his tongue stuck down Jessie's throat, looked over at Robert with pure intimidation.

Robert, thinking his uninspired tattoos were his way in, stuck out his hand. "Hi, I love your band."

Van begrudgingly shook his hand, not wanting to insult a fan. "Thanks, I appreciate that."

Van turned back toward Amy's drink to give her shit about the dangers of drinking Smurf pee, while dismissing Robert. The guys at the table Robert had been sitting at called him over, as a waitress sat down a round of shots. He squeezed my arm as he tried to look charming.

"I'll see you later, Faith. Maybe we can dance later." His gait was full of confidence, unaware he wasn't even close to pulling off the person he was pretending to be.

"Tool," Kill muttered walking up just as Robert left. "Slick, as your friend I have to say you have an uncanny knack for attracting the biggest poseurs, douche bags, and tools. You're like a beacon."

I turned to give him a piece of my mind, but stopped when his eyes went wide.

"Holy fuck, what're you wearing?" he asked breathless.

I glanced down to the dress I was banishing memories from. "Why, you don't like it?" I asked coyly.

Kill looked up to the ceiling as if he was praying for

146

patience. "You know you look fucking hot. It's like you added an extra strength light bulb to your douche beacon. Every douche for miles will be lined up," he said through gritted teeth, looking around the bar in search of the invisible line.

I laughed at the pained look on his face. Jet, and D walked up, thankfully ending the conversation. Jet moved the straws out of Amy's blue note and took a drink.

"What the hell is that?" D asked, his reaction so much like Van's I couldn't help but laugh.

"That's some yummy shit," Jet answered, before taking another drink.

"Jet, you know you're drinking something that looks like Smurf pee, right?" Van asked trying to get his point across, that ingesting anything blue wasn't natural.

"Dude, I have drank a lot worse than Smurf pee, believe me."

Jessie and I cringed, hoping he didn't clarify what that stuff would be. Everyone else cracked up, and I was glad the subject had changed from my attracting the worst of the worst.

The lights flickered, and Van kissed Jessie, telling her it was their cue to get the fuck backstage. Jet and Amy were kissing like he had just come back from war, and I turned my head, afraid of what would happen next.

D's face had an odd look on it. I slung my arm around his waist, wanting him to feel at ease with me. He seemed like he could never relax around me.

"Have a great show," I told him.

"Thanks. Don't let any douche bags hit on you while we're up there."

Kill snorted. "They can't help but gather around her, especially in that dress."

He pulled me away from D, putting his arms around me and resting his chin on the top of my head.

"I'm just saying, my friend likes to pull in the scum."

I pushed my head up causing him to snap his mouth shut.

"Well, my friend likes to pull in the skanks, so I guess we're just magnets for all the wrong people."

Jessie gave me the eye, but I ignored her. Van watched

Kill, and I was grateful not all the attention was on me. D looked from me to Kill, back and forth like he was watching a sideways tennis match.

Jet pulled himself away from Amy and looked at us, confused at what he had just missed, but then shrugged it off. He kissed the top of Amy's head and walked by Kill, punching him in the arm. "Let's rock this taco stand."

Van shook his head, and they followed Jet backstage. A group of girls were giving us stink eye, and I smiled, saluting them with my drink before settling in my seat.

"Just friends, huh? Be careful, Faith," Jessie warned.

Amy looked over at her, waiting for her to say more. I gave her a look, silently telling her to shut up, which surprisingly she did.

"What the hell's going on?" Amy asked, sucking down more of her drink.

"Nothing," I replied, making her go back to her drink.

"Amy, don't finish that whole thing, you're going to get alcohol poisoning," I warned, as she sucked down even more.

"It's mostly juice, and it tastes like candy."

I shook my head at her, hoping she was right. Amy eyed my chest then her drink, and I could almost see her mind turning.

"Hey, Faith, I bet we could fit one of your boobs in here."

Jessie snorted, and the table full of guys behind us laughed, obviously overhearing Amy's hypothesis.

"I get to take my glass home, we should try it."

I honestly didn't know how to respond, so I took a drink of my soda, or tried to, until I realized it was empty.

"Anyone want a refill before the boys start?" I asked, picking up my glass to help out the busy waitress.

Jessie eyed her half empty drink. "Yeah, get me another one of these. I don't know why, but I'm nervous."

She took a drink, and I patted her back before going to the bar.

When I had our drinks, the whole bar broke out into screams and chants, swarming the dance floor. Jet strutted out to the center of the stage pointing out to the crowd, making the

148

audience go insane.

Van settled behind his drums and pointed a drumstick toward Jessie. The women in the general direction of his drumstick screamed, thinking he was pointing at them.

D walked out during the insanity, and girls screamed his name. He gave them a shy wave.

Kill came out last. He had been talking to some guy, and didn't move until he nodded, agreeing to whatever Kill had said. Kill clapped him on the shoulder before appearing onstage, making the noise level rise to a dangerous point.

When his gaze landed on our table, his eyes narrowed. I stood there unable to take my eyes off him, immobile as people bumped into me. His eyes swept the crowd until they connected with me. He flashed his half-smile, and I tightened my grip on the drinks. They were heavy in my arms, and I struggled to stay upright as my legs turned to mush under his gaze.

He winked before taking the microphone and addressing the crowd. No longer locked in his gaze, I regained control of my body. Amy's drink was more than halfway gone, and Jessie made good on her last one, snatching the one I handed her and taking a huge gulp.

Every so often Kill looked over at our table, and I had to take a drink to cool off my heated body. After we finished our drinks, we headed toward the dance floor.

We elbowed our way through until we were as close as we could get to the stage without having to hit a bitch. Amy jumped around, flailing her arms and smacking into people, getting us more room on the crowded floor.

A pair of arms encircled my waist and pulled me toward their owner. I recognized the tattoos surrounding me immediately. Rolling my eyes, I turned, getting ready to launch into full bitch mode.

"Hey, Faith, I saw you out here looking all sexy, and I had to dance with you."

"Sorry, Robert, I'm dancing with my friends," I said, pulling out of his grasp.

That was when I noticed the guy Kill had been talking to before the show coming toward us.

"Well, what about later?" Robert asked, confident he would get a dance.

"Not tonight, sorry." I was still eyeing the guy as he came closer.

"That's ok. I understand you want to spend time with your friends. Maybe I can take you out some time?" he asked, leaning into me so I could hear him over the noise.

"I don't think so. I'm not dating right now."

"Alright, I'll leave you alone tonight, but I'll get you on a date." He winked and went back toward his table with enough swagger in his step to make him look like a total douche. I turned just in time to see the mystery guy melt back into the crowd.

The boys took a break, and we headed back to our table, sweaty from dancing. Jessie left to get the next round.

Amy threw herself at Jet, kissing him thoroughly. Van went to find Jessie, and D went along to help him carry the drinks. I had a smug smile on my face as Kill came toward me.

"Hey, Slick, are you having fun?" He glanced over at Robert.

"You guys are awesome as usual, but you know that. I'm afraid to compliment you in fear of your ego exploding."

He sat down and threw his arm on the back of my chair.

"So who was the guy you were talking to before you started your set?" I asked.

"A douche swatter." He had an impish smile on his face when he answered.

"A what?"

"A douche swatter. Kind of like a human fly swatter, but for douches."

"You asked someone to keep guys away from me?" I asked, secretly pleased.

"That's what friends are for. Did I mention you look amazing tonight?"

"Thanks, Killer," I said, bumping my shoulder into him.

Van, Jessie, and D came back. After handing out the beers, D pulled Jet and Amy apart.

A gaggle of brave girls approached the boys. Their eyes were glassy and I couldn't tell if it was from the alcohol surging through their system, or being near the boys.

"Oh my God, we love you guys so much!" the braver of the bunch exclaimed.

The others nodded their heads vigorously in agreement. I inconspicuously rolled my eyes at Kill, not wanting to piss off their fans.

"Thanks," he replied, taking his arm off the back of my chair so he could lean into them with his panty-dropping smile.

They started bouncing with excitement, and I had to turn my laugh into a cough. Kill grasped my leg under the table, leaving it there, causing heat to flood through me. I had to remind myself to breathe so he wouldn't see the effect he had on me.

"We're your biggest fans," one of the others said.

With the ice broken, they were becoming braver, checking out all of the boys. Kill leaned back and took a deep pull from his beer, and even I was affected by the sight of his throat moving as he swallowed.

The girls talked a while longer before wandering away starstruck. I couldn't blame them; being near Kill and the boys was potent stuff.

Kill left his hand on my thigh until it was time to go back onstage. He squeezed it before removing it, and I couldn't stop the sharp inhale when he did.

He stood up and winked at me from around his bottle as he finished it. As they sauntered off toward the stage, I, like the rest of the females in the bar, stared at them.

A girl in a black tube top and tight black pleather pants, walked up to Kill. She was beautiful in a "bad girl you don't want to piss off" kind of way. Her black hair was cut in a short bob not going past her ears and shaved at the back.

Both of her arms were covered in bright sleeves snaking around her collar bone. Her high heeled boots were laced to her knees, and when she touched Kill's shoulder, her blood-red finger nails gleamed in the light.

She leaned into Kill, her mouth close to his ear, and I was pretty sure after she finished with whatever proposition she offered him, she licked the outer shell.

I was watching intently, waiting for him to respond. I

know, I know, I had no right to be jealous, but I couldn't help the emotion as it flowed through me.

Hell, I practically pushed him toward any available skank, and the current one trying to get her claws into him was in the perfect package. My stomach squeezed painfully, and the soda I'd been sipping on burned next to the boulder.

He caught me watching. I didn't want to give him mixed signals; saying I only wanted to be friends, but don't touch anyone else, even though it was exactly what I wanted.

Well, if I was being truthful, I wanted him to tell me being friends was the stupidest idea ever, while throwing me on any available surface and erasing the idea of friendship from my head.

He cocked his eyebrow at me, cutting his eyes toward the biker skank. She saw him, and gave me the evil eye before turning back to Kill, placing a seductive look on her face. If I would have tried that look, I would have ended up looking like I was having cramps.

I tried giving him an encouraging look, letting him know it was ok if he wanted to agree to whatever she had suggested. His face turned to stone. He shook his head and said something to her causing her to pout, trying to get him to change his mind.

He walked toward the stage without another word. I let out a sigh of relief, wanting to get up and do a happy dance. I knew it wasn't fair for him to become abstinent because of our friendship, but I'm not going to lie and say it didn't make me feel fucking fantastic.

Biker skank turned on her heels, scowling at me as she stormed off.

"What was that about?" Amy asked when biker skank was out of sight, clueing into the outside world beyond Jet's naked body.

I shrugged.

"Faith, you need to be careful. Friends, remember?" Jessie warned.

"I know, Jess. So I have stupid feelings for Kill I shouldn't have, is that what you want to hear? I refuse to be one of his conquests, and because of that I need to steer clear of him. He's not who I thought he was. He's kind and thoughtful and so damn confusing, my brain has taken a vacation since meeting him," I rambled.

Jessie touched my hand as it fiddled with Kill's discarded bottle. Amy reached in her purse, which was stuffed with her now empty glass. After digging around she threw a bag of M&M's at me, which I took, grateful to have something to do.

"Friendship's all you should be offering him. He doesn't do relationships, and I can't see you get hurt again, " Jessie explained, while the boys started their set.

"Admit it, with his reputation, it doesn't make sense that he's turning down beautiful girls. I feel awful, but I also know seeing him with another girl would tear my heart out, even though he should be doing just that. I'm a bad person. I know I'm not ready for anything, but it's hard not to want him," I finished lamely.

Amy scoffed, tossing a Skittle at my head, I dodged it, and it lodged itself in the hair of a girl passing by. Her hair was teased so high she didn't realize it now had a colorful passenger. We stared at her as she walked away before bursting out laughing, wondering when she would find her little stowaway.

"You aren't a bad person, Faith. You're female, and we're complicated. Don't be so hard on yourself; it will all work out," Amy said, looking at Jet as he thrust his hips in time with the song, causing her to scream along with everyone else.

"Don't let his attention confuse you. He'll get tired of the chase and go back to easier conquests," Jessie ended giving me one of her briefer lectures.

I went to the bathroom when Jessie and Amy decided to do shots. While contemplating running into the lineless boy's bathroom, someone came up behind me.

"He isn't going to change for you."

I didn't turn around, thinking whoever was behind me was talking to someone else.

"I know you think your little innocent act will keep him happy, but it won't keep him around."

Ok, that was meant for me. I turned around to see none

other than biker skank sneering at me.

"I don't know what you're talking about. We're just friends. He turned you down for another reason besides me."

She let out a harsh laugh and narrowed her eyes. "He thinks you'll be different and you're worth changing for, but he'll get bored of it really fast, and when he does, I'll be waiting for him with open arms."

I snorted at her, trying not to let her know how close to home she was getting. "More like open legs," I retorted.

She just shrugged. "He'll be between those too, and you'll be at home like a good girl, never crossing his mind when he's buried in me."

Figuring she was right, I turned around and walked forward to close the gap in front of me.

"We're just friends because honestly I know you're right. I'm nothing special so I wouldn't even try a relationship with him. Because unlike you, I can't have sex with someone and not have feelings for them. I have standards, so if you can get him to change his mind, you're welcome to him."

She sneered at me and walked away, her mission accomplished. At the table the girls were a couple of shots in and feeling no pain.

When the set was over, and Van and Jet had pried their fans off them, they came over to us. Amy and Jessie were giggling, leaning heavily on the table. Van looked over at me with accusing eyes.

"I went to the bathroom, and when I came out they were taking shots," I defended myself, as Jet lifted up Amy.

She put her arms around him, and started snoring.

Jessie tried to get up to walk to one of the Vans she was seeing, but stumbled as soon as she stood. Van caught her and tossed her over his shoulder. They decided to take the girls home together so they could help each other. I fished Amy's keys out of her purse so I had a way home.

Kill was still loading the equipment. D came over to explain he needed to talk to the owner and to let Kill know if he didn't want to wait to just go home with me. Kill appeared later, looking confused.

"The girls had a little too much fun, so Van and Jet took

them back to the house in Jessie's car. D's finishing up with the owner. It's up to you, if you want to wait for him, or ride with me?"

Kill took the keys out of my hand and headed out of the bar. "Come on, let's get out of here."

I shivered from the temperature change when we emerged into the chilly Portland night. Kill put his arm around me, and I buried myself into his body, fully aware I wasn't just doing it for the body heat.

At the car he opened the door for me, not letting go until the last second.

Instead of driving home, he parked in front of a twenty-four hour diner. He didn't say a thing, swinging his long legs out of the car and came around to my door. Kill reached out, and I let him pull me out of the car as he tucked me back into his side.

"Come on, Slick, hurry your sexy ass up, it's cold."

He pulled me closer to him, and we hurried into the vacant diner. When we sank into one of the empty cracked vinyl booths, an older waitress came over, snapping her gum. She started to put the single page menu in front of us, but Kill waved her off.

"We would like a banana split, extra hot fudge please."

The waitress popped her gum in confirmation and headed off to make our order. I couldn't hold back the smile as he ordered, and almost moaned when he said extra fudge.

"Nice, Killer."

"That's what friends are for."

"I'm going to have an easy time getting used to this friendship thing. Did anyone ever tell you, you are by far the greatest friend any girl could ask for?"

His smile slipped, and I wanted to retract my statement to get it back.

"I wouldn't know. I've never done this before. I don't think it would be like this with anyone else." His voice had a serious note to it, and it took me a second to catch my breath. I was saved when the waitress came back, and this time I did moan when everything sin was made of was placed in front of us. There were two spoons sticking out of it, and we dug in before the waitress had turned around.

My eyes rolled back into my head at the gooey, sticky sugar mess. Kill laughed at my reaction, but I didn't care. I went in for another bite.

We were scraping the bottom of the bowl, and a spoon fight ensued, both of us trying to get the best of the leftovers. He would knock everything I gathered off of my spoon and scoop it up and putting it in his mouth before coming back to repeat it.

When the last of the ice cream was on his spoon, I stuck out my bottom lip. He stopped right before putting it in his mouth and turned it around stopping in front of me.

"Here."

I opened my mouth and tried to pull the spoon in but he pulled it back. Determined to get the last bite, I leaned over the table trying again to get the spoon in my mouth. He moved it further back. I lifted up, leaning my whole body across the table.

He had the last bite near his opened mouth. All thoughts of ice cream vanished; only the thought of Kill remained. His eyes were stormy with lust, and I was sure mine were the same.

I leaned in further, letting the spoon click on our front teeth, having only the width of it separating us.

When I was about to open my mouth to let the spoon and Kill slide in, a snap of gum brought us back to reality. I plunked back down, as Kill cussed under his breath, throwing the last bite back into the bowl.

"You all need anything else?" the damn waitress asked, and I wanted nothing more than for her and her noiseless shoes to go the hell away.

"Just the bill," Kill answered, not taking his eyes off of me. He threw a twenty on the table, once again tucking me into his side.

A group of girls piled out of a red Jeep Cherokee when we left the diner, and from the way they were leaning on each other you could tell they were in no condition to drive.

My heart seized when I saw biker skank stumbling out. Her glassy eyes lit up when she noticed us. I stiffened under

Kill's arm, and he muttered something under his breath.

She disentangled herself from her friends and staggered over. "Just friends, huh?"

She stood close enough I could smell the alcohol on her breath. "Remember my warning. I'll be waiting, because there's no way you can keep his interest for very long. He deserves someone that will keep him...."

Kill stopped her, his voice laced with anger. "You have no idea what you're talking about. You couldn't compare to her on her worst day. Stay away from her, and if I ever find out you talked to her again, you will regret it."

He let go of me so he could get closer, but I anchored my arms around his waist, keeping him against me. "Come on, Kill, let's go."

He tried to pull away again, but I held firm. He released a long breath, his anger deflating with it. By this time, her friends had ambled toward us. They apologized to us, explaining she was really drunk. As they towed her toward the diner, I pulled Kill toward the car, struggling to lead him away.

He cranked the engine, letting the heater do its work on the chilly interior. Kill's jaw was clenched as he worked through his anger. I watched him out of the corner of my eye, not wanting to interrupt.

"How did she know we were friends?" he asked, staring out the windshield toward the diner.

Ignoring his question, I stared out the windshield.

"Faith?" he questioned, when he realized I was not answering him.

I huffed out a deep breath. "She cornered me in the bathroom line," I answered, and he remained quiet, waiting for me to continue. "She told me I was stupid if I thought I could be enough for you and when you got bored of me, you would be falling into her open legs. When I tried to explain to her we were just friends, she didn't believe me."

He glared at the diner, and I was afraid he was going to confront her. His hand rested on the center console, and I placed mine on top of his, hoping I could get him home without more drama.

"Did she say anything else?" he asked through clenched

teeth.

I shook my head, and he opened the door to get out.

"If you won't tell me, I'll just go ask her."

"Wait, I'll tell you, but you have to drive home so I know you aren't going to freak out and get yourself arrested."

His face was hard, and I wasn't sure if he would agree. After a few seconds he put the car in reverse and backed out.

"I'm waiting. And by the way, just so you know, I would never hurt a girl."

"I know that. She said I would be stupid if I attempted a relationship with you because I wasn't good enough."

"You already said that," he growled.

"Fine, she explained if we were together, you wouldn't be faithful to me and while I'm at home like the good little girlfriend, you would be banging anything available with no concern for me. I agreed with her, and told her I knew I wasn't good enough, and that's why I'm keeping you away from my heart and only allowing you to be my friend."

He swerved off the road into the parking lot of a closed convenience store and threw the car into park. His chest heaved, and his eyes were a mix of fury and hurt.

"Do you really think so low of me that if we decided to try this, and you know there's something going on between us, I know you feel it, I would treat you like a piece of shit and not care about your feelings? Do you think I'm not capable of keeping my dick in my pants and being loyal to someone?"

I felt ashamed. He thought I was doubting his character, and I shook my head.

"It's not you, it's me. I don't think you would be able to be loyal to me because I know I'm not good enough for you. You're gorgeous, and I'm some broken girl with nothing to give. So yes, I don't think I could keep you interested enough not to stray."

"You have no idea what you make me feel. This is on you, Faith. When you're ready to find out who I am without making assumptions about me, then come talk to me, not some skank who's pissed off because I bruised her ego."

Looking down at my lap, I felt thoroughly chastised.

"I wish you could see what I do when I look at you," he

158

said as he eased the car back on the road. "I hope you get over your baggage soon, because you've been carrying it long enough."

His words hit me right in the gut. The rest of the drive was in silence, having said enough for the night.

Parking Amy's car on the other side of the street he got out, only stopping to hold the door open for me.

"I'm sorry. I didn't want to push you. I promised you I would be your friend. I guess I should have explained I'm willing to be your friend until you're ready for more."

Energy surged through my body at his words. I wanted to scream, cry, smash something, and rip off his clothes, but I wasn't sure which one I should do.

"It's not like I don't want something more. I just know you would destroy me if I gave this a chance. I can't see myself surviving you, so I can't let you in." My body shuddered at the sincerity of my confession.

"Well, I'm going to have to get you to trust me. Go to sleep. I will see you for our run tomorrow."

I wanted to give him a chance, but I was positive I wasn't strong enough to say the words pushing against my lips, trying to force themselves out in spite of my intentions.

"Go to sleep, Slick." He kissed the top of my head, before getting a beer and going into the living room to watch T.V.

I got ready for bed in a fog, putting on the big Ray's t-shirt I wore the night my life turned upside down.

I crawled into bed and plugged my headphones into my ears, forcing myself to fall asleep, instead of running downstairs to tell Kill I wanted him just as badly as he wanted me.

My vagina pleaded with me to go to him, but I shut her down, reminding her she was out of commission at the moment. His words ran through my head, and I hoped I could rid myself of my baggage soon.

# CHAPTER 13

I didn't want to get out of bed to face Kill. Last night ended without any real resolution, and I wasn't ready for the awkward reunion.

To buy some time after getting ready, I gathered a load of laundry and stuck it in the washer while chewing on a handful of Tums. Done stalling, I went into the living room to face Kill. He was on the couch, drinking his green protein shake.

He smiled brightly, making my insides go to mush. I planted my feet on the ground to stop myself from running to him and riding him like a cowboy escaping the law.

"Coffee?"

I shook my head, trying to push the mental image of me straddling him out of it. To create space I got two bottles of water from the kitchen, handing him one before sitting down.

"Do you want to eat?" he asked.

I shook my head again, but realized I was being an ass for not speaking while he was obviously trying to make an effort.

"No, I will eat after, so whenever you are ready, we can go."

He sipped his drink, showing he was in no hurry.

"What else are you doing today?"

"I need to go shopping. Do you want to go with me? We can pick up something for dinner."

"Sounds good." He rinsed out his cup, putting it in the dishwasher. "Ready?"

We jogged closer to each other than on our other runs, and at the end I was pretty sure we had recovered from last night.

Taking a quick shower, I straightened my hair and pulled it into a high ponytail. I hurried to get dressed, convincing myself it had nothing to do with Kill. Kill knocked on the door and walked in as I slipped on my neon green heels.

"Whenever you're ready, Slick."

Kill had moved Jet's truck while I got ready. His Mustang was in the driveway all hot and sexy. I grinned, happy I finally got to ride in his sex on wheels. He opened my door, and I sunk into the seat. He got in and smirked at me stroking the interior.

"See something you like?"

I let out a short laugh. "Kill, your car's almost as sexy as mine."

The engine roared to life, and just like its owner, my nipples harden from the sound. When we reached the stop sign, he looked over at me.

"Where to, Slick?"

"Bed Bath and Beyond."

The music was on low, but I caught the familiar strains to one of my favorite songs. Cranking it as loud as I could, when Lzzy Hale started singing '*I Get Off*,' I sang along.

Kill glanced over at me with surprise in his eyes. I loved this song too much to be self-conscious. Besides, friends get stuck with me singing when the urge hits me. When the song was over, Kill turned the music down.

"You're lucky we're friends. Most people wouldn't survive touching my stereo. Also, that was fucking sexy."

I rolled my eyes as we turned into the parking lot. "Halestorm's my favorite band. I would have sung any of their songs, it just happened to be that one."

"The fact you even know who Halestorm is, is sexy in itself, but your voice is awesome. Jessie was right. You need to sing more than just in the kitchen, which I still haven't heard by the way."

I blushed red, wishing I'd kept my mouth shut. Kill came up behind me and the shopping cart, putting his arms on each side of me. He leaned in and whispered in my ear, causing my whole body to break into goose bumps, a normal reaction when Kill was near.

"You're so damn sexy, and you keep surprising the hell out of me. I can't wait to see what you do next." He bit my earlobe, sending desire shooting through me.

"Come on, Killer," I replied breathlessly, pushing the cart forward.

I put my feet on the bar letting Kill push me, telling him when to stop. He made comments on everything, and a few times I picked up something random just to get a reaction out of him. Spotting a box boasting it was the "best corn remover," I threw it in the basket, making his eyebrows shoot up.

"See what happens when you wear those heels."

I laughed at his response. He snatched the box out of the basket and put it back on the shelf.

"And I know your feet are perfect, which is a miracle in itself."

I stuck out my tongue and found myself pressed into a display of comfy socks.

"I warned you, Slick."

He leaned in, making everything else disappear. Kill had his patented half-smile, and right before our lips met, he turned, kissing me on the cheek.

His face was smug, getting his payback for the stunt I pulled on my first day of work.

The cashier eyed Kill with lust in her eyes. Jealousy reared its ugly head, and I pushed it down, reminding myself I had no right to feel possessive over Kill. She leaned over to get my purchases, giving Kill a clear view of her cleavage.

I tried to get away so I wouldn't have to witness her eye-humping him in front of me, but before I could escape, Kill pulled me tight against his chest.

"Did you get everything you needed, sweetie?" he asked, kissing me on the top of the head while running his hands up and down my arms, leaving trails of heat as they passed.

The cashier shot me a dirty look and put more force than necessary into scanning my purchases.

Kill stopped me when I went for my wallet. He reached in his back pocket and grabbed his wallet, pulling out his card. "I got it, baby."

I pushed my elbow in his stomach, but he didn't move. With the receipt and my stuff in tow, he took my hand as we walked out of the store.

"What the hell was that for?" I demanded, trying to get my hand out of his.

He tried to look innocent, but the damn smile, carved by the devil, himself ruined it. "I was having fun. Friends can have fun together. Come on, where to next?"

He stored my purchases and hopped in the car, where I directed him to the Lloyd Center.

In Victoria's Secrets, Kill had the employees falling all over him. He held my hand the whole time, trying to get me into the fitting room for a private show, making his newly acquired entourage shoot death glares at me.

By the time we left the store, the salesgirls were head-over-heels in love with him, and probably plotting my death.

On our way to the food court, a pair of bright purple heels caught my eye. I stopped. Kill didn't notice I was no longer moving until his arm was jerked back from his forward momentum.

"What?" he asked, turning around. He scanned the stores, his face hard and the facial tick was back.

"Is he here?" He moved to get between me and whatever threat he thought lurked about.

"What? No he isn't here, I just saw a pair of shoes," I confessed, embarrassed my reaction to a pair of shoes had him going into bodyguard mode on me. The truth was, Jason hadn't crossed my mind. Kill had a way of making me forget the bad in my life.

"Shoes?"

I pointed at them with my finger, so he could see they weren't just a pair of shoes, but a work of art. "A pair of the most adorable shoes I've seen today, and I'm going to get them."

The sales girl stumbled over herself to get to us. I wasn't sure if it was because I had commission written all over me, or she wanted to get closer to Kill.

"Can I help you with anything?" she asked Kill breathlessly, answering my question as she ignored me.

Kill hauled me to his chest. "Actually, my girl saw the pair of purple heels with a black bow in the window, and I can't deny her anything, can I, baby?"

He rested his chin on my head, and I could feel the smile on his face.

"What size are you?" she begrudgingly asked me.

I told her, and she walked back to get them.

"Those are two hundred and fifty dollar shoes, Killer." I didn't want him to spend money on me just because he was playing boyfriend for the day.

"Shit, Slick," he groaned, as the girl came back shoes in hand.

I opened the box and fell in love. After trying them on, I dug around for my wallet. I was thankful for my tips at Ray's, which were triple what I made at Cool Beans. When I moved to hand my card to the sales girl, she was taking Kill's out of his hand.

"Wait, you can't pay for these. They're too much."

I tried to give the girl my card, but Kill took it and stuck it back in my wallet.

"Shut up. Those are fucking hot, and every time I see you in them I'll know I put them on your feet." He thanked her, taking his card and my shoes and walked out.

"Wait, are you Kill from the JackholeS?" Her voice was so high, I was afraid the windows would crack.

Kill turned and flashed her one of his smiles, causing her breath to shudder. "I am."

She ran around the counter, shoving a piece of paper and pen toward him. "Can I get your autograph? I love you guys so much. I try to get to The Note when you're there."

He signed the paper, and she took it clutching it to her chest.

"You should come see us at Ray's. We play every Friday and Saturday."

She nodded her head so fast she looked like a bobble head on a gravel road. "I will, oh my God. I can't believe I just sold your girlfriend shoes. Wait until I tell my friends."

I opened my mouth to correct her, but Kill kept talking.

"It was nice to meet you. I hope you come and see us. Come on baby, let's go home."

We walked to the food court hand in hand. I beat him to the cashier and paid for the food. I smiled at his frown, winking as I walked away, letting him carry the food.

At home I went upstairs to put my stuff on the bed. There was a pile of folded clothes on the bottom step. I smiled, happy my little system was working.

I put on a pair of black skinny jeans, a Ray's shirt, and my new shoes, doing a little happy dance when I looked at them in the mirror. On my second spin, Kill came in and I screamed. He leaned on the door jamb laughing his ass off, and my face burned from embarrassment.

"Were you just doing a happy dance?" he gasped when he got his laughing somewhat under control.

"Shut up. I have a deep affection for shoes. They make me happy."

He smiled widely, coming over, and tracing my cheek with his finger. "I like to see you happy, and those shoes look fucking hot on you. Come on, let's eat before you have to go."

He turned around and walked out of my room. I took a minute to make sure my legs had solidified, before following him.

Taking another load of laundry out of the hamper I saw it wasn't as full as the last time. In fact, the house looked like someone had scrubbed it clean.

"Hey, you sexy beast, where were you today?" Amy asked, stabbing a piece of chicken off Jet's plate and sticking it in her mouth as I came out of the kitchen.

"I had to get some things to replace what I had left behind."

The boys' faces went hard, so I tried to lighten the mood.

"And I got these killer shoes."

Kill smirked at my cleverly disguised description.

"Those are fucking sexy. You should let Amy borrow them so she can admire them while they're up in the air." Amy hit Jet in the back of the head, giggling while she did it.

"The dumbass is right, those are some sexy ass shoes," D piped in, surprising me.

I felt warm and fuzzy. He was letting me in. "Thanks, D," I responded.

Kill nudged me with his shoulder and whispered in my

ear. "I hope they don't give you corns. I will have to inspect your feet soon to make sure they're still smooth."

He went back to his food as if he didn't just make my whole body burst with sexual energy. I picked at my food, my appetite gone.

"Oh, I have something for you," I told him, handing him my rent check. I did it in front of everyone, so he wouldn't argue. His eyes went hard, and I could see his internal battle. I winked at him, my appetite magically appearing.

"Where's Jessie?" I asked, noticing she wasn't there.

Van's eyes flashed hard for a second, before returning back to the softy I knew and loved. "She went home to call her mom. I guess her grandma isn't feeling well, and she wanted to check on her."

"Why couldn't she call her grandma from here?" Jet asked, making Van flinch as D shot Jet a dirty look.

"She didn't want to explain where she was if they asked. Her mom's like a human lie detector."

"Why doesn't she want to explain where she is?" Jet asked again.

Kill leaned over and smacked him in the arm, trying to get him to shut the hell up.

"She doesn't think her family would approve of her spending time with me. Her parents own a bar, and they have been trying to keep Jessie from dating someone like me her whole life." Van's eyes were sad as he explained.

"Van, I love Jessie, and I love you two together, but don't ever feel like you aren't good enough. You're amazing, and when her parents meet you, they'll adore you." I encouraged.

I wondered briefly what my dad would think of Kill. I pushed the thought away, there was no reason to think about it. They were going to be discovered any day now.

"Thanks Faith." Van went to put his dishes away. "I'm going to take a nap. I'll see you later." He looked defeated, and when his bedroom door shut, we glared at Jet.

"What?" Jet asked in confusion.

"Idiot," D remarked, getting up to take his plate into the kitchen.

I followed him while Jet waited for an answer. Kill whispered to him, but I was too far away to hear.

I did a quick makeup check, wanting to get to work early so I could talk to Jessie. Waving goodbye to the boys I walked out. I opened my door, and Kill called out to me, jogging down the walkway.

Throwing my bag on the passenger side I waited for him to reach me. When he did, he rubbed the back of his neck, looking at the ground.

"Forget something, Killer?" I asked, not sure what to say.

He let his hand fall to his side and looked at me. "I just wanted to say have a good night and be careful. We'll be there about nine, so make sure to tell Catcher if anyone bothers you. Today was fun."

He leaned in and kissed my cheek. "Don't miss me too much, pretty girl."

With that, he jogged back to the house, closing the door without looking back. I knew this, because I watched him the whole way.

I was still blushing when I pulled into the parking lot early. Jessie's car wasn't there yet, so I waited, hoping to catch her.

My phone rang, and Trent's number flashed across the screen. My stomach tightened as I went to press the ignore button, but I changed my mind.

"Hello," I said.

Trent took a deep breath, just as surprised as I was. "Hey Faith, I wasn't expecting you to answer."

"I wasn't going to, and I'm not sure why I did. Please don't make me regret it."

"I'm so sorry about what I said; I didn't mean any of it. I understand you don't want to date right now, but I don't want to lose your friendship. Can you forgive me? " he begged, his voice filled with worry.

"I don't know if we'll ever get back to where we were, Trent. You said some pretty awful things, and I was just trying to tell you the truth. I'll try though; I don't want to lose you as a friend." My conscience warned me this was a mistake as soon as the words left my mouth.

"I'll take your friendship, and I promise I'll make it up to you," he was quick to respond.

"Why don't you come to Ray's tomorrow around ten?" I asked thinking it was the safest place to meet him.

When we hung up he seemed relieved. My doubting him so quickly into our mending didn't bode well for our reconciliation.

Checking to see if Jessie had pulled up, all the breath was knocked out of me when I saw Jason's car across the street. My hands shook, causing me to drop my phone; by the time I retrieved it, he was gone.

I sat in my car, playing with the mace on my key chain, trying to figure out what I should do. Kill's words flashed through my head. Jason wasn't going to give up so easily.

Frustration burned through me. Jason was always around the corner, able to destroy any progress I made on becoming whole.

Surveying the cameras mounted around the parking lot, I knew Jason would have been out of range. He was smart, and I was fairly certain if I measured where his car was, it would be beyond the distance the restraining order demanded he stay away.

Knowing I was still shielded by Jason's need to keep up the pretense of being Mr. Perfect calmed me. I reminded myself I was strong enough to get away and the panic subsided.

Jessie pulled up, and I went over to her, pushing Jason out of my mind. I didn't want her to know about Jason's cameo, and I definitely didn't want Kill to find out. Jessie was vigorously brushed her blonde hair. I knocked on her window, and she nodded her head, indicating for me to get into the passenger side.

In the car I got a good look at her. She had a wild look in her eyes. She brushed her hair so hard I was afraid she was going to pull it all out.

"Hey, what's up?" I asked, grabbing the brush from her hand, which fell limply to her side.

"I told my parents I was going on a date with Van," she told me, tears falling down her face.

"Honey, I think you two are doing a lot more than going on a date," I responded. Jessie had never lied to her parents so her little fib was a big deal.

"I wanted to test the waters." She let out a bitter laugh, and my heart hurt for her. "My dad told me he didn't want his little girl to date some wannabe rockstar who would never amount to anything except some gigs in rundown bars, while he's sticking his dick into anything willing to worship his mediocrity."

She put her face in her hands and sobbed. I put my hand on her back, rubbing it in circles.

My thoughts went back to earlier, wondering what my dad would think of Kill. I pushed it to the back of my mind along with Jason's appearances. Having enough on my plate, there was no reason to add to it.

"Jessie, they don't know Van. He adores you, and he wouldn't do anything to hurt you. They won't be some bar band forever; they're going to make it, and make it big. They just need to meet him."

She took her hands off her face. Her tears had dried up, but the wild look hadn't left.

"I know, and when they make it big, they'll have women throwing themselves at them. We were doomed from the start. I think I'm just going to have fun until then, and not tell my parents since there will be nothing to tell soon."

Jessie said this with finality. She took out her makeup to touch up what her tears had destroyed.

"Jessie, I don't think them hitting it big will change his feelings, and it's not fair to keep him hidden just because you're afraid he'll hurt you. I get you're afraid to tell your parents, but you should have more faith in your relationship."

My inner voice screamed that I was the biggest hypocrite in the universe, because I had similar thoughts about Kill leaving to pursue his dream. Jessie glared at me with the wrath of a cornered woman burning in her eyes.

"Faith, I love you, and I don't want to say something to ruin our friendship, so please stay out of this and let me handle it."

I wanted to grab her shoulders and shake her like a

169

British nanny would, but I nodded my head, letting her know I was there for her.

"Alright, Jessie, do it your way. I love you too, now let's get to work and make more tips than Bambi. That will make us feel better."

Jessie laughed, and some of the wildness dissipated from her eyes. I was reminded of how I had lied to my dad, and I fully empathized with her situation.

We walked into the breakroom, stashing our stuff before going out to the bar. Ryan laughed with Denise, and Bambi flirted with some guy wearing an expensive business suit.

Onstage, a karaoke station was set up and a guy in a portable DJ booth was putting people in queue after they chose their song. Wednesday and Thursday were karaoke night at Ray's. Jessie would always regale us with stories when we were at study group.

"Hey, you sexy bitches, are you ready for karaoke night?" Ryan asked.

Denise picked up her tray and winked at us before going to deliver her orders.

"I saw Mr. Wong signing up,"

Jessie groaned trying to spot the offending Mr. Wong.

"What does Mr. Wong sing?" I asked, looking around with Jessie, even though I had no idea who I was looking for.

"The Wong song," Ryan answered, cracking up at her bad joke.

Jessie pointed nonchalantly toward a short balding man in a striped button down shirt half tucked into his brown slacks.

"His wife left him years ago and took the cat. Once a month he drowns his sorrows and dedicates Whitney Houston's '*I Will Always Love you*' to Buttons," Jessie whispered as Ryan stifled a giggle.

"Buttons being the cat?" I guessed, causing Ryan to laugh so hard she walked away from the drink she was making.

The bar was busy, and I ran around trying to keep up. DJ Smoke, a dark Hispanic man, with black slicked back hair and a long beard got ready to start karaoke night.

My phone vibrated in my apron while I waited for my order.

### Miss me yet?

He had put his name in my phone under *Killer?* I wondered when he had time to put his name in my phone, and why he put a question mark after it.

Scrolling through my contacts, I saw he had put all the guy's numbers in my phone under the nicknames I had given them. I now understood the question mark since I never told him his nickname.

"What are you laughing at?" Ryan questioned.

"Nothing, Kill's just being an ass," I told her, hefting up my finished tray.

DJ Smoke began the introductions, calling the first group onstage. A bunch of women screamed as they danced to the stage. They were awful, but to their credit they had the whole bar singing along with them.

Mr. Wong must have been here early because he was number four onstage. His high notes sounded like he was stepping on the infamous Buttons.

Ryan sucked her cheeks in to keep from laughing, and the sight of her made me lose it. I leaned on the bar as Mr. Wong hit the last note, making my eyes water. Swiping my eyes, I tried to catch my breath. I took out my phone and text Kill back.

### Nope

I smiled as I sent it, wishing I could see his face when he read it. His reply came almost immediately.

### Liar

I giggled and typed.

### You wish, Killer

I stashed my phone in my pocket and looked up to see Ryan staring at me.

"Holy fuck, you're sexting, aren't you?" she accused me, trying to see down my apron.

"What? No. I was just texting Kill back. He's bored," I stuttered.

"I call bullshit. You don't get that look on your face when you're just texting, unless you're thinking about them naked," Ryan pressed on.

She shook her head when I was about to respond. "What can I get you, Bambi?" she asked.

I could have leapt across the bar and kissed her. There was no way I wanted Bambi in my business.

Bambi bumped into my shoulder, giving me an innocent look. "Sorry, Happy," she said in a sickeningly sweet voice.

"Her name's Faith, and stop being a bitch, or I will screw up your orders. You're on thin ice with Ray, so I suggest you play nice," Ryan reminded her.

I took my tray and walked off. Stupid Kill had put me in a good mood, and I wanted to keep it.

Hours into my shift, I couldn't believe how many people were still willingly getting onstage. The bell above the door clanged, alerting everyone their favorite boys had arrived.

The smile that had been playing on my face showed up in full force. Jet was Amy-less because she was tutoring tonight. He surveyed the bar like a ringmaster, instead of the clown he was. "Fucking karaoke night. Fuck, yeah."

The bar broke into cheers and cat calls. Van and D were side by side, more for D's benefit since he was looking down at his phone not paying attention to where he was going.

Kill came in last, and my heart beat faster from the sight of him. He was in a pair of black jeans and a long sleeve dark blue shirt. His hair flopped over his forehead, because like D, he was looking down at his phone. I heard a collective sigh of female appreciation and hoped mine blended in with everyone else.

He put his phone in his pocket, winking at me as he passed. I scrunched my nose at him and acted like the simple act of him winking at me didn't send my whole system in sexual shock.

Ryan was already placing beers on a tray for them. Jessie hung back, helping a group of women pick the best margarita. She was stalling, and I hated she was letting such a good thing crumble because of her fears.

My conscience tried to butt in, but I pushed it back not wanting to hear it. I tried to convince myself that my situation with Kill was different, and I was being smart to keep away.

After several attempts of Van trying to get Jessie's attention, she gave in. They smiled at each other, and after taking an order, she went to him. She kissed him on the cheek before going to the bar.

My phone vibrated, making my legs wobble as I fished it out of my apron.

**Wanted to put you out of your misery and show up. So you can stop daydreaming about me. Besides, I didn't want to miss the show.**

His smartass text made me laugh, confused what show he was talking about. My phone showed I missed a private call, making my stomach drop from the reminder that Jason was still lurking about.

Seeing Jason in the parking lot verified it was him at the grocery store. He was playing games, wanting me to break the restraining order, but I refused to take the bait.

I took my tray, wanting to ask Kill to about his cryptic message. Before I reached him, I got my answer.

DJ Smoke announced his next victim. "I need Faith to get her ass up here and rock my joint."

I searched out Kill with murder in my eyes. His head was on the table, his shoulders shaking with laughter. Van, D, and Jet chanted my name while banging their fists on the table.

"Faith, Faith."

Reaching over I smacked the back of Kill's head. I

snatched the beer I just put in front of him and downed half. He lifted up, still laughing while rubbing where I hit him, and smacked me on the ass.

"Get your ass up there, Slick." His words were coming out choppy as he tried to contain his laughter.

"I'm going to kick your ass," I hissed, as I went over to Ryan, hoping if I ignored him long enough the DJ would have to put someone else onstage.

"Get your ass onstage or I'll carry you up there," Kill said with challenge in his eyes.

I flipped him off on my way toward the stage. In the booth I figured if I was going to be a bear, I might as well be a grizzly; whatever the fuck that meant.

I didn't have time to be nervous because the song started immediately. Halestorm's *'I Miss the Misery'* began to play. I sang my heart out, letting the lyrics that always struck close to home flow out of me.

Everything Jason put me through was vomited out of me through the music. When I finished, I turned off the microphone and dropped it, deciding a drop and walk was the only way to finish off my embarrassing moment.

Scrambling off the stage, I stopped when I noticed the whole bar was quiet. DJ Smoke's mouth hung open and I hoped I wasn't awful.

The boys applauded first, screaming my name. Then the rest of the bar clapped, and some whistled as I made my way toward the boys. DJ Smoke got his senses back, saying he felt sorry for the person going after me.

I stalked over ready to kick Kill's ass for his little stunt. I had been inconspicuous for so long, being under Jason's rule. All the attention made me wary as if I was tempting fate by waving my newfound independence around.

I fought back the urge to keep myself from running to the bathroom and getting sick. Jet ran over and spun me around, I swallowed the bile rising up my throat. He put me down and slung his arm around my shoulder as he guided me to the table.

Van picked me up, pushing Jet's arm off my shoulder, and gave me a hug. I refused to look at Kill. My emotions weren't in check to deal with the havoc he caused me.

"That was awesome," D gushed.

"That was fucking hot," Jet added.

"Why didn't you tell us you could sing?" Van asked, plopping me down on the chair he vacated.

I tried to get up, remembering I was at work and I couldn't just sit on my ass while everyone else worked.

Jessie came over and kissed my cheek. "I've got your tables under control. Take some time to bask in your glory."

Van grabbed her before she could walk away and kissed her. She stopped herself before she got caught up in the moment and pushed away.

"You were awesome, Slick," Kill said. His voice was husky and my body quivered from the vibration.

I scowled at him. "You're an ass, Kill. I hate attention. Don't think just because I didn't bomb you're getting away with this."

He smiled widely at me, but D responded.

"Faith, you weren't even close to bombing! And don't get mad at Kill, it was partially my fault. Kill told me your voice would be perfect for a song he wrote. We figured this would be the best way to test you out."

I leaned over and kissed D on the cheek.

"You're free from my retribution, because I love you, and you apologized. I'm not singing one of your songs though. You guys are on a whole other plane." I looked pointedly at Kill. "You on the other hand, are dead."

Kill laughed, and I figured I had lounged around long enough.

"We'll talk about the song later," D said, as I got up.

I took the tray Ryan had filled up for Jessie to deliver. Ryan did a mock bow over the bar when she saw me.

"Fuck girly, I didn't know you had pipes like that. You got my panties all wet."

The guy sipping his beer at the bar, while staring at Ryan's ass, spit out his drink at her declaration. I got my instructions from Jessie as to where I needed to deliver my orders, while Ryan rolled her eyes and went over to clean up the mess.

People stopped me to praise my performance, telling me they couldn't wait for tomorrow night's encore. I tried to tell them it was a one-time thing, but the tips being shoved at me made me rethink my position.

Kill waited around for me with Van, who was waiting for a very skittish Jessie, as we closed down the bar. Jet left when he got a text from Amy, and I understood what Ryan was talking about earlier. Just from his face alone I could tell he had a picture of naked Amy in his head.

D left before last call, kissing me on the cheek and saying he would talk to me tomorrow about my duet. I wanted to argue with him, but I was afraid it would ruin the progress I was making on our friendship.

In the breakroom it took Jessie three times to get the combination right on her locker.

"Hey, are you ok?" I asked, hoping I wasn't stepping over the boundaries she set for me.

I understood being in a predicament you didn't want anyone to be involved in. I did the same thing to her with Jason, and I knew how much it sucked.

"I don't know," she replied, putting her forehead on her locker.

"Jessie, I love you and I don't want to overstep my boundaries. You respected mine when I didn't want to tell you about Jason. So I'm just going to tell you I love you, and I think Van loves you too."

She sighed heavily and turned around wrapping her arms around me tightly. "I think I love him too. It's just I've seen so many girls get hooked up with a band and watched them get their hearts smashed when they leave. My dad's right, it's not something I want again."

I wanted to ask what she meant, but she shook her head against my shoulder. And really, what right did I have to argue with her, I was having the same reservations about Kill.

"I've never disobeyed my parents or grandparents. I've always had their support, and them not agreeing with my decision to date Van is torture. I get why they're upset; there are things in my past that have made them cautious. I let my dad's doubts turn my feelings around and convince me I need to get as far away from Van as possible, but then I see him, and I can't remember what my dad said. Van's bringing up so many bad memories."

Hugging her tightly, I wondered if I could sneak in some advice.

"Jessie, they love you very much, and they'll come to terms with any decision you make because they want you to be happy. You should talk to them again; let them know Van isn't the average rocker."

My conscience rolled its eyes, declaring me a lost cause.

Jessie smiled at me through watery eyes. "I'll think about it. That's as much as I can promise."

The boys were talking to Catcher when we walked out. Kill caught my eye and winked. I rolled my eyes making him give me a half-smile. He had a paper bag in his hand, and he stuffed it behind his back when he saw me eyeing it.

Van gave Jessie a wary look as we approached, not sure how to act around her, since she had been standoffish all night. Jessie circled her arms around his waist, burying her face in his chest. Van let out a sigh, and I hoped he wouldn't give up on her. Catcher fist bumped Van and Kill before giving me a hug.

"You were great tonight, Faith. You should've seen all of the guys I had to keep from jumping onstage while you were singing. I can't wait for tomorrow night."

Kill frowned. When he caught me looking at him, he quickly erased the frown on his face.

Van told us he was going to drive home with Jessie, leaving Kill with me. Kill bumped my shoulder with his arm, and I tried to look annoyed.

"You're an ass." I told him while we were driving home.

"You loved every minute of it," he responded smugly, and I wanted to knock his ego down a notch.

"Actually, I didn't. I'm not used to attention. I always kept a low profile in hopes I wouldn't trigger Jason. I keep thinking about what you said; he isn't going to give up, and I don't want to trigger him into action."

Kill's face was filled with understanding as I pulled into my now designated spot and shut the car off. "I'm so sorry."

He looked pale, and I felt I may have went too far. Especially since I seem to already be on Jason's radar, and it had nothing to do with Kill's stunt.

"I should've thought about that. You were just so good in the car."

I put my hand on his leg as guilt surged through me. "It wasn't as bad as I thought it would be. I'm just mad at you for pulling that on me without telling me; although, if you did, I would have talked you out of it."

"You were so fucking sexy up there. I couldn't keep my eyes off you, and I almost had to kick some guys' asses that were staring at you."

I raised my eyebrow at his admission while my insides did a happy dance.

"Well, as your friend it's my job to stick up for you, right?"

"Yes, I guess that would be your job, and I appreciate you doing it so thoroughly."

We stared at each other, smiling like idiots. I yawned, and Kill laughed at me, reaching back to grab the paper bag I forgotten about while looking at him like a teenager with her first crush.

"Whatcha got there, Killer?" I asked as we strolled up the walkway.

His arm was around my shoulder, and I snuggled into his side siphoning off his heat. I reached for the bag but he snatched it back.

"Go sit down. I got this."

He wouldn't budge until I sat down in the living room. I flipped on the T.V, and channel surfed until I found *Remember the Titans*.

Kill came out of the kitchen with big plates of onion rings, french fries, cheese sticks, and nachos.

"Oh, shit. We're so going to have to run tomorrow," I told him while snatching up a chip and sticking it in my mouth.

"Shut up. You hardly ever eat. Always pushing your food around on your plate, thinking nobody's watching while you do it."

I smiled at him and took another chip, as he snatched a

fry. We sat in silence, watching the movie and gorging ourselves.

At the end, I was crying and remembered why I never watched that damn movie. I tried to let my tears fall silently down my cheek so Kill wouldn't see me, but in order to keep snot from running down my face I sniffled loudly.

"Ahh, baby, don't cry," he cooed, as he tried to hide his smile.

"Shut up."

I got up to take the almost empty plates to the kitchen. As I wiped my eyes on a napkin, he came up behind me and hugged me.

"Sorry, I didn't mean to make fun of you. It's cute you get all girly over a movie."

I nudged him in the ribs with my elbow, making him fall back, but he didn't let go of me completely.

"I'm a girl, what can I say?"

"I know," he responded under his breath.

Following him into the garage, I watched as he changed the clothes from the washer to the dryer, folding the dry clothes. He handed me my stuff and put the rest on the bottom stair.

Upstairs we lingered in the hallway, not ready to say goodnight, but not having a reason to stay with each other longer.

"Goodnight, Slick. I'll see you in the morning for our run. I don't want you getting all huge from our nightly snacks."

He winked at me, and I rolled my eyes, reining my tongue in. Even with my vagina telling me this would be the perfect time to unleash it from my mouth.

"Night, Killer."

I climbed into bed dressed in my running clothes. Just thinking of Kill made my heart speed up, and I smiled as I drifted off to sleep, with Pop Evil in my ears and Kill on my mind.

# CHAPTER 14

When I woke up I jumped out of bed, excited to spend more time with Kill. I rushed into the bathroom to get ready. Instead of skipping, I forced myself to walk downstairs. Afraid I'd look too eager. Kill was on the couch drinking his protein shake.

"Mornin', Slick," he said lazily, as if he had just gotten up himself, and was pushing sleep from his system.

"Shut up. I'm not awake yet." I pretend grumbled.

Coming back from the kitchen I handed him a bottle of water while peeling a banana, not wanting to argue over my eating habits so early. As I finished my food I tried not to look at him. It was futile. He was just so beautiful, and I couldn't stop my eyes from devouring him.

As we cooled down from our run, Kill asked, "What're you doing today?"

"I'm planning on working on my thesis. What about you, anything exciting?"

"I'm working on a new song, but nothing exciting," he said before we went our separate ways.

After my shower, I put on a pair of pajama pants, a sports bra, and tank top putting my hair up and securing it with a pen. While my laptop warmed up, there was a knock on my door.

Kill came in before I could tell him to. He had a notebook, similar to the one D was normally poring over, in his hand. Clearing some free space on my bed he sat down, leaning against the headboard.

"Thought you could use some company."

I scooted closer until we were touching.

"Get to work, lazy. When you graduate, I'm giving up the band and letting you take care of me."

"Oh, hell no! I'm expecting you guys to hit it big, eventually forgetting you even have this house, making it all mine. I already have my muumuu picked out, and I'm thinking about getting a bunch of cats....even though I'm allergic."

"You would look hot in a muumuu."

I laughed, before we lapsed into silence, both of us putting words down in our own respective ways. My playlist played quietly, and every so often, Kill would sing along softly.

His voice, no matter how low, was commanding, and when he would sing, I would stop typing to focus on him.

"Get to work, slacker," he demanded, when he caught me.

"Well, stop singing," I replied, secretly hoping he wouldn't.

"You don't like my singing?" he asked, pretending to be offended.

"For somebody so smart, you ask a lot of stupid questions," I told him, nudging him.

"You can't blame a guy for trying to get a compliment from a pretty girl. Especially when said girl refuses to give them to me."

"You're unreal."

Hours later, I couldn't concentrate any longer. He closed his notebook when he saw me shutting everything down.

"Did you get enough done today?" he asked nervously. He was worried he had disrupted me.

"Yes, Killer, you aren't as distracting as you think you are."

He gave me a wicked look before tackling me and tickling me until I was screaming. D opened my door and surveyed us as he leaned on the doorjamb.

"I told you to talk her into singing with us. I wasn't expecting you to torture her into submission." Displeasure was evident in his voice.

"I haven't asked her about the song. I was just going to call her a chicken when she said no. Maybe use the whole, '*we took you in and made you a part of our family and it's the least you can do*' argument."

Kill acted as if me being pinned under him was a normal occurrence. D shook his head and continued the conversation like I wasn't present.

"Sounds like a plan. If that doesn't work you could tell her it would mean a lot to me. Save me from the anguish I would endure listening to a bunch of singers, trying to find the right one, when we've already found her."

"Hello, I can hear you," I said, sticking my bottom lip out, pouting like a five year old.

"Good, then we don't have to repeat ourselves. Practice in fifteen," D yelled down the hall, getting Van and Jet to meet us downstairs.

Kill jumped up and adjusted his pants. I averted my gaze. He put his hand out, so he could help me off the bed. I slammed into him from the momentum of him yanking me at the same time I lifted up.

His eyelids went heavy, and he leaned toward me. My body flowed with desire as I leaned into him.

"Ahh, Slick. You don't have to throw yourself at me."

And just like that, I was able to get my desire in check. He winked, and I was pretty sure it was for my benefit, figuring I wasn't ready for what he was offering.

"Come on, I will help you with dinner so we can practice."

Nervousness skittered down my spine when I saw his obvious excitement from the thought of me singing with them. I followed him, afraid I was going to make a fool of myself. With dinner in the oven, I had forty-five minutes to embarrass myself.

"Come on, Slick, it will be quick and easy."

"That's what she said," I replied.

He groaned and put his arm around me. "And just when I think you're done with the surprises you throw out a 'that's what she said'."

Kill moved his car quickly, coming back into the garage giddy with energy. Amy was trying to sit still, waiting for practice to start.

"Where's Jessie?" I asked, right before she walked in.

She looked like she was trying not to cry, and I gave her a hug.

"What's up?" I asked, so only she could hear me.

**182**

"Later," she mouthed, and I gave her a look, letting her know I wasn't going to let her off the hook.

"Ok, let's start with the song I want Faith to sing," D explained.

Jet bounded over to me with his guitar strung behind him. "You're going to make this song so fucking badass."

Everyone nodded their heads in agreement.

"I don't know guys. I don't think I'm as good as you think. Promise me if I'm horrible you'll tell me; it won't hurt my feelings."

"Shut the fuck up," Jet yelled at me.

Amy caught my eye and gave me a thumbs up. The sight of her boundless energy lowered my anxiety.

On a stool next to the microphone was one of the many notebooks that floated around the house. It was open to a page with lyrics written across it.

"Ok, this is the song. We'll go through it once without you. Kill will sing it, letting you get acquainted. Then we will go through it with you, and tweak whatever we need to until it sounds right." D squeezed my shoulder before moving into position.

"You're going to be great. Just relax and do what you did last night," Van encouraged me from behind his drums.

I took a deep breath, pushing back the fear trying not to pass out.

"Deep breaths, Slick. It's just us. Focus on me."

Kill's voice was soothing, making the fear fade away. When my eyes connected with his, it disappeared.

"That's my girl." He smiled at me, signaling Van to start. Kill sang the lyrics as I read along. Signaling which parts would be mine.

The lyrics were heart wrenching. Every word burrowed into my soul. Kill sang about finding someone and as soon as they entered his life, he knew his world would never be the same. And no matter how hard being together was, there was no other option.

My whole being ached for the love he described. When the song ended, I was embarrassed I had to blink away tears shimmering in my eyes.

"Are you ready, Faith, or do you want to hear it again?" D asked, as I cleared my throat to get rid of the tightness.

"No, I'm good. I just hope I can do it justice; it's beautiful."

I wanted to study Kill's face, to see if he had experienced this all-consuming love, but I couldn't lift my eyes.

"You'll be perfect," he whispered, his voice husky with emotion.

When the song started again, I was lost in him. His body turned toward mine, and I heated up when the intimate words buried themselves within me.

When he reached the part, right before my verse, I started singing, feeling it was a better way to meld our voices. His eyes widened with surprise, a smile playing on his lips.

As the song continued, we gravitated toward each other, inches away from one another as we sang the last line.

Our voices ended on a breathless note, and for a moment, it was the two of us, but that ended abruptly when Amy and Jessie began clapping. We jumped apart like guilty teenagers. Jet picked me up, and swung me around.

"That was so fucking hot," he screamed, putting me down where I was immediately lifted into Van's arms so he could swing me around.

The girls jumped around, telling me how great I was. I glanced over their heads to see Kill's intense stare. He flashed me his panty-dropping grin and winked.

D broke into the girls' praise, ordering them to sit so we could finish.

"That was great. I liked you coming in sooner. It's unbelievable you have never heard this song. Honestly, it sounded like this song was yours." He gave me a one armed hug. "How's your voice?" he asked concerned, but unable to hide the excitement of another run through.

"It's fine; you have twenty minutes left before I have to get dinner."

"Let's do this then," D commanded, skipping back to his place.

Kill would stop throughout the song, making changes here and there, and by the fourth time, with all the tweaks, the song was even better.

After going over it one more time, Kill called it officially done. I had to admit, with the band backing me up, and Kill with me on vocals, it sounded pretty damn good.

I made my excuse about needing to finish dinner in order to get away from the boys' praise. I jerked my head toward the door, signaling Jessie to follow me. Amy nodded her head, so engrossed in watching Jet play, I wasn't sure she heard Jessie tell her she was going to help me.

I busied myself in the kitchen, giving Jessie time to get her thoughts together.

"What's going on Jess?" I asked when the silence got to be too much.

She leapt up on the counter while I made a salad. "I told Van I didn't want to tell my parents about him until after graduation," she answered, snatching a piece of tomato.

My heart hurt. She was handling this all wrong, and the heartbreak she was trying to avoid was going to hit her hard when it caught up to her. My conscience screamed, *hypocrite*.

"And I'm assuming it didn't go well?"

Her breath hitched, and I handed her a paper towel to catch the tears falling freely down her face. She shook her head until she got her voice back. "No, but he said he would respect my decision, as long as I made sure to tell them after graduation."

"Well, that's a good thing. He cares about you."

She smiled a watery smile. "He looked so sad. I think I broke his heart. He tried to act like it didn't bother him. He doesn't have the greatest relationship with his parents. They don't approve of his lifestyle. I feel like I'm letting him down by not accepting him, just like his parents. It's just I can't..."

She got off the counter, and cried on my shoulder. I swallowed my advice. She pulled back, wiping uselessly at the wet spot on my shirt.

"Jess, just make sure you let him know you accept him. If you're going to wait to tell your parents, make sure you let him know how much he means to you."

The music from the garage stopped, signaling the end of practice and our conversation. Jessie ran upstairs.

185

Her concerns mirrored some of my reservations I had with Kill. Not to mention, the band's impending break into the music industry. Their discovery was inevitable, and I refused to make him choose between me and his dream, especially if he cared about me like he acted.

I worried he was trying to fix his past by taking care of me, so he could right a wrong he felt responsible for. He needed to be set free from that burden, and he didn't need me teasing him with a relationship we weren't ready for.

The boys came in minutes later, their eyes shining with adrenaline. Van peered into the kitchen and I pointed upstairs, answering his questioning look.

Amy was riding on Jet's back, spanking his ass as they headed upstairs. I yelled at them that dinner was done, and Jet yelled back he only needed a minute.

There was a resounding crack from Amy connecting with some part of his body. "I was kidding, babe, we have a microwave."

D helped me finish getting dinner ready. I heard Kill's car start as he pulled it back into the garage, and my stomach flopped from the sound.

"You were awesome today. I knew you would be perfect for that song."

"Thanks. I actually enjoyed singing it. It's a beautiful song."

"I can't wait until we sing it at Ray's. It will blow everyone's mind." D grinned as he got out the salad dressing.

"Wait, what do you mean sing it at Ray's?" My squeaky voice in full force.

Kill came into the kitchen when I wheezed this out, and went over to D, punching him in the arm. "I told you to let me ease her into it," Kill told him, picking me up and sitting me on the kitchen counter.

"I'm not singing with you guys at Ray's. That was just for fun in the garage."

Kill had his stupid half-smile on his face, and for a moment I couldn't remember why I liked it so much. Now all I wanted to do was smack it off his face.

"Why do you think we had you practice and sing

karaoke?" D asked behind Kill, making him turn his head around so he could glare at him.

D's question made sense. I just didn't think they would actually want me to share the stage. I should have realized as soon as they put me onstage they wanted me to sing with them.

"Dude, shut the fuck up and let me handle this. Go tell everyone dinner's ready." Kill told D before turning back to me, making my panic morph into anger.

D walked out looking stunned, clueless as to what he said wrong.

"Hey, look at me," Kill requested in a soothing voice, making me want to tear his face off with my fingernails.

"Don't," I told him through gritted teeth.

"You don't get to throw your stupid charm on me and get your way. I'm not singing with you guys, so just drop it."

He put his hands on my waist anchoring me to the counter, when I tried to get down.

"I have charm?" he asked. He had an adorable look on his face, and I bit the insides of my cheeks to keep me from smiling.

"Please, don't act like you don't know you can just look at someone and get your way."

"But it doesn't work on you?" He cocked his head to the side, and I felt my resolve slipping.

"No, it doesn't work on me. I'm immune to you."

"What was the nickname you gave me when you first came into the bar?" His change of subject threw me off, not sure where he was going with this.

"Mr. Moody," I answered

For a moment his face was unreadable before he threw back his head and laughed. I punched him in the arm, and he held up a hand trying to get me to wait for him to catch his breath.

"You really are immune to me aren't you?" he replied, still chuckling.

"What? You aren't like Jet, are you? You thought it would be Sex God or something just as awful?"

He had his head down and glanced up at me through

his lashes, and now it was my turn to laugh.

"Oh my God, you did, didn't you?"

"Not exactly, I just thought maybe it would be sexier than Mr. Moody."

I put my hands on his face, squishing his cheeks together. "Ah, poor wittle Kill didn't get a big bad nickname to go with his big bad ego."

I pulled him forward and kissed his forehead before letting go of his cheeks.

"Now you have to sing with us tomorrow to make up for my deflated ego," he mumbled with a smile.

"No, Killer. Not going to happen."

"Come on, you already kicked ass onstage yesterday. And you're going to do it again tonight; what's the difference?"

"How do you know I'm going to sing again?" I asked, trying to look like he wasn't breaking my determination, even though it had pretty much crumbled.

"Because I already signed you up, and don't think for a second DJ Smoke isn't going to beg you to get onstage when he sees you."

He pulled me off the counter, not moving back so we were inches apart. I could feel the heat pouring off of his body and his scent was suffocating, making my brain go fuzzy.

"If you don't sing with us Jet will make your life a living hell, so you might as well give in." He tossed out his last argument knowing it wasn't necessary.

"Fine, but you're driving me tomorrow so I can drink."

He kissed the top of my head and took my hand, leading me out to the living room. D was on the couch pretending to be engrossed in the T.V. and not anxiously waiting for my answer, but the fact that Spongebob was on was a dead giveaway.

Wanting to teach them a lesson, I decided to make them sweat. "Dinner's done, help yourself," I said, going back to get a plate, not waiting for anyone else.

Kill chuckled and followed me back into the kitchen, knowing what I was doing.

"What the fuck Kill, did you talk her into it or what?" Jet yelled next to a flushed Amy. I heard him grunt from Amy punching him.

"No, he didn't talk me into it," I replied, stopping abruptly with my elbow sticking out, Kill unaware, ran into me causing my elbow to jab him in the gut.

"Ouch, well played," he whispered.

"Can you not let everyone know how easily manipulated I am?" I hissed back.

The whole band waited for me to explain why he wasn't successful. D and Van looked like they were going to grovel at my feet, and for a second I almost let them.

"You're so perfect for this song, and I think it would bring a whole other fan base to our band," D started in, about to launch into a million and one reasons why I should do this.

Kill put his hand on my shoulder and pulled me back to him, fitting me under his chin. "Stop D, please no statistics. She's going to do it. She's just mad at the way I approached the subject, and I'm sure she will punish me later."

I could feel his chin moving while he was talking, being it was pressing on the top of my head.

"I knew you couldn't say no to us," Jet stated, and I was afraid to hear his reasoning, but he surprised me. "You're a part of our little dysfunctional family. You're one of us now."

I stared at him with shock registering on my face, but then it split into a huge grin when I saw Van and D agreeing with him. Kill grunted behind me, which I assumed was his way of agreeing.

"I wouldn't want to be anywhere else besides here with my little dysfunctional family, but you can't get mad if I screw up tomorrow."

"Shut the hell up, Slick," Kill responded, letting me go and getting a plate, the others boys doing the same. Every one of them at peace with my acceptance into their family.

I stared at them, feeling serene, when Jessie came downstairs looking refreshed and utterly touched up. She put her arm around my waist. Amy came around to the other side.

"I don't know what I did to deserve all of you, but I must have done something fucking awesome," I said, low enough only the girls could hear me.

I made up my mind, with my best friends and new

family surrounding me, on what I needed to do to secure the safety of my new family. Jason's face flashed across my mind. My stomach knotted, but I knew what I had to do.

Jet's eyes glazed over with lust when he saw us. Before he could say anything, D punched him in the arm and dragged him out of the kitchen.

Van and Kill walked out next with their plates full. As Van passed us, he blew a kiss toward Jessie and she blew one back to him.

We grabbed what was left and went into the living room to sit with our boys. When dinner was cleaned up, I ran upstairs to get ready. My hands shook. I needed to end this. I just hoped my resolve stood strong.

Jessie was on Van's lap, running her fingernails over his bald head when I entered the living room.

"Hey, Jess, I need to run some errands before work." I said, startling them both out of the bubble they were in.

Jessie got up to walk me out. Right before I closed the door, Van yelled out. "Don't sing until we get there, Faith."

"Alright, Mr. Snuggles."

Jessie smiled at me.

"What?" I asked.

"They love you. I think you were just adopted by four big brothers," she giggled.

She was right, and it confirmed I was doing the right thing. I didn't want the boys to get hurt because they were trying to protect me. A shiver slivered through me at the thought.

I forced myself to think of something less daunting. Kill immediately came to mind. But once again dread filled me, realizing we were interrupted every time we were going to act on our undeniable attraction.

I allowed the doubt in my head to join the party, convincing me it was an omen of the relationship we would have if we tried. I couldn't help but think this was the universe, telling me I needed to do some repairing of my own before it would let me bring someone else into my life.

Not wanting to be caught on the cameras, I parked down the block from Ray's. As I stepped out of my car tremors racked my body, and I held onto my car until I could get them under control.

The firm grasp I had on my key chain mace became tighter with every step. Jason's car was in the same spot it had been in the day before, and my stomach pitched and turned as I advanced toward it.

Before getting out of the car I called 911, ensuring my safety. I hoped I could end this without anyone knowing, especially Kill.

If I was ever going to become whole, I needed to eradicate Jason from my life. When I reached Jason's car I took a deep breath and squared my shoulders. The mace was slippery in my hand from the sweat. I wiped them on my jeans before knocking on the window.

Jason was startled when he saw me. His gaze had been transfixed on the parking lot across the street. I expected to see triumph on his face, but he remained stoic. He was getting exactly what he wanted by me coming to him. When fear flashed across his face, my confidence faltered.

He looked nervous when he exited his car. His demeanor caught me off guard; this was not how I had imagined this encounter to go. Could it really be this easy?

I figured he would say what he had to say, getting in the last word. He could recreate his reality, making him the victim and banishing me from his thoughts forever. That was the plan at least.

"Hey, Faith, what are you doing? I can't be near you," he said, looking around.

"Jason, what are you doing here?" I asked, getting right to the point, knowing I didn't have a lot of time.

"I was doing some advertising work for this store," he answered, pointing to the business he was parked in front of.

Uncertainty roared through my body. Had Jason given up on me? Did my leaving him not affect him the way I thought it would? The daily private calls helped push some of the doubt away.

I reminded myself I needed to trust my instinct, particularly when it came to Jason.

"Listen, I don't know what you're doing here, but I can't

be near you right now, honey," Jason said, backing away from me, until he was pressed against his car, and as far away from me as possible.

"Jason, cut the crap. I know you're spying on me. I saw your car at the store the other day. You need to leave me alone. I called the cops to let them know you're violating the restraining order." I was proud my voice sounded strong and didn't shake.

Jason looked around again, and his face paled when I mentioned the cops. "Faith, honey, I was giving you space. You've been under a lot of stress. I love you. I don't know why you felt you needed to get a restraining order, but I'm not spying on you. We're meant to be. I'm giving you time before you come back to me." He reached out to touch me, but when I stiffened he let his arm drop.

"I will never go back to you. I'm free from your pain," I hissed.

I hoped the cops showed up soon. This felt wrong. My skin crawled being near him. I wanted to feel empowered by confronting him. Show him he had no hold over me, but standing in front of him drained my strength. I reverted back to powerless girl he molded me into.

Jason seemed genuinely surprised I was fighting him, and not throwing myself at his feet and begging for forgiveness. He still felt he owned me. I could see it in his eyes.

This was the first time I had ever spoken out loud about his abuse. He lived in his own reality and I had allowed him to, but not anymore. Never had I forced him to acknowledge what he had put me through, and it was terrifying to finally call him out on it.

"I don't know what you're talking about, honey," he said taking a step toward me.

His temper was surfacing, I could see it flashing across his face. I gripped the mace tighter and the nozzle dug into my palm, imploring me to use it. Reminding me I was no longer powerless.

"Jason, you know exactly what the fuck I'm talking about. You tortured me. You raped me. You broke me. I'll never come back to you!" I screamed.

I was seething, pissed he was still refusing to admit what he had put me through. I needed him to admit what he had done to me. I deserved the validation.

"You need to calm down, Faith. You don't know what you're saying."

Making sure we were still alone, he leaned into me, whispering in my ear. "You are mine."

His words pushed my temper over the edge. I saw red. The smug look on his face made me feel crazed. Confronting him was supposed to end his reign over me, allowing me to move on with my life and piece myself together. His denial took everything I needed to move on, away.

I lifted my hand, the mace poised and ready to go. I wanted to make him feel some of the pain he had made me feel. Hurt him like he had hurt me. Right before I could depress the nozzle, a cop car pulled up. I lowered my arm, stuffing the mace in my pocket.

I wasn't sure if I was relieved or annoyed I wasn't able to dispense my vengeance on Jason. When I glanced at Jason, I saw him visibly relax. The cop sauntered over, and Jason stuck out his hand.

"Hello, Frank. How have you been?"

My mouth hung open as they greeted each other.

"I'm good, been busy down at the station. What's going on here?" he asked Jason, not acknowledging me.

Jason had the nerve to look embarrassed, and I couldn't believe what was happening. I wanted to look around to see if I could find the hidden cameras.

"Frank, this is my girlfriend...err, I mean ex-girlfriend, Faith."

"You're the one that called the station?" Frank asked, finally looking at me.

"I am," I replied, confused on what I should do next. The whole situation was surreal.

"Dispatch said this was a restraining order violation. Is that the case?" he asked, looking between me and Jason.

"Yes. I have a restraining order against Jason, and he was sitting in his car across from my work." I explained, pointing over to Ray's.

"Jason?" Frank asked, waiting for Jason to explain, not letting me continue.

"It's all a misunderstanding. I've been working on an account at this building." He indicated the building with his head, not taking his eyes off of the officer. "I actually had no clue Faith worked over there. She saw me and thought I was violating the restraining order and confronted me," Jason answered.

He actually had the nerve to wink at me. What the fuck was happening? Sick of allowing Jason to take over this conversation, I pushed on.

"He has been following me. I saw him at the grocery store the other day, and his car was here yesterday, and today," I said, exasperated. I knew I sounded crazed, but I couldn't get a hold of my emotions. This whole situation was spiraling out of control.

"You came over to confront him?" Frank asked, before throwing Jason a smirk.

"I did."

Frank wouldn't allow me to continue. "It doesn't sound like you're scared of him. In fact, most people would have called us every time they saw the person they had a restraining order on, and never would they confront them." His eyes were accusing, and I stopped myself from reaching for my mace.

I wanted to scream I was not in the wrong here, but Jason butted in. "Don't be so hard on her, Frank. She has been through a lot lately, and I'm sure her friends were the ones to convince her to get the order on me. No harm done."

"Young lady, I suggest you stay away from Jason since you were the one that took out the order. Go on to work, and please don't confront the person you are *afraid of.*" He emphasized the last part, and I was so frustrated tears started to build in my eyes.

"Thank you for nothing, Frank," I hissed at him.

"I will be calling the station to explain how horribly you handled this situation," I said through clenched teeth. I turned to say something to Jason, but realized it was a lost cause and walked away.

In my car, I watched Jason shake Frank's hand before

driving off. I was shaking, and I kept blinking the tears back, refusing to cry. I couldn't believe how terribly wrong that had gone.

Jason's words haunted me. I wondered if anyone would believe me, Jason seemed to outsmart me at every turn.

As I sat in my car, I realized something.

I realized I didn't give a shit if anyone believed me. I knew the truth. I knew who Jason really was, and he would never have me back in his life. I had the support of my misfit family and I didn't need anything else.

That realization made me feel lighter than I had since the fateful day Jason saved me from that irate customer. I didn't need anyone to validate my choices. I was strong enough to validate myself.

I wasn't stupid. Jason was still up to something, of that I was sure. Next time, I would be ready for him. I wouldn't let him get the better of me; I had learned my lesson tonight.

Jason was limited in what he could do. He was stuck in the pretense he was living under. I, on the other hand, was free from limitations. I finally confronted him on the reality of our relationship, and that alone gave me the upper hand.

In the parking lot of Ray's, I felt a renewed determination to live my life without the shackles of Jason.

# CHAPTER 15

By the time Jessie pulled up, my panic had subsided. I gathered my resolve, refusing to allow Jason to break me.

Haze settled around the sun, bullying it until it submitted, no longer trying to warm the air. A tired waitress shuffled past us as we left the breakroom. She was a short Hispanic girl and even tired she was gorgeous.

"Rough day, Misty?" Jessie asked.

"Yeah, the baby's sick. I've been running on fumes," she responded, looking over and noticing me for the first time.

"Misty, this is my best friend, Faith. She just started."

"I should have recognized you. Ryan showed me the video of you singing, you were amazing. One of these nights I'll have to stay after so I can hear you sing."

My face heated, uncomfortable from the compliment. "Thank you. I'm just glad I didn't fall on my ass," I answered truthfully.

Misty laughed. "It was nice meeting you, Faith."

"It was nice meeting you too, and if you can stay for the show tomorrow, I'm singing with the JackholeS."

Her mouth dropped open, "Kill's going to share the stage? You must be amazing. I don't think he even likes to share the stage with the band."

Her look was skeptical as she eyed me up and down. My hackles rose as she badmouthed Kill, and from the assumption she had obviously made.

"I live with the boys, and they've become family. When they heard me sing, they figured it would be a better idea for me to sing with them instead of having some moron girl with the wrong idea do the part." My voice was sharp, wanting to express whatever she was thinking was wrong.

Jessie got in the middle of us, breaking our eye contact. "Seriously, Misty, it isn't like that and you need to get over your problem with Kill," Jessie scolded her.

Misty huffed and walked away. Jessie pulled me out to the bar to start our shift.

"Why does she have it out for Kill?" I asked, ready to go after her to defend him. My confrontation with Jason had left me full of nervous energy, and I needed to expel it on someone.

"I'm not sure. They fooled around, but that's most of Portland. Something happened between the two of them."

My stomach flopped from the reminder. The Kill everyone knew wasn't the same Kill who rubbed my feet and brought me brownies. It was hard for me to see him as the man-whore everyone else knew.

DJ Smoke pulled me out of my thoughts when he called my name. He pouted when I told him to fit me in after the boys showed up. His pout made him look like he was suffering from explosive diarrhea, instead of too adorable to deny.

The night went by quickly. The antics onstage had me giggling when the familiar vibration in my apron stopped me. I discreetly checked my message, eager to see what Kill wanted. My smile faltered when I saw it was from Trent.

The craziness of confronting Jason had made me forget he was coming by later. Resigned, I went over to Jessie while she waited for Ryan to finish her drink order.

"Hey, I forgot to tell you, Trent's going to come have a drink tonight."

"Why didn't you tell me this yesterday?" Jessie asked, her face filled with concern.

"You had other things on your mind, if you don't remember, and it slipped my mind until just now. I figured it would be safer to meet him here."

She twirled her hair, dissecting everything I had just said trying to find a hole in my logic.

"It makes sense he would come here. I know you don't want to end your friendship with him, but you need to be careful with him. I can't see you hurting anymore; you've had your share of that for a lifetime."

Jessie took her tray as I gave Ryan my orders, annoyed with Jessie's observation.

Sharp pains shot across my stomach as I worried about, well.... everything, I forced myself to take a deep breath, and threw myself back to work.

A table of frat boys were trying to get my number, almost as desperately as I was trying to get their order. After wrangling their order from them, I turned around and ran right into Trent.

"Hi. I wanted to get here sooner, but I was stuck in traffic," he rambled.

"Go find a seat, and I'll get your order in a second."

I practically ran past him. After seeing him my gut told me we were never going to be the same, or at least where I thought we were.

Ryan leaned over the bar and kissed me on the forehead. "Hey Sexy, are you singing tonight?"

"Yeah, I'm waiting for the boys to get here. I don't want to listen to them bitch if they missed it."

"Sexy and smart; will you have my baby?" she asked, causing a frumpy looking business man to spill beer down his cheek.

"Sure thing," I said.

When I approached the frat boy table, I noticed the gleam in one of their eyes. I could tell he came from money and was used to getting his way. He was scrawny and dwarfed by his friends, but the confidence he exuded made up for what he lacked in surface area.

"Here you go." I reached across the table, keeping distance from the one with the gleam in his eyes.

"Why don't you stay and talk to us for a minute?" He came over to stand next to me, causing my stomach to spasm with pain.

"Sorry, I have other tables. I'll come back and check on you in a little bit. Enjoy."

He grabbed my wrist squeezing it tightly.

"I said you should stay and chat." His voice was low, so he didn't attract Catcher's attention.

Memories of Jason flashed through my mind making me immobile. The determination I gathered in the parking lot shattered, paralyzing me as everything crashed down. I withered into myself, feeling pathetic I couldn't tell this pitiful jerk to back off. He was a bully pretending to be a big shot in front of his friends.

He ran his other hand down my arm, leaning in to whisper in my ear as the others around the table snickered uncomfortably. "I'm going to take you outside, and we're going to talk."

He pulled me toward the door, but thankfully, Catcher caught the panic in my eyes, and came toward us.

Kill crashed through the door making his grand entrance before Jet. He passed Catcher running toward me. Kill pulled Frat Boy away and tossed him to Catcher. Catcher motioned with his head for the others to get their stuff, eighty-sixing the group from the bar.

Kill yelled at Jessie to watch my tables and hauled me down the hallway. In the breakroom, he sat me down in a chair and examined the newly formed bruise on my wrist.

"Are you alright?" he asked, as he put both of his hands on my face, forcing me to meet his eyes.

I nodded my head, afraid if I talked I would start crying.

"Why the hell didn't you kick that little twerp's ass? He was smaller than you."

Kill removed his hands after I confirmed I was fine. He paced around like a caged animal, his hands fisted in his hair.

The truth of his words made me flinch. Everyone in the bar saw me back down, and now Kill was rubbing it in. I was still allowing others to dictate my actions. I wasn't as strong as I convinced myself in the car. Seeing Jason shook me to the core, and I sure as hell couldn't reveal that to Kill.

"He caught me off guard. I'm so damn sorry you had to come to my rescue again. I didn't mean to ruin your night with this minor inconvenience, friend."

I stomped past him, not stopping until I reached the bathroom. Locked in a stall, I sat on the toilet with my elbows on my knees and my hands locked behind my head as I tried to pull the broken pieces floating around my body into some form of organization.

Kill's reaction hurt more than almost being accosted by some lowlife rich kid. Seeing how upset he was at my reaction reminded me I wasn't good enough for him, or anyone for that matter.

He obviously wanted me to get over Jason faster than I was. I yearned to be someone whole, not a broken girl who crumbled with the slightest provocation.

Tears burned the back of my throat on a one-way track toward my eyes. Blinking like I had just walked into a dusty room, I tried to hold them back. Afraid if I cried it would officially ruin the night and there would be no saving it; why I was being optimistic was beyond me.

I went way past my allotted break time, but I was proud I hadn't shed a single tear.

Bambi's nasally voice echoed through the bathroom. "I'm so sick of the whole damsel-in-distress fucking act, it's getting so old," she sneered.

I hunkered back down in the stall, my stomach turned.

"Ugh, I know. She has the whole bar wanting to protect her. It's sickening," the other girl responded.

"Kill feels bad for her; he thinks she's fragile, so we have to keep our relationship a secret. He thinks she has a crush on him because he's constantly saving her stupid ass."

"Oh my God! You and Kill are together?" Stupid Bitch, which was what I dubbed her since I needed to call her something, shrieked.

If I hadn't been so sick from hearing Kill felt sorry for me, I would have rolled my eyes at her reaction. I wanted to believe she knew I was in here and she was making everything up, but I no longer trusted my instincts.

"Yes, but don't tell anyone, he doesn't want to hurt her feelings. Some girl, a long time ago, died and he can't get over the hero complex he has going on. We don't flaunt it. He doesn't want to upset his fans by having a girlfriend. He was so upset she got herself into trouble again I promised to blow him in the parking lot later."

Bile rushed up my throat. I gagged quietly and my eyes watered from the burning acid being forced down.

I was certain Kill didn't tell people about his past, and Bambi knowing his secret made me doubt myself. Was he just fucking with me? Telling me about his sordid past to get me to trust him because I was playing hard to get? Was I just a game to him?

I was stupid to think Kill was different from what I had heard about him. I had convinced myself he was someone else because I wanted him to be.

Kill was just using Bambi for any available orifice and would be done with her soon. Hell, he was already on the move, playing whatever game he was playing with me. She was stupid if she thought she could change him into the perfect boyfriend; something I was afraid we may have in common.

Bambi and Stupid Bitch giggled, and talked about her sexual escapades with Kill before finally leaving.

I washed my hands and splashed water on my face, wanting to get rid of the numbness that was spreading throughout my body as soon as I heard Kill's name come out of Bambi's mouth.

Pushing my shoulders back I gave myself a pep talk. I knew what he was before I met him, and this confirmation was the slap in the face I needed. In all honesty, I was falling hard for Kill, and I needed to get my feelings in check.

I wasn't convinced Bambi was telling the truth. She knew more than I expected, but it was Bambi. I wanted to talk to Kill. He was pissed the last time I listened to some skank without talking to him.

Back in the bar, I refused to show anyone I was beaten down by anything that had happened tonight. Bambi was talking to Kill, and he was laughing at whatever she was telling him. They got up and went toward the back entrance.

I wanted to run back into the bathroom and beat my fists against the tiled walls. I didn't know what was real anymore. They walked past me, and I refused to make eye contact.

I went over to Ryan; wanting to pull my weight.

My progress halted when familiar arms wrapped around my waist. The electricity that always accompanied Kill's touch was missing, but the unimaginative tattoos gave Robert away. I spun around as he tried to look charming and almost pulled it off.

Robert reminded me of diet soda; at first it almost tastes like a soda, and you are rooting for it to pull it off, but right before it reaches real soda taste, it misses the mark and you're disappointed.

"Hey, Faith, remember me?" he asked, knowing full well I did, but not for the reasons he was thinking.

"Uhm, Rodger, right?" I said, purposely getting his name wrong.

His smile deflated, but rallied back. "Robert, but you can call me anything you want if it gets you to keep talking to me."

He flashed that overconfident smile, and I wanted to tell him to give it up because he would never do it for me. The reminder of Kill and Bambi walking out of the bar made me rethink my stance on Robert.

"How did you know I would be here?" I asked, trying to look coy.

His lids went heavy so I must have done it right. "Your friend mentioned you worked here the other night. I wanted to see you again and ask you out."

He put on a sad face. DJ Smoke should take some lessons from him. Instead of turning him down like I should, I decided to get Kill out of my head.

"I'm off on Monday, would that work?"

Normally I wasn't this brazen, but I knew nothing would come from this. Robert was just a distraction. Robert's smile went into full wattage, right before someone bumped into him, causing him to stumble into me. His hands went to my shoulders to catch himself.

Trent stormed out of the bar, his drink and food barely touched. Guilt surged through me. I agreed to go out with Robert right in front of Trent; bad friend etiquette on my part.

"Are you ok?" Robert asked, running his hands up and down my arms, eliciting nothing, not even a spark.

"Yeah, I'm fine. Go take a seat. I have to get back to work. I took a long break, but I'll be around and we can finalize our plans."

Needing a moment to get everything in perspective, I walked away before he could respond.

Ryan had a concerned look on her face when I reached her. "So who's the douche with the bad tattoos?"

I laughed, loving her for not making a big deal out of

what happened earlier.

"Some guy I met at The Note. He asked me out, and I think I'm going."

She lifted her pierced eyebrow, and I reached over the bar to swat her arm.

"He's safe. I have no feelings for him. So it would be like a date with training wheels."

"Well, the bike's in good condition, but the decals are fucking awful."

Robert had taken residence at the table Trent vacated. He waved at me, his hideous tattoos taunting me from afar. I turned and bit the insides of my cheeks to keep from laughing. Ryan laughed full out, with no cares about who was watching her.

Grabbing my tray, I delivered drinks to my tables. I avoided the boys' table, knowing Jessie would keep them refilled. Besides, she owed me for ignoring Van most of the other night.

After I got my section in order and everyone refreshed, I made my way over to Robert.

"So what can I get you?" I asked, pulling out my pad of paper just in case he wanted something from the kitchen.

"Your phone number," he replied without a pause.

I smiled at him, wondering if his charms ever really worked. Although I couldn't judge since I willingly agreed to go on a date with him.

I scribbled my number on the pad, slapping it down on the table. "That was easy. Now, what can I get you to drink?"

He ordered a margarita, saying he wanted to hang out and watch me work. I wandered over to the bar, checking on my other tables to make sure they had everything they needed.

An older man was hitting on Ryan as she batted her lashes, mystifying him while he was filling out his receipt. The confusion on his face made it clear he was going to tip her heftily; his brain not focusing on math.

I waited down at the end of the bar while Ryan worked her magic. She skipped over to me, causing a couple of the guys at the bar to have heart palpitations.

"What do you need, sexy?"

I gave her my order, smirking at her. She knew full well what she was doing to the customer's sensibilities.

"So are you going to ignore those boys all night? Because Kill keeps looking at you, and I'm afraid he's going to throw you over his shoulder caveman-style if you keep it up."

I refused to look over at them, knowing if I saw his face there would be no resistance.

"He's worried about me after the little scene earlier," I said, trying to shrug it off.

"I'm just glad he was in the parking lot when I text him," Ryan explained, as she yelled at Dax in the kitchen.

"Wait, you text Kill?" I was flabbergasted.

"Yeah, he asked me to keep an eye on you and to text him if anything happened. He knew you would keep it a secret."

Kill stared at me, his face hard and unreadable, making me even more confused. Before I could get any more out of Ryan, DJ Smoke announced the singing waitress was up.

The regulars clapped and shouted for me. Breaking my gaze from Kill, I made my way toward the stage. I told myself I needed to keep it together long enough to get through this song and the rest of my shift. I ignored the questions flying around in my head; like what the fuck is Kill up to?

DJ Smoke smiled, revealing an enormous gap between his front two teeth, which surprisingly made him look like even more of a bad boy. "Are you ready, you sexy beast you?" he asked, while the person onstage finished up his rendition of 'Like A Virgin.'

"Yeah," I replied. "Although, I don't know how I'm going to top a bald biker with tattoos on his head singing 'Like A Virgin'."

Smoke just winked at me before he introduced me. "Let's give a big hand for Tiny and his Madonna impersonation. Alright, you guys are in for a treat. If you weren't here yesterday, one of our lovely waitresses kicked ass onstage. She's back for an encore. Please give it up for one of Ray's girls, Faith."

The bar clapped, and I heard the boys encouraging me. I took the stage and passed Tiny, who was anything but tiny, and got in front of the microphone.

The music to *'Coming Down'* by Five Finger Death Punch started, and I lost myself in the music for a moment, forgetting everything but the words. When I finished, I blinked my eyes back to reality; the bar was clapping, but most of it was drowned out by the noise the boys were making.

Robert came over and gave me a hug, grinning widely.

"You were amazing. I can't wait to get you to sing for me later. I'm definitely going to demand a solo concert."

He said it with such confidence, my skin crawled. I second-guessed my decision immediately. I told him I needed to check on my tables before my boss fired me and made my escape.

Swallowing my pride I walked over to the boys since Jessie was busy and didn't look like she had time to catch up just yet. They were all smiles as they talked excitedly to each other. I put my arm over D's.

"How are you boys doing?"

They grinned at me and the look in their eyes made me nervous. "What?" I asked with dread in my voice, certain I was not going to like their answer.

"We're just thinking of a couple more songs we want you try," Van said, as they nodded their heads in agreement.

I opened my mouth to tell them hell no, but before I could, Kill asked me. "Is that the guy that tried to hit on you at The Note?" He tipped his beer bottle toward Robert.

I feigned innocence. "Yeah, Amy let it slip I worked here the other night, and he came over to say hi."

I omitted the part where I agreed to go out with him. I felt guilty even though I had no reason to.

"Is he bothering you?" Van asked, in full big brother mode.

"No, he just wanted to say hi. He's harmless," I said, walking over to push Van back down into his chair.

Kill glared at me with narrowed eyes. I was sure he figured out I was neglecting to tell him something.

"Do you guys need anything?" I tried to change the subject.

Jet handed me his empty beer, and I took it, grateful for

the distraction. The others ordered another round too, and I scurried off to get them.

I took my time delivering the orders to the rest of my tables. I avoided the pity-filled glances from Bambi.

"Where did ole' Trent take off to?" Jet asked when I delivered their order.

I wanted to slap him in the back of the head for bringing up yet another subject I did not want to discuss.

"He had to go home; he worked hard today," I lied.

I glanced up just in time to see Robert making his way over. I took off to intercept him, not wanting to have to explain anymore. The guilt I felt because of Kill was confusing, and I didn't want to add to it. I cut off Robert before he made it to the boys, happy for the small miracle.

"That's all of the JackholeS!" he said excitedly, looking over my shoulder.

"Yep, they're my roommates," I muttered. I took his arm and pulled him back toward his table.

"Really? That's so fucking cool. Are you going to introduce me?" he asked as he tried to turn us back around.

"No!" I shouted. "I mean no, they're very protective, and if they find out we're going to go on date they won't be nice." I explained with a weak smile.

"Oh," he said, with a wink. "Well, then maybe another time. After they figure out how head over heels you are for me." He winked again, and I wanted to jab my fingers into his eyes so he wouldn't ever wink again.

"Well, I need to get back to work," I said, grateful when I was finally able to get him back to his table.

"Ok, I need to go anyway. I promised my buddies I would catch up with them later tonight."

I wanted to do a happy dance, glad I was going to get rid of him.

"Well, I'll see you later," I said, relieved he was leaving.

"You bet you will. I'll call you later." He winked again.

I had the urge to puke in his lap. I didn't. Instead, I went over to Ryan, who was staring at me with laughter in her eyes.

"Shut up. I know what you're going to say, and I'm hoping he never calls, so just hush."

She laughed at my rant, and I waited for her comeback. "Oh honey, you're stupid if you think that boy isn't going to call you. If I were you, I would come up with my excuse as soon as possible."

I flipped her off before grabbing my tray she had filled up while laughing at my predicament.

As I was walking off, she yelled after me. "Anytime, sexy."

I smiled at her as I rolled my eyes.

DJ Smoke packed everything up and the bar died down. Mentally I was exhausted from all of the drama. Jessie, Denise, and I closed up the bar, while Bambi sat with boys, flirting with Kill. She gave me dirty looks every time she caught my eye.

"If that girl touches my man one more time, I'm going to take one of these empty bottles and shove it somewhere most men have already been," Jessie snarled.

Her remark made Denise cackle. I stared at her, wondering where in the hell she buried my best friend, and if there was room next to her for Bambi's tiny carcass.

"Oh, honey, she doesn't have her sights on Van. Ever since Kill got her a job here her sights have been on him. They have something going on, I just can't figure it out," Denise responded, after she contained her laughter.

I whipped my eyes over to the table, Denise all but confirming Bambi's story. Bambi leaned over the table to give Kill a clear shot of her plastic surgeon's work. Kill looked her in the eyes, and I wanted to smirk since she wasn't getting the attention she obviously wanted.

Then I thought back to her conversation in the bathroom, and realized she was getting the attention she wanted, just not in front of fragile me.

"I wish her the best of luck," I said, as I went back to filling up the salt shakers.

Jessie and Denise looked at me like they didn't believe a word I said, but I just shrugged as I put more concentration than necessary toward my task.

"What's up bitches?" Ryan said as she plopped down in the seat next to me.

"We were just talking about what a great couple Kill

and Bambi are," Jessie responded, looking directly at me.

Ryan looked over at Kill, who was ignoring Bambi's silicone parts pressed near his face.

"I don't know how to respond to that. Except ewwww." She was staring at Kill, studying him. He looked over at us, and we quickly averted our eyes, knowing we were caught.

I groaned when his chair scraped the floor. Ryan giggled, and I kicked her under the table.

"Ouch, shit Faith, that hurt with those heels of yours." She bent over to rub her shin just as Kill approached us.

"So are you guys going to tell me why you were staring at me?" he asked, leaning on my chair.

I subtly inhaled his scent as I let it wrap around me. We looked up at him innocently. He stared at us intently as he tried to get one of us to break. He blew out a defeated sigh when none of us did.

"I should have known girl code would keep you silent. I will get it out of you later." He gave me a pointed look. "Almost ready to go, Slick?" he asked, as he grabbed the last salt shaker and filled it for me.

"Yeah, I'm done. Let me go grab my stuff." I hopped up off the chair.

"Ok, you're driving since I drank tonight."

We watched him walk away. Ryan had a huge, knowing smile on her face, and I was afraid to hear what was running around in that gorgeous head of hers.

"He can be dirty fun, Faith. As long as you go into it realizing it would be nothing more than hot, sweaty, monkey sex," she said, as she wiggled her eyebrow.

I didn't say anything to encourage Ryan's train of thought. None of them knew what I had overheard in the bathroom. Not wanting to explain what was going on between Kill and I, since I didn't understand it myself.

There were times he acted like he wanted to be around me, and then there were times he acted like he wanted to be inside of me. But with Bambi saying he was just worried about my fragile state, I couldn't help but doubt his actions.

Bambi sauntered to her locker, ignoring me, which was perfectly fine by me. As I moved to leave, she finally spoke, with her back toward me.

"You're stupid if you think he would want anyone like you. I've seen the girls he takes home and believe me, you're nothing."

I wanted to grab her by the hair and slam her into her locker, but I resisted. Jessie, Denise, and Ryan walked in. When Ryan saw Bambi, she made a crude gesture behind her back that had all of us holding back laughter.

"So, where are you staying tonight?" I asked Jessie, done with Bambi.

"Van wants to get something to eat. I'm not sure where we'll end up tonight." She glanced over at Bambi, giving her a clear message Van was off limits.

"Well, I guess I'll see you tomorrow. Night girls." I waved at them and went to find Kill. Catcher was demonstrating a chokehold by crushing D in his arms.

Amy must have just shown up. She hung on Jet's arm as she kissed his cheek. She waved at me with a bag of M&M's in her hands. I leaned on the table to get some of the weight off of my feet. It had been a long night, and my feet were making sure I felt every step I made them take.

"What's the matter, Slick? Are your torture devices getting to you?" Kill asked, coming up behind me and kneading my shoulders with his strong hands.

My eyes fluttered shut. He pulled me against him, and I was too tired to resist.

"Night Kill," Bambi said, her voice implying more than just a simple good night.

I stiffened and tried to pull away, but Kill held me tightly, resting his chin on my head.

"Night, Bambi, see you tomorrow."

I dissected every word, checking to see if there was a hidden meaning in them.

"Come on, Slick, let's get you home."

I resisted for a moment, not wanting to go anywhere with him. At least not until I got the answers to the questions I would never ask.

"Goodnight guys. I'll see you later," I finally said.

I waved a defeated goodbye. Ryan quirked her eyebrow

at me when she saw us. Kill hadn't moved from his position behind me, still holding me close.

"See you two later," she said with a wink.

I wanted to find a dark place to hide.

"Night," Kill answered.

I didn't respond, knowing full well what she was thinking. When we got to the car, Kill had my keys out and opened the driver's door.

"I like the mace," he said, eyeing the new addition to my key ring. "Are you alright to drive? You look dead on your feet. I can drive if you need me to," he said, as he ran his finger down the side of my face.

"I thought you had too many to drive," I replied. I wanted to ask so much more, but I knew this was as bold as I was going to get.

"I'm fine," he replied. He gave me a half-smirk, and I wondered if he knew what was going through my head. Without a word I jumped into the driver's seat. I needed to get my bearings, and driving would give me something to do.

He stood by my closed door for a second before he made his way over to the passenger side and slid in. I cranked the engine and headed toward home with both hands firmly planted on the steering wheel.

"Are you hungry, Slick?" he asked. He shifted toward me. His smell, as always, was intoxicating.

"No, I'm sleepy. I'm not used to working late yet, and I'm still adjusting."

I could feel his gaze on my face as I concentrated on the road. I wanted to get home, and safely in bed before I did something that would change my world.

"You don't eat enough," he murmured. His gaze was still on me, and when I looked over at him a frown was marring his face.

"I don't think I'll starve anytime soon. My body has enough to eat off of for quite some time," I replied, trying to lighten the mood.

"You have no idea how beautiful you are. That asshole sure did a number on you." He turned to focus on the road, his frown still in place.

I let out a shaky breath when I finally parked. Getting my bag from the backseat, I got out of the car. He was next to me as we made our way toward the house, neither of us saying anything. I wanted to escape under my covers, done with the day.

"Night Slick," Kill called out, right before I closed my door.

I opened it back up to see him standing in front of my door with a look on his face that made heat pool between my legs.

"Night Killer," I replied, giving him a halfhearted smile and closed the door.

I found a long t-shirt and ratty pair of gym shorts. Peeling off my work clothes, I changed quickly. Cracking my door open, I looked both ways to ensure Kill wasn't lurking in the hallway.

When I verified it was clear, I dashed to the bathroom and got ready for bed. After putting everything on the charger, I lay in bed and stared at the ceiling.

I made a pact with myself; I wouldn't let Kill get any deeper into my heart. I was going to accept his friendship for what it was, just a friendship.

Also, I made a promise I would deal with Jason; it was obvious he wasn't giving up on me. I couldn't keep ignoring him, and hoping he would go away. Turning on my side I buried myself deeper into the blankets.

Reminding myself I was strong enough to leave Jason, and because of that I was capable of fixing my messed up life. I felt better as I drifted off to sleep, hoping I was right.

# CHAPTER 16

My alarm went off, pulling me out of a very vivid dream starring Kill. Blushing, I looked around, paranoid someone would to bust into my room and accuse me of having a sex dream about my confusing roommate/friend.

In the living room, Kill waited for me. His hair stuck up artfully around his head, and I wanted nothing more than to run my fingers through it, tugging on it while making his lips align with mine.

He raised an eyebrow at me as I blushed.

"Morning, Killer. How do you always end up awake before me?"

"I can't give away all of my secrets, Slick," he said with amusement in his voice.

My vagina bartered with me to let her maul him. I chanted Bambi's name over and over again to get her to calm down.

"You need to eat more," he said eyeing the apple I was eating.

"I eat enough. I don't like a lot of stuff in my stomach when I run," I responded defensively.

"I get that, but then you don't eat when we get home, and when you make us dinner, you barely eat." His voice became agitated.

"Relax, Killer, I'm a girl. We don't eat as much. I eat enough; I just can't handle manly portions, making it look like I don't eat."

Proud of my excuse, I hoped he bought it. I didn't want to admit my breakfast not only consisted of the apple I munched on but also a handful of Tums. He shook his head not letting it go.

"I understand you're a girl; that fact has never been questioned. I also know you are full of shit, and if you don't start eating more, I will hold you down and force feed you."

He leaned toward me, his eyes shimmering with challenge. Anger simmered through my veins, needing to protect my secret.

"I don't need you mothering me. I've been taking care of myself for a long time. You're right, I could probably eat more, but my body's adjusting to my new schedule, so my appetite isn't what it normally is. Back off," I finished, leaning toward him also, accepting his challenge.

"Don't push me, Slick," he replied, anger coloring his voice.

Instead of making me back down it made me want to get in his beautiful face and vent all of my pent-up frustration.

"Don't bully me, Killer," I responded, my eyes narrowed as I shot venom through them.

The anger on his face vanished, replaced with hurt. I should have felt victorious, but instead I felt like a bitch for lumping him into the group of guys who used their physical dominance to get their way.

"I'm sorry. I'm just sensitive when people tell me what to do. I'll try to eat more, can we go run now?" I pleaded, wanting to run off the anger I wasn't able to expel.

He smiled his half-smile, but it didn't light up his face like it normal.

"Come on." He got up and cleaned his glass out, sticking it in the dishwasher. Noticing it was full, I walked over and started it.

I wanted to make it better between us, so I put my arms around his waist, burying my face into his chest.

"Don't be mad at me."

His chest expanded as he took a deep breath. I closed my eyes and breathed him in. "I'm not mad at you. You just bring out my emotions. You make me feel.... raw."

My heart squeezed, understanding exactly what he was trying to say.

"You make me feel the same way. That's why I need to be friends with you. My heart couldn't handle the amount of sensations you would bombard it with."

"Fuck! You can't say shit like that to me." He stared down at me. His eyes on fire with emotions. The sight caused me to suck in a breath from the pure unveiled, feelings pouring out of him.

"Come on. Let's go for our run before we say something we're both going to regret."

He let me go and went out the door. I got our waters with shaking hands and followed him outside into the muggy air. The air slapped me in the face. It clung to my body while it pushed me back. I tried to take a deep breath, but the heavy air stuck to my esophagus, coating it all the way down.

We stretched in silence, moving slower as we fought the thickness surrounding us. Together we moved to the street in sync with one another. He slapped me on the ass, his way of letting me know we were back in a good place.

We jogged slowly as we fought the muggy air for every step. We didn't increase our speed because the extra resistance made it difficult enough without pushing ourselves.

When we reached the house, I dropped to the ground on my back, sucking in the heavy air. Kill dropped down next to me, and I wanted to kick his ass since he wasn't breathing nearly as hard as I was. I shot him the evil eye, making him laugh.

"Why aren't you as winded as I am?" I whined, turning my head to face him.

"I'm in way better shape than you, what can I say?"

I reached over and punched him in the arm. "Ass," I laughed.

"But you love me," he responded, and I was afraid he might be right.

"Shut up, I need to work on my thesis before I go to work tonight."

He jumped up and reached down to help me. I stared at his hand, deliberating if I should take it or not. "Scared?" he taunted.

I scrunched my nose, and grabbed his hand, letting him lift me up.

"You don't like to back down from a challenge, do you Slick?" he asked, as we made our way into the house and closer to the beckoning shower.

"That's for me to know, and for you to never find out,

Killer."

I didn't want to admit he was the only one I had an ounce of fight with. All others I backed down from immediately, except for Bambi, but she's a bitch. Instinctually, I knew Kill would never physically hurt me. I was safe to explode around him.

After my shower, I lounged in a pair of cotton shorts and one of my favorite comfy bras with a ratty tank top over it. Everything was scattered on my bed as I started to work.

I glanced over at my door, wondering if Kill would join me. I intentionally left the side of the bed he was on yesterday clear, just in case. A little later there was a knock on the door, and Kill came in with his notebook. He noticed I had left a spot for him.

"Miss me?" he asked, as he sat down on the open area.

"No, I was actually expecting someone else, but I guess you'll have to do." I responded, not taking my eyes off of my computer screen.

"Liar," he whispered in my ear.

I jumped, unaware of how close he had moved. I wanted to wipe off his self-satisfied smirk, so I licked the tip of his nose, causing him to jerk back from me in horror.

He moved so fast he lost his balance, and ended up falling off of the bed with a bang. I scrambled over to see him sprawled on the floor, looking confused as to how he got there.

"You licked me," he cried in astonishment, not moving from the spot on the floor.

"You reacted like a girl," I retorted back, unable to hold my laughter.

"I don't think I have been licked on the face in.... well, forever."

I couldn't answer him because I was laughing so hard. He snagged my arm and pulled me off of the bed making me scream as I landed next to him.

"Now who reacts like a girl?" he responded, trying to look superior.

"I am a girl, haven't we had this conversation already?"

I got up and back on the bed, positioning my computer on my legs in an attempt to use it as a shield for whatever retribution he had planned. He got back on the bed and grinned when he saw me hovering over my computer, acting like I was engrossed in my forgotten paper.

"Truce?" he asked, putting his hand out to shake.

I reluctantly put my hand in his and he pulled it toward him, licking my whole forearm. Instead of making it a disgusting act of revenge, he languidly ran his tongue up my arm.

His eyes never strayed from mine as he completed his journey. Goosebumps broke out over my body, causing an involuntary shudder at his action.

My nipples hardened, and the panties I just put on grew damp. When he reached the inside of my elbow, he bit the skin gently before turning around and grabbing his notebook. He opened it and clicked his pen as if he didn't just ignite my body in a sexual inferno.

I tried to go back to my paper but ended up staring blankly at the last sentence I'd written. Frustrated I muttered, "Asshole," while I tried to clear my head.

He chuckled but didn't take his eyes off of the notebook. Why did he have to be such a man-whore and mess around with Bambi? I asked myself, all the while trying to get my vagina to calm the hell down.

We worked in silence just like the day before, and once I got his tongue out of my mind the words flowed. After a few hours, I packed it up. Kill was still engrossed in his notebook. I took him in, memorizing all of his features.

His eyebrows were furrowed as he read, and I watched as his eyes swept the page taking in every word. He was perfection. I couldn't blame him for not wanting to settle down. If I looked like him, I would also be going through Portland's hottest, like a hot knife through butter.

"See something you like?" he asked, catching me off guard.

"Doesn't everybody?" I shot back.

I was baffled he would want to sit in my room and work on a song instead of have some bleach blonde, surgeon-altered girl ride him like the last horse on earth. He closed his notebook, leaning into me.

"You shouldn't judge so quickly. It hurts my feelings."

"You confuse the hell out of me, Killer," I admitted, unable to hide the truth from him.

"Stop thinking so much." His eyes searched my face, wanting to see if I would obey his request.

"What happened between you and that waitress Misty?" I blurted out, needing to break the intensity of the moment.

He rubbed the back of his neck nervously before answering.

"One night awhile back, we had a really good night. The whole bar was buying us shots, telling us we were going to make it soon. Misty showed up crying because her baby daddy left her for some other woman. I felt bad for her and tried to make her feel better by complimenting her."

He held out his hand to listen to the whole story when I rolled my eye.

"I know, I know, not my finest decision, but I was plastered and thought it was what she needed. She started crying again, saying she should have fallen for someone like me, and then she kissed me, and I....well, I was drunk and I kissed her back. Before things went any further, her babysitter called and she had to leave. The next day she stayed after her shift and kept acting like we were a couple. I explained to her we weren't going to be anything. And to make sure I drove the point home, I took home some random chick right in front of her. She was pissed, and I can't blame her. I was an asshole, but I've changed. I hate that you have to know who I was, but I don't want to hide it from you."

He didn't look me in the eyes, and I could easily picture him doing something like that to Misty, and soon it would be Bambi. It was a good reminder. I needed to remain his friend, especially since I was trying hard to squash the jealousy bubbling up in me as he talked.

I refused to have a broken heart like most of the girls in Kill's life. He became nervous, fiddling with his notebook when I didn't respond right away.

"Are you ready to go start dinner?" he asked, coming around to my side of the bed so he could help me up.

He ran into his room to put his notebook away, and I went downstairs to get the laundry. Baffled by his sudden change in attitude, I tried to wrap my head around the fact he seemed to want me to believe he had changed.

I wished I could figure out what kind of game he was playing with me.

Kill stared in the fridge trying to figure out what we needed for dinner. Having no clue what I was going to make, he looked hopeless, waiting for something to magically appear. He heard me walk in and gave me sheepish smile.

"I was going to start dinner, but then I realized I had no idea what you had planned."

I wrapped my arms around him, wishing it could be different for us, but certain it never would be.

"Move over, Killer. Go sit down."

The front door opened and Jet called out, "Awesome has arrived."

Everyone came in the house carrying something.

"What's all of this?" I asked as they all made their way to the living room.

"We brought our star dinner. Can't have her slaving over dinner when she has to go up onstage later." D answered.

My stomach dropped at the reminder.

"Why did you have to remind her, dumbass?" Kill yelled at D, rubbing his hands up and down my arm. "Don't think about it, you'll do fine," he whispered in my ear, before biting my earlobe.

He moved out of the kitchen, calling dibs on half of a pizza. Taking a deep breath I tried to calm my nerves, unable to discern if they were from the fear of performing, or from Kill's teeth.

I had to stop thinking of him like that because it made me want to throw him down on any available surface and say the hell with our friendship.

I observed my newly acquired family, feeling a part of my broken heart heal. Kill nodded his head, indicating I should come over and join them. After dinner, the guys refused to let me clean up, telling me I needed to go get stage ready.

Jessie left after dinner, kissing me on the cheek and

telling me she would see me at work. Amy had a tutoring session, but promised she would be at Ray's in time to see my performance.

My stomach knotted up from the thought of being onstage with Kill and the boys. As I curled my hair, Kill leaned on the doorframe watching me in the mirror.

"See something you like?" I asked, throwing his earlier question back at him.

He grinned at me and scanned my body from the tips of my toes to my raised arm holding the curling iron. "Yep," he said, looking at me in the mirror.

The curling iron touched my scalp when all of my limbs went weak.

"Ouch," I cried, removing the iron from my hair and letting the curl fall on the side of my face.

"You alright?" he asked, not waiting for me to answer him before he started inspecting my scalp.

"I'm fine, get out of here. I'm already nervous enough. I don't need you around making it worse," I grumbled, grabbing another piece of hair.

He kissed me where I had burned my head and walked out of the bathroom. "You're going to be amazing, don't worry so damn much."

When he left, I stuck my tongue out at the empty doorway. Downstairs, the boys were on the couch playing a video game. Jet screamed at them to kill someone. They paused the game to assess me.

"Do I pass inspection?" I asked when none of them said anything.

"Fuck, we're going to be so hot tonight." Jet grinned, giving Van a high five.

D winked at me. I glanced over at Kill last to see him scowling. I gave him a questioning glance, and his face transformed into that damn half-smile.

"Let me go get my keys. I'm going to drive you tonight as promised, so you can get your liquid courage on."

"Not too much though, at least not until after your song, right?" D looked at me concerned, and I laughed at his worried face.

"Don't worry, dad, I promise to be a good girl."

"Sorry, Faith. I just want it to be as perfect as I know it will be."

"I'll be good, I promise," I said, crossing my fingers, making them laugh.

Kill walked back into the living room jiggling his keys. "Ready?"

"Yeah, see you guys tonight."

I bit my bottom lip, looking out the windshield and wishing I would have thrown my bottle of Tums into my bag before I left.

"You're going to be fine, Slick." He put his hand on top of mine, stilling it from drumming on my thigh. I turned my hand over and entwined it with his, relaxing from his touch.

"I'll be right there with you. I'm not going to let anything happen to you. Do you trust me?" he asked, taking his eyes off the road, waiting for my answer.

"Yes," I answered, without hesitation because as stupid as it may be, I did.

He squeezed my hand, and we lapsed into silence the rest of the way. He dropped me off at the back entrance and told me not to worry. His confidence actually made me feel secure, like maybe I could pull this off.

Jessie was waiting for me in the break room. Misty left out the back door. She didn't acknowledge me and I did the same.

220

# CHAPTER 17

The bar was busier being it was Friday, and the JackholeS were playing. I hadn't stopped since my feet hit the bar floor.

The clientele differed from karaoke nights on Wednesdays and Thursdays. This was confirmed by the small amount of fried food I served, compared to the cosmopolitans I was ceaselessly delivering.

Ryan moved at a speed that would make any bartender jealous. With little effort, she kept up with the orders incessantly coming from the bar and the waitresses. The bell clanged, announcing the boys' arrival. Everyone turned to see what grand entrance Jet had planned. He didn't let them down.

"Bow down subjects, I've arrived," he crowed. People laughed, and some actually waved their arms up and down in a bowing motion. His chest puffed out like a rooster.

Van and D pushed him out of the way when he didn't move from his post in front of the door. My heart sped up, knowing Kill would come in next. When he did, a possessive feeling came over me seeing all the women preening to get his attention. I stomped it down quickly.

He scanned the bar never meeting my gaze and making my heart drop. He took out his phone, frowning as he tapped on the screen and followed the boys.

Kill talked to the people who stopped him, but his frown stayed put. While I watched him walk through the bar, my phone vibrated.

***Where are you Slick?***
***You didn't chicken out***
***did you?  Because you can***
***run but I will find you.***

At the table he scanned the bar for me, and I then realized I was eclipsed by a bigger gentleman standing in front of me. Without moving from my spot, I text him back.

**Well if you can't find me in this tiny bar, Killer, your threat doesn't seem that scary.**

Bambi walked up to him, blocking my view when I was about to reveal myself. I shot the back of her head the evil eye before making my way to Ryan. My playful mood had vanished. Ryan had a tray ready for the boys.

I noticed there were three beer bottles on the tray instead of the normal four. I waited for her to get the last bottle.

When she made her way over, I pointed at the tray. "I need one more."

"Nope. Kill said he wasn't drinking, but I'm supposed to give you a shot in ten minutes." She winked at me before tending to her customers.

I moved at a slow crawl since Bambi had yet to move. When it was obvious her skinny ass wasn't leaving, I took a deep breath and pulled my shoulders back.

"Hey, Slick, where have you been?" Kill asked, looking past Bambi.

"I've been around. So, you're not drinking tonight? Admit it. You're trying to get me buzzed, huh."

He winked at me as Bambi ran her hand down his arm. He frowned at her action before glancing back at me. My emotions were at war, not knowing what to believe.

"I need to check on my tables. Later, Kill," she said, walking off, but not before giving me a wink, making my blood boil.

Handing out the beers, I was pissed at myself for getting worked up by a skinny bitch he was screwing with. I wanted to think she meant nothing to him, but what I didn't know was if I did.

"You ready for this, Faith?" D asked me, looking

concerned.

"As ready as I can be," I answered, while my stomach did loopy loops. "How will I know when you guys want me onstage?" I began to panic, realizing we never discussed this.

Would Kill call me over the microphone, like a little kid being summoned to the principal's office? Kill put on his half-smile, and the boys had matching shit-eating grins.

"You'll know," he replied without a care in the world.

The need to slap, and or kiss, the grin off his face made it impossible to be in his presence any longer.

"Ok, well let me know if you need anything. I need to get back to work." I hurried away, passing Jessie on her way toward Van.

The boys got onstage, causing people to abandon their tables to flood the dance floor. The noise rose as they tried to show how much they loved them with their voices.

I went over to Ryan since there wasn't anyone left to serve. All of us getting a much needed break. Ryan leaned on the bar and stretched her neck from side to side.

"You never came by for your shot. I need to make it up to you," she said, pouring me two shots. She mixed stuff together and the final result was a caramel-colored shot.

"What is it?" I asked, certain it wouldn't taste anything like my morning coffee even though the color was similar.

"It's a buttery nipple," she answered, making a bottoms-up motion with her hand.

In a fast motion I downed it. Jessie and Denise came over as I put the shot glass down.

"That was yummy," I said, disbelief coloring my voice.

"Drink up your liquid courage. I know the boys want you onstage soon, and you're going to need it," Jessie said.

I swallowed the second one just as fast as the first, knowing she was right.

"You're singing with the JackholeS?" Denise asked in disbelief.

"Yeah, D had an idea about one of their songs. He wants me to sing second vocal in it, and we're trying it out tonight." I toyed with the empty shot glass in front of me, embarrassed at the attention.

223

"You're going to rock it," Denise told me, as her smile widened.

"I hope so."

"You need another," Ryan said, taking the empty shot glass and refilling it.

I stared at the tiny glass while listening to Kill. He had the crowd in an uproar just by singing to them. With the pandemonium as a background, I took the shot, letting it slide down my throat, the sweetness lost on me. I implored the alcohol to do its job before I was up.

The boys announced they had a surprise for everyone when they came back from their break. The crowd went wild, curious about what the band had in store for them. I took the orders for my tables. With the alcohol burning through my veins I felt relaxed, even with my performance looming closer.

Every table I waited on had people whispering conspiratorially. They were all discussing what the surprise would be, some of the wilder predictions had me giggling.

The boys beamed at me. Well, all except Van, he was too busy staring at Jessie as she delivered his beer. "Thanks babe," he said, kissing her on the cheek.

Amy burst in looking rushed, the licorice in her mouth bounced as she ran over to the table. "Did I miss it?" she asked around her candy.

"Nope, you're just in time, Candy." Jet grabbed Amy and opened his mouth, guiding the licorice sticking out of her mouth into his until their lips touched.

My stomach churned, reminding myself I could fail miserably soon.

"Stop thinking," Kill whispered, pulling me out of my panicked thoughts. "If you keep thinking, I'll make Ryan shove more shots down your throat."

I looked over at Ryan who was making drinks for the crowded bar.

"No more drinks, my lips are numb," I said, pressing my lips together repeatedly to see if I could get feeling into them.

"You aren't too drunk to sing, are you?" D asked, freaked out as he watched me.

"Nope, I'm fine," I answered, looking over at him, then

224

added "I hope."

D groaned hitting his forehead on the table. Before he could go for another round, Kill put his hand between his forehead and the table, pushing it up when it connected.

"She's fine. Stop worrying. If you worry, she'll worry."

"Sorry, Faith."

"It's fine, I have to get back to work. I'll see you boys up there."

Jet surfaced from Amy's face long enough to put his hand out for a high five. Van gave me an encouraging hug while his eyes tracked Jessie's ass through the bar.

When the boys got back onstage, the bar was filled to capacity. I assumed everyone text their friends to say the JackholeS had something special planned for tonight.

The whole bar gyrated and bounced as Kill sang. For a second I considered another drink, but then they began playing a song I knew by heart. The reason I knew it so well was because I played it over and over again when I was younger.

Kill sang the first verse of '*Gotta Have Faith*'. The music was low, and Kill's voice caused my whole body to break into spontaneous goose bumps. I caught on fire when he whispered into the microphone he had to have me. The beat picked up, and the crowd chanted my name.

My body felt heavy, as if I was wading through the thick air again. Until I locked eyes on Kill, and time went into overdrive. I reached up to him, and he hauled me up onstage. The whole bar was electric.

Kill put his arm around me and pulled me close. His scent was stronger, mixed with sweat from performing, and it was intoxicating.

"This is Faith."

A shiver ran through me when my real name rolled off of his tongue.

"If you haven't heard about her, then where the fuck have you been?" he yelled into the microphone, making the crowd go wild.

I let out a nervous laugh at their reaction.

"She has agreed to get up here with our stupid asses and sing with us. So be nice to her." He kissed the top of my

225

head, letting me go, so we could take our places on either side of the microphone.

"I hope I don't screw this up," I said quietly, but the stupid microphone magnified it throughout the bar.

Cat calls and encouragements came from the crowd, boosting my confidence. Kill winked at me. Van started the beat, getting the band in sync. I closed my eyes, letting the music flood through me. When Kill began singing my eyes flew open.

The combination of being so close to him while people watched us was heady. The bar pulsated as people sang along since it was a revamped JackholeS song.

My eyes were fastened on Kill's, and his stayed glued on mine. Even with the deafening noise level, I was still able to get lost in him, forgetting everyone else.

When the song ended, Kill put his arm around me, and Jet and D came running over, jumping around me like puppies. Jet grabbed the microphone with a huge smile on his face. "Wasn't she fucking awesome?"

The bar clapped and screamed, and it was exhilarating. I smiled and waved at the crowd while making my way offstage.

"If you liked that, then you should come back tomorrow for her encore performance," Kill announced as I walked through the crowd.

People clamored to talk to me, and others asked for pictures. It was overwhelming, and I was reeling, wondering how the boys dealt with the constant attention.

When I made it to the bar, Ryan clapped, and I turned an even brighter shade of red. Some of the residents at the bar turned to see what had Ryan's attention. When they saw me, they clapped along with her.

I ducked my head, wishing they would stop. Kill was singing again, taking the vagina-owning crowd's attention away from me.

When the boys finished their set, Kill talked to the crowd and calmed them, but kept their adrenaline pumping. They were mauled by their fans, vying for their attention when they hopped offstage.

226

We shut the bar down as soon as last call was announced. Most of the crowd lumbered out, laughing and smiling, or letting the drama of their lives be vented into the night air. Catcher herded the lingering patrons out.

The three of us put the bar back together as Bambi flirted with Kill. Jessie made sure Bambi kept a large enough distance from Van.

Amy came over eating a Milky Way. When she reached us, I snatched the hand midway to her mouth, and took a bite. She smiled, happily feeding me sugar.

"Who's the skank?" she asked, pointing the rest of her candy toward Bambi, not trying to hide who she was talking about.

Denise laughed out loud while Jessie shushed her.

"That's, Bambi. She's an awful waitress and even worse person," Denise answered, also not trying to be quiet.

Amy nodded, agreeing with Denise's description.

"What are we talking about?" Ryan asked, while we tried to keep Amy and Denise quiet as they continued discussing Bambi.

"The skank hanging all over Kill," Amy answered.

Ryan laughed, plunking down on an empty chair next to me and leaning back against it to stretch her back.

"I don't understand what the hell's going on between the two of them. I know he got her the job, but I don't get why he puts up with her," Ryan said, as she extended her hand out to Amy. "Ryan, bartender."

Amy shook her hand. "Amy, best friend of these two." She pointed at me and Jessie. "And also humping Jet every chance I get."

"It's nice to finally meet someone who can keep up with Jet. Two down and two to go." Ryan said, looking over at the boys.

Bambi said something while bouncing on her toes, causing her cemented after-markets to almost move. We followed Ryan's gaze to see if her penetrating eyes would pull something out of him. He looked over at us, feeling our gazes on him. Kill raised his eyebrow and puckered his lips to one side. Unlike the last time, none of us looked away, all of us

227

searching for answers.

He came over to us, and we blatantly watched his progress, no one speaking, just observing. Bambi stared at his retreating back and stalked off to the breakroom, whipping off her apron.

"Are you ready?" he asked, kneading his hands into my shoulders and making me melt into the chair.

"Almost, but if you keep that up, you'll never get me home."

"Ok, but I'll continue when we get home." He squeezed my shoulders one last time before going back to the boys.

"Holy shit. What's going on between you two?" Ryan asked, looking over at Kill and me.

"Shut up Ryan, please," I begged.

"Just be careful. I've known Kill for a long time, and he's not the commitment type. Just don't get too caught up in it," Ryan whispered in my ear, once we had the bar shut down.

Before leaving, we went in to tell Ray goodbye since he had been holed up in his office all night. I walked back to the breakroom trying to find Kill. After changing and still not seeing him, I went outside. He wasn't by the car, and dread washed over me.

Under the light in the parking lot, I watched Kill climb out of Bambi's car as she hopped out and ran around the car, throwing her arms around his neck and kissing him on the cheek. She let go and got into her car, waving as she backed away.

I swallowed the bile as reality hit. I had just seen Bambi and Kill together doing exactly what she described in detail in the bathroom. Why the fuck would he tell me he wanted more when I was ready? All I could come up with was he wasn't used to having to chase a girl and he was enamored with the challenge.

I knew he wasn't relationship material, even though he kept asking me to give him a chance. The proof of his unchanging behavior was right in front of me. Ryan's stark reminder rang in my ears.

I blinked into the night air, refusing to let the tears threatening to fall leave my eyes. I knew who he was.

"Are you ok, Slick?" He put his arm around my shoulder, and as much as I wanted to, I didn't pull away, I reminded myself we were friends.

"Yeah, I'm just tired, the alcohol's wearing off, and all I want is my bed."

I let him lead me to his car and help me get in. I leaned the seat back and closed my eyes before he got behind the wheel. He started the engine, but didn't put it in gear I tried to slow my breathing to make it look like I had fallen asleep. He sighed and rested his hand on my thigh as he drove us home.

I forced the tears back. His hand on me felt right, and I couldn't keep taking comfort from someone who wasn't safe for my heart. When we got to the house, I was half asleep, getting out of the car and making it up to my room seemed impossible.

"We're home," he whispered in my ear, causing chills to run through me.

"I know. I'm too tired to move," I said leaning toward him until his lips met my ear.

He chuckled, climbing out of the car. I didn't open my eyes and hoped my toes wouldn't freeze off. Kill opened my door like I knew he would, saving my toes from detachment.

He leaned in with his patented half-grin. After he unbuckled me, he put his arm under my legs. "Put your arms around my neck," he said, making my sleepy body hum from his touch.

The alcohol relaxed me enough my muscles felt liquid. He lifted me up with no trouble, and I got a sense of how strong he was. I put my head on his shoulder as he took me into the house. The boys were on the couch. Amy and Jessie made a surprised sound when they saw us.

"Is she ok?" D asked as he came toward us.

"Yeah, she just had too much to drink, and the adrenaline's wearing off."

Someone touched my forehead, and Kill jerked me away. "She's fine, D."

"Calm down, Kill, we're just worried about her like you are," Van said, still on the couch.

"I know. I'm just tired," Kill responded, sighing. "I'm

going to get her to bed. See you later."

"Do you need to wash your face or anything?" he asked.

I shook my head on his shoulder, knowing I would regret it in the morning. He carried me into my room and pulled the covers back, putting me in. He took my shoes off, and my body felt like lead. I fumbled and unbuttoned my jeans, lifting my hips so he could peel them off.

"Shit," he muttered under his breath.

I drug my eyelids over my eyes trying to focus on him. The alcohol running through my body made me lethargic.

"Slick, I can't." He trailed off.

I let my hips hit the mattress, too tired to keep them up. "Fine, I'll sleep in my jeans," I said, my voice was slurred and close to a whisper, unable to exert enough force to make it audible.

"Fuck," he muttered, as he ran his hands through his hair. "Lift up."

His face had a pained expression as I lifted up. He grasped my jeans and took them off, throwing them on the dresser as he walked out. I got the covers up to my waist before letting my arms drop to my side.

I drifted off to sleep when I felt something warm and wet on my face. Struggling to swat it away, Kill stopped me.

"Sshh, I'm just wiping your face."

He had just claimed another piece of my broken heart. Was there any reason to put it back together since he seemed to be claiming it one piece at a time? As his retreating footsteps faded, I called out before he reached the door.

"Kill?" He stopped, but didn't respond.

Stopping myself from asking him something dangerously stupid, I finished lamely. "Never mind, good night."

My door clicked shut, he took off his shoes and crawled into bed. He guessed what I wanted to ask him, without having to vocalize it. I put my head on his chest breathing him in.

"You left your jeans on," I whispered, not wanting to shatter the moment by speaking too loud.

"Yep," he responded "Go to sleep. I'm really proud of you. You were amazing tonight, our male fan base just tripled from seeing your sexy ass up there."

I wanted to argue with him but I was unable to form words, I laid there with him in the darkness, feeling safe and whole.

In the morning my head rested on my pillow instead of nestled on Kill's chest. I considered maybe last night wasn't real, and he walked out of the room only to have me shift into a dream where he stayed.

My head ached, and my stomach felt like I swallowed acid. I leaned over and chewed on a handful of Tums from my nightstand drawer. When I leaned back onto my pillow I got a hint of Kill's smell lingering on it. Unabashedly, I pressed my nose into it, inhaling the haunting scent.

Uncertain if he stayed last night, or if his scent was just hovering from his time in my bed while he worked on his notebook. With slow, measured movements I got up, giving the Tums time to do their job. When I didn't have a sharp pain shoot across my belly, I inhaled, deeply relieved.

My phone beeped deep from within the bottom of my messenger bag on my dresser next to my jeans. Thoughts of Kill removing my jeans invaded my brain. My Ray's shirt barely passed my belly button. I was comforted when I saw I was wearing a purple boy shorts with pink polka dots spattered across them.

Retrieving my phone from the recesses of my bag, my mood soured.

## Hey sexy, It's Robert.
## I'm looking forward
## to Monday. What time
## can I pick you up?

I conjured up excuses to get out of it, but I figured there was no harm in one date, as long as he understood there would be no repeat.

I made a mad dash to the bathroom, not bothering to put my pants on, anxious for a shower. The hot water soothed my tight muscles into submission. Reluctantly, I pulled myself out and wrapped my pink towel around me. I opened the door

231

and got ready for another short dash to my room when I ran straight into Kill.

"Easy there," he chuckled before taking a slow perusal of my body still damp from my shower. "I'll go make coffee."

He let go of me and rushed downstairs as if the hounds of hell were chasing him and making progress. I watched him until he disappeared, mystified by his reaction, but when it came to Kill, that seemed to be the norm.

The light blue dress I put on cinched in the middle, making my waist look small, so of course it was one of my favorites. I brushed my hair and put it in a loose braid before heading downstairs barefoot, not having anywhere to go.

Kill was in his usual spot, and my heart warmed when I saw him finishing his protein shake. I went straight to the coffee pot. While putting the creamer back in the fridge, I realized a grocery trip looked to be in my near future.

I sat next to Kill and sipped my coffee, watching him as he toyed with his empty glass, looking uncomfortable. Fear rose in me, afraid he would tell me I was too much trouble and needed to leave.

"I have to go grocery shopping, is there anything special you want me to get?" I blurted out louder than I expected, causing him to jerk his head up and out of whatever he was thinking about.

"I'll go with you," he replied quickly. His face was expressionless, making my stomach knot when his famous half-smile didn't appear.

"You don't have to; I mean you probably have better things to do than go grocery shopping." I rambled. I snapped my mouth shut, afraid I was making it worse.

"I have nothing else to do, and it would be nice to get out of the house for a while. Finish your coffee and we'll go. We can take Jet's truck so we can load it up." He winked at me and the half-smile finally appeared, making my shoulders relax.

I chastised myself for being so paranoid, reminding myself Kill's thoughts didn't revolve around me. When I finished my coffee, he took our cups to the sink to wash them out. "Go get ready, I've got this."

I nodded my head to his back and walked upstairs to grab my shoes and bag. My phone blinked, announcing I had another text. It was from Robert again, and I chewed another handful of Tums while I read it.

**I just got reservations for my favorite restaurant at six-thirty. Where do you live, so I can pick you up?**

Anger welled up in me, in a weak moment I'd made a decision I was now dreading. I wanted to text him back, explaining I'd made a huge mistake. Picturing Kill getting out of Bambi's car made a life-sabotaging mood sweep over me.

I text him my address and slipped my shoes on before putting eyeliner around my eyes and slicking Dr. Pepper lip-gloss on my lips. I hated myself with every step I took back to Kill.

My phone notified me of another text. Kill sat on the couch, strumming his guitar, and humming to himself, lost in the music. I stood in the living room watching, spellbound. When he finished the song, he smiled when he caught me watching.

"Ready?" he asked, putting down his guitar and getting up.

"Yep. If you want to stay and practice you don't have to go with me. That was beautiful," I said, my nerves jumping all around me.

"You're going to give me a complex. That's the second time you've tried to get me to stay home."

"I was just trying to be a friend by letting you out of a boring errand, but if you insist on coming with me, who am I to try to stop you?"

He slung his arm over my shoulder, falling into step with me.

"What kind of friend would I be if I didn't go with you to make such a boring errand more exciting?"

True to his word, he made me laugh the whole shopping trip. On the way home, we sent jabs back and forth, and my sides hurt by the time we put everything away.

I told him I needed to work on my paper. He nodded his head, and I went upstairs; to my dismay, he didn't follow. Even though we didn't talk while we worked, it was lonely without him at my side. It took me longer to get into my paper, which irritated me. When I found my groove, after more attempts than I wanted to admit, I became immersed in my work.

I was stunned when I noticed how many hours had flown by. Kill sat in the living room with his guitar.

"I didn't want to bother you while you were working; I stayed down here so I wouldn't interrupt you." He looked self-conscious, and I wanted to admit it would have been less of a nuisance if he just played in my room, instead of making me wonder what he was doing, but I refrained.

"You wouldn't have bothered me. I have my music up so loud I wouldn't have noticed you," I lied; anytime he was near, I was aware of him.

Kill situated his stuff on the kitchen table and started strumming while I made dinner. He would stop every so often to write something in his notebook. When everything was cooking, I sat down across from Kill, listening to him hum while he perfected the song he was working on.

He looked up, blinking away the world he was just lost in. "It smells awful in here, Slick. Whatcha making?"

I shook my head since I had just made everything in front of him. Being so absorbed in his work, he was oblivious to his surroundings. When I tried to find out what he was working on he changed the subject, frustrating me.

"Stop pouting, I promise to tell you when I'm done."

I stuck my bottom lip out for a while longer, trying to sway his decision, but when I saw he wasn't going to budge, I sucked it back in.

"Fine, be mysterious, you have to have some ploy to keep a girl interested."

He laughed at my childish reaction, and the rich sound made me smile, although I tried not to. "You sure know how to make a guy feel good. You should teach classes."

"Don't worry, I'm sure your ego can handle it." I said,

mashing the potatoes.

"Yep, definitely should open classes."

I finished dinner and put it on the counter as Kill went upstairs to wrangle everybody up. Plugging in my curling iron, I opted to get ready while everyone was eating and just pick at the leftovers, so Kill couldn't monitor my food intake.

After I was finished, taking more time than normal since I would be onstage again, I swapped out the laundry. Everyone was watching T.V. and they looked full and content. Jet saw me first.

"That was fucking amazing. It reminded me of my grandma's meatloaf. I loved that shit when I was a little kid."

Amy sat on Jet's lap, unwrapping a Starburst; D snagged one from the package sitting on the table.

"I never used to eat candy until you, now I can't stay away," he complained as he popped it in his mouth.

"It just makes you sweeter," she told him before grabbing Jet's face, and they mauled each other.

"I made you a plate, it's in the microwave," Kill said, grinning, knowing he had beat me at my own game.

"Thanks," I said, defeated this round. I grabbed my food and sat next to Kill on the floor, making a valiant effort to finish the majority of it.

"Are you good, or do you need liquid courage tonight?" D asked, stealing another candy while Amy was preoccupied with Jet's lips.

"Ugh, no alcohol tonight. I barely remember getting into bed last night."

Kill had an amused look on his face, and I once again questioned if he really slept with me last night.

"You did great last night, Faith. I knew you would. My best friend's awesome," Jessie announced, making Amy remove her face from Jet's long enough to whine.

"What about me?"

"You're awesome too, but last night was all Faith."

"I can't wait to see how many guys show up tonight to see you sing. I bet you quadrupled our fan base," Jet said, before guiding Amy back to his lips to continue sucking on her face.

"I highly doubt that," I replied, rolling my eyes. "I just hope I didn't make you lose any. I don't think I'm as good as you think I am."

Van's face got red, startling me because I hadn't seen his anger pointed at me before. "Faith, you need some self-esteem. You're like a sister to me, and anyone that talks shit about you will get their ass kicked, even you."

"Sorry, it's a knee-jerk reaction."

Van moved Jessie off of him and got down next to me, pulling me into a big hug.

"Don't let him win; you're better than that, believe in yourself," he whispered in my ear, squeezing me before going back to Jessie. He grabbed her hand and put it on his head, moving it around until she rubbed it on her own accord. Satisfied, he leaned into her hand reminding me of a needy cat.

I put my plate away and stood staring at the sink. Was I letting him win? That question made me second guess every choice I had made, since escaping Jason.

"What are you thinking about?"

"Nothing," I replied, not sure how I felt about Van's statement. He tried to be encouraging but the truth hurt.

"Liar," Kill taunted, as he stepped closer to me.

"Van told me I need to stop letting him win. Now all I can think about is that I wasn't as strong as I thought I was by leaving him." My brain reminded me of my confrontation, but I countered it by reminding it how it ended.

Kill put his arm around my waist and pulled me in front of him, placing his forehead on mine. "He doesn't want you to go backwards from the progress you've made. What you did was extremely brave. We see the effects of what he did to you, and we want you to break those habits. It's going to take some time to get him out of your system, but we want to help you, because you deserve to be free of him." His gaze was unwavering, and that look alone made me feel invincible.

"I don't think my system will ever be pure of him," I whispered my fear, wanting him to take it away and soothe me.

"Then take what's swimming around in you and make something good out of it," he said into my hair.

"What?" I asked, hoping he could give me some

guidance.

"You're a smart girl, you'll figure it out. Give it time." He let me go, and I wanted to grab his arms and wrap them around me like a seatbelt, keeping me safe, holding me together as I sped through this life-altering change.

When we went back into the living room, Jessie crawled out of Van's arms. "Are you ready to go?" Jessie asked.

"Yeah, are we driving together?" I asked, wanting her to say no, so I would have the alone time to get my mind focused.

"I'm taking my car so Van and I can go out to dinner after work. So, it's up to you, if you want to ride with me and go with the boys after, or you can take your car," she answered, leaning over and kissing Van's head,

"I'll drive over. I'm not drinking tonight, so I'll be fine to drive home."

"I'll take you, and then you can ride home with me tonight." Kill took his keys off of the counter.

"It's ok. I don't mind driving," I replied, not wanting to be alone with him.

"If I drink too much tonight you can drive my car."

The boys collectively inhaled at his offer.

"What the fuck, Kill, you won't let any of us drive your car." Jet said, looking pissed off.

Kill flipped him off and grabbed my arm, steering me toward the garage. He snatched up my bag hanging by the staircase and carried it with him.

"You didn't have to drive me, you know."

"I know, but I didn't want you stewing in your thoughts while driving. It's not safe, and you still have a crazy ex out there. Have you heard from him lately?" he asked.

I shrugged and looked out the side window. My mind went to my encounter with Jason.

"Don't shut me out. We are friends remember, and if you renege on your deal, then I'm pulling over and fucking you, until I'm all you can remember, which is what I've been dying to do from the moment I saw you, looking sexy and lost when you walked into my bar."

My thighs clenched, and I wanted nothing more than to take my friendship away just to feel him sliding into me, making me forget everything, but I denied myself.

"I've had some private calls, but I can't be sure they're from him, and I haven't had one of those in a couple of days." I said, and even with his sunglasses on, I could feel the disappointment radiating off of him.

"That doesn't mean anything. He's probably switching his game plan wondering if you'll come to him if he waits you out." He was questioning my resistance toward Jason, and it made me mad.

"I'm not her! I'm not going back to him. If I did, he would own me forever or until he ended me," I snarled.

It was a low blow to bring up his past regrets, but I felt it was fair since he kept pushing them on me. Of course Jason was still out there waiting for me. He made that much clear when he showed up at Ray's.

"I know you aren't. I'm sorry I was being an ass, I just.... I just worry about you."

Realizing this conversation was useless, I changed tactics. "Did the great and powerful Kill just apologize? Where are the paparazzi when you need them?"

I pretended to try and get a glimpse of the elusive paparazzi. Getting his half-smile in place made me feel like I just accomplished something worthwhile.

"I'll never admit it, and if you tell anyone they won't believe you anyway. I'm the consummate badass."

We pulled up to the back of the bar, and he put his car in park to lean into me. I could smell the mint from his gum lingering on his mouth and wanted nothing more than to swipe my tongue across his full lips.

"No more thinking tonight. I'll see you later and when you're onstage with me tonight, let all the crazy emotions swirling inside you, out."

I focused on his lips, watching the words leave them, wanting to inhale them. At that moment I couldn't remember why I had resisted him for so long.

As I leaned into him there a knock on the driver's side window, breaking the connection. I was ready to shoot lasers from my eyes at the person who interrupted us, but when I saw who it was, it felt like a bucket of ice water had been dumped on me.

Bambi leaned down to peer into the window scowling at me, but when Kill turned his head, she was all smiles, squeezing her arms to her sides, causing her boobs to pop out.

Kill sighed and rolled down his window. I seized the opportunity to get my stuff and scurry out of the car without saying goodbye. I escaped as fast as I could so I didn't give into the temptation to listen to their conversation.

# CHAPTER 18

Because I was in such a hurry, I didn't see Misty until I practically ran her over. I caught her arm to keep her from falling on her ass.

"Faith, are you ok? You were running so fast, I expected a man with a hockey mask to be chasing you."

It took me a moment to notice she was being civil.

"Listen, I've been a bitch to you and I'm sorry," she apologized. "I'm still pissed at Kill, but I realized he isn't going to change, and I need to accept that. Besides, I heard he's with Bambi, and I had the wrong idea about the two of you." Hurt flashed through her eyes, but it disappeared in a blink.

I understood she wanted to make our encounters less awkward, and this was her peace offering, but it didn't ease the pain slicing through my stomach when she spoke.

"Bambi thinks they'll last. I wanted to tell her Kill never stays with one girl for too long, but she wouldn't have listened if I tried. Have a good night."

And then poof, she was gone. Her words branded my heart with the painful truth I needed to remember in order to keep my heart in place.

I walked to the breakroom in a fog, wishing Kill would be the same guy he was with everyone else; it would make it easier to keep my feelings from growing. They didn't see him as I did; considerate, funny, loyal, and passionate, well, I'm sure most of the females in Portland were aware of his passion, but the other things he showed me on a daily basis, seemed to be lost on everyone else.

Bambi flounced in as I stared blankly into my locker, hoping the contents would bring me clarity. Like when you walk into your kitchen and open the fridge numerous times, hoping it had sprouted something edible while you were away.

"Kill just feels sorry for you. Stay away from him," Bambi hissed, as she pulled her shirt down to show the edge of her bra.

I hated that someone like her could hurt me. Jessie came running in looking flushed.

"Where have you been young lady?" I teased, ignoring Bambi and her cutting remarks.

"Shut up," she snapped, kissing me on the cheek. We walked into the bar together, leaving Bambi to primp and preen by herself.

"Have you talked to your parents?" I asked, as we walked over to Ryan, who was pouring a bright green concoction into a glass, while a girl with a tiara and bride-to-be sash giggled with her friends.

"No, not yet." She looked so sad. I put my arm around her waist to give her a quick hug.

"Why don't we go to lunch on Monday?" she asked, hugging me back.

When she mentioned Monday, I flinched. Remembering I needed to check my phone for Robert's response.

"Monday's fine, but I have a date at six-thirty," I said, cringing when she screeched at me.

"With who?"

"Remember that guy, Robert, at The Note?"

She nodded her head yes.

"Well, he came in here and asked me out, and I said yes." I took my tray ready to run off, not wanting to discuss it further.

"Monday, you and I have a lot to talk about. I'll let you avoid the subject until then, because I'm avoiding my own stuff right now, but Monday we need to have some serious confession time."

I took the order from table of giggling couples, ordering drinks with sexual innuendos in them, each trying to one up the other. In fact, I was pretty sure the last drink didn't exist. Before I could leave to put their orders in, one of them stopped me.

"Are you, Faith, the singing waitress?"

My cheeks flooded red from the recognition. "I'm Faith, and I sang with the JackholeS last night. So, I guess I am," I said, unsure how to respond.

"Oh my god. We have the singing waitress at our table. Can we get a picture?"

One of the girls intercepted Bambi, asking if she could take the picture. Bambi looked like she wanted to bitch-slap the girl, and I had to bite the inside of cheek to keep from laughing. I posed in the middle with them, not having to fake the smile on my face as Bambi snapped the picture and set the phone on the table with a loud bang and walked away.

"So, is she the bitchy waitress?" The guy sitting next to the girl now checking her phone for damage asked.

"Yep," I replied, feeling giddy as I walked away.

"What the hell is a double penetration?" Ryan asked when I handed her my order from my now favorite table, besides the boys' of course.

"I don't know. They were trying to one up each other with sexual innuendos, so have fun concocting it, I don't think they care."

Ryan had an evil glint in her eyes, as she put together the drink in her head. "I will have it up for you in a minute."

She rubbed her hands together, and I was scared for the guy that would end up with whatever concoction that facial expression was inventing.

When I came back, my tray was full for my second favorite table, and there was a drink on it that was bright red on the top, and purple on the bottom.

"Don't ask what's in it; just tell him if he wants another he will be cut off because two's the limit on these. Get it, double penetration?" Ryan giggled evilly as I took my tray to the waiting table.

When I gave him Ryan's warning, the rest of the table ordered a double penetration for their next drink. By my sixth picture request of the night, my face didn't flame fire engine red anymore, it was now a much subtler wine-cooler pink.

The bell above the door rang, but before Jet could make his announcement, the bar chanted for the JackholeS. Amy took the Tootsie-Pop out of his mouth, putting it in hers so he could greet his fans properly.

"The awesome has arrived bitches. Are you ready to get rocked?"

The bar exploded, and the newly acquired male customers looked around, not knowing what was going on. I laughed at their expressions, most of them looked like they had bitten off more than they could chew by coming here.

The rest of the boys followed, and I made sure I wasn't hidden when Kill entered. I wanted to see where his eyes landed first, me or Bambi. I felt sick resorting to such teenage games, but I couldn't help it.

Kill's eyes swept past Bambi first and they smiled at each other. My heart dropped into my stomach, keeping the boulder company. He continued his scan until they landed on me.

I tried to keep the scowl off my face and probably looked constipated from fighting it. He gave me a questioning look and came over to me.

"I told you not to think tonight, Slick." He pulled me into his arms giving me a hug. My nose planted into his chest so I could inhale the scent I craved.

"I didn't agree to your request, but you were too busy with other things for me to tell you," I responded into his chest, my nose vibrated when he chuckled into my hair.

"Sorry about that, Bambi requires a lot of attention, and if I wouldn't have talked to her, she would have caused a huge scene."

I stiffened at his reply. In my mind he had confirmed there was something going on with him and Bambi. And him allowing her to be clingy, without moving on to the next available vagina made my stomach squeeze, trying to evacuate its contents.

I swallowed, not wanting to vomit on his shirt, or maybe I did. I debated vomiting for a second before deciding against it.

"I understand you wouldn't want to make her upset." Placing my palms on his chest I tried to push away from him.

"Are you jealous?" he asked.

I wanted to slug him, because even though I couldn't see his face, I was certain he was smiling.

"Please, Killer, we're just friends remember?"

He let me push off of him. I scurried over to Ryan

without a backward glance.

"What's going on between you two?" she asked.

"We're just friends," I said defensively, hating the word friend every time I said it.

"Ah-ha. Just remember to be careful," she replied, as I hefted the tray full of the boys' beers.

Most of the bar had shifted their chairs so they could get a glimpse of the boys. Jessie caught up and we walked over together. Before we reached the table she took a bottle and handed it to Van, kissing him in the process. Kill smirked at me when I handed him a bottle.

"Thanks, Slick."

"I knew you would increase our male fans. Look how many more there are tonight," D said, surveying the bar, and I could guarantee he would be able to tell me the exact percentage it had grown.

"I don't know, D, it's Saturday. I'm sure they're just here because it's the weekend."

"Nope. Faith, they're here for you. I have been asked by most of the males; mind you none I've ever seen before, if you were the singing waitress, and if I could introduce you to them," Jessie said.

D and Jet laughed, but Kill searched around the bar, glaring at the new customers, making me cock an eyebrow at him.

"Whatcha, looking at, Killer?" I asked, curious at what he would say.

"Just making sure none of these douche boxes need an ass kicking. Where's Catcher?" he grumbled, grabbing his bottle and scraping his chair on the floor as he went to look for him.

"That guy needs to get laid," Jet said, Amy nibbling on his ear. "Ever since he's taken on protector role, he hasn't had time to get any." Jet's eyes rolled back in his head, and I knew his input was done until his ear was returned.

I wanted to correct him, and tell him Kill was getting plenty from a certain busty waitress with a perpetual bad attitude, but I kept my mouth shut.

"It isn't Faith's fault," Van stated. "He's growing up.

244

Look at you. I've never seen you so hooked on a girl before. Besides, it gets tiring having a different girl every night, especially when all she wants is your rock 'n' roll persona, and not the real you." D fist bumped Van in agreement.

"Well, then he needs to find someone like my Amy, take her somewhere and bang the shit out of her, and claim her as his own."

Amy giggled. Jessie stared at Van as if he had grown two heads. Her eyes welled up with unshed tears. I dragged her away before anyone saw, telling the boys we needed to get back to work and would check on them soon.

"Are you alright?" I asked, as she pulled her cheeks down, trying to get the tears to go back to where they came from.

"I don't know. What Van said just now, sometimes it feels like he's too perfect. He always says the right thing, and I'm not sure he's for real. Maybe this is his game." Her voice was laced with panic.

"Van's falling in love with you, or is already there. You need to talk to him. Not everyone's walking around with an agenda."

"Faith, I need to tell you something about Texas." Her face was pale, and she kept glancing over at the boys.

"Whatever it is, it will be ok. Do you want to talk tonight, or wait until Monday?" I tried to placate her, wanting the panicked look on her face to go away.

She closed her eyes and when she opened them, her face was the picture of calm, having pushed all her emotions away. "Monday. Can you come to my apartment? Candice won't be there."

"It's a date. I love you, Jess."

"I love you too, Faith."

We took off to deliver our orders. When people asked me about the red and purple drink, I blushed every time I told them the name. I gave them the rules and kept a mental tab on whom and how many each person had had.

The boys went onstage, and the bar emptied to the dance floor. I stopped and admired them in all their glory. I leaned on the bar, and rested my feet since my tables had abandoned me. Denise and Jessie leaned next to me.

Thankfully, Bambi stayed over by the gaming area, staring at Kill like she wanted to unhinge her jaw and swallow him whole. Ryan stood behind us, handing us each a bottle of water. I accepted mine gratefully and guzzled it without taking a breath.

"Nervous?" she asked, taking the empty bottle from me.

"I almost forgot I was going up there again. I've been going nonstop since I got here." I admitted, taking my eyes off Bambi, and back to Kill.

"Do you want a drink?" Ryan asked.

I shook my head, certain my stomach couldn't handle two nights in a row.

"You will be fine. This will be your fourth night onstage, and the other three you were incredible," Denise said, touching my arm for encouragement.

"Karaoke was for fun. I didn't care if I messed up. I'm afraid last night was a fluke, and I'll mess up and hurt the boys."

"Those boys will make it no matter what happens tonight. Don't worry about them. They're big boys, and they know what they're doing. You need more confidence." With her wisdom dispensed, she took off to clean the empty tables.

"I concur," Ryan said, wiping down the bar during the lull.

I took off to help Denise with the tables. Jessie was staring off into space, and I let her have some time.

When the boys jumped offstage, the crowd scrambled back to their tables. I had already put bottles on their table when they ended their song and kept busy with my other tables.

The break didn't last as long as I wanted, and my nerves were on edge. My intro song started while I cleaned a deserted table. Chills broke out over my body when Kill sang my name as if we were the only two in the bar, all the while making the crowd go wild.

When I reached the stage, he lifted me up as he continued to sing. He sang the last verse directly toward me. The bar broke out into whistles and cat calls. People yelled at

Kill, telling him he was the man and other encouragements.

"You lucky mother fuckers are in for a treat. If you're back from yesterday, then you can tell the person next to you they're about to become addicted." Kill walked around the stage, getting the crowd into a frenzy.

"Marry me, Faith," some random guy called out from the crowd.

Before I could spot my would-be fiancé, Kill was back by my side.

"You're so fucking sexy," another guy yelled out.

"Sorry, buddy, I don't go that way," he responded, making the crowd burst out laughing.

"Not you, Kill, that fucking fine ass girl next to you," the crowd tossed back.

Kill smiled, but his jaw was ticking. Luckily, it went undetected to everyone but me. My shoulders stiffened, recognizing he was uncomfortable onstage, and guilt washed over me. I was ruining one of the places he felt at home.

Van led us into our song, unaware of my thoughts. As soon as I heard the first strains of the music, my muscles relaxed. I let the familiarity of the chords wrap me up and protect me from everything else. Kill watched me as I melted into the song, and the twitch in his jaw vanished. He winked at me before starting.

I gave him my version of his half-smile, making his eyes widen. I was afraid he thought I was having a stroke by his reaction. By the time the song ended we had gravitated toward each other. The crowd was more frantic than they were last night, mauling me when I got offstage.

Jet yelled in the microphone, telling everybody to back up and let me through. I tried not to panic, but having people pushing and cornering me, triggered memories of Jason. My breath came out in bursts, and black spots appeared in front of me.

"Get back, or our show's done," Kill yelled from behind me.

The anger in his voice brought the people closest to me back to reality, and they immediately backed off. I tried in vain to catch my breath, fully aware I was seconds away from passing out.

"Easy, Slick, take a deep breath."

I focused on Kill's voice, hating I was the damsel-in-distress again. The black spots turned to blinding bright lights when I closed my eyes, and my stomach somersaulted against the sensory assault.

"Hey, you need to breathe, come on, Baby. I promise to never make you come back onstage again. I'm so sorry I did this to you."

His self-depreciating attitude snapped me out of the darkness, and I turned to him.

"Shut up and get your ass back onstage and rock the rest of this fucking show. If you want me to sing with you next week I will, but if you don't, it better be because I sucked tonight, not because you're trying to protect me."

I pushed him back up the stairs while he kept looking back, trying to figure out if I was really ok. Catcher was waiting for me. I looped my arm though his and let him lead me safely back to the bar.

"Ok guys, you need to promise me you'll be nice to Faith, or she won't come back again." Kill chastised the crowd. Some of the culprits looked guilty, making the non-offenders smack them. Jet wagged his finger back and forth looking disappointed.

"Alright, I understand your attraction to that gorgeous girl, but please keep your hands to yourselves. If I have to, then so do you."

The crowd stopped looking chagrined, and got back into its insane state of hero worship. Van started into a well-known JackholeS song and all was forgiven. With most of the bar on the dance floor trying to make nice with Kill, I relaxed at the bar with the girls.

Three guys shuffled up. One of them pushed another in front making him the official spokesperson. I made sure Catcher was close, just in case.

"Uhm, Faith, we were just trying to tell you how awesome you were. We didn't mean to scare you." They looked guilty; the one in front looked like he might cry.

"It's ok," I said and hugged him, hoping he wouldn't cry.

The other two circled us, and I found myself in a very uncomfortable hug. When they let go, they asked for a picture. Ryan snapped the picture and told them to move along.

"Thank you; I didn't know how to get rid of them."

"No problem, baby doll. Are you ok? I saw them rush you and then I couldn't see you, there were so many people." Ryan handed me another bottle of water, and I took a drink before answering.

"Yeah, it was overwhelming, but Kill got me through it."

I didn't see Bambi standing next to me until she spoke. "You're so stupid. The whole "save me, I'm so lame" bit will only get you so far." She sneered at me, and I hated Kill saw something in her. Even if her vagina was ribbed for his pleasure, I still wouldn't see her appeal.

"Bambi, you need to back the fuck off, now." Ryan growled at her quietly, so she didn't attract too much attention.

"Ahh look, even the lowly bartender's sticking up for you. You're so pathetic."

"Bambi, I don't know why you feel like you need to pick on me, but when your mouth opens, my ears shut off. I don't give a fuck what you think of me. You need to leave me alone and back the fuck off," I whispered softly, keeping with Ryan's example.

Bambi opened her mouth to respond but Jessie, Amy and Denise stepped up.

"If you don't leave her alone, we'll tell Ray how you've been making extra tips." Denise said, making Bambi storm off.

"I think I just fell in love with you," I told Denise.

"That was hot," Ryan exclaimed, and we laughed, causing Bambi to turn around, most likely thinking we were talking about her.

She slid up to a well-dressed man on the edge of the crowd and ran her fingers up and down his arm. I couldn't take my eyes off her. How could someone who had Kill look at another guy?

The boys wrapped up their set and jumped into the middle of the crowd.

"I can't wait until Monday," Jessie said staring at Van, before turning her head to look at me. "I hate this feeling of holding it all in, it's eating me up. Faith, promise me you won't judge me." The tears she had fought earlier were back with a vengeance.

"I wouldn't judge you, or anyone for that matter, because I wouldn't want anyone to judge me. I love you Jess, don't worry, I promise it'll be ok."

Tears fell down her face, making her look like the most heartbreaking beauty queen the world would ever witness. I put my arms around her as she cried on my shoulder.

Van made his way toward us, but I shook my head, stopping his advancement. He ran both of his hands over his bald head, looking like he wanted to hit something, being the only thing he could control at the moment were his actions.

D and Kill came up to each side of Van, putting their arms around his shoulder and guiding him toward their table. Denise took them their filled tray, giving Jessie time to compose herself.

Amy was on Jet's back as he tried to get to the boys, having been held up in the crowd. Being Jet, he couldn't deny the attention he was receiving, although to his credit he looked torn between the attention and Van.

When he made it to the table, he put his arms around Van and kissed his head, making Van jerk up and slug him in the arm. Jessie sniffled and pulled away, getting herself together and turning red when she realized where she just broke down.

"Did Van see?" she whispered, turning away from the boys' table to stare at the wall.

"Yeah. He wanted to come over here to check on you, but I signaled him to give you a moment. Jess you need to talk to him. He looked ill not being able to comfort you."

I put my arm around her waist, facing the wall; both of us planning our escape from the hole we had put ourselves in.

"I will, but I need to tell you first," she sighed, wiping her eyes one last time to make sure her mascara was still in place. She plastered on a fake smile I was familiar with, and went to the bar asking Ryan what she needed to do.

Ryan glanced at me silently asking what she should do, and I shrugged, unsure what was best for Jessie. Then I thought about what I would want, and mouthed to keep her busy. Ryan gave a sad smile, but then put Jessie to work. Jessie went on her merry way, with her fake smile etched on her face.

Van watched every move she made, his wounded look showed he was suffering while she shut him out, and as much as I loved Jessie, I wished she would get her head out of her ass and see how much he loved her.

I helped Ryan put the bar together as she yelled last call. Most of the bar had cleared out when the boys finished their set.

A few stragglers lingered, either having too much fun to leave, or hadn't nailed down who they were going home to *get it on with* yet.

I watched a guy pull up his courage and talk to the girl he'd been gawking at all night. He was pale, and I was afraid he would pass out on his way over, but he made it without incident.

Catcher ushered everyone out, assisting some into the waiting cabs outside. The guy that had screwed up his courage landed the girl. She giggled at whatever he was whispering to her. I gave him the thumbs up when I caught his eye. He looked puzzled, but returned the gesture.

We circled around our normal table when Kill dragged a chair over to help. Ryan looked at him. "Did you get hired as the help and entertainment?"

"No, but I figure if I'm over here, you won't talk about me," he responded, leaning over and nudging me with his shoulder. "Besides, I'm tired and want to go home."

"Oh, and I get to drive your car." I did a happy dance in my chair, and Kill went pale.

"I didn't drink that much, Slick. I'll be fine to drive."

"Nope, you had alcohol, and you don't need a mark on your record when you're about to be rich and famous. You can buy hundreds of the same car and give me yours when you're discovered."

Kill mulled over my suggestion. "The car's yours when we hit it big."

"I'm going to get sex on wheels soon!" I exclaimed, and it must have been with more enthusiasm than I thought,

251

because the boys turned to look at me.

"You're giving her your car?" Jet was staring at Kill in horror. He took Amy off of his lap so he could come over and join our conversation.

"Yep, I get it when you guys hit it big." I put out my pinky. Kill gave me a questioning look. "Pinky swear."

He grinned, hooking his pinky with mine. "Pinky swear, the car's yours when we hit it big."

"You have that much confidence in us, huh?" Kill asked, still holding my pinky, staring intently in my eyes.

Jet was behind Kill, looking like my answer would hold the fate of the band. In fact, all of the boys were staring, waiting for my answer.

I stood up on my chair, so I towered above everyone, hoping I didn't fall on my ass doing this stunt, but wanting them to know how much confidence I had in them.

"I declare, I'll have that car before I graduate."

The boys went crazy, and even Catcher got caught up in the mood and pounded his hands on the table. Ray walked out from the back room.

"What are you doing up there, young lady?" He looked like we had gone crazy, which I was sure was exactly what we looked like clapping, hollering, and standing on his furniture.

"I just predicted the JackholeS will be discovered before I graduate, and Kill's going to give me his car."

Ray laughed, but then sobered immediately. "How soon are you going to be graduating?"

"I will be able to get my degree this summer."

Ray groaned and ran his fingers through his silver hair. "I guess I'll have to find a new band soon." The guys cheered louder, and Jet ran over, picking Ray up and swinging him around.

Kill yanked me down off the chair, causing me to shriek when I collided into his hard body.

"I hope you're right, but what are you going to do with your new car when you're on tour with us?" He smacked me on the ass as he walked back to the table. "Stop screwing around; get back to work, slacker, I want to go home," he yelled over his shoulder.

I stood there and watched him walk to the table, in shock he would assume I would go on tour with them. Ryan cleared her throat while Denise giggled.

"I know it's an amazing view, but can you help us so you can get that fine boy home."

We put everything away as Catcher and the rest of the boys helped us put the chairs on the table for the cleaning crew. Once we were done, Kill followed me to my locker and sat at the table.

Bambi walked over to stand in front of Kill. "Hey, Kill, wanna come out to my car again?" She looked over at me and back at him, batting her heavily laden eyelashes.

"Not tonight, Bambi, I'll be here tomorrow, maybe then." He looked from her to me, in what I assumed was a reminder I was near.

"Fine, I understand." She looked at me again, and I almost told him to go out and fuck her so she would stop being such a bitch, but I didn't because.... I'm not that stupid.

"Ready to go?" he asked, shouldering my bag, as he handed me the keys to his car. With his keys in my hand, my mood lifted.

"Yep, let's go Killer. I want some of the chocolate ice cream we bought." It was a childish jab with Bambi still standing there, but I couldn't help it.

"That sounds good. You can scoop me a bowl when we get home." He slung his arm around my shoulder, leading us out the door. "Night, Bambi. I'll see you tomorrow."

"Alright, Kill, see you tomorrow." She put a lot of emphasis in her words, and her sentence sounded dirty.

After we shouted our goodbyes, Kill led me out of the bar. I bounced on my toes the closer we got to his car.

"Are you happy?" he asked amused at my reaction.

"Yep, I've been thinking about this all night." I got into the car and adjusted the seat, since he was taller than me, and he leaned his seat all the way back. "How do you drive so far away from the steering wheel?" I asked, finally getting the seat adjusted. Just then nerves shot through me.

"Getting cold feet?"

"You know what, you didn't drink too much. Maybe you

should just drive."

"What's this about, Slick?"

"I don't know," I said, thinking this was a mistake.

"Talk to me, please."

"I know how much you love this car, and I'm afraid I'll do something stupid. I was told I'm not the greatest driver," I confessed.

"You'll be fine. I trust you, and I do love my car, but it's just a car. You're going to be fine. There's nobody on the road right now, and there's a bowl of chocolate ice cream waiting for us." He gave me his half-smile and winked, a deadly combination. The engine rumbled to life, and I took a deep breath before driving out of the parking lot.

With every block, I became more relaxed. When I turned on our street, I was sad it was over.

"You look hot driving my car," Kill remarked, as I parked in the garage.

"Thank you." I took the keys out of the ignition and handed them to him. He slapped me on the ass as we walked into the house.

"Now go get me a bowl of ice cream."

The alpha attitude wasn't going to fly with me, and I wanted to put him in his place. "Fine, I'll make you a bowl, but I'm tired. So I'm just going to go to bed."

His eyes widened, and he came closer. "Are you feeling ok? Do you want me to help you get to bed?" He went to pick me up, and I couldn't hold back the laughter.

I slapped him on the ass. "Gotcha."

"What the hell?"

"Well, you were acting like a badass rocker, so I wanted to put you down a peg or two."

He lifted me up, and threw me over his shoulder, carrying me to the kitchen and placing me on the counter. Kill got out two bowls from the cupboard as I looked around to see a spotless kitchen.

"Who cleaned?" I asked, looking out into the living room noticing it was sparkling too.

"We have a lady. She works around our schedule."

"That makes sense. I wondered why the house was so

254

clean when I first moved in. Honestly, I was surprised a bunch of rocker boys lived here."

He grinned at me and pulled the ice cream out of the fridge.

"Kill, I was just messing with you. I can get my own."

"I know you can, but you were right. I was being a sexy alpha ass to you. So sit your pretty little ass on the counter and watch my sexy ass make you a bowl of ice cream."

While the hot fudge warmed up, he took out the whipped cream. I watched him work and smiled when he made a happy face with the whipped cream. "Stay there," he ordered.

He put everything away and took the two bowls to the living room. Coming back, Kill picked me up off the counter and carried me to the couch. He handed me a bowl and took the other for himself.

"What do you want to watch?"

I put the spoon in my mouth and bit back a moan as the hot fudge and cold ice cream collided together. "Huh?" I asked, forgetting what he asked me.

He gave me a half-smile and grabbed my hand with the next bite on it and guided it into his mouth, sucking the spoon clean before releasing my hand.

"Why did you do that? You have your own." I pointed my now spotless spoon to his bowl.

"You seemed to be enjoying yours more, so I wanted to see if yours tasted different." He exchanged our bowls.

"What the hell?" I screeched, reaching for my stolen ice cream.

"I want yours."

He stuck his tongue out at me, and ate his stolen treat with vigor.

"Be careful there Killer, next time I see that I'm going to suck on it until you moan," I retorted.

He stuck out his tongue again, leaning into me.

"You're an ass," I replied breathlessly.

"But you still love me." He looked back at the T.V. and flipped through channels. I finished most of what he had scooped for himself, but threw in the towel groaning.

"Done?"

I nodded my head, and he took both of our bowls to the kitchen. I toed off my shoes and tucked my feet under me, leaning on the side of the couch.

Kill came back and asked, "Feet, or head?"

I couldn't figure out what he was asking.

"What's going to end up in my lap?"

"Oh, not my feet. I've been on them all night, so I guess my head."

"I don't care," he responded, trying to pull my feet out from under me.

"I do," I said, flipping around and putting my head on his lap.

He found something to watch while I snuggled into him. He ran his hand through my hair, and my eyes got heavy. "Are you falling asleep?"

I jerked a little, blinking my eyes to get them focused. "No," I said, the sleep evident in my voice.

"You were snoring."

"I don't snore," I replied "Do I?"

He laughed, pulling me up to him, so I sat on his lap, with my head pressed into his shoulder, and my face in his neck. "No, you don't snore, but you have to have some faults."

I wanted to look at him as I listed off my many faults, but the position I was in was too comfortable, so I answered into his neck. "My faults would take a lifetime to list."

"I don't believe it, give me one," he taunted, rubbing circles on my back with his palm.

"I'm a horrible judge of character," I sighed into his neck, which seemed to be the center of where his delicious smell came from, and I loved that I currently had an unlimited supply of it in this position.

"Ahh, come on. Give me something good."

I shook my head, burying my nose further into his neck, hoping I wasn't impaling him. "Nope, you asked for one. That's all you get tonight, Killer." I was hit by a huge yawn making my eyes water from the intensity.

"Do you want to go to bed, Slick?"

"I know I should say yes, but is it bad I'm comfortable right here?" Sleep made the truth easier to admit. His hand went still on my back, and I was afraid I said too much.

"I'm comfortable here too. How about we go and lay down in your bed, and I'll stay there until you fall asleep. Like last night?"

Finally, after wondering all day, he confirmed he stayed in my bed. The speeding in my heart increased.

"Slick?" I had been so distracted by his confession, I forgot to answer him.

"Are you sure? I don't want you to think you have to." I squeezed my eyes together, so when the blow came I could fend it off.

"Shut up." Was the only response I got as he shut the T.V. off and carried me toward my room.

"You know I have legs, right?" I asked, trying to alleviate the tension.

"Didn't I tell you to shut up?"

I smiled into his neck and bit my tongue before I let it slip out of my mouth to take a taste, positive it would be an instant addiction.

"And yes, I have noticed your legs, often," he rumbled.

In my room he put me down on my bed. Running his hands through his hair. He was having an internal struggle, and I wanted to comfort him. I let him off the hook of trying to undress me again.

"I have to wash my face, or I'll have pimples all over it. Why don't you go change, and I'll meet you back in here."

His damn shit-eating grin returned, and I wasn't prepared for his response. "I sleep in the nude."

My whole body flushed red picturing him in bed naked. He waited for me to respond, and I resorted to sarcasm. "Well, Killer, I know you have gym shorts. Please don't go into shock that there's a girl in this world who doesn't want to see you naked."

He moved so our foreheads touched. "Liar," he whispered, licking the tip of my nose.

"Ass," I replied, just before he walked out of my room, to which he responded by smacking his butt.

I got my clothes and sprinted into the bathroom. After I changed and performed my nightly routine I went back to see if I had beat him, he was smugly sitting against my headboard in a pair of gym shorts.

"What took you so long?"

"I was hoping if I took long enough you would fall asleep, and I wouldn't have to talk to your dumbass."

I climbed under the covers, trying to keep the drool pooling in my mouth from leaking out at the sight of his naked abs, defined in all the right places. Wanting to trace every line with my tongue.

"You get mean when you're sleepy." He lifted his hips up so he could move the covers down and pull them over him. He crawled closer, pulling my arm around his waist as I fit my head on his chest.

When I was comfortable, I tried to make myself fall back to sleep, but my body wanted nothing to do with sleep. Kill ran his fingers up and down my arm while I listened to his heartbeat.

"You were amazing tonight. You didn't get hurt, did you?"

From that simple statement, another piece of my heart belonged to him.

"No, I didn't get hurt. It was just overwhelming. I'm not used to having attention thrown at me. I like being in the background, and since I've met you, I seem to be in the spotlight more than ever."

"Did you mean what you said about getting back onstage with us next week?"

"I did. Unless I was super awful, and you're trying to spare my feelings."

"You don't know how to take a compliment do you, Slick?"

"It's easier to believe the bad, but I'm always wary of the good, unsure if they're being honest, or they just want something." I was tracing little circles around his stomach, focusing on making each loop the same circumference while I told him yet another one of my faults.

I felt like the biggest hypocrite since I'd just told Jessie not everyone had an agenda even though I felt the same way.

"Well you're going to have to get used to it. You fucking

**258**

rock, and everyone's going to want to tell you. Personally, I think you sound like a dying cat."

I laughed messing up my circle pattern. "I always thought you sounded like a dying cat too, so I guess we make a good pair."

He chuckled, and I gave up on my circles, placing my hand flat on his hard abs. "Thanks. I was afraid my ego was going to inflate, but you seem to keep it in check."

"No problem, Killer, I'll keep you in line."

"I'm counting on it," he mumbled. His eyes were closed, concluding the conversation. He switched to rubbing my back, and my eyes became heavy, and I went willingly as sleep dragged me away.

# CHAPTER 19

My phone rang in my bag, pulling me from my dreams. I ignored the disappointment I felt at waking up alone.

The screen flashed "private," and my stomach dropped as I hit dismiss. How stupid of me to expect Jason would back off after our confrontation.

Chomping on my morning Tums, my phone rang again. How did he still have so much control over my life? In a moment of insanity, I answered the call. I wanted him to know the routine had been changed, and he couldn't presume my reaction. Placing the phone to my ear for a second before my sanity returned, and I pressed end.

In the bathroom I got ready for my run. Just the thought of Kill made me smile, Jason's phone call forgotten for a moment.

Kill didn't get as many cracks at my ass as usual, during our run. Once upstairs, I took a shower, keeping my hair down so it would dry before work. After getting dressed, Kill came in carrying a plate of sandwiches.

"Hungry?"

"Whatcha got?"

He sat on the ground, propping his back up against the bed. I scooted next to him. He handed me a sandwich, and I grinned when I took a bite.

"Peanut butter and jelly, huh?"

"Nothing but the best," he replied, digging into his sandwich.

"I haven't had one of these in forever. I forgot how good they are."

"Really? The girl who eats peanut butter on her pancakes and in her cereal. Hell, I figured you lived off these things," he responded, finishing his and putting the plate on the dresser.

"That was awesome, thank you," I said, sitting back in

front of my computer.

We were lost in our work when a phone rang. It took a moment to realize it was mine, by the time I got to it the call had been sent to my voicemail. I sighed internally when Robert's number was displayed. Kill craned his neck to read the screen, not even trying to hide his actions.

"Who was it?" he asked, trying to sound casual.

"Just some guy."

"Any more private calls?" he asked, not digging for details.

I was embarrassed at the hurt I felt when he didn't seem to care about some random guy calling me.

"I had two this morning. I answered the second time, but I hung up before he said anything."

The tick came back, and I focused on his flashing dimple. "Faith." He shut his mouth and ran his hands through his hair. He looked so lost. I crawled over my papers to reach him and put my arms around him. "This being friends thing's fucking hard," he growled.

Dread washed over me, thinking he was fed up with my drama. "If you don't want to be friends, I understand. I won't like it because you have become such a big piece in my new life, but I won't force you."

He stood up, breaking apart my encircled arms, grief prominent in his eyes. "I need to go practice. They want you to come and practice later. See you." He rushed out of my room, and my eyes prickled with tears I would never let fall.

Ugh, I can't believe I let myself become one of those girls that pined for a guy. I gave myself a pep talk, pulling up my big girl panties so I could be someone I could be proud of.

I didn't leave Jason to let another guy screw with my emotions. Putting everything away, I was certain I wouldn't get any more work done. I contemplated hiding out in my room, but sucked it up. If the boys needed me to sing, then I would, no hiding.

It was my fault for letting myself become too emotionally attached to an unavailable, sexy as hell boy, and the band shouldn't have to suffer. Van and Jessie were snuggling on the couch when I made it downstairs.

"I thought you were practicing right now?" I asked.

He gave me a puzzled look, and Jessie sat up extricating herself from Van's grasp. "We were later, right before you left for work. So you could sing your song before you left, and I know D wants to try another one, but we weren't doing that until tomorrow," Van answered, trying to grab Jessie and bring her back.

"Oh." Kill lied to get away from me. Jessie pulled me toward the kitchen, telling Van she was going to help me with dinner.

"Are you ok? You turned as white as a ghost when you saw us on the couch," she asked, feeling my forehead like I was a feverish child.

"Yes, I'm fine, it's just, well..." I stopped, unsure what to say, she just nodded understanding what I couldn't verbalize.

"We have a lot of catching up to do."

I hugged her, seeking comfort.

"So, since we're pushing all of our emotions down until tomorrow, what's for dinner?" she asked, sitting on the counter, waiting for me to put her to work.

With dinner in the oven, we ran upstairs to get ready for work. I always marveled at how Jessie could look at herself in the mirror for a long period of time; maybe she didn't hate what looked back at her as much as I did.

I put my makeup on in a rush, only checking to make sure I didn't look like a five year old armed with a box of crayons attacked me. I left to go check on the food while Jessie finished up. As I walked out, Amy and Jet emerged from Jet's room all smiles.

"Hey wife number one, is dinner ready? Wife number two's insatiable."

Amy smacked him in the back of the head, before grabbing his neck and sucking on his tongue, the whole time holding onto a licorice stick. I answered him before I made it to the bottom of the stairs.

"Dinner will be ready in five minutes." I heard a grunt and wasn't sure if it was confirmation they heard me, or they would be late.

"It smells great," D said, walking into the kitchen,

262

peering at the food.

"Thanks, D. I'm ready for work, so I can do a run through before I have to go."

"You're awesome. Did Kill tell you there's another song we would like you to try?"

"I've heard rumors of this elusive song, but nothing has been confirmed." I teased, trying to loosen him up.

"We'll practice it tonight while you're at work, so all we have to do is work on the vocals tomorrow."

"It isn't one of your old songs?" I asked, surprised.

"No, we've had it for a while, but could never get it right. Now we know it was just missing you."

"I kind of have plans tomorrow."

"Don't worry. We'll work around your schedule. We just need to go over it a couple of times, it shouldn't take more than an hour."

"Alright, why don't we do it after my run with Kill?"

"Perfect," D said, right when Kill walked in.

"What's perfect? Besides me," he asked, coming over to scope out dinner.

"Faith's going to practice the new song tomorrow after your run, before she has to go out," D answered, filling up a plate.

Kill tried to get the answers to his unasked question by mentally pulling them out of my head. When he was unsuccessful he relented and asked. "Where are you going tomorrow?"

Before I could respond, Jessie and Van walked in, and Jessie answered for me. "We have a date tomorrow. We haven't had a girl's day, and I need one."

"I told D I would practice with them after my run, and before our girl date. Is that ok?" I asked, wanting to kiss her for saving me from telling them about my date with Robert.

"Yep, sounds good," Jessie replied.

"What sounds good? The three of you kissing?" Jet asked, as he turned into the kitchen with Amy on his back. Amy rolled her eyes but smiled, like... well, Amy in a candy store.

Jet put Amy down and pushed Kill out of the way. Kill pushed him back and a wrestling match ensued.

"Not around the food," Van reprimanded, splitting them apart.

Jet and Kill picked up their abandoned plates acting as if nothing had happened. Jessie and Amy got in line after the boys, filling up their plates.

"Don't make me make you a plate," Kill whispered in my ear.

"I'll eat, but I'm still full from the peanut butter and jelly," I replied, hoping to get him off of my back. I was still pissed at him for lying about band practice and escaping from my room earlier.

"That was hours ago. Don't mess with me. I'll win."

"Fine. Neanderthal," I shot back, putting the smallest piece of chicken on my plate and adding everything else while he watched.

"Happy?"

He eyed my plate

"This is it Kill, take it or leave it." I refused to put more on my plate, knowing my stomach would howl when I put all of it next to the boulder.

"Fine, but please eat, you worry me." His words made me soften. I wasn't used to people taking care of me. I had been the caregiver when my mom left, helping my dad to make his life stress-free.

"I know you are. You're a good friend, Killer."

After dinner was cleaned up, I followed the boys out to the garage. Kill and I were breathing like we had just finished one of our runs when the song ended. D came over and clapped Kill on the back,

"She's great," he said, "I can feel the emotion pouring out of you. I'm not sure what you're thinking, but I can tell you're personally attached to the song."

I blushed, afraid to look at Kill, hoping he didn't use his mind reading ability to figure out I was thinking about him. "Thanks, D. I need to get going; you guys are going to come over later, right?" I asked, backing up and walking into Jet. I turned around, getting more flustered by the second.

"Easy there, girl, let me move my guitar before you back that ass up," Jet cooed into my ear, easing some of the tension.

Jessie kissed Van, and Amy munched on a bag of gummy bears as I disentangled from Jet. Kill snagged me by my middle, hauling me to his chest.

"What, no kiss for me?" I closed my eyes and turned around, brushing my lips across his cheek before escaping.

Just like the last Sunday, the bar wasn't as busy, and I delivered more food than drinks. Since the bar was so empty, I ended up at the bar with Ryan and Jessie. Denise had the night off.

The three of us stood at the bar watching Bambi, taking bets on if she would show nipple or not, when the bar door pushed open. Jet and Amy entered first. As usual, Jet rang the bell.

"You're welcome." Once he felt he had received enough attention, he led Amy to their table, nibbling her ear as they went.

Van, D and Kill seemed to be arguing with each other. Jessie shrugged when I caught her eye, just as in the dark as I was. She took the boys their tray, arriving before they did.

Bambi bounded up to Kill and took him by the arm, and out of the discussion he was in. The boys didn't wait for him and went to their waiting beers. Jessie leaned down to talk to Van. She glanced at me, making me even more curious.

I went to find out what the hell was going on, but Ryan called out one of my food orders. With one more glance at the table I went and delivered the food, ignoring Bambi as she dragged Kill toward the back of the bar.

"What's going on?" I asked when I made it to the boys.

"Should we wait for Kill?" D asked, looking around the bar.

"He's busy with Bambi at the moment. She dragged him out of the bar," I said, trying not to sound bitter.

Jessie looked toward the back of the bar, to see if Kill would magically appear.

Jet laughed, "Oh, well I guess we can start. Who knows how long Bambi will keep him."

I wiped my face of any expression. They shook their heads as if Kill and Bambi being together was nothing new. I wanted to ask them what Bambi was to Kill, but I didn't have the courage to hear the answer.

"What's going on?" I asked again, my voice harsh from the burning acid searing my throat.

"We were practicing the new song, and it's going to be fucking classic when we add your vocals to Kill's," Van said, twirling his beer around on the table, and not making eye contact.

"We also have another song we want you to sing," Jet spit out, looking at Van, confused why he was keeping this information from me.

"Another song! I can't do three songs with you guys," I cried out.

"Why the fuck not?" Jet asked, and Van looked at him like he wanted to duct tape his mouth shut.

"Because, I don't know. I just can't," I sputtered, looking around trying to find someone who hadn't gone off the deep end.

"Sure you can, Faith. You'll be awesome, just wait until you hear the songs." D was using his manager voice, and I hated that he acted like it was no big deal.

"I don't want a lot of attention on me, especially after...." I veered off, not wanting to say an abusive relationship, afraid to sound pathetic. I switched tactics. "Ray isn't going to let me take off for three songs on the busiest nights of the week," I argued.

Jessie patted me on the shoulder. Instantly, I knew it was the wrong argument.

"I already talked to Ray. He would love for you to do more songs. Besides, the bar's on the dance floor when we're onstage. So it isn't like you're leaving anyone in a bind. Ray was ecstatic with the influx of male customers you brought in," D finished, smiling at his logic.

I wanted to smack the smug look off of his face. I forgot why I wanted to be friends with him in the first place.

"Why don't you want to do this for us?" Jet asked, genuinely hurt with my obstinate behavior.

"I'm not a fan of attention," I replied lamely, and Jet looked at me perplexed.

Being the huge attention whore he was, me saying I wasn't a fan of attention was like explaining I didn't like ice cream to a toddler. "I'm afraid if I do this, I'll be back on Jason's radar," I lied, since I was never off it.

Jet finally got it, at least for a second. "Fuck that guy. If he comes anywhere near you, we'll kick his ass," Jet said, and Van agreed with him. "Come on, Faith, we need you. Please," Jet pleaded his puppy dog eyes turned on high.

"You know you aren't going to deny them. So you might as well just get over it and say yes," Jessie stated, still behind me.

"Have I told you guys I hate you?" I said, pouting.

"Kill said you two would skip your run tomorrow so you could have plenty of time with Jessie," D said, acting like that would soothe me.

"Oh he did, did he? How accommodating of him," I said through gritted teeth.

D and Van coughed into their hands, pointing with their eyes. I spun around to see Kill and Bambi coming back into the bar. Bambi said something to Kill, and he laughed.

I seethed, wanting to claim him as my own and tell her to *back the fuck off.* Kill noticed me and winked before saying goodbye to Bambi and walking toward us. Bambi saw me standing by the table and smiled before watching Kill's ass as it moved away. Kill put his arm around my shoulder when he reached us and took a drink of his beer.

"Faith's going to do the three songs," D said proudly, causing Kill to swallow the wrong way.

He choked on his drink, and I smacked his back harder than necessary, until he got his breath back. "Oww, Slick," he mumbled.

I looked at him innocently. "Sorry," I replied, smiling brightly at him.

He gave me a questioning look, before remembering what caused his coughing fit in the first place. "I told you to let me talk to her about it," Kill growled, glaring at the rest of the band.

"Well, now you don't have to. We told her you would skip your run tomorrow so she would have time before her girl's day." Jet said smugly, snatching the licorice out of Amy's mouth and putting it in his.

Amy glared at him for a second, and he kissed her on the nose. Appeased, she reached in her bag and pulled out another one.

Kill ran his hand over his face; his jaw twitching, and I'll admit, I was enjoying his frustration. "Slick," he started, but I stopped him, wanting him to stew for a while.

"I have to get back to work. Talk to you guys later." I checked on my tables to make sure they didn't need anything. With my orders, I went over to Ryan, not ready to let Kill off the hook just yet.

It upset me he knew I would be pissed off, like he knew me. Because if he knew me so well, he would know to stay the fuck away from Bambi.

"Are you hungry?" Ryan asked, pulling me out of the rant in my head. She pointed at my mouth. I popped my lip out, not realizing I was gnawing on it. "What's up? Do I need to stab a bitch?" Ryan looked around the empty bar, ready to kick ass for me.

"No, you don't need to stab a bitch for me, but I appreciate you love me enough to get all stabby for me."

"Of course, doll. Now what has you so upset you're chewing on your lip like a dog with a bone?"

"The stupid boys want me to sing two more songs with them," I grumbled.

Ryan looked puzzled, and I'll admit when I said it out loud, it didn't sound as bad as I was making it out to be.

"I hate the attention. I don't want Jason to know anything about my life, and I feel like this is just asking for trouble," I explained.

"Fuck that guy; he isn't going to mess with you anymore. Those boys love you, hell, we all love you, and we all have your back."

I smiled at her, wishing she was right. Kill came over when he saw me smiling and put his arm around my shoulder.

"Am I forgiven?" he asked into my ear.

I held back from leaning into his touch since Ryan was watching us like she was trying to put together a puzzle. I shrugged his arm off my shoulder, but he just put it right back.

"I'm doing it for the boys, because they asked," I responded.

My body stiffened when Bambi walked over. She shot an evil glare at me and then smiled at Kill. Ryan rolled her eyes, making me giggle. Kill looked down at me with his half-smile in place.

"What's so funny?"

"Oh, we were talking about this pathetic girl that comes into the bar, and how glaringly obvious she is," Ryan answered for me, causing me to giggle even harder.

"I like it when you laugh," Kills said, pulling me closer. Bambi stomped off, and I gave Ryan a high five. "Why do I feel like I'm missing something?" Kill asked, looking back and forth between us.

"Because you are," I responded, causing Ryan to go into a fit of giggles.

"What's so funny?" Jessie asked when she walked up.

"The hell if I know," Kill said, and this time I couldn't hold back my laughter.

"It's ok, Killer, just stand there and look pretty."

He hugged me, and I had to stop myself from inhaling him in. "I'm not pretty," he scoffed, sounding offended. "I'm fucking sexy, some would say even God-like."

The three of us girls laughed at him, and I squeezed him tighter before letting him go.

"I'm out of here. You women are insane." He walked off, but Ryan had to get her last jab in.

"Really? God-like? How can that ego of yours fit in this bar?"

He turned around and winked at me, causing my insides to ignite from the heat that one little look caused. "Slick keeps it in control for me."

"Faith, is there something going on with you and Kill?" Ryan asked, looking at me intently so she didn't miss any signs when I answered her.

"We're friends," I responded with complete honesty, not wanting to go into more of an explanation.

Jessie bumped my shoulder with hers. "Let's get this

over with so tomorrow can come faster." She skipped off to tell Catcher we were going to shut some of the bar down since there weren't very many people left.

When everything was put away, Jessie, Ryan, and I went to the breakroom, while Bambi fawned over Kill. I contemplated taking Ryan up on her offer at getting all stabby on her ass.

Bambi sauntered in looking smug, and I wanted to smack that look off her face. "Night ladies," she said, with false cheerfulness.

None of us responded as we walked past her. She just wanted an opening to start in on her bitchiness.

"Hey, Faith, tell Kill thanks for tonight," Bambi sneered, when we were almost out of the room.

I felt like I just got punched in the stomach. Jessie and Ryan looked over at me with worried expressions. "Cramp," I hissed, bending down to rub my calf, trying to look convincing.

Kill saw me bent over rubbing my leg. "Are you ok?" he asked, bending down so he could see my face.

"Just a cramp. I'll live."

"Here."

Before I could register what he was going to do, he lifted me up and threw me over his shoulder. I squealed, even though I should be used to him handling me like this by now.

"Night, guys. I have to get our little performer home," he told everyone. They all said goodnight to my ass, as he walked me out of the bar.

"I can walk you know?" I mumbled, angry he would act like this toward me after doing whatever he did with Bambi earlier.

"Night, Bambi," Kill said as we went by the person I was just cursing in my head.

"Uhmm, why are you carrying Faith?" she asked, in a sickeningly sweet voice.

"I can't trust her to walk by herself," he responded, making me want to kick him for being sarcastic with her about me.

"Oh, well, see you later then? Thanks for tonight, uhm, well you know." I saw her hand reach out and stroke his arm, and I wanted to beat them both.

"Anytime, see you later, Bambi." He moved out of the bar, and I hung there limply, figuring there was no use in fighting him.

"Are you ok to drive?" he asked, digging my keys out from my bag.

"Not really, can you?" I admitted, too frustrated to be operating heavy machinery.

"Yeah, I'm good. I didn't even finish the one beer. Are you ok?" He rubbed my calf muscle, and my traitorous body melted into his hand.

"Yep, it's just been a long week," I answered breathlessly.

"You'll get used to the late nights soon enough, but let's get you to bed."

Kill put his hand on my leg as he drove, and heat flooded through my stupid body. I kept repeating in my head, he was messing around with Bambi, but my disloyal body didn't care.

All the while, my vagina was swinging around on a stripper pole. We made it home and I was surprised when Kill let me walk inside.

"Are you hungry?" he asked, leading me toward the kitchen.

"Not really," I replied, needing space between us.

"But if you are, eat. I'm just going to bed."

"Nah, I ate before we went to the bar. Meet you back in your room." He went into his room, not giving me time to refuse him. I gathered my night clothes and decided to waste time and take a shower.

I procrastinated as long as I could. Shaving everything I could possibly think of and meticulously applied lotion. Kill was under the covers fast asleep when I made it back to my room.

I put my stuff on the charger, deleting the missed call from a private number, and the one from Robert. I shut my phone off, not wanting to deal with any of them just then.

Crawling into bed I stared at Kill. The moonlight filtered into my bedroom, giving me just enough light to see his face. It wasn't as intense when he was asleep, but he was just as beautiful asleep as he was awake. Though I preferred him awake, the intensity and confidence he exuded made him irresistible.

Kill rolled over and reached out. My heart sputtered, wondering if he was reaching for me in particular, or if he was just used to having a warm body in his bed. He dragged me into him, exhaling when he had my body positioned where he wanted it.

I was on my back, and he was on his side, his arm and a leg thrown over me, securing me to him. I waited for the fear I should have felt from being held down, but it never came.

As I contemplated why I felt so safe, I drifted off to sleep enveloped in Kill's arms.

# CHAPTER 20

Pounding on my door jolted me awake in an empty bed. I couldn't dwell on Kill's abandonment, as the banging on my door persisted.

"What the hell do you want?" I yelled, just as the door swung open.

Kill stood there smiling which made me scowl, making him smile even wider. "Wake up, sleepy head." He bounced on my bed, causing me to flop all over.

"I'm up, just stay still for a minute," I grumbled, and he stilled, leaning over to whisper into my ear.

"I almost got caught," he admitted sheepishly. "You're too comfortable," he continued.

My body heated up when his hot breath washed over my neck. As nonchalantly as I could, I pulled the covers over my head to hide my reaction.

"I slept better than I have in years. We need to add this to our friendship agreement. Now get up and get ready. I really want you to practice these other songs." His face lit up with excitement, and I couldn't help absorbing some of his energy.

Pushing him over, I got out of bed, probably looking like a demented psych patient that just escaped the asylum. I lifted my hand to my hair trying to smooth it, knowing it was a useless endeavor.

"Give me ten minutes. I will meet you in the garage."

"Ok, hurry up."

He slapped my ass on the way out. I tried to pretend to be upset at his retreating form, while grinning like an idiot. In my room I powered up my phone, reminding me of the dreaded date with Robert.

I hit delete as soon as I saw the private missed call, cursing Jason. Shame hit me as I deleted it. I should save these calls for evidence, but couldn't bring myself to do it. Conjuring Officers Frank's unhelpful face in my mind, I knew I would have to do this on my own.

My silence had to be torturing Jason, removing the control he had become accustomed to must have been driving him insane. Jason played the perfect boyfriend for so long, I was positive he would never break character. The cage he put himself in was my security. He was planning something, but until he could make it happen, he was stuck.

My phone notified me I had missed a call from my dad. Smiling, I hit my voicemail and my dad's gruff voice rang through as I chewed on my morning Tums. "Hey, baby girl, it's just me, dad, calling to check on you. I haven't heard from you in a while; call me when you get a chance. Love you."

My dad still thought voicemail was like an answering machine. The beginning of his voicemail was always loud, hoping I would hear him, and answer the phone. I was about to call him back when Jet yelled from downstairs.

"Woman, get your ass down here, or I'm coming up there."

Afraid of what Jet would do if I didn't hurry, I opted to call my dad later. When Jet saw me, the smile on his face fell.

"Damn, I wanted to come and get you. Kill said you might be naked."

"Sorry, maybe next time," I said, patting him on the back as I passed.

Kill came in from moving his car, holding a load of folded laundry. I skipped over and punched him in the arm since he couldn't protect himself.

"What was that for?" he cried out, putting the laundry on the bottom step and rubbing his arm.

"You said she would be naked," Jet whined, punching Kill in the other arm before running upstairs, "I'm gonna get Amy."

"Alright, I guess I deserved that." He winked, taking my hand and pulling me into the kitchen. He snaked his arms around my waist, hoisting me up on the counter. "What would you like for breakfast?" He expanded his arms to encompass the kitchen. "Your wish is my command."

I stared at him, wondering how many women in Portland, or the U.S. for that matter, had fallen in love with him? Because looking at him, it was impossible not to.

"I can just have a banana and be happy," I replied, hopping off of the counter.

"You can't just have a banana. I'm offering to make you food. What's your poison?" He was so eager to make me breakfast I couldn't deny him, hungry or not.

"Anything I want?" I asked.

"Yep, what would you like?"

"A toasted peanut butter and jelly sandwich," I replied, smiling at his baffled expression.

"What the hell is that?" he asked, looking around the kitchen with a perplexed expression.

"Just what it sounds like. You make two pieces of toast and then put peanut butter on one side and jelly on the other and squish them together."

"That's what you want?" he asked, incredulously.

"Yep, it was my favorite thing my dad made me when I was little, and I loved them. In fact, I forgot about them until you made me a peanut butter and jelly sandwich."

"Where was your mom when this masterpiece was being created?"

"She left when I was four," I responded. My stomach flipped, being I didn't normally talk about my flake of a mother.

His eyes went wide, and I readied myself for the pity, but his eyes never expressed it. Instead, they filled with understanding, and my heart fell into his hands, no longer able to hold it back.

"Well, let's get you breakfast so we can get this show on the road." He turned around and made two sandwiches, allowing me a second to collect myself after my confession.

When the rest of the boys came in to see what we were eating, they made themselves one too. Except Amy, who refused to eat something that *disgusting,* as she waggled her licorice stick at us.

Jessie arrived as we were going into the garage. Van opened the door, hugging her tightly and kissing her softly. "Perfect timing, babe. We were just about to practice. Are you ok?" he asked, noticing her pale skin, which made the dark circles under her eyes more prominent.

275

"Yeah, I think I'm getting sick," she told him before giving him a reassuring hug. She gave me a tight smile. I could only hope after she purged her secrets, she could move on and emerge from the darkness around her.

The boys had everything set up, and D was beyond energetic. He led me to the microphone where Kill stood. Opening a notebook and setting it to the right page.

"Ok, Faith, this is the first song. We practiced the music for it yesterday. So now all we need to do is fill in your part and tweak it, just like last time. When we have this one down, we'll try the next one." He turned the page with another song written on it. "Are you ready?" he asked, vibrating with energy, and I wondered if Amy's candy addiction had claimed another victim.

"She's fine, D. You need to switch to decaf man," Kill told him, stepping between us and pointing to D's normal spot.

D shot me a guilty expression. I smiled, trying to convey I was good with his instructions. I read the lyrics, getting acquainted with the words. The song caused my heart to ache. The passion evident in every verse.

The song was a story of someone who felt as if they were unlovable to the world, only wanted for what they could give, but never for who they were.

After I had the lyrics and the lump in my throat under control, I nodded my head, signaling I was ready to begin. Kill motioned for Van to start. I studied the notebook, reading the lyrics and matching the words to the music.

When Kill's voice broke into my thoughts, I was rendered useless, I fell into the hypnotic trance his voice created. The emotion pouring out of him made me wonder if he felt he was unlovable.

I softly sang my words when it was time. So caught up in Kill, by the end of the song, I was singing right along with him.

We were both tangled in the song's web, until D came over, breaking our trance by putting his arm around my shoulder and giving it a squeeze. "That was awesome. You were perfect. We need to make a few changes, but you sounded spot on."

Kill's eyes were sparkling; all the passion of the song had melted off of his face. "Alright, D, stop praising her. You'll give her a big head. Her ego barely fits in this house as it is," he said grinning.

The exhilaration of singing with him made me giddy, so I couldn't stop the giggle that escaped me. "My ego would fit just fine if yours didn't take up every corner of this city."

D let me go to slap him on the back. "How does it feel to find a girl who doesn't fall for your bullshit and jump into bed with you?"

Jet answered before Kill could. "D, that boy can find more pussy with his eyes shut than you can with a spotlight and a pussy detector. He doesn't care that Faith doesn't want to sleep with him. She's like our little sister."

"But she isn't our little sister," Kill and D said, at the same time.

They looked at each other in surprise. Tension radiated off of them, but it dissolved quickly when they started laughing. Kill punched D lightly on the shoulder, dissipating the rest of the tension.

D rolled his eyes, reverting back to professional mode. "Alright, let's run through the song again. This time, Faith, let it all out like you did at the end. Ok?" he asked.

"Yep, let's do this," I answered, setting my focus back on Kill.

Kill winked at me, and I rolled my eyes. Once we had perfected the song to D's satisfaction, Amy and Jessie were clapping and whistling. I curtsied at them as D came over to change the notebook to the next song.

Kill nudged D over with his shoulder. "She can turn a page, D. Give her some room."

I glanced over at him, uncertain why he was so snappy.

"Stop being an ass. I'm just trying to help," D snarked back. His voice had an edge to it I had never heard before.

Feeling stuck in the middle of something and not really sure what it was, I tried to make light of the situation by snapping right back. "Ok, back up for a second. Let me get familiar with the words," I replied, not bothering to look at either of them.

Nothing else mattered though when I read the lyrics. Only the black words slashed across the lined white paper existed. They wound their way around my heart until the essence of the song itself was woven into my soul. It was tragic, and my eyes blurred as they filled up with tears.

"Are you ok, Slick?" Kill whispered in my ear. His voice was laced with tension, and I could only nod as I went over the words written in front of me. Kill had filled the page with verses of immense longing, heartache, and love.

It was a journey of someone who had finally found the person that made them whole, but they were too afraid to let them in because everything they touched, they destroyed, and the thought of destroying something so precious was unfathomable. The verses explained they were going to keep a distance, but kept slipping up, just to get a taste of perfection.

"When did you write this?" I asked quietly, since we weren't alone. None of them were paying attention while I became familiar with the song, but I still didn't want them to overhear.

"The other day," Kill answered, rubbing the back of his neck.

Jet chimed in before I could think of a response. "Are we going to do this shit? I have a hot piece of ass I would like to get into sometime today."

Amy blew him a kiss that he caught in the air and placed on his crotch.

"Yeah, let's get this done, I have a hot date." As soon as the words left my mouth, my face flushed red.

The boys got into their places, Van started the beat slow and heart-wrenching. Kill sang. This time he wasn't looking at me, and I was relieved because I didn't think I would be able to have a coherent thought if he thrust those lyrics in my face.

I didn't break into the song like the last. I listened to where I was supposed to sing, trying to get the emotions lodged in my throat like a dry cracker to go down.

The song ended, and I wanted to drag Kill out of the garage and strip us both naked while I demanded answers. The desire was so strong; I curled my toes into my flip flops and dug my fingernails into my palm so I didn't act on it.

"Are you ready to step in this time?" D asked, bringing me back to the present. I nodded my head, and D smiled widely.

"Let's get this shit going," Jet responded behind me, breaking the strain.

My part was right at the beginning so I got lost in the music sooner than the rest of the songs they'd had me sing. The lyrics ripped me into jagged pieces, and my voice was huskier because of it.

When we finished the first run-through, Kill put his arm around me and pulled me into his side, letting me sag into his strength, as mine was sapped out of me as each word left my mouth.

"Are you up for another round?" he asked, as D, Jet, and Van circled around me to check on me.

Not long after they were surrounding me, Jessie and Amy were in the circle also.

"Man you guys make this look easy, give me a second." I tried to make my voice sound stronger than what I felt. My stomach was in my throat with my heart, trying to escape because the emotion swelling in me had left no room for anything else, and if I wasn't careful, all my other organs would follow.

"Are you sure you're ok? You look pale." D asked, bending so he could look me in the eye.

Kill tightened his grip, and I leaned further into him, wishing everyone would stop looking at me like I was some newly discovered creature.

"She always looks like shit, D," Kill replied, and a hint of smile appeared on my face when they looked at him with shocked faces. I nudged him to acknowledge he had been successful.

"Kill, that was fucked up! You don't look like shit," D responded with a horrified expression.

"I would fuck you," Jet said, trying to make me feel better.

Kill snorted at Jet's statement. "Dude, you would do anything with a warm hole." Seeing Amy, Kill began to sputter.

279

"Well, not since you've been tamed."

Amy sent Jet a salacious look. "I haven't tamed the beast; he's just too tired to prowl after having me all night," Amy explained. Jet ran over, hugging Amy as his tongue checked her tonsils.

"Alright, we've finished the TMI portion of this segment, let's run through the song again," I said, shrugging out of Kill's hold.

Jet extricated himself from Amy's mouth. Van tracked Jessie as she moved away. He shook his head and sat behind his drums looking dejected. D stood in front of me, watching me as I watched Van push his emotions aside. He blinked suddenly before moving to his spot without another word.

"Are you ready, Faith?" Van asked from behind me.

"Yep, let's rock this," I replied, with fake confidence. I decided to adopt the saying *fake it, until you make it.*

Once again, I got sucked into the process of fine tuning the song, not allowing myself to dwell on the lyrics. We got the song where the boys liked it, with my input I might add, which gave me one more reason to love my rock stars in shining armor. They listened to me and considered my opinion, instead of dismissing me immediately.

"Alright, Slick, you are dismissed," Kill said, grabbing me and pulling me into a hug. The other guys ran over and put their arms around us again.

"You're going to fucking rock it," Jet said somewhere near my ear, Van and D agreed with him.

They let me go, Kill being the last. His arms lingered on my back longer than necessary, leaving me in chills when he removed himself completely. Jessie stood behind me, and Van was off to the side staring at her like she was something behind glass he wanted to touch, but couldn't.

I nodded my head over in Van's direction when I caught Jessie's eyes, and she looked conflicted. After a few seconds she walked over to him and put her arms around him. Van sighed into her hair.

Jessie's fear of her past was holding her back. I just hoped after she unloaded her story, it would help her move on. Van was adorable, in a bad boy way, and wouldn't stay single

280

for long, and it would be her fault if that happened.

"We're going to finish practice, so get your asses out of here," Kill said next to me, watching the interaction between Van and Jessie. He leaned in and whispered into my ear, causing my knees to go weak, from having his lips so close. "He really likes her. I don't want him to get hurt."

I turned around so I could face him. He didn't move, so our lips were centimeters from each other's, making mine tingle at their proximity. My brain screamed at me to move. I leaned around his beautifully pouty lips, and reached his ear. "I'll do my best. I don't want either of them hurt."

I decided I needed to stop denying myself every pleasure in the world and bit his earlobe before walking toward the door. Kill was right behind me, pulling me into his body. My back was flush with the front of him, and it made moving awkward.

"I'm going for water, anybody want anything?" he asked, ushering me out of the garage, not waiting for anyone to respond.

He abruptly released me when we entered the kitchen. He leaned on the counter with his back facing me. I placed a bottle of water in front of him. He uncapped it and downed half of it in one drink.

"Ok, have fun with Jessie," Kill said, walking back to the garage, not once looking at me.

What the fuck just happened? I was about to storm out to the garage and ask him what the hell that was all about, when Jessie walked into the kitchen oblivious to my inner turmoil.

"Ready to go?"

"Let me change, and I'll be down in a second."

I took my clothes from the pile on the bottom step and ran upstairs. I hurried to meet Jessie back in the kitchen.

"Let's take two cars," Jessie said.

I took the alone time to give my dad a call and check on him. "Hello," Martha answered the phone and my mood lightened happy, my dad had someone to keep him company and in line.

"Hi Martha. I was calling to check in with dad, so he

doesn't send out the search team."

"Hi, Faith. We were outside working in the garden, and I came in here to get us something to drink. Do you want me to get him for you?" she asked, and I could hear her moving around the kitchen getting down glasses from the squeaky cabinet.

"No, if he stops working, it will be hell getting him started again. Just tell him I called and I'm alive. I haven't been kidnapped or held against my will."

Martha laughed and told me she would be sure to give my dad the message. We said our goodbyes just as I parked at Jessie's place. Her evil roommate's car wasn't in its usual parking spot, and I breathed.

Jessie was uncommonly quiet, so I sat down on the couch, allowing her time to get her thoughts together. Nothing had changed since the last time I was here. The couch was a micro-suede light blue material with recliners at both ends. There was a coffee table made of wood and glass, and looked too scary to touch. The T.V. was on an entertainment center matching the scary untouchable coffee table. The carpet was the normal apartment beige, and there was nothing on the walls. I mean nothing, even though they had lived there for years.

Candice had one more semester and she would be moving out, giving Jessie the apartment to herself, unless she got another roommate. I wasn't sure she would, after living with the hell Candice had put her through.

Jessie grabbed two diet Pepsi's and motioned for me to follow. I sat on her bed, popping the top of the soda and taking a sip just to have something to do.

I promised to let her get herself together before asking her to talk, but if she didn't do it soon I would go nuts from the buildup. After she paced the room so many times I had lost count, I lost my patience.

"What's going on Jess? You can tell me or someone else, but you need to get this off of your chest soon. It's ruining you."

She looked as if she had forgotten I was there. She finally sat, leaning against the headboard. "You're right, and it's stupid Van's fault. He makes all of these feelings I never wanted to feel again come surging through me, and I don't know what to do."

She was helpless to stop the tears streaming down her face. I touched her ankle trying to give her silent support.

"Did you know I have a sister?"

I shook my head because she had told me she was an only child.

"I do, well I hope I still do. I haven't heard from her in years, not after she left with Eric," she scoffed but continued. "She fell in love with Eric, a drummer in a band, participating in the Battle of the Bands competition we hold every year at the bar. Once his hooks were in her, we couldn't get her back. They took off when we tried to intervene in their relationship.... he was a lot like Jason, honestly that was how I knew what was happening to you."

"Is this why you don't want to be with Van?"

"There's more," she stated flatly.

"You don't have to go on if you don't want to, Jess," I said, giving her an out, knowing the worst was still to come.

"No, you need to know, so you don't hate me when I push Van away. I'm trying so hard not to, but it's inevitable."

"Jess, I'm not going to hate you. If you don't want Van, then that's fine. I could never hate you, but you need to stop hating yourself."

She took a shuddering breath and continued. "I wanted nothing to do with guys for a long time. I refused to let someone break me the way Eric broke my sister. Then I met Brock."

The way she said his name made me tense, my body prepared for the next blow.

"Brock was a drummer." She laughed bitterly, falling back into the past. "Because of Eric I was wary of musicians, especially drummers. So when Brock hit on me, I turned him down immediately. He was relentless and wore me down. He was perfect, and he had my whole family fooled. I thought we would be together forever, and then I got pregnant."

She focused on her breathing before she continued.

"I was nervous, but certain Brock would take care of me. We had talked about a family; I just figured we would start it earlier than expected. It never occurred to me he was not who he portrayed to be when he was with me. I can't tell you how surprised I was when I walked into his apartment, and he had his dick in his PR lady."

I tried to hide my shock when she dropped that bombshell. She spit it out quickly, wanting to get it over with.

"I stormed out of his apartment, and he followed after me, telling me this was for our own good. Once the band was signed all of our dreams would come true. I told him I wanted nothing to do with him ever again, and went home."

She closed her eyes squeezing the pillow she was holding tight against her abdomen.

"I lost the baby that night. I had to escape the worried looks I saw every time I caught my family staring at me." She finished her story, and we sat there letting what she had revealed sink in, crying for what she had been through.

I understood her family's hesitancy in accepting Van, and her constant need to keep him away from her heart. Two drummers had ripped her family apart, and she refused to let another destroy what they had mended. Van had two strikes against him, and he hadn't done anything wrong.

"Well, I understand why they don't want you anywhere Van." I said, nudging her ankle with mine, wanting to stop her from falling into the darkness she was on the precipice of.

"It isn't just my family, it's also me. Van's so perfect; he says the right things and he's beyond romantic. He reminds me of Brock so much, all I can do is push him away. When I'm with him, he makes me forget what I've been through, but as soon as I'm away from him it all comes flooding back. Sometimes I feel like I'm letting down my baby by falling for someone just like its daddy." She cried, and I held her, letting her release her grief.

"But Van's nothing like Brock," I said when she calmed down enough she could hear me over her anguish.

"How do you know?" she asked into my shoulder, sounding exhausted.

I didn't have an answer for her. In my heart I was positive Van wouldn't hurt Jessie, but at the same time, a person could never be sure of another's intentions. "I can't promise you'll have a happily ever after with Van, but I can tell you he cares about you, and I think you should tell him so he can let you know where he's coming from. You can never guess the future, but you can't be scared to try."

Jessie shook her head on my shoulder, and my heart dropped, because until she told Van everything, they didn't have a chance. I wondered if I was doing the same thing with Kill. Then I thought of Bambi. I was unsure of their relationship and refused to ask Kill, afraid of the answer.

"Promise me you won't say anything," Jessie pleaded, looking up from my shoulder.

"I promise. This is your story to tell Jess, but you need to think about telling him if you want a relationship."

She searched my face, making sure I would keep my promise. When she saw confirmation, she crawled under her covers and put her head on the pillow she had clutched the whole time she told me her story.

Her eyes were red and puffy from crying. I got her a bottle of water and some Advil. Jessie was almost asleep when I returned to her bedroom.

"Thanks," she said, when I handed her the medicine.

"Go to sleep. I'm going to go," I said, putting the covers over her as she snuggled in.

"Getting ready for your hot date?"

"Ugh, why'd you have to remind me?"

"Sorry, at least you'll get a free meal out of it," she said, yawning loudly.

"I'll lock the door on my way out," I told her before walking out, not waiting for her to respond.

On my drive home, I let her past run through my head. I was proud to be her friend; she was a survivor. I was surrounded by amazingly strong women, and with their support, I felt secure I would conquer my demons.

285

# CHAPTER 21

Robert text me when I pulled up to the house.

## Can't wait 2CU ;0

What the hell was I thinking?

The boys were playing a video game in the living room. They yelled at each other, "*get out of the way or shoot someone*!" I tried to get by them unnoticed, but Van and Kill looked up as soon as I walked in.

"Back already?" Van asked, craning his neck to see if Jessie had followed me.

"Yeah, uhm....she fell asleep." I turned my head, not wanting to give anything away. I meant it when I told her it was her secret to tell.

"Do you want to come play video games with us, Slick?"

I faltered, afraid to tell him I had a date. "No, I have plans later."

Moving fast, I didn't stop until I was in my room. I went through my clothes, trying to find something that implied I would not be having sex tonight. I chose a pair of black leggings and a long purple sweater with a black belt cinching it in the middle.

When I opened my door, Kill was coming upstairs. I childishly dashed into the bathroom before he could catch me. While washing my hair the door opened, making my eyes snap open, which of course made soap rush into them.

"Son of a bitch," I cried as I rinsed them out.

"You ok?" Kill asked.

"Why are you in here?"

"I just wanted to ask about your day. Why are you getting dressed up?"

I didn't answer.

"What are you up to Slick? If you don't answer me, I'm

coming in there."

My vagina begged me to stay quiet. "I agreed to go to dinner with Robert," I said quietly into the shower.

"What?" he roared. "Why the hell would you do that?" he asked through gritted teeth.

"Because he asked me out, so I said yes. I wasn't aware I needed to confirm my schedule with you first." I sounded like such a bitch and I hated it, especially when I didn't want to go in the first place, but Kill had me on edge. His fluctuating attitude, and his relationship with Bambi had my emotions scattered.

"You're right," he replied, leaving me alone in the cooling shower.

With more force than necessary I shut off the water. I was being an asshole, but I convinced myself it was partly his fault I was going on this date, fueling my anger. Yes, it was a cop out, but I was sticking with it.

While getting ready, I kept thinking I should have listened to Ryan and faked being sick. Kill busted in, not bothering to knock.

"Can I help you?" I asked as my heart beat wildly.

I needed to apologize for being so shitty to him, and my vagina had images of him allowing me to lick him all over as my penance.

"Why are you going out with him?" he asked, stalking closer as I backed up, not wanting to be near him.

If I was honest, I didn't trust myself when I was near him. "I don't know," I responded, and his twitch kicked up on his jaw.

"Not good enough."

"Because I was mad at you," I said, no longer retreating.

Screw him for thinking he had a right to be angry at me, especially given his extracurricular activities with Bambi.

"Why were you mad?" he asked, running his fingers through his hair while his cheek jumped in an angry staccato.

"I know about you and Bambi. She told some skank in the bathroom, in detail I might add, about your sexual exploits. Right after my ears stopped burning, Robert asked me out, and I agreed. It's confusing, one moment you act like you care about me, but in another you're fooling around with Bambi in the parking lot," I seethed, staring at our shoes. They were almost touching, and I was surprised I told the truth while being so close to him.

"I'm not doing anything with Bambi," he answered, stunned.

"But I saw you getting out of her car," I replied, trying to grasp at something that made me look less like an asshole.

"I was helping her. Her steering wheel was locking, and I checked on it. Her brother and I went to school together. He joined the military, and asked me to keep an eye on her. She also let me read a letter he sent her." Kill stepped back from me, and I wanted to take the step back toward him, but I didn't. "If you ever have a question, just ask me. We're friends, and I promise never to lie to you. I thought I made it clear you should talk to me instead of crazy women with a vendetta against me. You still don't get it, do you?"

His face filled with disappointment, and I hated myself for putting it there. I jumped to conclusions without asking him, again, and it wasn't fair.

"You're right, but if it makes you feel any better, I don't want to go on this date," I admitted, right before Jet yelled upstairs there was a douche box at the door for me.

Kill let me walk ahead of him, not responding to my last minute confession. All three boys stood around Robert, glaring at him, and it made me giggle at how oblivious he was to their dislike.

My eyes zeroed in on a bouquet of red roses and I froze on the steps, causing Kill to collide into me. He wrapped his arms around me to keep me from falling. I held my breath in a vain attempt to keep the smell from entering my nostrils.

"Walk," Kill whispered in my ear, I inhaled through my mouth before moving.

Robert thrust the offending bouquet toward me, and I backed further into Kill. With great reluctance I took them, and my stomach pitched forward.

"Thank you; I'll just put these in water."

I took them into the kitchen, holding them far away from my body. In a panic, I thought of how to get rid of them.

Kill came in and put his hands on my shoulders, pulling me to him. I sank into him as my panic disappeared.

"I can't have these here," I whispered. "Jason used to...."

He stopped me by hugging me tighter, silently telling me he understood. "I got it, Slick, they won't be here when you get back."

I stayed in his arms, relishing the feel of him. When I pulled away, the smell of those retched things made me gag. I turned into Kill, burying my nose into his shirt so all could I smell was him.

"Come on." He led me out of the kitchen. The boys stood around Robert glaring at him. He relaxed when he saw me.

"No more roses there, big boy," Kill said, letting go of my hand.

I waited to see what he would say, grateful he was doing it.

"She's allergic," Kill explained, looking back at me winking.

"Sorry, I didn't know. Why didn't you say something?" Robert asked, putting his arm over my shoulder.

"She didn't want to hurt your feelings, and well, it doesn't fucking bother me," Kill responded.

Robert stiffened beside me at Kill's words. "You weren't kidding when you said they were protective."

"Nope, and if you do anything to her, we *will* hurt you," Van replied menacingly, while the other three nodded their heads.

"Ok, point taken. We need to get going if we want to make our reservations," Robert said, leading me toward the front door.

"Night, Faith. Night....What's your name?" Jet asked, just as Robert turned the handle.

"Robert," he answered as we stepped outside.

My blood ran cold when I noticed a silver Honda Civic parked across the street. Robert saw the horror on my face and chuckled.

"I know you expected a tough guy like me to drive something with more power, but what can I say, it saves on gas."

I relaxed, realizing it wasn't Jason waiting across the street for me, but being that Robert drove the same car as Jason, and brought me roses, made me want to end the date right then.

My steps felt wooden. He opened my door, and I got in. The guys stood at the kitchen window. I gave them a weak wave as Robert drove off.

"How is it living with the JackholeS?" Robert asked, sounding star struck.

"Great, actually. I love them, and they watch out for me," I said, calming just mentioning them.

"Sorry about the roses. I guess I'm not good at that sort of stuff. I wanted to make a good impression. I'm too much of a bad boy."

The retort *just because you have stupid, unoriginal tattoos going up your arms doesn't make you tough,* tried to fly out of my mouth.

When we got to the restaurant, he offered me his arm and I reluctantly accepted it. He walked straight up to the hostess and put on a smile that made me want to hit him for trying so hard. When she explained it would be ten minutes to be seated, he went into complete asshole mode.

He demanded to talk to the manager. I'm not positive, but I had a feeling he was flexing his arms, making sure people noticed the ink covering them. By the time the manager came out and apologized for the inconvenience, the table was ready, and Robert acted like he won a prize.

I bit my tongue to keep myself from explaining his little tantrum lasted the ten minutes we were going to have to wait. Robert sat next to me, and my already annoyed state ratcheted up higher.

"Sorry, I don't wait," he said in my ear, his self-important attitude making my skin crawl.

I opened my menu, not responding. When the waitress came over to get our drink orders, Robert ordered an obnoxiously complicated drink. I shot her an apologetic smile before she left.

"Sorry about that," he said, leaning into me so he could

look at my menu instead of opening his.

"About what?" I asked, wondering what behavior he felt deemed an apology, or if he was lumping the whole date into one.

"The waitress," he looked at me like I was an idiot. "She was hitting on me; it's the ink. They all want a piece of me." He put his arm around the back of my chair. "Don't worry, I only have eyes for you tonight," he replied, interpreting my stunned reaction incorrectly.

When the waitress brought our drinks, Robert took a moment before he approved his. She tried to take our food order; he once again changed everything, making it a custom meal. The waitress was beyond annoyed by the time she left.

I excused myself, needing to get away from Robert's ego and his wandering hands. While washing my hands, I stared at my reflection in the mirror asking myself what the hell I was doing. I'd just escaped Jason, why was I punishing myself by going out with someone I had no chemistry with?

Kill's words revolved in my head. I'd assumed the worst of him but gave a stranger the benefit of the doubt. Taking my phone out of my purse I dialed Jessie, wanting to get out of here. Thankfully she answered on the second ring.

"Hey, Faith, how's the date going?"

"It's awful. Can you please come get me? I'll buy you ice cream, candy, or whatever you want, just please hurry. I'm at the little Italian restaurant downtown, please hurry," I begged, as an older woman came into the bathroom giving me a disgraceful look.

"Hold on," Jessie said, clicking over to the other line. I leaned on the bathroom wall waiting for her. "Faith, I'm so sorry."

"You can't come get me?" I whined into the phone, as the old lady hurried and washed her hands to get away from me.

"It's not that. I was on the phone with Van; I clicked over to tell him I needed to go get you." My stomach dropped, already knowing what she was going to say. "Kill's on his way."

My laugh bounced off the tiled walls.

"I'm so sorry, Faith." Jessie sounded like she was on the

291

verge of crying.

"Don't worry about it Jess, as long as I get out of here, I don't care who comes to get me," I lied.

For a brief second I wondered if I should tell Robert I wasn't feeling well, or if I should explain I wasn't feeling a connection, and throw some cash on the table.

I sat next to him contemplating what to do, while he told me about the women who came to our table to proposition him while I was gone, all of which he turned down; what a gentleman.

As I was checking my phone for what felt like the millionth time Kill walked up behind me, scaring the hell out of me.

"Ready, Slick?" he asked in my ear, causing me to jump and hit my knee on the table.

"What are you doing here?" Robert asked, grabbing my leg under the table, causing me to jerk it away and bang it on the table again.

"Shit," I said, scooting back so I could assess the damage.

"This date's over, Romeo," Kill said as he shouldered my bag.

"What's going on, Faith?" Robert asked, reaching for my hand, trying to stop me.

"I'm sorry, Robert, but this wasn't working so I called Kill to pick me up. I know it sounds awful and I really am sorry, but I need to go."

His face turned red with fury. I edged closer to Kill's side. "I don't believe this," Robert screamed, claiming most of the restaurant's attention.

Kill put his hand on his shoulder, pushing him down onto his chair as he tried to move. "Sorry about this, but it wasn't working. She doesn't want to embarrass you, but I don't give a shit. I suggest you stay in your seat."

Kill threw money on the table and steered me out of the restaurant as everyone watched us leave. When I sank into the passenger seat, I was relieved I was out of that situation, but scared of the new one I just entered.

His cheek twitched, making his anger apparent, and he

had every right to be. Taking a deep breath to settle my nerves, I launched into a much deserved apology. "I'm sorry, Kill. I shouldn't have assumed Bambi was telling the truth. You're right. I should have asked you, but she didn't know I was in the bathroom, and she knew things that made it easy for me to believe, and then I saw you getting out of her car and... I'm a shitty person." I couldn't stop rambling.

He didn't say a thing, and I watched his dimple fade in and out.

"Thank you for saving me," I said trying one last ditch effort to get him to talk.

"I hate you think the worst of me. I've done nothing to show you I'm the person you think I am. Yes, I was an asshole. I screwed any girl that offered, as long as they understood I didn't do reruns, but I haven't done that since I met you. You just got out of something, and you need time, I get it. When you went on a date with that asshole, it pissed me the fuck off. Why would you give him a chance when you refuse to give me one?" he asked, pulling into a drive-thru.

He ordered food, and I didn't answer him until we were on our way home, giving him the well-deserved truth.

"I agreed to go out with him because I knew he was safe. I knew I would never lose my heart to him."

Kill looked over at me with a sad expression. I reached out to run my hand through his hair on the back of his head. He leaned back into my hand, as I let the silky strands run through my fingers.

"When you're ready, you will give me a chance. I understand it might be a while. Agreeing to go on dates with guys you know aren't going to mean anything to you shows me you aren't ready, but when you are, give me a chance. No more going out with pussies. You already have one, and really, there's no reason to have two."

I took my hand from his head and placed it on my chest with a shocked expression. "Did you, the man-whore of Portland, just try to convince me having multiple vaginas is a bad thing?"

"Well, you know what I mean," he said, rubbing his hand over the back of his neck.

"I'm scared you would destroy me," I whispered to him, reiterating my fear.

"Did you ever think you could destroy me?" he replied quietly before pulling into the garage and shutting off the car. We both turned so we were facing each other.

"No, honestly it never occurred to me. You could have anyone you want, why would you want me?" I asked exasperated.

"Because you're the one I want," he answered.

His eyes blazed with emotion. Not wanting to hold back any longer, this time both my heart and brain were silent, letting my body gravitate toward him. I was throwing caution to the wind, not caring any longer about protecting my broken heart.

Our lips brushed lightly. His taste was intoxicating. My tongue slipped out tracing his bottom lip, asking for entrance. He growled, reaching out to pull me toward him. My seatbelt held me firmly in place.

We were panting, our desire evident in our reactions. I quickly reached to release my seatbelt, ready to climb on top of him. Kill put his hand on my shoulder to stop me.

"Not yet, I'm not letting you regret us. When this happens, I want it to be real." He kissed the tip of my nose and climbed out of his car, holding the food, while I got the drink carrier.

The guys were in the living room watching T.V. when we walked in. They jumped up when they saw us.

"Food!" Jet cried, trying to snatch the food out of Kill's hands, but Kill yanked it away and went into the kitchen.

"Do we need to kick sissy boy's ass?" Jet asked, punching his palm and eyeing me to make sure I was still in one piece.

Van came over and hugged me.

"No, I just couldn't stand to be away from my boys any longer," I explained. D had a wounded expression on his face, so I gave him an encouraging smile to let him know I wasn't hurt.

"No more dates," Van declared, kissing me on the head, before taking his food and going into the living room.

Kill handed D his food next, and Jet whined.

"Why are you being so mean? Give me my food. My woman will be here soon, and I need to get fueled up before I unleash the Sex God on her."

Jet thrust into a kitchen chair, and Kill handed him his food to get him to stop molesting innocent furniture. Kill took our food and motioned for me to follow him, which I did, not wanting to upset him more. As we ate, I gave them the gory details of my date.

Amy showed up as we were finishing up, and jumped on Jet's lap, kissing him soundly. I moved to throw our trash away, not wanting to see Jet show Amy his new moves he had been perfecting on the kitchen chair.

Kill followed me, and soon Van and D were huddled in the kitchen as we heard Amy and Jet making noises I didn't want to explain.

Van yelled out, not moving from his post in the kitchen. "Go to your room, we don't want to see that."

The moaning stopped and Jet answered back. "Of course you do, everyone wants to see the Sex God in his prime, but I want none of you ogling my woman, so we'll be in my room. Don't bother us." We waited until Amy's laughter faded before we deemed it safe to leave the kitchen.

"Have you ever played Band Hero?" Van asked, pulling out all of the instruments.

"Nope, I'm not good at video games. I put too much pressure on myself, and it becomes more stressful than fun."

"This is different. No saving the world, just hitting the right notes."

"Ok, I'm game." I inspected everything as Van set it up.

Van explained all the buttons and different things I needed to do to score. I made the boys go first so I could watch them. Not long after I was singing along and playing the instruments beside them. I hijacked the guitar from D, determined to play it.

When I started fumbling around, Kill pretended to get frustrated. He put his arms around me and guided my fingers to the correct keys. I was flush with his body, and I couldn't concentrate. Giving up, I let him take my hands and guide my fingers as I leaned into him and soaked up the heat radiating off of him.

"Not fair, you're cheating," D cried, snatching Kill off of me, making my body weep.

"I was just helping her," Kill said, laughing as he put D in a headlock, and they wrestled around the living room while Van and I took cover on the couch.

While they were screwing around, I scooted closer to Van. "You were on the phone with Jessie when I called?" I asked, wanting to get the lowdown.

"Yeah, I want to thank you."

"For what?" I asked, not sure what he knew and afraid I would say something I shouldn't.

"She said you tried to convince her give me a chance. I'm falling in love with her, and it's ripping me apart that she won't let me in."

His face was full of anguish. Kill and D were on the floor doing some contest where they locked legs and tried to flip each other.

"If you love her, you need to prove it to her; she's been through some shit."

He opened his mouth, and I answered him before he could ask. "It isn't my place to tell you her story. But I can tell you, if you're willing to be patient, I can see you two having a happily ever after."

Van rubbed his head, frustrated I wouldn't reveal what I knew.

"I'm rooting for you Van, but if you hurt her, there will be hell to pay."

"What if she hurts me?"

It was a good possibility that would happen. It didn't go unnoticed how similar this conversation was to the one Kill and I just had. I was afraid once a person had been through trauma, they were never able to fully trust again, shutting themselves off from opportunities to find happiness.

"Then I'll buy you chocolate and let you pick out any chick flick you want."

He laughed and pulled me into a hug. I leaned on his side as we watched Kill and D wrestle. When they were both

296

tired and laying on the floor trying to catch their breath, Kill glanced at us, and raised his eyebrow.

"Trying to steal our new singer?" he asked, getting up and plunking down on the couch, making me bounce off of Van.

"Shut up, asshole, she's like a sister and besides, it would be stupid to mess with someone living with us," Van explained, as if it were obvious.

Kill's half-grin was plastered on his face as he responded, "Who said any of us were smart?"

"You're a dick, Kill." D decided to put his two cents in now that he had his breath back.

"Faith's way too smart to fall for your fake '*I'm a good guy act.*' We all know you can't commit to anything longer than the chase." D got up off the floor glaring at Kill.

"What the fuck's your problem?" Kill asked, anger simmering off him. Before he could get up, I launched up and landed on Kill's lap, forcing him back to the couch.

"Enough, there's way too much testosterone in this house. You two need to stop, or I'll make you kiss and make out."

All three of them stared at me like I grew another head, and I gave them a smug smile.

"Don't you mean, make up?" Kill asked, looking horrified, and I shook my head.

"Nope, you guys are throwing barbs back and forth like there's some sexual tension between you. Hell, Van and I just watched you engage in foreplay."

"You're fucking crazy," Kill said, turning my face toward him so he could look straight at me.

"Yeah, but I got rid of the tension didn't I?" I stated matter of factly.

"Yeah you did," he said, winking at me.

I wished everyone around us would disappear so we could engage in some acts of foreplay of our own.

"You aren't going to make me kiss him, are you?" D asked, sitting as far away from Kill as he could.

"No, but you guys are friends, and I don't like it when friends are being mean to each other," I answered, hoping nobody thought it was odd I was still perched on kill's lap like I belonged there.

"So what are we going to do?" D asked, eyeing me as I ignored his questioning glance.

I tried to move off of Kill, but he held me, anchoring me to him. "Where are you going, Slick? I think your bony butt has imprinted in my thigh, and if you move anymore, I'm going to bruise."

Van chuckled, flipping through channels to find something to watch.

"I was getting off you so my bony butt doesn't do permanent damage to your scrawny legs, although it would be satisfying to see your pretty body damaged." I pressed my ass into his leg, and he howled in agony, and I collapsed onto his chest laughing.

"Damn, that hurt. Stay still and watch T.V." He pulled me further into him so I was leaning on his chest.

"Let me up, I don't want to hurt you. You'll never stop bitching if I do, and I can't take any more of your whining."

"Fine," Kill agreed, and stupidly I thought he would let me up, but instead he opened his legs so I plopped onto the couch and fastened his arms around me. In this position, my head was under his chin as I reclined on his chest.

"Are you really going to keep me hostage?" I asked, hoping he said yes.

"Yep, you threatened to make me make out with one of my best friends. I figure with you in the middle, I can keep you and your evil thoughts contained."

"Good thinking," Van said, propping his feet on the table as he stopped on a movie.

"I'm not making out with you, so you're safe from me," D responded, sounding pissy.

"Well, this way I know I'm safe. Not that you aren't sexy D, but I prefer my kissing partners to be dick-free," Kill replied.

We settled in to watch the movie when D's phone rang. He left to go upstairs speaking in his manager's voice. Kill put his hand on my stomach and rubbed his thumb up and down, the heat of his hand penetrating through the material of my shirt.

My body was on fire, and I couldn't stay still from all of

the energy building up inside me. I shifted slightly trying to get rid of the ache, and I ended up brushing against Kill's groin, which seemed to be having the same problem, except with his outdoor plumbing, his was obvious. He hissed out loud, and Van looked over at him.

"Her belt's digging into my stomach." His voice was ragged, and I was impressed he was able to come up with a plausible excuse.

"Sorry, I'll go change," I said, taking the opportunity to get away.

I ran upstairs, contemplating not returning. I pulled out a pair of Batman jammie pants and a black tank top over a sports bra, figuring if I didn't want my nipples letting everyone know what being close to Kill did to me, I needed to reign them in.

I sat on my bed and deliberated what to do when Kill knocked on my door and opened it.

"Are you coming back down?" He leaned on the door jamb, and if I hadn't just eaten, I would have devoured him whole.

"Yeah," I answered getting up off of my bed.

"Batman?"

"Don't talk about Batman," I warned him, ready to go rounds for my superhero.

"Wouldn't even think about it. Those are sexy." He grinned at me as he slowly perused my body. I applauded myself for thinking ahead and putting a bra on to hide my arousal. I quirked an eyebrow at him, letting him know his line was too cheesy even for me.

"Really, my pj's are sexy? You need to get out more," I said, walking around him wondering if he heard my rapidly beating heart.

"You need to look at yourself in the mirror more," he replied, pulling me against him.

We stayed that way for a moment before he let me go. I was grateful my escape gave me time to get my sexual tension down to a simmer, but it made me sad I wouldn't be able to cuddle with Kill anymore.

Van was passed out on the couch, with the remote

dangling from his hand. Kill kicked his feet off of the table, startling him awake. "What the..." Van sputtered, looking around, trying to get his bearings.

"You were passed out. If you stay like that, you won't be able to move your neck just like the last time," Kill said, grabbing the remote from his hand.

"Shit, I was up late with Jessie. I guess it's catching up with me," Van answered, rubbing his hands over his face.

"Go to sleep, big man, we have a show tomorrow, and I need you at your best," Kill said, pounding him on the back, like boys do when they don't know where to put their hands.

"Yeah, I need all the sleep I can get to keep your ass in tune," Van remarked, getting up and stretching his arms to the ceiling. "'Night Faith," he said as he sluggishly made his way upstairs.

"'Night Van," I responded, before he disappeared.

Kill pulled me down so we were lying on the couch with my head in the crux of his arm. He put his hand under my tank top and circled my belly button with his finger. With every revolution, the fire in my belly intensified, and I was breathing harshly, matching his ragged breaths.

His finger made bigger and bigger loops until they were brushing the waist of my pants. I held my breath when he grazed the elastic band, silently begging him to go further. I turned my head and saw his eyes smoldering with desire. My inner thighs were damp and imploring him to continue.

"Slick," he whispered. We were so close I felt the air escaping his lips when he spoke.

His hand flattened on my belly, his pinky resting slightly under the elastic band, I held still when all I wanted to do was buck up to get his hand to slip under the barrier.

"I want you so much. I can't think straight when I'm near you; all I can think about is getting you naked and touching every inch of your body."

My body shuddered at his words.

"You need to tell me to stop, because I'm not strong enough to do it on my own. I know you aren't ready for this, and I don't want to screw this up, so please tell me to stop," He pleaded with me; his hand was branded into my skin.

My tongue darted out of my mouth to wet my lips, and his eyes zeroed in on the movement, the tick in his jaw was evident as he clenched his jaw shut. "Kill."

His eyes returned to mine waiting for me to deny or invite him to finish what both of us wanted. I opened my mouth not sure what would come out when D closed his door and made his way downstairs. We scrambled apart positioning ourselves on opposite sides of the couch, pretending to watch the movie.

Kill sarcastic laugh sounded harsh to my ears, and I glanced over at him to see him staring intently at the T.V. while his dimple danced on and off of his cheek. D, ignorant of what he had once again interrupted, sat in the middle of us.

"That was the guy who wants us to sing in the music festival on Thanksgiving. He's positive he can get us in," D said to Kill, enthusiasm evident in his voice.

"That's great," Kill growled, causing D to look at him like he was ready to go for round two.

"What's your problem, man? I've been busting my ass to get us into this thing, and you're being a complete prick," D yelled.

Kill's shoulders slumped, and he looked over at him apologetically. "Sorry, that's great. I'm just tired."

Guilt speared through me. I was the reason he was being so short with his friend, even though I wasn't doing it on purpose. I was basically a tease.

Every time Kill and I were about to start something somebody walked in on us, or I gave him the 'let's be friends spiel.' I was an asshole. My thighs clenched when I pictured Kill's hand suspended on my stomach, creeping slowly toward the center of my heat.

He mentioned I wasn't ready to start something, and as much as I hated to admit it, he was right. I wanted to believe he wanted me, but my self-esteem was too damaged to trust him. Kill was an amazing person, and he deserved someone who could give him their whole being.

D blocked my view of Kill. His words came back to haunt me. He told Kill I was too smart to fall for his good guy act, and once I gave in to the chase, I would be dropped for the next hunt, but I doubted I was as strong as D thought I was.

The back and forth my heart and brain were doing made me want to scream. I would never ask Kill if it was just the chase or something more, and if I did, I wouldn't believe the answer anyway.

I stared blankly at the T.V., no longer trying to keep up the ploy of watching it as thoughts ransacked my brain, making me feel like my skin was too tight.

"Do you want to watch another movie?" D asked me, and I blinked, bringing myself back from my whirling thoughts to see the credits rolling.

Kill leaned over so he could see me, both were peering at me.

"No, I think I'm ready for bed." I stood up quickly, only my foot had fallen asleep, so when I stood, it felt like it wasn't there, and I went down as soon as I was up. Kill reached across D and caught me before I collided with the table.

"Easy there." He pulled me to his side, and I leaned on him, still not recovered from the lack of feeling in my foot.

"My foot fell asleep," I mumbled, glaring at it like the traitor it was.

Kill laughed, and D got up to stand on the other side of me.

"Are you ok? Do you need help getting upstairs?" he asked, his hands hovering over me.

"I'm fine. I think I can walk now," I said, putting weight on it, satisfied it would hold me.

"I got you." Kill lifted me up, putting me over his shoulder and walking toward the stairs.

"I can walk, Kill, put me down," I said halfheartedly.

D was frowning as we ascended the staircase. I gave him a what-can-you-do look, and pain registered in his eyes. I hoped this didn't set our friendship back.

"Night D. I'll see you later, hopefully while I'm standing on my own two feet without this caveman throwing me around."

Kill walked into my room and pulled the covers down before putting me down. He began taking off his shoes, and I stopped him.

"What are you doing?" I hissed.

"Getting into bed," he answered as he reached down to take his shirt off.

"D's still awake. If he doesn't see you coming out of my room he's going to know you're sleeping in here, and he isn't going to understand this is just a friend perk," I whispered, pointing at the door as I spoke.

Kill looked over at the door and then back at the bed. "But I'm tired," he whined as he picked up his shoes and shoved his feet into them.

"Sorry, Killer, you don't want them to think that I'm giving it up to you, do you? That isn't what friends do," I said as he finished putting on his shoes.

"No, I don't want them thinking anything about us until you and I figure out what this is." He waited for me to argue, but I kept my mouth shut.

"I can't promise I'll be back. If I wait for D to go to sleep, I might fall asleep before I can get back in here."

"Your side will be waiting for you if you come back," I said, rolling over because my resolve was melting fast from the heat of his stare.

"Night Slick."

"Night Killer. Sweet dreams."

He shut my door, and I listened to his footsteps as they moved to his room. I turned on my back and stared at the ceiling wondering if he would come back. I reached for my iPod and put on my headphones.

My mind went over every nuance of my encounter with Kill, when I felt my bed dip, making my eyes fly open.

"You scared the shit out of me," I hissed to him, hitting pause.

The music stopped, plunging us into silence.

"Sorry, I was trying to be quiet, so I didn't wake anyone up. I whispered to you, but you didn't answer. I thought you fell asleep without me." He sounded upset, and when I rolled over to cuddle him, his body was rigid. I ran my hands up and down his arm and waited until his body relaxed under me.

"I didn't hear you," I confessed in the darkness. "I had my ear buds in."

"I thought you were asleep, and it pissed me off because I couldn't sleep without you. I was afraid I was more addicted to you."

"It's the bed," I said, storing this information in my file of confusing things Kill said, to review later.

"What were you listening to that could drown out all sound?"

I yawned before I answered him; his warmth was making me feel drowsy. "Slip Knot."

"Only you would listen to rock to relax enough to fall asleep."

"The louder, the better. With all that going on, my brain can't keep me awake. It inevitably has to surrender to the music," I said, falling deeper into him as my limbs became heavier.

"What's keeping you up at night?" Kill asked, his mouth was touching my hair, and I felt pieces shifting as he spoke.

"You," I responded, as another yawn attacked me.

"I don't want to cause you sleepless nights. Well, unless I'm not in bed with you. I don't mean to complicate this. I promise to be a better friend and to stop trying to get my hands down your pants."

He tried to make a joke, but when he mentioned his hand and my pants, heat shot through me.

I wanted to tell him the problem was I couldn't stop thinking about how I wanted his hand, and other appendages on his body, in my pants. But sleep had its grasp on me and didn't let go until I relented.

# CHAPTER 22

There was no sign of Kill when I woke up, but there was a blueberry muffin and a bottle of orange juice on the nightstand. I was so screwed. After swallowing my morning Tums, I tore into the muffin with a smile.

I finished what I could before getting ready. With my trash in hand, I tried to curb the spring in my step as I went downstairs. Kill was in his normal spot on the couch and smiled when he saw me. When I came back from throwing my trash away his smile was still in place.

"Morning, Slick," he said, taking a sip of his protein shake, his eyes trained on me.

"Morning, Killer," I responded, feeling like a giddy teenager in front of her crush.

"Are you going to eat breakfast?" he asked taking another sip, so he could hide the grin on his face.

"I already have. The breakfast fairy visited my room this morning."

"Are you sure it was a fairy? Because I'm pretty sure breakfast is delivered by an extremely handsome, godlike creature."

"So Jet brought me breakfast?" I asked, pretending to be confused.

Kill laughed and got up to put his glass away. "Brat," he said, coming over and putting out his hand for me to take. When we reached the door D came downstairs, and I quickly slipped my hand out of Kill's.

"Where are you guys going?" he asked, looking at our workout clothes.

"For a run," Kill said, throwing an arm over my shoulder. "I have to keep her ass motivated, or she would never leave the house." I nudged him in the side.

"You don't have to always put her down."

Kill's arm flexed around me. "I was just messing with

her. She knows I'm just playing."

"If you want a running partner that doesn't insult you, let me know. I ran track in high school," D explained. He went toward the kitchen, and Kill watched his retreat.

"Ready?" I asked, bringing his attention away from D.

"Yep, let's get going."

At the end of our run when the house came into view, my heart dropped, not wanting our time to end.

"You're getting fast."

"I would be a lot faster if I had a better running partner; the one I have now is lazy."

He laughed and tried to put his arm around me, but I dodged it.

"Eww, you're all sweaty," I cried, as I maneuvered away from his next attempt.

"Come on, Slick, you're hurting my feelings." He pushed his bottom lip out, and I stopped myself from latching onto it with my teeth and sucking it into my mouth.

"You don't have feelings," I said, my voice shaky from the visual I just had.

"I do, and you hurt them all the time." He put on the puppy dog face. I giggled and threw my arms around his waist.

"I'm sorry, Killer. Are you going to live after the torment I've caused you?"

"I hope so. I never would have agreed to let you in my house if I'd known you were a bully."

"You'll survive. I haven't lost a victim yet," I said, unhooking my arms and pinching his cheeks. "Poor wittle Kill, getting picked on by a mean girl."

He pulled my hands off of his cheeks and dragged me into the house. There wasn't anyone around, and I was sure Kill wouldn't have stopped if there was. He acted like a man on a mission as he pulled me into my room.

"What has gotten into you?" I asked as he closed the door behind us.

When he let go of my arm, it dropped lifelessly to my side. My heart beat wildly, the sporadic pulsing pooled blood to my lower region. I stepped back, wanting to put distance between us as my body screamed at me to go forward.

Kill moved toward me; his stride was bigger than mine, swallowing up the distance. I took another step back and continued until the back of my legs hit the bed, and his eyes lit with amusement.

He slowly stalked me, watching every move I made, calculating the amount of pressure I could stand without freaking out. He didn't stop until we were toe to toe. Desire surged through me, and my vagina was in her cheerleader uniform pom-poms ready.

Kill's pupils had expanded, pushing the color into a sliver along the edge. I forgot to breathe. I dropped to the bed, my legs no longer accepting orders to hold me up. His nostrils flared, and the predatory glint in his eyes made my inner thighs clench with need. He leaned over, and I fell back on the bed. His eyes exuded pure lust, causing my body to tighten with want.

All the feeling in my body was centered on the pressure between my thighs. He climbed onto the bed, hovering over me, his legs on either side of me effectively trapping me with his body.

"Are you ok, Slick?" His voice was ragged, and my nipples puckered from the sound.

I nodded my head, my mouth too dry to speak. My body diverted all the fluids to the boiling heat between my legs. He moved his legs, so his knees were holding my arms down and he was perched on my stomach. I looked down at my arms, and when I turned back to him his face had changed from lust to mischief, putting me on full alert.

"You know what I do to bullies?"

I shook my head, not wanting to find out. One corner of his lip lifted as he raised his hands into the air above his head, stretching his fingers out. He let them fall slowly toward me, his fingers wiggling as if they were spider legs descending on its prey.

I squirmed under him, trying to buck him off me as my eyes stay trained on his hands. He didn't budge at my attempt.

"No, Kill, please don't," I begged, my voice small, and I pushed into the bed when his fingers were inches from my neck. I tried to press my chin into my sternum to hide any open skin, and he let out an evil laugh.

"Sorry, it's the punishment for being mean."

"I won't do it again, I promise." I squirmed around the small amount of wiggle room I had.

He stopped his hands and cocked his head to the side as if he was considering my promise. "Really, you can refrain from hurting my fragile ego?"

I opened my mouth to respond, giving him access to my neck, and he pounced. He tickled me as I tried in vain to escape.

I screamed and laughed, begging him to release me when D came bursting in with panic in his eyes. D's entrance distracted Kill, and I took advantage of his negligence. I thrust up with my hips, dislodging him to the side so I could scramble away. My actions were disoriented and clumsy because I was laughing so hard.

"What the hell's going on? I was on the phone when I thought Faith was being murdered."

Kill laid face up on my bed giving me a wink before turning his head to D. "She was being mean. I was attempting to tickle the meanness out of her. From the looks of it, I tickled her back into her awkward teenage years."

I kicked out, jabbing his side with my toes, and he jerked around, looking at me with a shocked expression. "Oh my God," I squealed, pouncing on him and tickling his sides as he jumped off the bed, making a cross with his fingers while backing away.

Giving him an evil grin, I extended my finger moving it in a come here motion, but he shook his head still backing away.

"What? Are you scared of me?" I said, batting my eyelashes for the full innocent affect.

"This isn't over," Kill said, putting D in front of him as a shield, making me laugh even harder.

"Bring it on, Killer," I taunted, looking at him with a smirk on my face, knowing I was playing with fire.

Kill winked at me, and I left the smirk on my face, not wanting to go any further with whatever game we were playing in front of D.

"Kill, leave Faith alone," D said as he pushed Kill out of

my room.

"You good, Faith?" he asked, and I nodded, my eyes focused on Kill, making faces at me like a five year old.

D looked me over again before closing the door behind him.

I sat on my bed smiling like fool. My phone beeped, showing me I had a missed call from a private number and a text message from Robert.

I debated deleting the message. The way I left him at the restaurant was awful, and I knew his message was going to be dreadful. Convincing myself this was my punishment, I forced myself to open it.

**I am so glad I didnt go**
**hme with u last nite, UR**
**a whore that has the whole**
**band in her. I went hme**
**with the waitress she was**
**hotter then u and a**
**better FUCK**

I reread the message two more times, cringing at the grammatical errors, thanking my lucky stars Kill came when he did.

Jessie's name flashed on the screen right before I sat my phone down. "Hey, sexy, what are you wearing?"

"Let's see. A pair of shorts and a tank top, because it's actually hot today," she replied.

"Oh, that's sexy. What's up?"

"Get ready I'm coming to pick you up. You owe me confessions."

"What are you going to buy me for this top secret information?" I asked, getting a blue and white striped summer dress out.

"Coffee."

"Done, give me twenty."

"That's all it takes? You didn't even barter for a scone."

"Yeah, about your friend Faith. I hate to tell you this,

but she's kind of a whore," I said, causing her to sputter with laughter.

"I know, but I love her anyway."

"Ahh, I love you too, Jess. Now I have to go. I have to get ready for a hot date."

"See you in twenty," she responded.

I dashed to the bathroom to take a quick shower. Pulling on a dress and blue heels with little red anchors on them, I was ready to go. Jessie was on the couch with Van when I got downstairs.

"Ready?" I asked after standing in the living room, shifting awkwardly when they didn't notice me right away.

Jessie jumped up and ran over, giving me a hug. "You aren't in jeans and a band t-shirt. I'm so proud of you."

I pushed her off of me. "Shut up. I own dresses," I defended my beloved band t-shirts.

"I know but you never dressed cute unless you were allowed."

"She looks cute in her band t-shirts," Kill said from behind me, making me jump.

"You need a bell around your neck. You scared the shit out of me," I said with my hand at my neck, my pulse beating madly underneath it.

"A bell? Really?"

"Yes, a bell: that way you can't sneak up on people."

"I swear, I never know what to expect to come out of your mouth. Why are you all dressed up?" he asked, changing the subject as he eyed me up and down, causing a small fire to burn between my legs from the way his eyes traveled appreciatively over me.

"Jessie's taking me out on a date," I said, taking a step toward him. My body instinctively gravitated to him.

"Ah, are you going to need me to come and save you again?" he asked, laughing when I gave him an evil eye. He put his chin on my head and hugged me close.

"So, are you guys going to come to The Note later?" he asked, looking over my head at Jessie.

"No, I was planning on force feeding Faith ice cream, and making her watch chick flicks all night."

Kill let out a sound of mock horror, and I elbowed him in the stomach.

"Girls night sounds perfect," I said, still snuggled up to Kill, wishing I could make a Kill body suit that just wrapped around me.

"Good, now let's get out of here." She walked to Van, and kissed him. Kill didn't let me go, and I didn't try to move.

"Are you going to be here when I get home?" Van asked, pulling her onto his lap so he could give her a proper good bye.

"I'm not sure. I have to do some stuff before I go to work tomorrow," Jessie responded, becoming rigid on his lap.

Kill squeezed me when he saw Jessie pull away from Van, knowing we couldn't continue holding each other any longer without raising suspicion.

"I can help you tomorrow if you want?" Van asked.

"I will let you know. I promised my mom I would call tomorrow, so let me see how long that takes," she said, not meeting his eyes, and missing the hurt flashing over his face.

"Alright, have fun," he responded dejectedly.

Jessie looked over at me. "Ready?" she asked. Her voice was full of emotion, and I knew this was hurting her just as much as it was hurting Van.

Kill let me go, and I walked out of the warm safety of his arms. I couldn't stop the shiver that racked my body from the temperature change.

"Bye, let me know if I need to come save you," he said, as we made our way out of the door.

Jessie was walking hurriedly in front of me, fleeing the house as if it was on fire.

"Bye, Killer. I'll be fine, go buy a bell." He laughed as I shut the door.

Jessie had her car started by the time I reached it, and she was down the road before I put on my seat belt. My stomach churned, remembering the last time we escaped in her car like this, although this time it was Jessie running from *her* demons.

When we reached our coffee shop, her eyes were glazed over from unshed tears, and it wrenched my heart to see her in such pain. Her feelings for Van were tearing her

311

apart, allowing buried memories to surface.

"Well, are we going to sit in here all day or are you going to buy me that coffee you promised?" I asked when we parked at the coffee shop, assuming she wasn't going to figure anything out today, so I might as well try to get her mind off of it.

She blinked back her tears and gave me a wobbly smile. "Yep, come on, let's get you caffeinated so you can dish out the good stuff."

# CHAPTER 23

Jessie ordered our drinks while I found a place to sit. I nabbed a quiet table in the corner and waited for Jessie. I greedily accepted the mocha frappe she handed me. She sipped hers as I put my finger in the thick whipped cream and licked it off.

"Ok, what happened last night?" she asked, her eyes shining with the prospect of getting lost in someone else's drama.

I told her everything from Robert showing up with roses, and the boys surrounding him like sharks and like he was a bucketful of bloody chum, all the way to Kill interrupting his wandering hands. Then to put the cherry on top, I handed her my phone to show her Robert's text message.

"I can't believe he came into the restaurant instead of texting you to tell you he was there," Jessie said, wiping her eyes with a napkin.

"I know. He was so cool about it too. His voice never changed. It was kind of awesome."

Her eyes lit up, and I realized I went too far and was about to be bombarded with Kill questions.

"So how's the *friends* thing going?" she asked with worry, putting her empty cup off to the side and giving me her full attention.

"I don't know," I replied, and she was about to argue with my weak answer, but I put my hand up to stop her, letting her know I needed to gather my thoughts first.

"We're friends, but I know he wouldn't push me away if I propositioned him. He accepted that I can't just be a fuck buddy."

I bit my bottom lip as my mind went to his hand inching closer to my waist band last night, and my face burned from the memory.

"What aren't you telling me?" Her eyes were like lasers.

"Nothing really, we flirt but.... I think that's just inherent in Kill's personality. We have been on the verge of making out a couple of times, but we've been interrupted every time, and I think it's a sign we shouldn't cross that line."

Jessie squealed loudly, and everyone in the coffee shop stared at us. "You have what?" she screamed, and I leaned over putting my hand over her mouth to silence her.

"Can we not let the entire coffee shop in on my drama?" I asked, not removing my hand until she nodded in agreement.

"Sorry, but you can't just throw out that you and Kill have almost made out on more than one occasion, and not expect me to react," she hissed, her disappointment evident.

"He told me last night he would stop trying to get into my pants and be a better friend." I said, sucking up nothing, being I had finished my drink. "He also made me promise when I was ready to date again, I would give him a chance."

"Holy crap," Jessie said loudly, garnishing more attention from her latest outburst.

I threw away our empty cups, knowing I needed to get her out of there. We walked to her car and away from the curious stares of the people in the coffee shop.

"Where to now?" I asked, trying to steer the conversation to anything un-Kill related.

"Shopping!" she answered, I laughed at her enthusiasm. "I'm not going to warn you about Kill again. I just want you to be careful....and that's all I'm going to say. Well, and I don't want to see you get hurt again."

My stomach plummeted along with my heart. Why did it seem like everyone and everything was against us?

We walked around the Lloyd Center, trying on hundreds of outfits and shoes. I text Kill asking what they wanted me to pick up for dinner. As we went on a junk food run, my phone notified me that I had new messages from Kill.

**Have fun, try not to miss me too much. Let me know if you need me to come get you. The boys want**

314

**Jimmy Johns.**

And the second,

> **Did you buy anything**
> **you need to model**
> **for me?**

    I rolled my eyes at his response, but couldn't quite keep the smile off of my face.

    While Jessie was down the aisle trying to decide on the best popcorn, I text him back.

> **No, I didn't get anything**
> **I could show my friend.**
> **I'm going to have to wait**
> **and model all my new**
> **lingerie for someone else.**
> **Do you know anyone?**

    As soon as I sent the message my phone lit up, and I laughed before I even read his reply. Jessie looked at me questioningly.

    "The boys want Jimmy Johns," I explained.

    "Ok, we'll get it when we're done here," she said, now perusing the sodas on the other side.

> **I just spit my drink**
> **all over D, and now**
> **he's all pissy. As a**
> **friend, I should see everything**
> **you bought first, so I**
> **can tell you how horrible**
> **you look before making**
> **some poor, unsuspecting**
> **douche have to lie to**

**you and tell you how great**
**you look. Just being a friend. :)**

I stifled my laugh, not wanting to make Jessie suspicious. I text him back quickly.

**Now I am self-conscious,**
**and I think I should just**
**take it all back.**

Kill responded just as quick.

**Why waste your time,**
**you should let me help you.**
**That's what friends are for.**

I bit the inside of my cheek as I responded.

**Ask the boys what they**
**want from Jimmy Johns**
**and text me the order. I**
**just found a leather bustier**
**I need to try on for the**
**salesman in the store.**

Kill's response did not disappoint.

**As your friend, I strongly**
**suggest you stop saying**
**stuff like that if you don't**
**want me hauling you**
**out of the store and kicking**
**some poor guys' ass.**

Jessie came back with the cart full of junk as I put my

phone away, letting him stew. My phone vibrated as we checked out, and I tapped down the desire to reach for it.

When Jessie rushed into her apartment to drop off her stuff and pick up some movies, I dove into my bag for my phone. There were three messages, and I was giddy when I opened the first one.

**Slick, you are about to get some poor guy murdered. As a friend, I suggest you text me back, and keep your clothes on. I can tell you leather is uncomfortable, and you will look awful in it.**

I chuckled as I opened the next one.

Alright, you know you won't
look awful in leather,
but now I have to sit
here on the couch and
lose my video game because
my FRIEND gave me a
freaking boner.

The rest of the text was the boy's dinner order, and I opened the last one before Jessie came back.

**Ok, I finally got my raging boner down but when you get home, you're trying everything on for me, as a friend of course. This can also be considered bullying, so be warned, I will retaliate.**

I had a smug smile on my face as I text him back.

**Sorry, Killer, I was busy
with the sales guy, didn't
hear your text. I'm glad your
little problem's down, and
you could get back to your game.
I don't know if I will have
enough strength to try on my
new clothes for you, I'm tired out.**

Jessie came out of her apartment, and I read his reply before she got back into the car.

**There's nothing little about my
problem, that you caused,
by the way.  I hope you didn't
hurt the poor boy when you
called out my name.**

I wished he was here so I could give him my retort in person.

**I'm sure the boy will be sore,
but he had a smile on his face
when I left. Why would I call
out your name?**

Jessie threw the movies in the backseat, before backing out of the driveway. My phone beeped, and I snatched it up, having no willpower.

**Because I'm the only one
you think about, and I'm
holding you to your promise.**

My heart sped up as I typed out.

## Am I the only one you
## think about?

But before I hit send, I deleted it, not wanting to give my heart any hope when it came to Kill.

"Did the boys send you their order?" Jessie asked as she found a parking spot.

"Yeah, I have it. If we went in and ordered the whole menu, it would match what they want."

My phone beeped with another text when we were almost home.

## Where are you, smart ass?
## I'm hungry.

I typed back immediately.

## It's ok to admit you miss me,
## I'm pretty awesome.

I stashed my phone in my bag and helped Jessie haul the food and my purchases into the house. Van opened the door before we reached it. He took everything out of her hands and kissed her on the nose as he moved into the kitchen.

The boys pounced on the food when my phone notified me of a new text. Jet looked over at me as I tried to maneuver the stuff in my hands, so I could get to it.

"Not you too," Jet yelled at me, "Kill has been texting all night and made me lose my damn video game because he was so fucking distracted, and now your ass is scrambling to get your phone out. You people make me sick. Always on your phone, not caring about people you're supposed to be helping kill terrorists."

"Don't listen to him. He's just a sore loser, and I wasn't on my phone the whole time," Kill replied, slugging Jet in the arm.

"Dude, if you weren't typing on your phone you were scowling at it until you got a text back, and then you would smile like a fucking idiot."

"Shut the fuck up, Jet," Kill growled, walking into the living room.

"Dude, you were all kinds of pussy-whipped over your phone," D replied smugly, and I laughed out loud.

"I'm going to put my stuff away." I ran upstairs and dropped my bags on the bed scrambling for my phone, eager to see his reply. I let out a cry of victory when I found it. My door opened, and spun around to see Kill with his damn half-smile. I must have looked like a maniac clutching my phone to my chest, wide eyed.

"I was not glued to my phone," he said sternly.

I laughed at his serious face. "Good, because as a friend, I would have to confiscate your phone if you were mooning over it. Especially if it was over some girl."

Kill took my phone from my hand, placing it on my night stand, his eyes alight on the bags sitting on my bed. He started reaching for my stuff.

"Stop, dinner's here, and you have to go soon," I protested, taking a bag out of his hands and putting it back on the bed.

He lunged on the bed, snatching another bag and landing on the other side out of my reach. He pulled the lid off of my new heels. They were matte black with little studs on the back and down the heel.

"Fuck.... these are hot."

"They go with the leather bustier," I said, admiring my pretty new shoes.

"Which bag's it in?" he asked, trying to find the mysterious bustier.

"It's not."

"Come on, tease, let's go eat. You can model for me tomorrow."

We walked downstairs, bumping into each other on the way down. Everyone was in the living room, and looked at us when we entered.

"We were about to send out the search crew. I thought

you were going to get her," D said.

"Sorry I couldn't get her ass down here. She kept insisting she show me her new bustier."

"Shut up, you wanted to wear it."

"Man, you two have a fucked up friendship," Van said, shaking his head in confusion.

"Right, it's weird to see Kill talk to a girl he isn't trying to get his dick into," Jet responded, sticking the last bite of his sandwich in his mouth.

With my food in hand, I sat next to Kill on the floor. Jet and Van argued over the video game they lost. When everything was cleaned up, the boys went upstairs to get ready for their show.

"You guys aren't coming tonight?" Amy asked, rummaging through her purse for a bag of sour gummy worms.

"No, we're going to stay in and do girls' night. Do you want to join us?" Jessie asked. "We've got plenty of candy," she taunted, when Amy looked at her like she was crazy.

"No, I promised Jet I would come and cheer him on."

"You two are getting along really well," Jessie said, stealing a worm from Amy.

"Yep, he makes me come more than anyone ever has. I love him," she said dreamily.

"I'm happy for you. I mean that you're in love, and I guess for the orgasms too," Jesse replied blushing, and Amy just handed her another worm.

"Dork," I said, as Jessie threw the other half of her worm at me.

I plucked it off of my dress, and threw it in my mouth. The boys came down while we were talking.

"Ready, Candy?" Jet asked, as Amy ran over and jumped on him, wrapping her legs around his waist.

"I guess she is," Van said, trying to get around them.

When he finally got around them, he walked over to Jessie. He was hesitant as he put his arms around her. "I wish you were coming tonight. Go to sleep in my bed, don't drive."

Emotions warred in her eyes, wanting to trust him, but the memory of Brock held her prisoner. "I will, but don't get mad if I have the covers wrapped around me when you come home tired," she warned, kissing him on the nose.

"I would let you have all the blankets I own if you would stay in my bed every night," he replied, giving her a desperate kiss.

I turned away to give them some semblance of privacy. Jet carried Amy to D's car. I stood around awkwardly trying to ignore Jessie and Van as they whispered to each other. D and Kill came down, discussing something in a notebook. D rolled his eyes when he saw Jessie and Van, and Kill looked at them, hopeful.

"Jet and Amy just went toward your car, D. You might want to check on them before they christen it for you."

D looked horrified at the prospect of them going at it in his car. He thanked me for the warning and rushed out of the house. D screamed at them to unlock the door, and Van backed away from Jessie.

"I better go help him before he breaks a blood vessel." He kissed her lightly on the lips and went to help D before any fluids were leaked on his interior, or at least that's what he was screaming.

"Have a good show," Jessie yelled.

He turned around and winked at her. "Thanks, babe."

D soon quieted down, so whatever Van did was helping. Kill looked outside, laughing at whatever they were doing to halt Amy and Jet.

"Aren't you going to go help them?" I asked, going over to him just in time to see Van haul Jet out of the Highlander, and D bent over to make sure his interior was semen free.

"Nah, they had it handled," he replied, laughing when Jet got behind D and pretended to hump him. D pushed Jet off of him, still inspecting the interior.

"See you later tonight," he said in my ear.

"I don't know if I'm going to be able to stay awake," I said, certain I would.

"Well, then save me a spot," he whispered in my ear, before walking out of the house. "Bye, friend."

"Bye" I replied, to the closed door.

"Be careful," Jessie said startling me.

"We're friends." I responded, going into the kitchen to

gather the junk food we bought.

"Friends who whisper sweet nothings in each other ears? What did he say?"

"He wants to wear my leather bustier I bought," I told her.

"But you didn't buy one."

"I know, it was a joke."

"Van was right. You two do have a weird friendship."

"You have no idea," I replied. "Do you want to watch the movies out here, or in my room?"

"Let's go in your room and binge," she replied, filling up two large cups with ice.

"Ok, we'll have to take this up in trips."

When we had the loot in my room, I threw my purchases on the floor, and we changed into comfy clothes.

"Which one do we watch first?" Jessie asked, as we looked over our selection.

"*Bridgette Jones's Diary,* or *Love Actually,*" I responded, going for the British comedies.

Jessie picked *'Love Actually'* and put it in while I stacked the discarded movies on nightstand. We watched *'Crazy Stupid Love'* next. Both of us sighed when Ryan Gosling did the *'Dirty Dancing'* move.

We decided we needed to watch *'Dirty Dancing'* next, and recited the lines verbatim. We passed out before the movie was over, and I was cuddling the popcorn bowl when my door opened.

My eyes snapped open, and my heart thundered in my chest. Memories of Jason attacking me while I slept viciously invaded my brain.

My eyes adjusted just in time to see Kill at his side of the bed, which Jessie now occupied. I sat up quickly, clutching the empty bowl so it didn't make a noise.

"Hey, I didn't mean to wake you up," Kill whispered.

"Kill, stop."

He froze, confused.

"Jessie's in here; we fell asleep."

His eyes went wide when he registered Jessie's sleeping form. He came over to my side and kneeled down. I turned over so we were face to face.

"This sucks," he whispered, and I smiled at him.

"I'm sorry."

Jessie stirred, so I leaned in closer not wanting to wake her.

"I waited until all of the boys went to bed before I snuck in here. Come get in bed with me," he said, his eyes lighting up to the idea.

"What if Jessie wakes up and I'm not in bed with her?"

"I don't know if I can sleep without your snoring."

"I'm sorry. I tried to wait up for you, but I had a sugar crash. If it makes you feel any better, I don't want to sleep without you."

I felt brave enough to admit this in the dark. A hint of a smile appeared on his face, confirming it was the right thing to reveal.

"How was the show?"

Jessie moved again, and I glanced over to make sure she was still asleep. When I turned around, Kill picked me up off of the bed. He shushed me when I tried to protest. He took me downstairs and deposited me on the couch.

"What are you doing?" I hissed, not wanting to wake anyone up.

"My legs were getting tired crouched down like that, and if I can't sleep with you, at least I can tell you about my night before I have to go to my big bed alone. If Jessie wakes up you can tell her you couldn't sleep, and came down here to watch T.V. with me."

He turned on the T.V. to make his excuse as truthful as possible. Kill pulled me on his lap and I snuggled in.

"I'm glad you brought me down here. Ok, tell me how the show went?" I asked as his hands brushed through my hair.

"Me too, I missed your smart ass tonight."

"I know. I was afraid without being insulted by me all day, your ego would overrun the city."

His chest rumbled, in that delicious way it does, when he chuckled. I put my hand flat on his chest, wanting to catch every movement.

"Well, I think your text messages kept it at bay, but it

wasn't as good as the real thing."

"So the show, the way you keep avoiding answering me makes me wonder if you didn't screw up completely. I told you practice doesn't always make perfect. And to be honest, I don't know if your voice is ever going to be good, practice or not."

He tugged on my hair lightly.

"It was good. There were a lot of people tonight, and some asked about you."

"Me?"

"Yes, you. They heard about your performances at Ray's, and wanted to know if you were going to sing with us at The Note."

"Did you explain I only sing at Ray's because I'm messing around with you guys?" I said, panic rising up inside of me.

"No, I told them you would come next time."

"What?" I screeched, moving my head so I could glare at him.

"Slick, you're good, and you give the band another facet that will help us get discovered. You need more confidence."

"Kill, I can't." I couldn't keep it the terror out of my voice.

"Hush, we'll talk about this later. I don't want to argue with you." He rubbed my back soothingly, and guided my head back to the spot on his chest. I bit his chest lightly, causing him to jump.

"What was that for?"

"For telling people I would do something without talking to me first."

"I told them because I know I can talk you into doing it. So what would be the point of telling them no?"

"So sure of yourself, aren't you?" I asked, offended he thought he could manipulate me so easily.

"No, I'm sure of you. I know you don't want to let us down, and if that didn't work, I was going to offer to buy you a new pair of shoes."

"New shoes?" I perked up, making him laugh.

"You're so easy, Slick."

"You know, that's the second time today somebody told

me that," I grumbled.

Kill laughed, and I nipped his chest again. "You do that again, and it's going to be very uncomfortable on my lap."

I snorted into his chest. "So.... about those new shoes?"

"Alright, if you come with us next Tuesday, I will buy you a new pair."

"I'll go on Tuesday, and you don't even have to buy me a new pair. You already bought me a beautiful pair, and I can't take advantage of you. Let's just say you prepaid for my services."

"I don't mind buying you anything, Slick."

"It's fine, Killer. Tell me more about tonight," I said, changing the subject, not feeling comfortable with him shelling out more money on me.

"Nice try changing the subject. We'll talk about the shoes later."

I picked up my head from his chest ready to argue, but he pressed it back down.

"It was different without you; in the audience, or onstage. I kept glancing around the bar looking for you."

"You missed me. I think you like me," I teased.

He grabbed my hand and nipped the tip of my middle finger, sending electricity zinging through me and making my breath hitch. I yanked my hand back, tucking it in between us.

"I did not miss you. I missed your smart ass. You keep fishing for me to tell you missed you. Are you projecting your feelings on me?"

I laughed so hard, I had to wipe the tears from the edge of my eyes.

"Did you really just psychoanalyze me?"

"What, you didn't think I knew what projecting was?"

"Shut up, that's not what I meant."

"Ok, well, maybe I missed you a little, but only because I had nobody smart enough to come up with witty comebacks. I honestly thought I would to have to give people a ten minute reprieve to think of something clever."

"Ahh Killer, that's the nicest thing you've ever said to me. I missed you too," I admitted into his chest.

I could hear his powerful heartbeat through his t-shirt,

and it sped up after my confession.

"You're kind of addicting. I think your snoring has special powers, because while I waited for the boys to fall asleep, I was wide awake."

"I can record it for you so you can listen to it while you're in your room. I wonder if I could market it for other egotistical, moody musicians that can't sleep," I snarked back, snuggling deeper into him as he ran his fingers through my hair.

He laughed quietly into my hair, and my eyelids dropped down, too heavy to keep open. "Nope, you're my discovery for sleeping soundly at night, and I refuse to share. I missed that day in kindergarten."

"Kill, I can't keep my eyes open," I said, my voice thick with sleep.

"Go to sleep. I'll wake you up before everyone else wakes up, and if Jessie asks where you were, you can just tell her you couldn't sleep and fell asleep on the couch."

"What about you? Aren't you tired?" I asked, ready to fall asleep as soon as he gave me the reassurance I needed.

"I sleep better with you near me, but I'm a light sleeper. If I hear anyone coming, I'll move you off of me and make it look like we fell asleep watching T.V."

He yawned and slipped his hand under my shirt, touching my bare skin and causing a small fire in between my thighs. If sleep hadn't been so consuming, I wouldn't have been able to bank my desire so easily.

"Are you comfortable like this?" I asked, my voice slurring from the amount of effort it took to speak.

"I'm fine, don't worry about me."

"We can lie down so you will be more comfortable."

"Are you sure?" he asked.

I nodded my head, too close to falling asleep for words. He shifted us around, until we were spooning. My brain registered I was no longer buried in his chest, and his smell was fainter. I turned, burying my nose in his chest. I hitched my leg in between his, so we were properly intertwined.

"Better?" he asked, and I could hear the smile in his voice as I nodded my head.

327

"Night Slick."

"Night Killer, I hope my snoring lulls you to sleep."

Not much later, I felt Kill shifting me around so we were no longer tangled together.

"Where are you going?" I mumbled, reaching for his hand.

"I'm going to make my protein shake, don't get up just yet; sleep some more."

He brushed his lips over my forehead, and I burrowed further into the couch where he had been.

I felt a hand on my shoulder. I nudged it off, wanting to stay in my current dream of Kill. After another nudge, I recognized the electrical current accompanying the touch, Kill stood above me with a smile on his face.

"Morning, do you want some coffee?" he asked, his half-smile doing naughty things to the lower half of my body.

"Water," I croaked. "I had so much sugar last night that anything but water sounds wrong."

Kill pulled the blanket off, taking my hand and hauled me off of the couch. "Come on, let's go get you your water."

My stomach knotted up from moving so fast, and my bottle of Tums was nowhere nearby to help me. I winced from the pain.

"Did I hurt you?" he asked, his face coated with worry as he searched my face.

"No, my stomach hurts from all of the junk," I explained, giving him the half-truth.

His face relaxed when he realized he hadn't done anything to cause me pain. "Come on, let's detox you then. We'll skip our run today."

"I'll be fine after I drink some water. We don't have to skip our run," I replied, not wanting to be the broken girl anymore.

"Alright, let's get you hydrated."

"I'll meet you in a second. I'm going to go change and check on Jessie."

He nodded his head and went to the kitchen as I went upstairs. Jessie was still asleep, and I didn't think she had moved from the position she had been in when I left with Kill.

I was shaky, and weak from the short walk upstairs. I threw a handful of Tums in my mouth as I pulled out some workout clothes. I got ready in the bedroom, not wanting to wake Jessie up. I hoped she would never be the wiser to my nocturnal abandonment.

I gathered everything we didn't annihilate last night and took it downstairs for the boys. Kill was at the kitchen table with his protein shake when I came down with my arms full of leftovers. He helped me put it away.

"Jeez, no wonder you don't feel well. Did you buy the whole store?" he asked, handing me a bottle of water.

I took a long drink, letting the cool liquid coat my parched throat.

"We did, in fact, I'm the new owner of Target," I quipped back as we made our way toward the table.

"Nice to meet you. I love your store," he replied.

"Are you hungry?" My stomach rolled, causing the boulder to dislodge and trample my already painful stomach.

"Judging by the fact your face turned green at the mention of food, I'm going to take that as a no," Kill responded, concern etched on his face. "We don't have to go running today."

My skin was clammy as my abdomen started an acidic burn. I took another sip of my water, trying to dilute it.

"I'll be fine," I said, but my voice sounded just as shaky as I felt.

"Nope, you look like you're about to pass out. We're not running today and you're resting until you have to go to work. You haven't been working this schedule very long. You need to allow your body to adjust."

I hated to see the worry on his face, but I couldn't focus on making him feel better, as the water was now traitorously stabbing my abdomen with the tiny swords it had stowed away unbeknownst to me.

I put my head on the cool table, as the urge to vomit ran through me. Kill got up, and turned on the faucet. A wet cloth was placed on the back of my neck, and the shock brought me away from the precipice of fainting.

Jessie came downstairs, and when she saw me

plastered on the table with Kill hovering over me she ran over.

"Faith, are you ok? What happened?"

I went to answer her, but bile started to rise, so I snapped my mouth closed.

"She had too much junk food last night, and she couldn't sleep. We watched T.V. downstairs until we both fell asleep. She didn't get much sleep though, and I don't think her body's taking the lack of sleep and *sugar shock* very well." Kill's voice was calming as he explained, and my stomach stopped trying to revolt.

I carefully lifted my head, but when the room spun, I clamped my eyes shut and put my head back on the table, groaning.

"I'm so sorry, Faith. What can I do?" Jessie pleaded.

"I'm fine. I think I just need to drink some more water, and maybe sleep for a couple more hours." I put my hands flat on the table, letting the coolness seep into my wrists. My stomach rolled around, upset I moved.

"I'm going to pick you up and take you to bed," Kill said, removing the cool cloth on my neck.

"I can walk, Kill, you don't have to carry me." My voice was weak, and I hated he once again had to rescue me.

"I know I don't have to. I want to. Let me be your friend. You can pay me back by letting me wear that leather bustier," he replied as he lifted me up.

I pushed my face into his neck, breathing him in as my body revolted from the movement. He stood there for a moment letting me adjust to the change.

"Ready?"

I nodded my head, and he gently carried me upstairs. Jessie followed.

When he put me on my bed, I immediately curled up into a ball.

"Do you want me to stay with you?" Jessie asked, sounding frantic.

"No, you need to go crawl in bed with Van."

"Faith, I want to make sure you're ok," she whined.

"Jess, you aren't going to stay still, and I can't handle movement right now. I'll be fine, I just need another hour or two. Go get in bed with Van, and make him a happy boy."

"Are you sure?"

"Go on Jessie, I'll take care of her," Kill urged, as he led Jessie out of the room.

I took the alone time to grab my bottle of Tums and chomp on a handful, not wanting him to discover my secret stash.

Kill came back just as I swallowed, and I was thankful I didn't have to explain why my bedside partner was a bottle of Tums. He got into bed, making as little movement as possible. He placed the cloth on my forehead, and I slid over until I was pressed on his side.

"I'm sorry. I should have let you sleep longer."

I reached out a shaky hand and placed it on his stomach. "It wasn't your fault. I had too much junk, and not enough sleep the past couple of weeks; it all just compounded on me. I'll be fine after a couple more hours of rest. You don't have to stay in bed with me. I'm just going to sleep."

The second round of Tums seemed to be doing its job, and I was already feeling better.

"I know I don't have to, but this is what my friendship entails, so get used to it."

"You can turn on the T.V. if you want," I told him, already letting my body sink into a healing sleep.

He flipped through channels as I drifted off to sleep listening to the T.V. drone on in the background.

# CHAPTER 24

I woke up groggy, and sprawled on top of Kill. He slept with his arms over his head. I studied him, reveling in him for a moment, afraid if he woke up and saw me staring, he would consider me a stalker. His lip curled up on one side, and I leaned in closer.

"Do you see something you like, or are you plotting my death?" Kill asked, not moving from his position.

I let out a startled breath. "Just wondering if you snore," I quipped back, trying to keep my voice steady.

He peeked at me with one eye, before closing it. His lips twitched as he held back a smile. "So, do I snore?"

"Oh, not from what I could see, but I just began my observation when you so rudely interrupted me."

"I could feel your eyes probing my dreams."

"Sorry," I said, rolling away.

He caught me and brought me against him. "Do you feel better?" he asked, rubbing my back, and I arched into him.

"I do, how long have I been asleep?" I asked, not wanting to leave the comfort of his arms to check the time on my phone.

Thinking about my phone reminded me of the unread text I had from him.

"I don't know. Honestly, you were out for a couple minutes before your snoring lulled me to sleep."

"You want to go on a run before I have to get ready for work?" I asked, not wanting to leave him just yet.

"Not today."

"Ok," I responded, trying and failing, to hide my disappointment of us parting ways, even though I couldn't blame him. He had been with me since he got home last night from his gig.

He tilted my chin up with his finger. "You kind of scared the shit out of me this morning. You were white as a ghost. I honestly thought you were going to pass out right in front of me, and if you tell any of the boys I said that I'll tickle you for hours." His face was sincere, and he had worry lines on his forehead.

I reached out and rubbed his forehead with my finger, smoothing the lines away. "You shouldn't frown so much. You're going to get worry lines, and I don't think you can have any more strikes against you in the looks department if you want to make it in the music industry. You can barely sing as it is."

He smiled and grabbed my hand still rubbing his forehead, placing it on his chest over his heart.

"I need to do something productive today. I feel like a complete failure in the female department, having you save me more times than I want to count," I said, needing to get out of my room before I listened to my vagina's requests.

"Well, get your ass ready and meet me downstairs. Do your hair and the other shit, so all you have to do is get your work clothes on later."

"Where are we going?" I asked, excitement surging through me.

"Just get ready and meet me in thirty. Hurry your ass up," he commanded.

I hopped off the bed and ran into the bathroom, showering as quickly as I could.

Dressed in a pair of corduroy shorts and a Rob Zombie concert t-shirt, I shoved my feet into a pair of white flip flops. I dried my hair and stuck it in a messy bun. I smacked on some makeup and threw my bag over my shoulder digging out my phone.

Ignoring the three missed calls from a private number, I opened the text from Kill, aware I was almost out of the allotted time Kill gave me.

**I would never tell you
if I did miss you, and
you're obviously too full
of yourself by claiming you're**

333

**awesome. We definitely need
to limit our time apart so
I can keep you from getting
an ego as big as mine.**

I smiled, as yet another piece of my heart leapt out of my chest in search of Kill. Van was on the couch when I made it downstairs.

"Where's Jessie?"

"She went home. Her mom called. She told me to tell you to call her when you wake up." He looked me over with brotherly concern, moving to give me a hug. "Are you good, Faith? Jessie said you looked like death warmed over."

I pulled out of his embrace. "Yep, just not enough sleep, and too much crap. I'm fine, Mr. Snuggles," I said, patting his cheek.

"Ready to go?" Kill asked, coming downstairs.

Van gave him a questioning look. "Jessie said you two were up watching T.V. at all fucking hours of the night. D would kick your ass if he figured out you're corrupting our new superstar with your bad habits."

Van glared at Kill and I felt bad, being it was really my fault, and they didn't know the real reason why I had almost passed out today. So, I stepped in. "It wasn't Kill's fault. I thought I was adapted enough to my new schedule, but I guess I wasn't as good as I thought. He took care of me, and he even got me to agree to do next Tuesday's show at The Note."

Van and Kill both had shock registered on their faces.

"How did he talk you into that?" Van asked, looking at Kill in awe.

"I promised to get her a new pair of shoes."

I opened my mouth to argue, but stopped when Kill raised an eyebrow waiting to see how much I was going to reveal to Van about our weird relationship. I snapped my mouth closed.

"Nice job. You're going to be awesome onstage. We'll practice more tomorrow before you go to work," Van said, squeezing me tightly.

I held my breath, because his strong arms were trying

334

to force it out of me. I tapped his back, and Kill came up behind me.

"Let her go, Van. She isn't as strong as you are. I think she might be tapping out."

"Did I hurt you?" he asked, letting me go.

"Nope, Mr. Snuggles." I got on my tip toes and kissed his cheek, wondering how Jessie could resist him.

"Alright, let's go," Kill snapped.

I gave him a questioning look, making his hard expression change to his half-smile right before my eyes.

"Let's go," I said, wondering what the hell was going through his mind.

"Where are you guys going?" Van asked, going back to lounge on the couch.

"I don't know. He won't tell me."

"Well, let's get out of here so you can find out," Kill replied, taking my hand and pulling me toward the garage.

"Have fun," Van yelled after us. I was barely able to say bye before I was propelled outside.

Kill got in his car after depositing me in the passenger seat, and hit the garage door opener as he started the engine. Jet's truck was parked right behind us.

"Shit!" he exclaimed, taking the keys out of the ignition. "I'll be right back." He jogged over to the truck and moved it out of our way.

Back in the car, we drove to our surprise destination. He saw me eyeing his key ring and gave me a half-smirk.

"I took his keys and made a copy. I'm telling you, the thought of having to see him naked again is motivating."

I was relieved happy-go-lucky Kill was back.

"So, what was that back there?" I asked, knowing I didn't need to clarify.

His jaw clenched, and his dimple flashed. "It was nothing. I'm sorry. I was being stupid, which for some reason seems to be the status quo when I'm with you."

I wanted to ask him more, but I didn't want him to get upset, so I let him have his secrets.

"So, where are we going?" I asked, leaning into the passenger seat and watched the bustling city around me.

"We are going to get you something to eat."

My stomach growled at the mention of food, and he chuckled at the affirmation he just received.

"What are you in the mood for?" he asked, stopping as the metro passed.

"I'm not sure what I want. Are you craving anything?"

His eyes went to my body, lingering on my legs and making them ache with need. I clenched my legs together, making the pressure even worse. He swallowed hard and returned his eyes to the road.

"Actually, I know where we can go," he responded with a smile on his face, his voice unable to fully hide the desire he was trying to mask.

I giggled when we pulled into the parking lot of Incredible John's, which is basically a Chuck E. Cheese on crack.

"Are you up for it?"

"Let's go, Killer."

He intertwined our hands, and pulled me into the insanity of the restaurant. After we filled up on the buffet, Kill practically vibrated in his chair, wanting to go play. I tortured him with the slowest bites in history.

"Come on," he whined, making me laugh at him.

"Go without me," I challenged him. I expected him to jump up and run off without a backward glance.

"They have pinball, and I know you want to get your name on that high score. Don't think I haven't seen you play at Ray's when you have a chance."

At the mention of pinball, I sucked down my drink, while on the move.

"Hell, if I would have known that was going to get you up, I would have mentioned it a while ago."

He swung his arm around my shoulders and led me into the massive play area. He pointed me toward the empty bank of pinball machines. I kissed him on the cheek before I made my way toward the machine I was about to make my bitch.

Satisfied with my high score, I turned around to see Kill standing behind me with a huge grin on his face.

"How long have you been standing there?" I asked,

feeling my cheeks heat up.

He walked slowly up to me, and stopped when we were just inches from each other.

"Well, as a friend, I had to make sure nobody was watching you while you made that machine submit."

My cheeks burned. He laughed at my reaction and put his arm around my shoulder. I tried to push it off, but he kept it firmly over me.

"Sorry, it was adorable though. Come on, I'll let you watch me beat you at air hockey."

"I'm pretty damn good at air hockey, Killer."

As we made our way toward an open table, a little boy ran straight into Kill's leg, sobbing. Kill got down one knee so he could face him.

"Hey, buddy, are you lost?" he asked, soothingly.

The little boy nodded his head, his bottom lip trembling as he tried to hold in his tears.

"My mommy.... I can't find her." He sniffled as big alligator tears streamed down his face.

"Ok, let's see if we can find your mommy. What's her name?" Kill asked, and the little boy looked at him, like he just asked the dumbest question ever.

"Mommy," he replied, hiccupping as he held back another sob.

Kill smiled throwing me a wink over his shoulder. "Ok, buddy, let's go find your mommy. This is my friend, and she has special mommy-seeking powers, so it's a good thing you found us."

The little boy eyed me, trying to determine if I actually had special mommy-seeking skills.

Kill held the little boy's hand, and I took the other. We hadn't made it more than two steps when a woman ran up to us, grabbing the little boy and hugging him tightly.

"I told you not to move, Jack. I was so scared." She picked him up and cuddled him closely.

"Sorry Mommy, I wanted to play the light game," he said, burying his face in her neck.

"Thank you so much. I only took my eyes off him for a second," the mom told us, after verifying her little man was safe.

The little boy smiled at me. "She has special powers that find mommies," he explained, pointing his little chubby finger at me.

Kill chuckled, and pulled me close.

"Thank you so.....Holy shhh....oot," she exclaimed, changing the word that was going to follow holy when she spotted Jack looking at her. "You're Kill, from the JackholeS. I love your band. I went and watched you a month ago for my sister-in-law's bachelorette party." She gushed over Kill's presence, and Jack watched him with curiosity, as his mommy fawned all over the man who saved him.

"I am. I'm glad you like us," Kill replied and rubbed Jack's head. "Alright buddy, stay close to your mommy. I have to go beat this girl at air hockey. It was nice meeting you," Kill said, as Jack's mom just stared at him open-mouthed.

I felt sorry for her, understanding exactly how it felt to be caught in the presence of Kill. She giggled and attempted to push her hair behind her ears while holding onto Jack.

"Bye, thank you for finding my mommy," Jack said, hugging his mommy tightly after he mentioned her name.

"No problem, little buddy."

With that we were back to the air hockey table. I tried not to stare at Kill. The way he had been with Jack, I was absolutely positive he would be an amazing dad when he found the right girl.

My heart stopped beating, from the pain since I would never be that girl. I could never give him, or anyone else, a baby. I quickly shoved the thought away, not wanting Kill to notice my mood change.

We were tied after four games. Kill glanced down at his phone and looked back at me.

"Ok, Cinderella. I have to get you home so you can get to work on time." He dropped his arm around my shoulder.

"Come on, I'll beat you later."

"It's on. Anytime, I'll take you down," I taunted back, making him laugh.

As we drove home, we talked about poor little Jack and his mom. When we turned onto the street, I sat up straight in my chair.

"Shit, I forgot to get the boys dinner," I said, as I mentally went through what I could make in the little time I had before I work.

Kill put his hand on my thigh, and any thoughts I had running through my head went blank from his touch.

"Don't worry. I text them and let them know I would treat them at Ray's tonight after practice."

"You're pretty damn good at this friend thing," I said, and he smiled back at me.

"Yeah. I'm pretty awesome."

I ran upstairs and changed quickly. The boys were on the couch watching T.V. Amy was in her normal place perched on Jet's lap, eating a bag of gummy bears.

"Hey, sexy bitch, you better not sing until I get there."

All I could do was roll my eyes at them. Amy launched a gummy bear at me, and by some miracle I caught it and popped in my mouth. She pulled back to launch another one, but I threw my hands up in surrender.

"Ok, I promise I won't," I said, and she put her arsenal in her mouth, satisfied with my retreat.

"You're so hot when you're bossy," Jet said, pulling her face to his, causing all of us to groan.

"Jessie said she would just meet you at work," Van told me, as I tried to ignore my friend being mauled, and doing some mauling of her own.

"Ok, I have to get going so I won't be late. I'll see you guys tonight."

I felt Kill's presence right before he slung his arm over my shoulder. "You better not sing until we get there," he growled in my ear, causing goose bumps to rise all over my body, and I cursed him in my head, knowing my nipples were now rock hard.

"I won't. Don't miss me too much," I responded, unlocking my car and throwing my bag inside.

He noticed my new shoes. "I'm not going to miss you, but those shoes are a different story. Fuck, those are hot!"

I got into my car, because if I stood by him any longer I wouldn't be able to leave. "Thanks for today, Killer, I had fun.

See you tonight," I said as he gave me his stupid half-smile, making me want to tear his clothes off.

He closed my door as I cranked my engine and drove to work, begging my nipples to calm down.

When I got to work, Jason's car was just leaving the spot where he supposedly worked. Instead of feeling the fear I normally felt, anger welled up in its place. This constant reminder he was still lurking in the background was pathetic.

I wanted to laugh in his face, knowing he was stuck in his perfect persona, and I finally had the upper hand. I tamped down my emotions and crazy daydreams of beating him at his own game, and went to work.

Work went smoothly, and I made sure DJ Smoke didn't add my song to the line-up until Jet came in expressing how fortunate everyone was, he decided to grace them with his presence.

Jessie made a point of ignoring Van, and he watched her like a lost puppy most of the night. When I pulled her aside to ask her if everything was ok, she explained it was harder to see him after talking to her parents. They reminded her of how much they'd been through.

When work was over, my arms were sore from playing air hockey and carrying heavy trays of food all night. After closing up and changing, I dug my keys out of my bag and handed them to Kill, who was at the table, talking with the boys and Catcher.

"Are you ok?" he asked nervously, pulling me to his side.

All of the boys watched me closely, making sure I didn't pass out in front of them.

"I'm fine. I'm just tired. If you don't want to drive, I will," I retorted, pushing him off me and reaching for my keys.

He jerked them away and pulled me back to his side. "Sorry, I told the boys about today, and we're worried about you."

"Don't be. I'm fine. But I'm ready to go home."

Kill tensed when I said home, but his face showed no emotion. "Alright, let's get you home," he replied, turning me around so we could head out of the bar.

"Night guys," I yelled out as Kill put his hand up to wave.

Bambi walked out of the breakroom. She plastered on a fake smile as we walked by.

"Have a good night Faith. Night Kill." She went by us, and I turned my head, trying to see any trace of demon tail or marks to indicate she had been possessed.

"Whatcha looking for, Slick?"

"Trying to see if there's a scar from the exorcism," I replied, turning my head back as we headed toward my car.

Kill tried to turn his laugh into a cough. We got in the car, and as he drove, I was still trying to puzzle out Bambi's new attitude. I thought about tonight and realized she hadn't said anything rude to me.

"What are you thinking about?" Kill asked as I ran through the night again to see if I missed anything.

"I was just thinking how odd it was that Bambi hadn't said anything mean to me. You don't think she's sick?" I asked, the only plausible explanation I could think of.

Kill cleared his throat, looking uncomfortable. I knew right away he had something to do with Bambi's new attitude.

"What did you do?"

He rubbed the back of his neck with his hand, confirming my suspicions. "Don't get mad at me, but I talked to her and told her back off."

I stared at him with my mouth open in shock, pissed he once again rescued me. "I can't believe you did that," I said, my voice barely above a whisper since it had to pass by the lump lodged in my throat.

"Don't be mad," he pleaded as he parked the car and shut off the engine.

"I'm not mad," I replied, telling him the truth. "I'm just wondering how many more times you're going to rescue me before you recognize how one-sided this relationship is."

Kill's face was calm, but his jaw twitched, indicating I struck a nerve, and he was trying to rein in his emotions.

He didn't say a word, making me fidget. I waved my hand back and forth in front of his face. He blinked and caught my hand. He linked our hands and placed them in the middle of us, his jaw still clenched.

"Are you alright?" I asked nervously.

He sighed deeply and threw his head back onto the seat before answering me. "I've already told you I'm not rescuing you, and it bothers me you would think I would keep track. You're my friend, and I want you to be protected. It eats me up inside I wasn't there sooner. This is my selfish way of making me feel better, since I can't do anything to change the past. Please, just accept I'm the most awesome friend you'll ever have, and I'm going to blow your mind with how great I am at this shit."

"Sorry, you're right. I'll stop worrying about you protecting me. It's just hard for me. I'm always waiting for the other shoe to drop and become disappointed. That's my issue, not yours, and I'll stop pushing it on you."

"I'm not going to disappoint you, Slick. I know he's waiting for the right time to come after you. I'm on edge because I don't know when it will happen, I just know it will. But I'll be there, and he will not hurt you again."

My heart lurched, silently begging him to keep his promise. We made our way into the house, both of us going to our rooms and changing before meeting back in the living room. The boys filed in, and once they had made their way upstairs, we snuck into my bed and fell asleep tangled around each other.

# CHAPTER 25

The next day after our run and a much needed shower, I practiced with the boys until deemed worthy. Instead of sitting around watching the rest of the practice, I went upstairs and worked on my thesis.

I was petrified because I was done, and another chapter in my life was ending.

It was lonely working without Kill, and I kept looking over at the empty spot he usually occupied. As I read over everything I had written, I hugged his pillow tightly, inhaling his scent embedded in it.

After dinner, I got ready for work. Amy gave me the same warning, not to sing until they got there, and I agreed so I wouldn't have to dodge any sugary treats.

The night was busier than last week, and some of the customers were there to hear me. A lot of them were men that loved the JackholeS, and were interested in their new female singer. I tried to explain I wasn't the new singer, just backup for a couple of songs, but they didn't seem to care.

Some of the female customers were openly hostile toward me, sneering and making snide comments while I was in hearing range. Most of it was the same insult; I wasn't pretty enough, but the one that bothered me most was the rumor I allowed the whole band to penetrate me at the same time.

I told Ryan, trying to figure out how it was anatomically possible. Ryan was happy to show me, demonstrating with straws how it wouldn't be hard at all. The guy next to me ran off. We watched him walk toward the bathroom with his hands in front of him and laughed when he was out of sight.

"That poor guy. He'll probably have a wet spot on his pants." I tried to chastise her, but I couldn't stop myself from giggling.

"Ahh, I'll over-pour his next beer so you can spill it," Ryan said, causing me to go into another fit of giggles.

"Ryan, you're a saint."

Denise walked by, and I just shook my head, not wanting to explain. When I was on my way back from delivering my drinks, Ryan had her straws back out, and Denise was studying them intently. I decided to wait, already scarred from the first demonstration and not wanting an encore. I caught up to Jessie and walked with her.

"Hey sexy lady, how are you doing?"

Her face deflated. She had bags under her eyes, and I could tell from the amount of concealer around them she'd been crying.

"You need to tell him, Jess."

I was about to say more, but the bell above the door rang, and everyone stopped to wait for Jet's arrival.

"Suck it, bitches. I know you're thirsty for my fame stick," he crowed.

I rolled my eyes as he walked over to the table, with his arm wrapped around Amy. Van saw my arm around Jessie, and his shoulders dropped in defeat. I took their beer to them and kissed Van on the top of the head. He looked up at me with a lost look on his face.

"Ask her to talk to you, but I didn't tell you that."

He smiled and saluted me with his beer.

"I want a kiss, and for you to whisper naughty things in my ear too," Jet whined, already wincing before Amy's hand even connected.

I blew him a kiss. Kill watched me intently, and the ferocious look on his face startled me. I put my arms around his shoulders, feeling the tension radiating off of him.

"Are you ok there, Killer?"

"Yeah, I'm fine, just have a lot on my mind," he responded gruffly.

I let him go when I felt his shoulders relax, and now it was D staring at me intently. Who would have thought living with a bunch of boys would be so full of drama.

I walked over to D, but before I reached him, I caught a glimpse of the table that insinuated I let all four of them in at once. They whispered to each other while pointing at us.

I smirked as I put my arms around D and kissed him on

the cheek, never taking my eyes off of them. D tensed up, and his cheeks turned bright red.

"Come on, Faith, you can't leave me out," Jet said, looking at me with his puppy dog eyes on full blast.

"Well, according to some people, I didn't," I replied, still looking at the table, which was now in a frenzy.

"What's that supposed to mean?" Kill asked, pulling me away from D.

"Is somebody bothering you?" D asked, looking around the bar for the culprit.

Even Van scanned the bar with his face hard and scary.

"Stop. There was some speculation as to the reason I'm singing with you guys, is because I allowed you to....uhmm.." I tried to think of how to describe it, when Jet chimed in.

"That we made you airtight?"

I hoped he wasn't going to describe what he just said, and also made sure there weren't any straws near.

"I'm not sure what that means, but I think, yes," I answered.

Jet moved his hands like he was going to explain, and I stopped him quickly.

"Please don't," I begged, while Kill chuckled next to me.

"You know, we fill every hole, making you airtight."

I could not believe he just said that out loud.

"What's wrong with you?" I asked.

The boys laughed at me, and I knew I was a deep shade of red.

"I was just giving them a show by hugging all of you. Trying to let them know I don't care what they say."

The women were still talking and pointing. Kill got up, and I pushed him back down in his chair.

"Don't," I ordered.

DJ Smoke requested my presence before he could protest. Kill gave me an innocent expression I was not buying.

"Don't let him go over there," I commanded Van and D, before walking up to the stage.

Van and D kept their promise, and didn't let Kill walk over to the table of women, that unfortunately lingered until last call.

When we drove home, I felt exhausted, since I kept one eye on Kill most of the night. The worst part was every time I would check on him, he was staring at me. He would wink when our eyes connected, making it almost impossible to work with the haze of sexual tension between us. My nerves were shot, and I got goose bumps so many times I looked like a plucked chicken.

Van and D loitered longer than normal, and I had to fight to keep my eyes open as we waited them out. When they finally left the living room, Kill and I let out a collective sigh, making us laugh at ourselves.

"Ready?"

"Yes, please," I answered, yawning loudly.

"Don't scream."

I didn't have time to ask him why before he threw me over his shoulder. I bit my lip so I wouldn't make any noise, not wanting our wait to be in vain.

In my room Kill threw me down on the bed, and I held a pillow over my face to muffle my laughter. He jumped on the bed, making me bounce, and I held the pillow even tighter. He snuggled up to me and lifted the pillow so he could talk into my ear.

"What's the matter?"

Wanting revenge, I pulled the pillow off of me and leaned over, licking him on the nose. His eyes went wide, but I put my finger on his lips making sure he kept quiet.

"Alright, Slick," he said, putting out his hands to keep me away from him. He smiled and pulled me into his chest, and put my head down on him. "That tongue's going to be the death of me."

Heat flared between my legs, and I had to work on keeping my breath steady. Repeating silently in my head the stupid word, *friends*. I listened to his heartbeat, unable to fall asleep from the heat surging through my veins.

"Are you asleep?" I whispered, not wanting to wake him up if he was.

"No," he replied, with amusement in his voice. "You know I can't sleep without your snoring."

I bit his chest lightly through his t-shirt.

"I can't sleep," I said, rubbing the spot I had just bit.

"Well, you need to fall asleep so your snores can put me to sleep. What can I do to help?" Kill asked, rubbing his hand up and down my back.

I shrugged, knowing what would calm my body, and too chicken to ask him to quench the desire pulsing through me.

"Do you want me to sing to you?"

"I couldn't do that to you."

"Why? I use you for your snoring so in your own way you are singing me to sleep."

"I don't snore," I grumbled. "But yes, please."

He chuckled into my hair, and sang softly. His voice was incredible. I was so used to him belting out lyrics with intense emotion, hearing him sing softly took my breath away.

I took a deep breath and let it out slowly as he continued. My body liquefied, and I melted into him as his voice calmed me enough to slip into a dreamless sleep.

When I woke up, Kill was gone. I found him downstairs sipping his protein drink.

"Morning, Slick."

On our run, he smacked my ass more than needed, and we were laughing during our cool down.

Jason had been pushed out of my mind, and I felt like I was moving on with my life. Jason's ominous statement he wouldn't give up on me was pushed away every time it tried to surface. I wasn't stupid, I knew my final showdown with Jason was going to happen. I just wasn't going to allow it to ruin my life.

We took showers separately, as much as my vagina begged me to invite him to save water. He came into my room later while I reread everything I had written, making changes here and there before sending it to one of my favorite literature professors to proofread it.

Kill looked over at the bed that wasn't littered with my normal clutter.

"I finished my paper," I answered his silent question. "I've been working on it for a year and a half," I explained.

He smiled at me and hopped onto the bed, leaning

against the headboard, opening his notebook and taking out a pen.

"How do you feel to be on the final leg of something you've been working on for a year and a half?"

"Honestly?" I asked, and he gave me his half-smile.

"Always."

"Scared to death. I've worked on this for so long and have had this concept in my head even longer. To finally be done, to let someone read what I have put together so they can criticize it, and have their own opinions makes me want to vomit. Also, when I turn it in, it will be the end to a crucial part of my life, and I don't know what I'm going to do when I don't have to write it any longer."

He studied me for a moment, taking in everything I just rambled on about. He asked for the truth, so I didn't feel bad unloading.

"Write something else," he answered, like it was the most obvious answer.

"What?"

"I've watched you write, and you're happy when you're lost in your words. I get the same feeling when I'm onstage. Your true passion's writing. Have you ever thought maybe the reason you took so long finishing it was because you enjoyed it so much you didn't want the experience to end?"

My inner voice screamed he was right. I did enjoy putting a paper together. I'd always envied authors that could sit down and write a story so powerful you became lost in the characters.

"What would I write about?" I asked, unable to think any further than his suggestion, but excited at the prospect.

"I don't know. I'm sure you have a story or two in your head you could put down on paper, and make your own." He touched my forehead with his finger and ran it down to the tip of my nose, tapping it.

He turned his attention to his notebook, like he hadn't just blown my mind with an idea. An idea that made me feel as though something essential had just been put into place.

I stared at my computer, no longer reading the words in front of me as my mind turned a mile a minute thinking of the possibilities. I figured I would work in a field revolving around my biology degree, and my literature degree was something to enjoy on the side. The prospect of doing something with it was a notion I had never entertained.

"What are you thinking about?" Kill asked, pulling me out of my thoughts and back to reality.

"That you're right."

"Well, of course I am. I'm always right, but you need to be more specific since the range of my correctness is so vast."

I hit him with a pillow. "I love writing. I love putting my thoughts on paper and seeing them in front of me. I never thought about writing a story, because I never had much of an imagination. When my mom left I had to grow up fast. Every year I would take on more responsibilities, so my dad wouldn't have to work so hard to raise me. Sometimes, I wonder if I wasn't misbehaving to make sure he wouldn't leave me too." I whispered the last part, never actually voicing that out loud.

"I never played with the other kids, and *pretend* was something I didn't have time for. Honestly, you kind of turned the plans for my future upside down."

He shut his notebook and scooted closer to me, pulling me toward him so I was resting on his chest. "That's the most you've ever told me about your childhood. I'm sorry you went through that, but I don't believe for one second you don't have an imagination," he said, running his fingers through my hair.

"I don't want you to feel sorry for me. I had a great childhood. My dad was amazing, and I never wanted for anything. He never asked me to help out, I did that on my own. I don't like talking about it because I don't want pity," I said, trying to get up from his chest.

Having him rescue me was bad enough without pity attached to it. He gently pushed me back down, not letting me get up when all of my instincts told me to run.

"I didn't mean it that way. Stop trying to run away. I just meant I'm sorry you had to go through that, but it has made you the person you are, and you're a strong, smart, beautiful, stubborn, woman with the snore of a lullaby. I would love to hear more about you as a little girl, because I bet you were just as spunky as you are now."

I listened to his words, making sure they were truthful and he wasn't trying to placate me.

"What about your childhood?" I asked, realizing he was right; neither of us had revealed much about our past, and at that moment I was done talking about mine.

"Another time when there's lots of alcohol," Kill replied, turning on the T.V. and finding a comedy.

I shut off my computer and put everything away. Kill's arms were out waiting for me to return and I happily went. We watched T.V., and when I told him I needed to go shopping, he volunteered to drive.

As I cooked dinner, Kill sat at the table with his notebook, he would get up and steal a piece of something I was cooking to test it to make sure I wasn't poisoning his band. After dinner, I went over my three songs, and once they agreed I was ready for the stage, I ran upstairs to get ready for work.

Jessie hadn't been around all day, and I text her to make sure she was doing ok. She called back, frantic because her parents had met a boy they thought would be perfect for her, and she didn't know how to tell them about Van.

It took me awhile to calm her, and I tried to get her to meet me early before work to talk, but she brushed me off. I knew she was avoiding me and I was fuming. Then I realized how hypocritical I was being and gave her a break.

Jason's car wasn't in its normal stalking spot, and fear shot through me. I'd thought I figured out his routine, and with this little change-up, I was wary of what was to come.

Work was packed. Jessie didn't show up until right before her shift, and with the bar being so busy, I was unable to talk to her.

When the boys walked in, everyone cheered, drowning out whatever Jet had prepared. Jet was visibly upset nobody heard his entrance. Van whispered something into his ear that made his eyes light up.

I raced over to Ryan and took the pre-made tray to their table. Kill got up to follow me after I delivered their drinks.

"Hey Slick, it's crazy in here," he said into my ear, causing my body to flush with heat from the warm air of his words on my skin.

"Yeah," I answered him, my voice sounding husky, betraying my thoughts about both of us naked on some sturdy surface, instead of in a busy bar.

His lips turned up at the sound of my breathlessness. "You're hot," he replied, snuggling further into my back so his full length was pressed against me.

My nipples pebbled, making my breasts seem heavy and uncomfortable, confined in my bra. His voice caused the ache associated with Kill's presence to flare to life.

I pulled away, my heart beating wildly, and I flushed from embarrassment, since I could feel dampness between my thighs.

"Friends," I grouched, trying to reprimand him.

"What did I say?" he asked, trying to look innocent, but the half-smile on his face ruined it. "I just said you look hot."

I glared at him. He knew full well what he said, and how he wanted me to interpret it. I glanced over to see one of my tables searching for me. Using this as my escape, I walked over to them and away from Kill.

Jessie kept to the other side of the bar, trying to act like she was too busy to go talk to Van, but I caught her staring at him several times. I curbed the urge to throttle her ass, and kept my tables happy instead.

"Why don't you go over there? You need to talk to him." I finally broke my silence when I caught her at the bar.

"I want to. When I'm with him he makes everything better, but so did Brock," she replied, looking over at Van at the same time he glanced over at her.

He winked at her before going back to his beer, giving her time to come to him.

"Fudge. Why does he have to be so perfect?" she cried softly before heading over to the table, grabbing his face, and kissing him.

When she pulled away, Van had a big smile on his face. Jet put out his hand to get a high five, telling Jessie something I could only assume was extremely inappropriate. The boys made their way onstage. The whole bar gravitated to the dance floor, screaming their undying devotion to them.

Jessie, Denise, and I converged at the bar, slumping on the stools exhausted.

"I'm too damn old for this. I need some rich man to come and sweep me off of my feet," Denise griped, and all of us nodded our head, agreeing a rich man at this moment sounded like heaven.

I spied Bambi across the bar leaning on one of the pool tables, talking to a guy wearing clothes that screamed *I have money*.

"I think she had a bitchectomy. She hasn't been horrid the past couple of days. After a hundred more treatments, she could almost be considered human," Ryan said when she saw me looking over at Bambi.

"Kill talked to her," I admitted.

When I didn't go into further detail, Ryan got pissed. "What did he say? You can't just give us that little gem and not tell us everything you know."

"I don't know what he said. All he told me was she shouldn't be bothering me anymore. I didn't ask what he said, because I was pissed at him for feeling he needed to protect me from a hundred pound, silicone-filled bitch."

"Holy Crap. I would have loved to be there when he talked to her," Jessie giggled.

"That boy has it bad for you," Denise said, and I felt my face heat up.

"We're just friends," I insisted, turning toward the stage, not wanting to look at her stupid, smirking face.

"Shut up, Denise. She doesn't need someone like Kill as her rebound," Jessie said through clenched teeth.

"Honey, I've known that boy for a long time, and he doesn't do friends," Denise replied, ignoring Jessie.

"He's friends with you, and you," I argued with Denise, and I glanced over at Ryan trying to make a point.

"Well, honey, I think I'm too old for that boy, and I was dating someone when I met him."

Ryan was pretending that wiping down the bar was the most interesting thing she had ever done. My eyes went wide.

"Did you....?" I couldn't finish my sentence, wishing I hadn't started it.

"Ryan," Jessie hissed at her, making her finally meet our eyes.

"I never had sex with him," she said, causing my whole body to relax, but the look of guilt on her face told me she still had more to say.

"We made out one night. When I told him I didn't want a one night stand, he stopped immediately, and told me to come back to him when I changed my mind."

Kill glanced over at me as if he could feel my gaze on him, and winked. When I didn't respond back, he gave me a confused face before pouring his attention to the crowd.

"Why didn't you sleep with that boy? He's delicious," Denise asked after Ryan's admission. "Sorry Faith," she apologized.

"We're just friends," I cried a little louder than I meant to, but with the boys onstage and the fans screaming their fidelity to them, it went unheard except for the girls.

"I decided I was sick of one night stands," Ryan answered, as she shook her head looking defeated, but wiped the look off her face quickly. "I want the fairy tale," Ryan admitted, blushing red.

The badass bartender wanted to find true love. I knew we were friends for a reason.

"Ahh, that's so sweet," I cooed, and the other girls giggled as Ryan hit me with a bar towel.

Van started the intro to 'Gotta have Faith,' and my legs trembled as Kill's voice caressed my name. I ignored everyone, except the beautiful man onstage singing to me.

Kill gave me his half-smile, making the crowd go wild. He beckoned me with his finger. Some of the braver audience members touched me, but none of them were bold enough to gather around me, afraid of the wrath Kill would inflict on them.

When I reached the stage Kill hauled me up next to him, making the crowd go insane. I threw my head back and laughed at their exuberance.

"Hey, everybody, I'm so glad you came out to see us tonight. As most of you know, this is Faith, and she fucking rocks."

The crowd screamed, and Kill waited for them to quiet down before he addressed them again.

"We have two new songs we would like to share, and we're going to debut one of them here tonight." After the shouts calmed down, Kill continued, "The other one, we will sing tomorrow night.... if you're interested, that is."

The crowd chanted my name, and my face burned from the attention they gave me.

"I think they want you to sing," Kill responded. "Want to show them what we've been working on?"

"Let's fuck this shit up," Jet cried, causing the audience to go into a frenzy.

The song started and I jumped into it. The crowd fed me their energy, yelling and telling me how much they loved me. Kill winked at me, executing his lyrics to perfection. When the song was over, the whole bar was on their feet screaming and clapping. I laughed, riding the high.

"We're going to take a break. Don't worry, we'll bring her back up before the night ends."

Jet jumped down so he was in the middle of the crowd, soaking up the attention. I was happily surprised when I saw him turn down a pair of underwear with a phone number on it. Van and D hopped off the side stage where they could walk to their table without having to wade through most of the crowd.

"Which way do you want to go?" Kill asked into my ear.

The audience looked at Kill, wanting his attention. Taking a breath, I pointed toward the stairs where he would have to walk past the bulk of the crowd.

"Are you sure?" he asked, the apprehension evident in his voice.

"Yep, I don't want to deny your fans a chance to grope you, although they'll be disappointed if they grab too far down."

I smirked, and he pulled me into his chest and whispered, "I'll get you for that later."

We made our way through the crowd, and I was surprised by how many people wanted to talk to me. When I noticed Jessie and Denise running around like mad women trying to keep up with the crowd, I took off toward the bar taking orders as I went.

The relief in Ryan's eyes made me feel guilty I had procrastinated with Kill, when I should have been working. When all the customers were satisfied, I tried to apologize to the girls.

"I'm so sorry I didn't run straight down here to help you. I promise it won't happen again."

"Shut the fuck up. You did awesome by the way, I just didn't have time to tell you. Besides, if you wouldn't have stopped to talk to them, all of their dumbasses would be crowding my bar and pissing me off," Ryan told me, while her hands moved a mile a minute keeping up with orders.

"You help us more than Bambi, and she doesn't jump onstage in the middle of her shift. Don't ever apologize again," Denise said, heading off to hydrate her parched customers.

"I love you, Faith, and it makes me happy to see you up onstage and not hiding in your hoodie anymore. No more apologizing." Jessie blew me a kiss and headed off with her drinks.

"See, I told you. Now shut the fuck up, take your tray, and do your job, slacker," Ryan ordered.

After the rush, I ran over to check on the boys, since Jessie was in avoidance mode again.

"There's our sexy singer," Van said.

"I've been sitting by you this whole time," Kill responded, making the table groan.

"You fucking rocked it. I swear if I wasn't in love with Candy, I would so be trying to crawl up in you," Jet said, as he kissed Amy on the head and whispered something in her ear, making her blush.

I stared at him with my mouth wide open, and when he looked over at me, he saw the confusion on my face.

"What? Don't act like you don't know I would hit that."

"Did you just say you loved her?" I asked, wondering if he didn't realize.

"Of course I fucking love this girl. She tastes like candy, and I mean everywhere. She's smart and can make me come with a touch. What's not to love?"

"Ahh, baby," Amy cooed, straddling him as she showed

him just how much his words meant to her.

They were oblivious to their surroundings, lost in each other. Jealousy reared up, and I had to tamp that sucker down quickly. I put my elbow on Kill's shoulder, leaning on him giving my feet a rest.

"So are you guys good, or do I need to get you anything before you go back?"

"I need a bottle of water, but don't worry, Slick, I'll get it."

"Don't worry about it. I have to do a last minute check before you go up anyway. I can bring it to you," I said, getting back on my feet. "Van, are you good?"

"Yep," he answered, leaning back in his chair trying to find Jessie.

I didn't bother asking Jet, because he seemed to be fine with Amy all over him. "What about you D?" I asked, noticing he'd been quiet.

"No, I'm good," he replied, dismissing me and turning his attention toward Kill. "So did you hook up with that girl the other night? The one all over you at The Note?"

I tried not to stiffen from the pain that lanced through me.

Kill stared at him sharply before responding, "No, she was too easy. I'm starting to like the ones that are harder to get," Kill ground out through clenched teeth. "You know, I think I'll go with you and get that water."

I didn't argue, but my stomach burned with jealousy, and I bit my tongue hoping to tame it.

He put his arm around me, steering me toward the bar, not letting me get away. His jaw twitched with tension, and his eyes burned with frustration. He looked like the rock star he was, perfect, untouchable, and I ground my teeth in frustration and embarrassment for thinking I would have a chance with him.

"Whatever you're thinking, stop."

One of my tables called me over before I could tell him I was giving myself a dose of reality. They fawned over Kill as I took their order, I tried to slip away, but Kill grabbed my arm, keeping me next to him.

"I have to get back to work," I said, trying to get around him.

"Excuse me, ladies. I have to make sure she gets her work done so she can get back onstage with me." He led me toward the bar when one of the ladies asked him the inevitable.

"Are you guys together?"

"Not yet," he answered.

My heart pounded against my chest. He winked at me as the table sighed.

"Why did you say that? Now they're all going to wonder what's wrong with me for not taking you up on your offer," I huffed out, hitting him in the arm.

"They're already wondering about you, the whole bar is in fact. This way they aren't gossiping about you being a slut," he explained, like it was obvious.

My stupid, hopeful heart dropped like a stone when I realized he was just trying to steer the rumors with a positive spin. I reminded myself he wanted me to give him the first chance, but my heart still hurt. The two conflicting emotions beat each other for supremacy, until I had to suppress them both.

"We need to talk about what D said."

My stomach lurched at the reminder of the girl at The Note, and I walked faster toward Ryan, as if she was a beacon.

"Don't worry about it, Killer. I totally get it, but I do need to get some of these orders in and you need your water."

I ducked out from under his arms right before we reached the bar, and Ryan lifted her eyebrow at me. Kill's face was hard and I could tell he was angry, but he refused to start something in the middle of a crowded bar.

"He needs a bottle of water," I said, taking my full tray.

"Slick, we're going to talk about this later."

I nodded my head as I went by him, not wanting to look at him until I had my emotions under control.

The boys went back onstage, and the dance floor was bombarded with frantic fans, recharged from their break. I smiled as Kill addressed them, hating things couldn't be easy between us.

We had our hang ups, and it was all from our pasts. Until we could overcome the damage inflicted on us, we wouldn't have a chance. If we took our relationship to the next level, he would hold back, waiting for me to run back to Jason, and I wouldn't be able to trust.

I would be waiting for the blow to my heart at every turn. We weren't ready to take that step, but watching him onstage, commanding everything, made it hard to remember the arguments to stay away.

Jessie put her arm around me as we watched Kill. He shot me his half-smile, and my traitorous body returned it.

"They're going to make it soon," Jessie sighed next to me, and I nodded my head.

"Van told me D's trying to get them in the music festival on Thanksgiving. A lot of bands have been discovered there, and he said D heard a couple music industry big wigs have been asking about the JackholeS."

She sounded as dejected as I felt. They worked so hard, and they were such amazing guys, I wouldn't want them to be denied the success they worked for.

"Jess, he wouldn't hurt you; you need to tell him everything. He would understand. You're shredding his heart every time you shut him out."

She shook her head vigorously, and I closed my mouth, knowing it was useless.

"If they play in that concert, they're going to be gone by the end of the year. He'll be surrounded by fame-sucking whores. I can't ask him to stay away from all of that. He wouldn't be a rock star if he kept it in his pants while he was on tour, but I also refuse to share. It's almost July, and Thanksgiving will be here soon. The only reason I told you about Brock is because you're my best friend, and I know you aren't going anywhere. I can't tell him what happened to me, when I can't ensure I'll be with him longer than a couple of months."

Since Jessie had been with Van, he hadn't looked at another girl when they swarmed the table after their sets, or on any other day. Women dressed in practically nothing threw themselves at him, and still his eyes never strayed from Jessie.

"Jessie, nothing's promised, and I get why you don't want to let yourself trust, but if you're ever going to love again, you need to take some chances."

She huffed, but I stopped her. "I get it if you aren't ready, but don't push him away if you have feelings for him. Finding someone special doesn't happen often. If you don't think you can handle it though, you need to let him go."

Kill caught my eye, signaling he was ready for me. He crooked his finger in the *come here* gesture while he finished up his song. I kissed Jessie on the cheek and went toward Kill.

I pulled my shoulders back, and stood up straight as I made my way through the parting crowd. I acknowledged the ones giving me encouragement, and ignored the rest. They didn't know my story and they could never hurt me. I refused to give anyone that power over me again.

Kill pulled me up like it was the most natural thing to do, and using the stairs never occurred to him. Jet gave me a high five.

D stared at me intently. I gave him a small smile not knowing what else to do. I blew Van a kiss. He caught it, pretending to put it in his pocket. Jet yelled he didn't get one. I turned around and blew him one, in which he pretended to catch and rub on his crotch, making everyone go crazy.

Kill pulled me toward the microphone, his arm around my shoulder, and the heat radiating off of him sank into me.

"Are you ready for another dose?" he screamed, and insanity ensued. "Ok, let's get this girl singing. I know you want it."

The crowd went wild over the revamped JackholeS song. When it ended, I made my way toward the stairs, but Kill had me take a bow with him. The boys made sure everyone let me through without a problem. I was bombarded with questions and picture requests, and it seemed like it took hours to get back to the bar where Ryan, Denise, and Jessie waited for me.

"God, you're sexy when you're up there," Ryan said, puckering her lips like she was making out with someone. I giggled and accepted the bottle of water she handed me.

"You really are good, sweetie. What are you doing

waitressing with us when you could be making it big with those boys?" Denise asked when I finished my water.

"Hey! What's wrong with us?" Ryan complained, and Jessie laughed at her offended look.

"Nothing's wrong with you guys, and I like waitressing with you," I responded.

"I like being up onstage, but I couldn't imagine doing it all the time. It's fun messing around, but I don't think I could be as dedicated as they are. It's their dream, not mine. I'll do it as long as they're here at the bar. Oh, and they want me to do a couple of songs next Tuesday at The Note."

"What....No way, they want you to sing with them at The Note?" Jessie sputtered, looking at me like it was the first time she had seen me.

"Yes," I answered, wishing I would have kept my mouth shut because now all of them were staring at me with awe on their faces. "What?" I asked, as the boys announced the next song would be their last.

The crowd begged for more, and Kill laughed at them, telling them they would be back tomorrow.

"The Note's a big deal; a lot of bands have played there. With you up onstage, they're basically stating you're a part of the band," Denise answered.

"I'm not part of their band...." I said, trying to think of how to describe me. "I just make cameos."

"You're in denial," Ryan laughed, mopping down the bar top.

Denise patted my shoulder as I stared at Ryan, trying to think of a good comeback.

"You're more to that band than either of you are willing to admit. Let it progress naturally and go with it. You deserve happiness. And you do too," Denise said, giving Jessie a stern look. "You need to let that poor boy in, Jessie, before I lock you two in a closet."

I felt better now that I was off the hook, as another person got lectured. Amy came out from the middle of the crowd. Her face sweaty from bouncing around supporting her man. I walked over to her as she took Jet's empty seat.

"Hey chickie, do you need anything?" I asked, as she

rummaged through her purse for a bag of cinnamon bears.

"Water," she panted, as she popped a bear into her mouth. I nodded, nabbing one of the spicy candies. I brought her water to her as the boys ended their set and made their way back to the table.

My section was rapidly filling up with sweaty fans. I took their orders as they tried to squeeze in their drinks before last call. Ryan got everything together as we threw our orders at her. I had to wade through the fans surrounding the boys to deliver their drinks. Of course, they were all gorgeous females vying for their attention.

I was proud of myself for not hurting the ones openly staring at Kill. We made eye contact, and I could tell he hadn't forgotten about finishing our earlier conversation.

The bar died down, and I couldn't help the happiness I felt when the girls around the table thinned from the rejections they received. I wouldn't ever get used to having Kill surrounded by gorgeous women. For that reason alone, I would never be able to give him the chance he wanted. I was done making stupid decisions when it came to men.

I lingered at my locker after the bar was shut down, preparing myself for my inevitable showdown with Kill. Sure enough, he stood at the end of the hall when I came walking out. He pushed off the wall, determination on his face.

"Ready?" he asked, putting his arm around my shoulder, not allowing me to respond.

In the car, Kill took my hand, nestling it in his larger one and rested it on my thigh as he spoke.

"Listen. I don't know what the hell D's problem is lately. I have a feeling, and fuck, I hope it isn't what I think, but I didn't do anything with anyone at The Note. I haven't done anything with anyone since I met you." His voice was laced with sincerity.

"But you should," I responded, swallowing the bile caused by that sentence. "You're waiting for me. What if I'm never ready to trust another guy? You're gorgeous, and you shouldn't have to deny yourself anything while you wait for something that may not happen. I don't want you to resent me while you turn down girl after willing girl. I've seen them draped over your table, and I know I can't compare to them anyway."

"Look at me."

I shook my head, refusing to give in. He let go of my hand and put it on my chin, turning me around so I was facing him with my eyes closed.

"Open your eyes or I'll lick you," he threatened, and I could feel him moving closer to me.

When I opened my eyes, his tongue stuck out and he crept in closer.

"I'm not denying myself anything. I've done those girls. I was trying to find something in them and they were willing to let me, even though I knew it was a hopeless cause. You're different, and I feel like when we finally do try, I won't be searching any longer. You're right in saying you don't compare to those girls, because you're so out of their league it's ridiculous to see them try."

My heart beat so hard, I was afraid my sternum would become dislodged from the force of it. I let everything he just told me sink in. The thought crossed my mind that maybe he was too perfect, and Jessie may be on to something. I was confused, not knowing if I could trust my decisions, afraid Jason had permanently ruined me.

"Are you hungry?" he asked, switching the subject.

"I could eat, where to?"

We decided on the all night diner where we had our banana split. It occurred to me he never explained what he was insinuating with D, and it made me curious.

"What do you think is going on with D?" I blurted out when we finished our food.

The smile left his face right before the tick in his jaw started. "It's nothing. Are you ready to go?" he asked, throwing some cash on the table, putting an end to our conversation.

As we drove home, I tried it again. "Are you going to tell me, or am I going to have to torture it out of you?"

"I think I'm going to go with the torture option. It sounds interesting and kinky."

"Come on. You can't just say something like that and not expect me to ask you what the hell you're talking about."

"Can't you just let this one go?"

"No," I answered, and his jaw clenched so tight his dimple stayed on his cheek longer than a flicker.

"I think D has a thing for you," he finally responded, not unclenching his jaw as he spoke, making the words come out harsh.

I laughed at him and rolled my eyes. "D does not have a thing for me, we're just friends," I said, wondering how someone so smart could be so dumb.

"Friends like us?" Kill asked.

"No.... we're different, and you know that. D has never done anything to make me think he wants something more than my friendship. I think you're way off on this one," I responded primly.

I touched his cheek, hoping to alleviate the tension. He sighed loudly, looking at me through tired eyes.

"Like I said, I hope I'm wrong, but I've known D for a long time, and he's never been vicious toward me, or anyone, for that matter. It seems every time you're the subject, he has to throw in a jab. It's not like him, and the only thing I can think of is he has a thing for you." He entangled our hands, letting them rest in between us.

"Are you sure you haven't done something to piss him off? Maybe you messed around with a girl he was hot for, and he's just pissed at you," I tried to reason with him.

Kill gave me his half-smile and squeezed my hand. "Maybe that's what it is," he responded, with no conviction in his voice.

"Are you ready to see if we procrastinated long enough?" he asked, his smile still on his face. He tried to look like he wasn't bothered by our conversation. "Come on, let's get you to bed."

He let go of my hand and jumped out of the car as I reached to get my stuff. Kill opened my door and helped me out. I hoped we wasted enough time, because the thought of cuddling up with Kill sounded like heaven. When we walked in, the T.V. in the living room was on, causing my heart to plummet.

# CHAPTER 26

D was on the couch with his feet propped up on the table. His forehead furrowed when he saw us. "Where have you two been?"

"Kill took me to eat. I was too keyed up to come home right away," I answered, since Kill's jaw seemed to be locked shut.

"Where did you guys go?" D asked, seemingly oblivious to Kill's mood.

"We went to the diner by the bar," I answered, and my body was racked with another vicious yawn.

"Looks like the adrenaline's wearing off. You look like you're about to fall asleep on your feet," D said.

Kill put his arm around my shoulders. There was something in D's eyes that kept me from melting into Kill like I wanted. "Come on, Slick, let's get you to bed."

Kill pulled me in tighter since I wasn't doing it on my own. D studied us, and I had a feeling if I didn't get them away from each other soon, Kill was going to pee on me to mark his territory.

"Come on, Killer. I'm exhausted, and I need to get these shoes off. Night D, see you tomorrow."

I nudged Kill with my shoulder as he walked us toward the stairs.

"Night D, see you later," Kill said in a forced tone.

"Night Faith, have a good night's sleep. You did amazing tonight," D said as we made our way up to my room. "Hey Kill, can you come down here? I want to ask you something."

Kill stopped, his body tensed.

"Go talk to him. I'll get ready for bed and get it nice and warm for you," I said quietly as I shrugged out from under his arm.

Nodding my head toward the living room, I gave him a pointed look before going to my room without him. I pried my shoes off of my feet and put them away, getting my jammies and going to the bathroom.

I tried to listen to music, but my body was too hyper to settle down. The whole interaction downstairs had me keyed up. I switched on the T.V.

I examined all of my conversations with D to see if there was any evidence to support Kill's claim. He did seem to be more hostile toward Kill, but I wasn't positive Kill hadn't done something.

I heard footsteps come upstairs. "Night D," Kill said, before the footsteps continued down the hallway.

I let my breath out slowly. Of course he couldn't just walk in my room with D still up. I settled on a show where a massage therapist gave more than massages, trying to keep my mind from Kill and D.

I was on the second episode when Kill walked in, shutting the door quietly behind him. His half-smile made my heart stutter before restarting and beating wildly.

"Miss me?" he asked, sauntering over to his side of the bed and slipped under the blankets.

"Nope, I was just thinking how nice it was to have the whole bed to myself without you hogging it," I responded, curling into his side as soon as he was settled against the headboard.

"How can you say that when you're basically on top of me the whole night? " he threw back.

I pulled away, so I could check if he was being serious, but his arms banded around me, holding me close.

"I was kidding. I don't think I could sleep without you wrapped around me, snoring in my ear."

I bit him lightly on the chest. "What did D want to talk about?"

"He wanted talk about a song I've been working on. I honestly thought he was going to bring you up," he explained, sighing as he ran his hand over my back.

"I think you're seeing something that isn't there. Maybe you aren't completely used to this friend thing yet."

"What the hell are you watching?" he asked.

I looked over at the screen just as the massage therapists hands slipped under her client's towel. I explained the premise of the show while my body heated.

"What are you thinking?" Kill asked. His voice husky and I knew the risqué behavior on the T.V. was affecting him as well.

"Nothing," I replied quickly, not wanting to tell him what I was picturing doing to him.

"Slick," he commanded, trying to cajole the truth out of me.

"I was thinking those girls are hot, and I need to start running more and maybe stop eating altogether."

"You're wrong," he said, pulling me tighter. "They have nothing on you."

"Ok, I'm not blind, so don't even try and pull that shit on me," I said, sarcasm lacing my voice to disperse the desire his words caused.

"Really, you have no idea how fucking sexy you are. Yeah, those girls are sexy, but look at the makeup they have coated on. I've seen you just out of bed with no makeup and you're gorgeous."

"You think I'm pretty?"

He reached out tracing my face, running his finger gently down my cheek until it rested on my chin. "No," he responded bluntly, and I furrowed my eyebrows, making him chuckle. "I think you're beautiful and sexy."

My heart stopped. He still caressed my face as he gazed into my eyes.

"It upsets me that you don't believe me. Never be surprised people find you attractive inside and out. I hate him every day because he did that to you."

"I think you're beautiful, too." I wanted to stuff the words back into my mouth as soon they left.

He tried to look offended. "I'm manly sexy, but not beautiful. You're going to ruin my reputation if you keep throwing those words around."

"Manly sexy, that's almost as bad as crotchel area."

"Shut up, and watch T.V., besides, I still need to get you back for referencing my crotchel area tonight," he said, sinking further into the bed getting comfortable.

Soon, my eyes were heavy as Kill ran his hand up and

down my back. When the episode ended, Kill turned off the T.V., blanketing the room in darkness.

"Night Slick," he said, kissing the top of my head.

"Night Killer."

I barely got the words out before falling asleep, feeling protected and safe in his arms.

The next morning I woke up alone. I shamelessly grabbed the pillow he slept on and inhaled deeply, wondering if I could bottle his scent and take it with me.

Kill and I went for our run, taking our time just so we could prolong our time together. Near the end, I jumped on his back, letting him carry me into the house.

The guys were on the couch, with Amy sitting on Jet's lap. We were laughing so hard Kill could barely stand up. He leaned my back against the wall, squishing me in the process. I wiggled and tried to get down, but he locked my legs around him.

"Let me down," I ordered, trying to get my legs away from him.

"Say the magic word." I bit his neck, shocking him enough to get out of his grasp.

"You're so dead," he yelled as I took off running upstairs.

When I heard him come after me, I let out a very girly scream. I tried to slam the door and lock it, but Kill was faster. I pushed my full weight against it, but he opened with ease. I couldn't stop laughing long enough to come up with an exit strategy as I ran to the bed.

"I'm sorry," I said, but my hysterical laughing didn't make it sound sincere.

"Oh, you will be." I ran toward the door but he jumped across the bed, catching me around the waist and pulling me down.

"No. Please. Don't. I'm sorry," I begged, trying to get away from him, but I was so weak from laughing, even if he let go, I wouldn't get very far.

I stopped laughing when I saw a red blotch marring his neck. Reaching out I touched the irritated skin. A primitive feeling rushed over me, seeing my mark on him. My body burned, while my vagina begged me to claim his whole body

"I marked you," I whispered, still running my finger over it.

He walked over to the mirror. My passion dissipated as I worried over his reaction. I reached out and hesitantly touched his back.

"I'm sorry. I didn't realize I bit you so hard." I cringed when he turned around, my body automatically waiting for punishment.

Kill reached for me and pulled me to the floor. He straddled me to keep me still, which wasn't hard because I was stunned. He licked his lips and focused on my neck.

"What are you doing?" I asked in a breathless voice. My body tingled from his nearness.

The look on his face made my inner thighs clench, and I could feel my nipples brushing against my sports bra. He bent down and licked my neck, causing my eyes to roll back in my head as I moaned.

I tried to free my hands, wanting to run them over him, but he had them pinned to the floor. He sucked on the spot he had just licked and gently scraped his teeth over it as he slowly released it out of his mouth.

I held back another moan, unsure what was happening, but afraid if I made any noise the moment would be over. He licked the same spot again and sucked the skin back in his mouth.

My whole body was on fire, and I couldn't stop myself from pressing every inch I could against him. He bit down on the skin he'd been teasing and the pain of his teeth pressing into the sensitive skin sent lightning bolts straight in between my legs, causing my hips to jerk up.

When he pulled back, he had desire pulsing in his eyes, and his breath came out in harsh pants. The bulge I'd felt when I moved against him was evidence I wasn't the only one wanting to throw our friendship out the window and rip our clothes off for a marathon sex session.

A slow smile spread across his face. My brain was too hazy to figure out what was happening.

"There, now we match," he said, his voice filled with

lust.

I had to stop myself from wrapping my arms around him and pulling him back so he could lick, suck, or bite on whatever he wanted.

"Match?" I asked, figuring if we got this talk over with, he would get back to what we were in the middle of.

"Yep, look at your neck." He got up and adjusted the bulge in his pants as I shamelessly stared at his hand moving the engorged muscle into a comfortable position.

He chuckled, and my eyes darted up to his amused expression, knowing I'd been caught. Helping me up, he placed me in front of the mirror.

"You marked me?"

"Yep," he answered, pulling me into his chest as I continued to stare at the newly formed hickey.

"Why?"

He shrugged his shoulders, his half-smile was in place, but his eyes were fierce with emotion.

"Kill?" I whispered, watching our reflections in the mirror.

"I've been resisting kissing you since the moment I saw you. I know you don't trust me completely, I can see it in your eyes, but you make me insane. I need you to figure it out soon, Faith. I don't have much restraint left." He kissed the top of my head and moved away from me. "Go take a shower. We want to practice before you go to work."

He left my room with his half-smile on his face. I shook my head, trying to clear the Kill-induced cobwebs. In the shower I begged the water to assist me in understanding what had just happened, while my vagina lectured my eyes to exude trust anytime Kill was around.

After my unhelpful shower, I dressed and made my way downstairs. The boys were on the couch playing a video game. Amy, noticed my new accessory first.

"What happened to your neck?" she asked, causing D to glance up at me, making me turn bright red at his scrutiny.

Jet yelled at D to pay attention, but D's eyes were trained on my neck, and Van paused the game.

"Kill got revenge. I accidentally left a bruise when I bit

him," I answered Amy.

"What the hell did you do that for?" D asked Kill. The hostility in his voice made me flinch.

"It isn't a big deal. It will go away soon enough. Don't be mad at Kill, I started it."

"Well, that was stupid," D said, throwing down his controller and getting up off the couch, done with the game.

Van tried to stop him, but D shrugged him off. He stopped in front of me and inspected the red area.

"Back off, D," Kill growled, and D looked over at him, his eyes burning with anger.

"It's not a big deal," I said, putting my hand on D's arm, getting his attention, not wanting this to escalate even further.

"I don't like seeing marks on your body; it reminds me of what you looked like when you came to us." His face was sad, and I felt unexplained anger shimmer up my spine. How long would I be that girl, the one who allowed her ex to use her as punching bag?

"It's *nothing* like that," I responded, more harshly than I meant to.

Kill bounded off the couch, noticing the change in my demeanor. "What did you say to her?" Kill asked, wrapping his arms around me.

When I saw D's stricken face I pulled away, but not completely, needing Kill's comfort more than I wanted to admit.

"It's ok, D. I understand. Thank you for being such a good friend." He gave me an awkward one arm hug since I was still partially in Kill's grasp.

"No problem, Faith. I'm here for you."

"We have practice in ten minutes," Van said, looking between Kill and D to see if they would object.

"Ok, I just need to get something out of my room." D ran upstairs not looking back.

I stepped back into Kill's embrace, knowing it was weak, but not caring.

"Are you ok, Faith?" Van asked.

I nodded my head.

"What the fuck's happening between you and D, Kill?

You looked like you were going to rip each other's heads off," Jet said.

"He's afraid I'm going to hurt Faith, and I think he just wants to protect her," Kill replied, pulling me even tighter.

Van's eyebrow quirked up, doing some weird boy telepathy with Kill I couldn't hear.

"Are you going to hurt Faith?" Jet asked with a perplexed expression, because he couldn't hear the silent conversation happening between Van and Kill either.

"No, Jet, I'm not going to hurt her," Kill answered through clenched teeth.

"What's going on between you two?" Van asked, finally ending his silent conversation.

"It's nobody's fucking business," Kill growled

"Well, Faith's our business because we'll kick anyone's ass that fucks with her, even yours." Even though Van's words were harsh, he smiled like he was just let in on a secret.

"Enough. Are we ready for practice?" Jet asked, sick of not having any attention focused on him.

"Yep," Kill said, leading me toward the garage, not waiting for the rest of the band.

D was the last to file in. We ran through my three songs, working a little longer on the one that would be debuted tonight. When my part was done, I decided to leave and let them have some quality band time, opting to start dinner.

With everything in the oven I ran upstairs, thinking this would be the perfect time to call my dad. I had a text waiting for me, and my stomach lurched as I rushed to my bottle of Tums.

### I left you something, go
### check your car.
### ALONE.

Jason knew my car was my pride and joy, and if he messed with it, I would be devastated. Walking slowly downstairs, I held onto the railing, not trusting my legs. I seized the doorknob, afraid to turn the handle and see what was waiting for me on the other side. If he did something to my car, I would let the boys have full access to him.

Opening the door, I cried out in relief when I saw my car parked prettily by the curb with no visible damage. I sprinted toward her, checking her over, making sure all of the tires were intact and there weren't any scratches or dents.

The piece of paper under my windshield wipers went unnoticed until I was fully convinced there wasn't any damage. My stomach rolled, causing the boulder to sway back and forth. I snatched the paper and began to unfold it but stopped, wondering if he was watching me.

Returning to the house I held my head up high, not wanting him to see how affected I was by his new tactic if he was still lurking about. In my room I locked the door, knowing the boys were going to be wrapping up soon, and I needed to get myself together. I unfolded Jason's new means of ruining my life.

**You were always meant to be mine. I will wait for you to be done with whatever this little rebellion is you have going on, but don't make me wait too long for you, Faith, my patience has started to wear thin. You are a good girl, and I will be with you, you are mine.**

As I read it, my anger rose. He was fucking delusional if he thought I would come back to my senses and return to him. I couldn't show this to Kill, because in some bizarre way this would solidify his fear of me returning to Jason.

Shoving the note into the bottom of my t-shirt drawer, I slammed it harder than I needed to, with a new conviction that I would prove them both wrong.

They jumped on dinner like ravenous animals as soon as they exited the garage. I poked at my food. Kill watched me walk out of the kitchen after depositing my plate in the dishwasher. I planned to play off my sour mood by explaining I was nervous about the new song.

372

I went into my room, avoiding the dresser drawer. The note mocked me as I tried to figure out what to do. I wondered if I should go to the police, but figured they would consider it circumstantial, and with my last encounter, I really didn't have much confidence in them.

I chucked a handful of Tums in my mouth as I headed to the bathroom. The spot on my neck remained cover-up free, because in some sick way I liked that Kill claimed some portion of me. Pathetic, table for one.

Kill sat on the toilet, watching as I curled my hair.

"Can I help you?" I asked, when I was done with my hair.

I bent over the sink to get a better look as I applied my eyeliner, taking more care than I normally did so I didn't have to look him in the eye.

"What's going on with you, Slick?"

"What do you mean?"

He sighed and placed his elbows on his knees, running his fingers through his hair. I was purposely being obtuse, and I felt bad because it wasn't his fault.

"You barely ate anything and your face is paler than normal. Explain."

I cursed myself for never investing more money in makeup so I would have more to do. I leaned on the wall behind me so I could look at him.

"Nothing's up with me. I'm fine, except I'm a little nervous about tonight's performance. The high note is really high."

He knew I was lying, and I held my breath, waiting for him to call me out on it.

"The high note's nothing and you know it. Tell me what's going on with you."

I smiled sadly, loving he called me out on my shit, even though I wished he wouldn't.

"Jason contacted me today, and I was upset he still hasn't given up."

His jaw twitched, and his eyes were fierce with anger. "What did he say? Where's your phone?"

I went over to him, so he couldn't get up without

373

running me over. "I erased it after I read it. It was the same old stuff he's been saying since we've been together. It just got to me today, that's all."

His eyes flashed with fury, and he stood so we were inches apart. "Why are you erasing those? You're removing any proof he's still contacting you and going against the restraining order."

His jaw twitched furiously, his dimples appearing and disappearing quickly. My anger rose along with his. I was frustrated from today's events, and seeing a proper outlet for venting, I gave it to him.

"I erased it because it came from a blocked number like normal, and I was angry he's still trying to have some say in my life. I'm so sorry I don't want to keep that shit on my phone. Please forgive me, next time I want to remove something off my phone, I'll be sure to ask you first."

I was on my tip toes so I could be closer to his face.

"Fuck, why can't you let anyone help you? I just want to help you. We're friends, remember?"

His face was bright red, and he was bent toward me just as much as I was, our noses were almost touching. I opened my mouth to yell right back at him, but my stomach decided this was the perfect time to twinge, and I winced, wrapping my arms around myself.

The anger on Kill's face vanished, and he pulled me tightly into his body, rubbing my back. "I'm sorry. I didn't mean to yell at you. I was being stupid, I didn't mean to scare you."

"I wasn't scared of you. I'm just so sick of everyone feeling like they need to protect me. I'm a big girl and I can take care of myself," I said, muffled into his t-shirt.

"Well, you're going to have to get used to it. When we love someone, we take care of them, and you're a part of our family and our band. Can we please stop having this conversation? It's getting old."

He was right, and I needed to get over my hang ups about accepting help. It was harder than I expected, knowing anyone I decided to trust had the ability to let me down.

"You're right," I said into his shirt, not wanting to move from his embrace.

"I'm always right. You just haven't figured it out yet. Let us help you. You're stuck with us," he said releasing me.

"I feel sorry for you guys because you're stuck with me."

He made a face feigning horror. "Oh, geez, you're right. We totally got the bad end of the stick."

I pushed him, and he pretended to fall over, making me roll my eyes. "I have to go. I can't be late for work. I'm sorry I erased it, but it was a silly text message, and honestly the more he contacts me, the more likely he is to get caught and blow his cover."

His jaw was so tight I worried about his back teeth. I wrapped my arms around his waist. His body was rigid, so I hugged him tighter until I finally felt him relax.

"We just worry about you, that's all."

"Well, I appreciate you guys worry about me, but it's uncalled for. And I'm not part of the band," I said, wanting to get this straight.

"Ok, you have songs you sing with us, you practice with us, and you get onstage with us. What the hell was I thinking, saying you're a part of the band?"

I smiled at his sarcasm and bit him lightly on his rock-hard pec. He tensed up, and I wondered if I bit him harder than I thought, but when he shifted his lower body away from mine so he could hide his reaction, I realized what my teeth did.

"Get ready for work; you don't want to be late."

We went into my room, and he sat on my bed as I grabbed everything I needed.

"Why's my pillow on your side of the bed?" he asked.

"How do you know which one's your pillow?" I asked, buying time as I thought of a plausible excuse, my face flooding red from his discovery.

"Because it doesn't smell like you," he said, throwing the wrong pillow back to his side and laying back down on the one I used.

"Well, if you think about it, I really don't use a pillow since you have started sleeping over," I said, cocking an eyebrow at him, hoping to get out of this with some dignity.

He grinned at me and plumped the pillow higher under

his head. "I like to take naps on the pillow that smells like you. Since I don't get your snoring it's a consolation prize."

"You take naps in here?" I asked, floored he lounged around in here without me.

"Sometimes, not very often," he answered, not meeting my eyes, and if I didn't know better I would think he was embarrassed.

"Why don't you sleep in your room?" I asked.

He just shrugged his shoulders. I noticed it was time for me to go.

"See you later, Killer," I called out walking out of my room, but instead of staying put, he followed me down.

"What are you doing?" I asked, as we got to the bottom of the steps. I waved goodbye to the guys and Amy as we headed toward the door.

"Walking you to your car," he answered, putting his arm around me.

"You don't have to walk me to my car." I said, scanning my windshield quickly to make sure there wasn't anything there.

"What are you looking for?"

"Nothing, I was just love my car," I said, guilt eating away at my stomach as my head screamed I was a horrible liar.

"See you later, unless you want me to drive you?" he asked, and the hopeful look on his face made me want to take him up on the offer.

"No, I'm fine, go take a nap on my pillow and I'll see you tonight."

His face dropped, and he didn't do anything to hide it. "See you tonight." He kissed my forehead. I reveled in the tingling sensation his lips left on my skin.

"See you later, Killer."

# CHAPTER 27

On the drive to work, I fished out my Tums, pleading with my stomach to behave.

The rumor mill was on high as people tried to guess what my relationship to Kill was. The speculation was downright disturbing. Jet came in later doing his normal entrance.

While they made their way to the table, I grabbed the pre-made tray and delivered it before they reached their table, so I could avoid Kill a while bit longer.

I wasn't sure why I was avoiding him. I was becoming increasingly dependent on Kill, which terrified me.

My depending on people didn't happen very often because they either left like my mother, or they hurt me like Jason. As I delivered a tray of appletini's and cheese fries, I felt Kill's presence behind me. The electric current between us never seemed to diminish.

"Hey Slick."

I turned around to see him staring at the floor, rubbing the back of his neck with his hand. My heart flipped his face was so unsure.

"Hey."

It was my fault things were awkward between us. He'd laid it all out for me; it was me holding us back. He wanted me to trust him completely, and I wasn't sure I would ever be able to give him that.

His face lightened when I smiled, and I wanted to kick myself in the ass for doing this to him. I was just as bad as Jessie.

"People are wondering how long I'm going to let you work here. You know, since you're pregnant with our love child."

I noticed the people nearest us watched us intently.

"The sad thing is, that isn't the worst one I've heard

tonight," I replied amused.

"Oh, I know, but it's my favorite one," he said, winking at me before walking away, as I stared at him with my mouth hanging open.

"Oh my God, you're pregnant," the lady closest to me whispered loudly.

"Nope, sorry guys," I said, turning around and walking back to the bar.

"Don't worry, honey, we won't tell anyone," the lady that was supposed to keep my secret loudly drunk whispered.

"What was that all about?" Denise asked, her honey eyes curious.

"They think I'm having Kill's baby," I said with disgust in my voice, trying to hide the hurt.

When Kill said me having his baby was his favorite rumor, for a split second I was excited, before reality crashed down. If we ever moved forward from this friendship to something more it would never happen.

"Is that such a bad thing?" Denise asked, confused at the vehemence evident in my voice.

I opened my mouth, then shut it, not wanting to confess anything. Denise patted me on the shoulder as we finally made it to the bar.

"What the hell's on your neck?" Ryan asked when she saw me.

I swatted my neck like a cracked out ninja, trying to get whatever the hell had made Ryan's face look that horrified, off immediately. Denise caught my swatting hands and held them firmly in hers.

"The hickey," she said, letting go of my hands so she could point at the spot which held everyone's attention. Ryan leaned further across the bar to get a good look at it.

"It's not a hickey," I hissed, giving the people at the bar my best evil eye so they would mind their fucking business.

"What are you talking about?" Jessie came over, giving Ryan her orders even though Ryan made no attempt to start filling them.

"Faith's hickey," Ryan replied.

"It's not a hickey," I said, keeping my voice low. "I'll

explain later. Let's just get this last order out before the boys are done setting up."

Ryan and Jessie glared at me, making sure I was not trying to get out of my duty to dish. Denise patted me on the shoulder but helped me out. "Come on girls, let's finish this up so we can get the dirt."

This spurred Ryan into action, and she made all of our orders and screamed at poor Dax in the kitchen. We set off to deliver our orders. I moved back to the bar slowly, not wanting to relay the events of how the non-hickey was formed.

"So?" Ryan said, when I didn't launch into the details right away.

I was positive the stories they'd conjured in their heads were going to be a lot saucier than the real one, because there was no way in hell I was going to tell them exactly how Kill felt on top of me; sucking, licking, and biting, while he placed the damn thing on my neck.

"It's not a hickey," I reiterated, and Jessie moved her hand like she was trying to hurry me up. "It's more of a revenge mark," I explained, making Ryan's and Denise's eyes light up.

"That sounds hot. Who gave it to you?" Ryan asked, making me laugh at her eagerness.

"After our run, Kill gave me a piggy back ride into the house."

"Oh yeah, Kill all sweaty," Ryan said, and Denise fanned herself.

"Kill gave that to you?" Jessie screeched, eyeing the stage as he thanked the crowd.

"Let me finish," I said, assuming the thought of sweaty Kill got these girls hotter than watching him onstage.

"He pinned me to the wall, and wouldn't let me down so I bit him. It left a mark, so he decided to give me a matching one." I shrugged like it wasn't a big deal, and I wasn't getting turned on thinking about him hovering over me.

"You two are so hot for each other, you need to just fuck and get it over with," Ryan said, disappointed I didn't give her a better story.

"What? No, she needs to stay away from him," Jessie

said shocked Ryan would suggest anything between me and Kill.

"It's going to happen eventually," Denise chimed in.

The three of them discussing my life as if I wasn't there, or didn't have enough common sense to make my own decisions, had anger running through me.

"Hello, still right here."

"Sorry honey, your relationship with him just confuses us, that's all," Denise explained watching the boys as they played. The crowd jumped up and down screaming at them.

"You aren't the only one," I mumbled, under my breath.

"You just got away from that scum bag, I don't want to see you get hurt, especially by a musician," Jessie said, wrapping her arm around my waist.

"But she can have fun, and who's to say he won't fall madly in love with her and they won't get married and have dozens of gorgeous babies," Ryan threw back at Jessie, and I stiffened hearing the "b" word again.

I was saved from continuing the conversation when Kill segued into 'Gotta Have Faith.'

I didn't bother with the stairs, walking straight toward Kill. There were a couple of cat calls from the audience, and some shouted a request for us to kiss. Kill winked at me, showing me he had no problem kissing me. I rolled my eyes, not knowing what else to do.

Van started the intro to my first song, and I was thankful I had something to concentrate on instead of the perfect fullness of Kill's lips. When the last note faded, I moved away, but Kill pulled me back toward the microphone.

"Where are you off to so quick?" he asked, and the crowd yelled out suggestions on what they thought we should do.

"I thought you were done with me," I answered, making the crowd frantic.

"Not nearly," he said, and I was embarrassed how turned on I was.

The insides of my legs were wet from our banter. He knew exactly what he was doing to me.

"Are we doing another one with Faith?" D asked.

Kill clenched his jaws but recovered quickly, and nodded his head as Van began the song we debuted last night. When it finished, I peeked at Kill, wondering if we were going to do the last song right now. He explained to everyone, including me, we would perform the newest song later. The crowd's reaction was mixed emotions, some were boo's, while others were uncontrollable screaming.

"All right, you're off the hook. Now get your sexy ass to work."

I pretended to glare at him, and the whole crowd went crazy, some of them liking the dominant tone, while others told me to kick his ass.

"Just kidding. You know I wouldn't make you work unless you wanted to."

He glanced down at my stomach quickly, and everyone erupted at the implication he just made. The sea of people parted for me, not wanting to hurt Kill's baby momma. When I finally made it to the edge of the crowd, I glanced over to see Kill watching my progress while he sang. He winked, and I gave him the finger.

The girls stared at me with open mouths. Bambi's gaze was glued to my stomach, trying to become the first naked eye ultrasound tech.

"What the hell's going on?" Ryan questioned.

"Nothing, Kill's fueling the rumors so more people will come to the shows," I said, as they all glanced at the packed bar unconvinced. "Ok, I don't know. If you want to know why Kill's playing this game, then you're going to have to ask him," I said, sounding bitchier than I meant to. "Sorry, I really don't know what's going through that boy's head," I grumbled.

Bambi rolled her eyes and walked off, pissed she didn't get more of a story.

The boys ended their set, and Kill hopped offstage into the middle of the fray along with Jet. Everyone rushed him, trying to get more information about our supposed love child.

When he caught my eye, he winked at me with that damn infuriating smile. I took the tray Ryan had made up for them and stalked over to the table. I was surprised most of the skanks normally circling the table weren't around.

"Hey Slick," he said, taking his beer while putting his arm around my shoulder.

"Why did you do that?" I asked him, keeping my voice low so nobody could hear us.

"To keep the girls at bay. It's exhausting having to tell them no night after night. I figured if they thought I had something going on with the hot new girl in our band, they would back off. Besides we are going to happen eventually."

Tears flooded my eyes. He pulled me into his chest so my face was buried in it before quietly asking me. "Is it so bad, Slick?"

One rogue tear spilled over the edge of my eyelid soaking into his t-shirt. "I can't have kids," I admitted, and blinked rapidly, not letting any more tears fall.

His whole body went still, and my heart fractured, prolonging him from owning it completely. I pulled out of his grasp, running off into the busy crowd to do my job.

The boy's finally went back onstage, and everyone abandoned their seats to get closer. I went to the bathroom, taking my time.

Jessie came in looking concerned. "Are you ok, Faith?"

My bottom lip trembled, and I bit it to make it stop. Jessie ran over and put her arms around me. I glanced at the ceiling, hoping gravity was working inside the bathroom.

"I can't have kids," I blurted, knowing how stupid it sounded in the middle of a dirty bathroom, but I had to get it out or I would never tell her.

"Oh, Faith...."

I stopped her before she could give me the condolences I couldn't handle. "Don't be nice to me."

She looked at me, making sure I hadn't lost my mind completely.

"I can't handle you being nice to me. I still need to finish working, and I have to get onstage soon. I need to hold it together, so please don't be nice to me right now," I pleaded.

"Fine, get your butt back to work. Who do you think you are taking a break when we aren't busy in the least? Other people have worries too. Look how stressful Bambi has it, having to be a bitch all the time. It has to be exhausting, poor thing; bless her heart."

"I love you, and you said bitch," I said, putting my arm around her as we made our way out of the bathroom.

"I know, you made me resort to the big guns."

I could feel Kill's eyes on me as soon as we rounded the corner. Kill eventually called me, and when he pulled me up, he held me longer than necessary. He had the fans in a frenzy as he introduced the new song. When everyone was foaming at the mouth from excitement, Van started and I lost myself in the song.

When the set ended, Kill wouldn't let me leave while he ended the performance. He walked with me offstage, not letting me get far away. The boys watched Kill's behavior and when we finally got through the drunken crowd and to the table, they pounced.

"What's wrong, Faith. Is Jason bothering you?" Van asked, scanning the bar and stopping for a second when his eyes landed on Jessie.

"No, I just didn't get much sleep last night," I responded lamely.

"Sit down a second," D said, getting up to offer me his seat.

Jet and Amy watched me, and I knew Amy wanted to call my bullshit, but she wouldn't because she was a good friend.

"I need to go help with the last call rush."

"We can finish it up for you." Jet said, starting to get up.

I pictured the mess he would make, and I gave a real smile. "No, I got it."

Kill's arm was still around my shoulder, and I shrugged out of it, lifting up on my toes and kissing him on the cheek.

"You guys are awesome," I said. My new protective family was amazing.

"I know," Jet replied.

I was ready to go home as soon as the bar was shut down, but not ready to have to face Kill's questions. Kill hadn't said a word since we closed the bar down and the silence was suffocating.

"What are you thinking about?" I finally caved.

I had always been able to talk to him easily, and the awkwardness between us felt wrong.

"I'm upset you didn't ask me if I was hungry. We drove by like a dozen food places, and you didn't stop at one."

At a red light, I stared at him, shocked. The pout on his face made me laugh. Verifying the road was empty, I made an illegal u-turn, pulling into the first fast food place I saw.

I ordered for myself and waited for him to give me his order. Instead of telling me, he leaned over me and gave his order to the crackly box.

My nipples hardened at his nearness and I had to regulate my breathing. When I got back to the same stop light, he still had a pout on his face.

"What?" I asked exasperated.

"I wanted McDonalds."

I rolled my eyes and the light finally turned green.

Van's car wasn't there, and I hoped Jessie was finally opening up to him. Jet's truck was also gone, and there was no telling what he and Amy were up to.

"We should have called D to ask him if he wanted something," I said as we got out of the car.

"Nah, he only eats at McDonalds. I was going to get him something there, but you refused to go."

Unsure why he wasn't bombarding me with a million and one questions, I was grateful he tried to make me laugh instead of letting me dwell on it.

"Well that's good, because I was going to offer him your food," I said.

He gripped the bags, pulling them to his chest and looking offended. "You're a bad person."

D was on the couch on his phone. We rummaged through the bags on the kitchen table, and D got up and walked upstairs.

"Well, since we kicked him out, want to eat in the living room?" Kill asked, already taking his food to the couch.

"Take me to bed or lose me forever." Kill said, reaching for the remote and turning off the T.V.

"Did you just quote '*Top Gun*'?" I asked, making my way toward him.

"Yep, go get ready for bed, and I'll lock up the house," he said, slapping me on the ass softly.

I didn't know how he was able to turn my night around, but I was going to go to bed happier because of him.

After I crawled into bed, Kill opened my door, but D stopped him. "What are you doing?" he asked Kill, and I held my breath, trying to hear everything over my breathing.

"She wasn't feeling good, so I was just checking on her before I went to bed."

"You need to leave her alone, Kill. She isn't just one of your conquests you drop once you get her. You can't fuck with her like the other ones. I won't let you hurt her."

I closed my eyes, wondering how stupid I was being for letting him sleep in my bed, stealing a little piece of my heart hourly.

"Mind your fucking business," Kill responded, through clenched teeth.

What was left of my heart plummeted to my feet. I wasn't expecting him to confess his undying love for me, but the fact he didn't even try to correct D was painful.

My door clicked shut, confirming Kill hadn't come in. I tried to watch T.V., but the stupid screen was blurry from unshed tears. I gave up, putting my ear buds in and turning the volume up to let my mind get lost in the rapid beat.

After an absurd number of songs I drifted off to sleep. I was startled when my bed dipped down as Kill got in with me. Neither of us reached for the other as we normally did. Kill shifted next to me as he pulled the ear bud out of my ear.

"Don't listen to him Slick," he whispered, as tears tracked down the sides of my face to hit my pillow. "Shit," he whispered, pulling me to him. I went willingly. He owned my heart, and denying him would be impossible.

"When you're ready, just give me a fair chance. Please, don't let everything you have heard color your judgment before I can even prove myself."

"I'll try," I told him truthfully.

He sighed, taking out my other ear bud and turning off my iPod. His heart beat was now the music I fell asleep to, and so far, I hadn't heard a better lullaby.

385

# CHAPTER 28

The next day it took a while for us to get our normal banter back. We went shopping to get out of the house.

Later a text informed me of another note on my car. I searched the block to see if anyone watched me, but it was clear. It was a picture of Kill kissing my forehead after one of our runs Kill's face was burned away. Under the picture was scrawled.

**You are mine.**

I shivered as I stuffed it in the back pocket of my jeans. I didn't want to be scared. How could Jason still dictate my life? I'd convinced myself I was safe, and Jason was stuck in the cage he had made for himself. It seemed he was flexing the bars more each day.

I slipped it in my drawer with the other note and went downstairs to practice and get dinner ready.

Work was slow, so all of us girls convened together at the bar to gossip. The boys came in later, Jet announcing the king had arrived. The night crawled, and I was so glad when it was over, and I would have two days off. The next two days Kill and I hung out.

I didn't get another letter until the day I was supposed to sing at The Note. It was another picture of me and Kill. This time while we were running, and Kill was smacking my ass. It pissed me off Jason would take something that was ours and soil it. I crumpled the picture and stored it with the others, wondering if I could do something with them if I got enough proof.

My nerves were on edge from the threats and my looming performance. Jessie came over to dress me properly. She wanted me in a dress, but I got her to agree to a pair of tight shiny jeans, and a red halter top.

Jessie curled my hair, pinning the top part with a red

flower. She made it reminiscent of a pin up girl, complete with the bright red lipstick.

When we arrived at The Note, there was a line winding around the building. Luckily, I stashed a bottle of Tums in my bag. We went through the back door, avoiding the line altogether.

Amy beelined it to the bar, on a mission for another blue note, and Jet kissed her, telling her he wouldn't drink tonight so he could take care of her. It was weird to see them together. The love shining in their eyes was undeniable. I couldn't understand how they could have the healthiest relationship out of all of us.

I was mortified when I saw Robert and his friends at the same table as last time. I turned around quickly before he saw me and ran right into Kill.

"What's up?" he asked, his voice tense.

"It's Robert," I whispered using my eyes to point to the table where Robert was.

Kill's face split into a wide grin. He put his arm around my shoulder, pulling me close.

When we reached the table, he didn't let me go like I expected. Instead he kissed me on the top of my head and held on. Jessie glared at me, and I was certain she was going to break into the *lecture Faith* portion of the night soon.

Kill nodded his head toward Robert and his friends. I giggled nervously when the boys registered who Kill was nodding toward.

"Do you want to move?" Van asked, moving in between me and the table to block my view from Robert.

"I don't know. I don't think he'll come over here. I embarrassed him by walking out of the restaurant instead of finishing the date." I shrugged under the weight of Kill's arm, but not enough to dislodge it.

A slow smile spread over Jet's face. "He just noticed us. He can't see Faith because Van's blocking her, but he knows you're here," Jet said, rubbing his hands together like this was the best thing that had happened to him all day.

"Well, he knew we were playing tonight, and he knows I'm protective of Slick," Kill said. His voice was light but he held me tight, proving he wasn't as laid back as he pretended to be.

Amy came back with her ridiculous blue drink, sipping on it happily, with no clue of the drama around her.

"You're driving home tonight, Killer." I snatched one of the many straws in Amy's drink and took a huge gulp.

Amy smiled, happy to provide sugar and alcohol to friends.

"Don't go too overboard, or at least not until you've finished your set, and even then, I still wouldn't recommend it because you'll be watched since you're with the band," D said in his *I am the manager* voice.

"I'm not, D, I'm just trying to relax, don't worry. I wouldn't do anything to purposely embarrass me or the band."

"Sorry, I didn't mean to say it like that. Forgive me?" He gave me a shy smile, and I returned a weak smile back, pawing for the straw again.

"She's good D, I've got her. You don't have to worry about her," Kill said, once again trying to keep his voice light, which was not matching his body language.

"I know she's fine, but we all worry about her, Kill." D said, his voice pitched high and his face bright red.

Van changed his stance in between me and Robert's table and went over to stand near D. He shot Kill a look behind D's back, trying to get him to stop the pissing contest they were locked in.

Kill sighed heavily. "I know, D. I didn't mean anything by it. I'm just a little on edge. When I went to pick her up his hands were all over her, and it pissed me off."

D's face faded back his normal color, and I took another sip, wishing I could disappear. Kill led me to a chair far away from Amy's drink. She was right; it tasted like candy. I wasn't sure if it was the sugar or the alcohol running through me that made me giggle.

I bit my bottom lip to keep myself under control, so I didn't get in trouble with D. Kill's eyes glittered with laughter and his face broke me, and I giggled harder.

A chair near us fell over. I turned toward the noise and saw Robert pick up his chair and storm off. He was swallowed by the crowd his friends looked at our table accusingly.

Kill moved like he was going over to them and Van shifted, ready to follow, but I held Kill in place. His cheeks twitched from the pressure of clenching his jaw.

"They're not worth it; I don't give a shit what they're saying about me. Go get ready for the show, and I'll meet you up there soon."

Kill shot them a death glare, in fact the whole table was giving them a similar look, even little Amy glared at them over her fish bowl. He put his hands on my shoulders and kneaded them gently. I leaned into his touch, craving it like a drug, and too weak to refuse a free hit.

Not as many girls came over to offer themselves as sacrificial lambs as they had at Ray's, and I was relieved I didn't have to deal with them.

I sat back with a grin just as enraptured with Kill as the rest of the place. Kill introduced me after he sang 'Gotta Have Faith.'

I waved to the insane crowd, laughing at some of the things they were willing to say, and do, to get the band's attention. When the song was over, the fans were on the verge of pandemonium, and I received some marriage proposals from men and women in the crowd.

We made our way to the table with Kill and Van in front, muscling most of the people back, but also trying to give them the respect they deserved for being such loyal fans.

Once we made it to the table, the drinks I stole out of Amy's fish bowl were pressing down on my bladder. I excused myself and went to the bathroom, figuring my bladder would be pushed to the breaking point waiting in the long line.

As I suspected, the line was down the hallway, so I settled in behind some drunk girls that appeared they were going to do some experimenting with their sexuality later. They kept touching and complimenting each other.

I turned my head to people watch, trying to give the experimenters some privacy. One of the guys at Robert's table spotted me as he came out of the men's bathroom, with the non-existent line, I might add.

I glanced away and noticed the two girls in front of me weren't waiting until later, and had their tongues stuck down one another's throats. I tried not to stare, afraid I'd look like a freak voyeur watching two people get down in public.

There was a tap on my shoulder. Robert's friend was now standing next to me, I realized my luck was not going well tonight, and I worried what that meant for my straining bladder.

He became distracted by the two girls, who were now dry humping against the wall. A gap had formed in front of them, and I tapped on their shoulders to tell them to move ahead.

One of the girls turned her head and glared at me, so I just stepped around them, crossing my legs together, about to do the potty dance. Smarmy guy broke his gaze from the two girls and followed me, glancing back to make sure they hadn't progressed.

"So, Robert told me you're Kill's girl, but you guys don't mind sharing, and I just wanted to introduce myself." He held out his hand as I stared at him, my bladder forgotten for a second.

"He told you what?" I asked, venom dripping off my tongue.

Someone behind me yelled that if I didn't start moving, they were going to pee on me. Thankfully I was next for the bathroom. Shaking my head, I ignored his outstretched hand.

I barely made it, and for a moment everything was forgotten except the feeling of relief. It had taken me so long to get into the bathroom the boys were already onstage, and Kill had the crowd fired up.

Taking Amy's almost empty fish bowl, I finished it, letting the sugar and alcohol wind through me, wanting to get the giggles back.

"Are you alright, Faith?" Jessie asked, scooting closer to me so she could hear me over the noise.

"Yeah, I'm fine," I lied, and by the look on her face she knew it. "I don't want to talk about it, Jess, but I promise it's nothing," I said, not wanting to get into it.

"Alright, but I'm here if you want to talk," she said, patting the hand clenched around Amy's now empty drink.

I looked at Amy sheepishly and handed her back her

glass. "It's good isn't it?" Amy asked, not caring I had mooched her alcohol all night.

"Yeah, it's pretty good for Smurf pee," I answered.

A horrified expression crossed Amy's face. "Do you think Smurfette has a blue period?"

Unable to even start to pretend to understand where she got her ideas, I started laughing. It was so much better to laugh than mope around with drama I had no control over, so I decided to go further.

"I don't know, do you think their cum's blue?"

Jessie tried not to laugh, or get in our conversation in order to maintain her southern belle status, but she couldn't stop herself from giggling. Kill was trying to see what we were laughing at from onstage. D looked at me concerned, and I'm sure he saw me down the rest of Amy's drink.

"Are we going to be able to coax you back up onstage? You look like you're having a damn good time over there," Kill asked over the microphone, making most of the people on the dance floor turn their heads.

I waved at Kill and blew him a kiss, thinking maybe I drank a little too much after all. Kill threw his head back and laughed.

"Come on up here," he said, motioning me with his finger.

I wobbled a little when my heels hit the floor. Once I was steady, I eyed Amy's now empty fish bowl, regretting our quick affair.

The fans squealed in delight, and people cheered. I searched for Kill, and spotted his head above the crowd, making his way through the throngs of people.

He emerged after causing chaos among every one he passed. He smiled as he approached, and I giggled at the pure determination on his face. When he reached our table, he addressed Jessie and Amy as I tried to quell my giggles, while holding on to the table to make sure I didn't fall on my face.

"Ladies, I'm going to have to steal your friend for moment. Her services are required."

The people close enough to hear him made lewd comments on the services they thought he required.

"Take her," Amy said, jumping around in her seat, loving the attention focused on the table.

"Thank you," Kill said, throwing me over his shoulder as he made his way through the dance floor.

I laughed while staring at the amazing view of his ass, and thought I should petition to have this as my means of transportation from now on.

When we reached the stage, he sat me on the edge, and he hopped up, helping me stand. Jet gave Kill the thumbs up, and Van laughed behind his drums. D smiled and played along, knowing the antics would help the band's image, but there was a tightness around his eyes and mouth.

"Well, I got you up here, the least you can do is sing for us," Kill said, and the crowd chanted for me to sing for my ride.

I signaled for Van to start before Kill could, more in the moment then normal. Van laughed at Kill's surprised expression.

We sang to each other, not looking at the audience as much as we had done in the past, and I was hypnotized by his lips as they formed the lyrics. The song ended, and the fans erupted into applause and whistling.

When they calmed down, Van segued into the last song I would sing tonight. He extended the intro allowing the screams to die down so we could actually be heard.

When my set was over, Kill summoned a chair from a stagehand. I wondered if he was tired, and thought he better be ok to drive because I wasn't. When he saw me start to walk away, he stopped me.

"Where do you think you're going?"

I pointed to the girls, trying to figure out why he would ask such a dumb question. The chair finally made it up onstage, and he placed it off to the side so it wasn't interfering with band, and then led me over to it.

"Sit here; you deserve the best seat."

The audience screamed their agreement. I sat down on the chair as the boys finished their set, unable to wipe the smile off of my face.

Jet, not wanting to disappoint, jumped into the waiting arms of his lingering fans. Van held his drum sticks, coming over to me with Kill and D behind him.

Van reached me first swinging me around and telling me how great I was. He put me on the ground and kissed the top of my head, making me wobble from all of the movement.

Kill put his arm around my waist, keeping me steady. "I gotcha', Slick," he murmured in my ear.

"Sorry, Faith, I was just so excited," Van said.

"Shut up, Van, you know you can swing me around whenever you want. Amy's drink hit me harder than I expected it to."

As Van got offstage, he was surrounded by bar girls trying everything they could to get his attention. Jessie stiffened when she saw him surrounded she snatched her purse off of the chair, ready to make her escape.

Van spotted her retreat and ran straight toward her. He picked her up, swinging her around in the same fashion he had with me, except when he set her down, instead of kissing her on the head he kissed her full on the mouth.

"Do you need anything, Faith?" D asked. He kept looking at me as I leaned on Kill, letting him do the pesky job of keeping me upright.

"I'm good, thanks D. I'm ready for bed," I said, yawning widely and snuggling further into Kill.

"I can take Faith home if you want to stay and party for a while, Kill?"

I was too tired to register D's suggestion, the sugar and alcohol were pushing me into a wall. Kill held me tighter, and I yawned again, just wanting to go home and crawl into bed.

"No, I got it D. Thanks," Kill said.

"Are you sure? I know Gemma was looking for you. You seemed really interested in her last time," D said, and I put my hand on Kill's chest, trying to assume our normal sleep position while standing up.

"Kill, that drink's making me crash." My voice was small because it was taking all the effort I had left to speak.

"Alright Slick, let's get you home," he said into my hair. "Can you pack up without me? I'm going to get her out of here," Kill said, already moving me offstage.

"Yeah, but Gemma's going to be upset," D said loudly.

"D, stop. Now!" Kill growled, as we walked off.

"Hey Kill, want to come back to my place?" A seductive voice asked, as Kill tightened his hold on me. Her voice was husky, and I moved my head to get a glimpse of who was prolonging my sleep. My body physically lurched from the perfection standing in front of me.

She wore a low cut, tight black shirt, and a short, red leather skirt with fuck me heels. I pulled away from Kill, not wanting to show any weakness, but Kill wouldn't let me go. I tapped into the energy reserves I was trusting my body to have stored, just for situations like this.

"Hey Gemma, remember what we talked about?" Kill said.

She focused on Kill, pretending I didn't exist, and I used the time to pull myself together. I wasn't strong enough to watch women throw themselves at Kill.

I realized a relationship was never going to happen between us. I could never be secure enough for him to be surrounded by women. I wished he would take her up on her offer so I could hurry up and get my heart broken.

"Hey Kill. I'm really tired. Maybe I can get one of the girls to take me home so you can stay."

I refused the tears wanting to form, telling myself it was bound to happen.

"No, Slick, I got you," he said. His face was emotionless, but his eyes told me there wasn't a chance in hell I was going to be anywhere but with him.

"Alright," I sighed, defeated.

"Gemma, I have to get her home." Kill flashed her his performer smile. I remained standing up straight, even though all I wanted to do was slump into Kill.

"I'll be here whenever you need me," she purred, and kissed him on the cheek.

A primal urge ran through me to push her off him and claim his as mine. I knew it wouldn't be fair to either of us if I pretended I was ready in order to get some skank off him.

Kill turned his head, causing her to leave a lipstick smear as her lips trailed over it. She leaned back and put on a fake smile, but her eyes glowed with anger.

"Are you alright, Slick?" he asked, in my ear, and I nodded my head, not trusting my tongue to form words other than, '*back off bitch, he's mine.*'"

He sighed as we made our way to the table. "Hey guys, I'm going to get little Miss Lightweight home. She's crashing pretty hard from the sugar, alcohol and adrenaline."

Van and Jet both told Kill to get me home and not to worry about packing up. Amy sat at the table looking like I felt. She was practically wilted on her chair, staring off into the distance.

"Actually, can you take Amy home for me?" Jet asked, putting his arms around her.

"Yeah, no problem. Jess, do you want to ride home with us?" Kill asked.

"No, I'll ride home with Van." Her eyes drooped, and I didn't know how much longer she was going to be able to sit upright.

"No, Jessie girl, go home with Kill and get in our bed. I'll be home soon," Van said, pulling Jessie up into his arms.

I waited for her to argue, but I guess the night had gotten to her too, because she allowed Van to guide her, along with Jet who was carrying Amy, and me, snuggled into Kill out the back door to the car.

When we got home, I helped Kill wake the girls up so we could shuffle them into the house. They walked upstairs, bumping off each other and the walls as they made their way up to their boyfriends' rooms. I leaned on the wall in front of the stairs, trying to find the energy needed for the journey I was about to make.

Kill came up behind me and chuckled. I tried to turn my head, but it had become so heavy the thought of moving it gave me a headache. Kill carried me as I melted into him. When we got to my room, he put me on the bed, and I cuddled into the pillow on his side.

"Come on Slick, you can't wear that to bed," he groaned.

I opened an eye, glaring down at my still dressed body, hating clothes at the moment. Taking off my shoes, I let them fall to the floor and hoped I wasn't scuffing them with my mistreatment. I went to take my shirt off, but Kill stopped me as my hands started to rise.

"Hold on," he said, sounding panicked.

"Come on Killer, you've seen plenty of naked girls. Am I so deplorable you can't see me naked?" I asked pouting.

"That's it Slick, I don't want to see you naked because you're deplorable. Shit, only you would use the word deplorable while you're drunk," he complained.

"Then why won't you help me get undressed?" I asked, flopping back on the bed to unbutton my jeans so I could shimmy out of them.

"I've been trying to be a good friend to you. The self-control I've used while around you should have me on the way to getting my sainthood. I know you feel it too. The jealousy coming off of you when Gemma kissed me was palpable. We're too close for me to hurt my chances now. So please, get undressed and put something on, or I'll go get one of the girls."

"Fine, don't go get the girls. Go get changed, and by the time you get back, I'll be dressed," I said.

"Alright, I'll be right back."

I got up quickly taking off my jeans, shirt, and bra and throwing them on the dresser. Picking up my shoes I put them back in my closet, apologizing to them for being lazy earlier.

Using all the energy I had to throw on a sports bra with my underwear. I contemplated putting on something more, but my energy was spent. Crawling under the covers I put my head on Kill's pillow.

I barely remembered Kill slipping under the covers and pulling me into him. Caught somewhere between sleep and awake, I dreamt of Kill touching my naked skin on a private beach, when he cussed at me for making his resistance falter by only wearing underwear and a bra.

I wanted to argue it was a bathing suit, but realized I was only wearing a bra and underwear in bed in real life, and before I could determine what was real, I fell asleep again.

# CHAPTER 29

The next two weeks were on fast forward. Rumors of our love child died down, but every once in awhile I would catch a customer staring at my stomach. Since I was done with my thesis and waiting for my professor to get back with me, I didn't stay in my room as often.

Kill and I sometimes would go to the park. I would read while he wrote in his notebook, or take out his acoustic guitar and strum it as he hummed along to a new song. Those were by far my favorite days.

One day, we wasted all day sitting at home in the living room singing. We made a game where I tried stumping him with songs, thinking he wouldn't be able to play them off the top of his head. I hadn't been able to get him yet.

Other days, we would go on an adventure, ending up at the Zoo, or in Washington for the day, shopping or people watching. The more time I spent with Kill, the more I recognized I was an idiot to think I hadn't already given him my whole heart. I had a sneaking suspicion he had from the moment I met him.

I practiced with the boys when they needed me, and was now in the rotation to sing with them at Ray's and The Note every week.

I no longer saw Jason's car across the street from Ray's, but I continued to get notes on my car at least three times a week. By sheer luck, I was able to collect them without the boys finding out.

Martha had moved in with my dad, and I had a feeling they were going to get married sometime soon. Amy and Jet were still going strong, spending the night at Amy's house most of the time, and only coming over for practice and dinner. Dinner became one of my favorite times of the day, except for at night when I could snuggle into Kill.

Jessie and Van were up and down in their relationship, and I could time their fights by whether or not she had talked to her parents. She still hadn't told Van about her past, but her calls to her parents were fewer than they used to be.

Anytime I would try and broach the subject, she would get upset and tell me she would do it on her own time. Trent had tried to call me a couple of times, and I refused to answer. I felt bad for avoiding him, but I just wasn't ready for him.

After I had sung at The Note, Ray's seemed to be even more crowded. With the influx of customers, we were running around trying to keep up with the demand.

I was talking to Ryan, Jessie, and Denise, when a group of business men came in. They were well dressed, so we assumed Bambi would pounce on them like the gold digger she was. None of us bothered moving as we gossiped about Denise's new man.

One of the men gave us impatient glare at the same time I looked up to make sure Bambi was taking care of them. When our eyes connected, he made an irritated *what the hell* gesture with his arms.

I shrugged off the bar and walked toward him since Bambi had magically disappeared. When I reached them, Mr. Impatient rolled his eyes, obviously annoyed. "About fucking time," he glowered, making his friends laugh uncomfortably.

"Sorry, the waitress who handles this table has disappeared. What can I get you?" I asked, wanting to placate them.

"Nice, blame it on some invisible person, because you're too incompetent and lazy to do your fucking job."

It astonished he would say something like that in front of people. I was used to Jason pretending to be a good guy in front of people, seeing an organic asshole in the wild took me by surprise.

"I'm sorry. What do you guys want?" I asked, looking around for Bambi.

"Ok, I get it, if I talk to you like the piece of shit you are, I get you motivated enough to take my order," he sneered, smirking at me.

Turning around, I refused to deal with him. Tears formed not because of the way he was talking to me, but because I was letting him. I wished I had the gumption to turn around and tell him off, but instead, I allowed myself to back down.

I was so busy trying not to let my emotions take over, I didn't see Kill standing behind me until I ran into his chest.

Once again, I was the damsel-in-distress and he was going to fix it for me. Why was I so pathetic? I hated myself for being so weak.

"Is there a problem here, Faith?" he asked. His voice was menacing. I pulled away from him and plastered on my fake smile, sick and tired of having to be rescued.

"Nope, I was just helping Bambi by taking one of her tables, but she should be back soon enough," I said, wondering if the guys at the table had enough sense to keep their mouths shut while Kill was staring them down, ready to maim.

"Are you sure, because it didn't look that way from where I was standing."

I took his arm and escorted him away from the table, done with the drama. Kill relented, and let me steer him toward his table. "Where are the boys?" I asked, noticing the table was empty, and I hadn't heard Jet enter with his usual exuberance.

"They're still at home. Jet and Amy were....doing what Jet and Amy do. Van was moping around because Jessie had to call her parents, and D was on the phone. I decided to come over early and get some food."

His face was tight, and the whole time he talked, he stared at the businessmen, who were now giving their orders to Bambi, and from the look on her face, they seemed to be behaving toward her under Kill's scrutiny.

"Well, what can I get you?" I asked, trying to pull his attention from the table of douchebags because nothing good could come of it.

He didn't answer me, because he was busy keeping watch. I snapped my fingers in front of his face.

"Hello," I said, finally getting his attention.

"What do you want to eat?" I asked, exasperated with the situation as a whole, and taking it out on him.

"What?" he asked, trying to keep his attention on me, but his eyes keep flitting away.

"Nothing, let me know if you decide to order," I snapped and turned on my heels.

"Hey sexy beast, what are you doing?" Ryan asked when I slid up to the bar. She didn't move her eyes to look at me. She stayed steady as she poured a drink with different layers of purple.

"What the hell is that?" I asked, mesmerized at her pouring, like everyone else at the bar.

"It's a purple haze," she said, finishing the different layer's and standing back to admire her creation proudly.

"Put it on the tray for me, hun. I don't want to mess it up," Denise said, eyeing it with worry.

Ryan laughed at her wariness and put it on the tray, she walked away slowly, trying not to jostle it. Ryan noticed Kill sitting at the table by himself, or as by himself as he could get. There were a couple bar floozies surrounding him, tossing their hair and pushing their after markets in his face.

"When did Kill get here?" Ryan asked. "Did he come in here alone?" She questioned when she had searched the whole bar and didn't locate the rest of the JackholeS.

"Yeah, the guys were busy, so he decided to come in early to get something to eat," I explained.

"What does he want? I will put it in for him," Ryan asked, and I realized my mistake too late.

"He didn't know just yet," I said, as nonchalant as possible.

"You mean to tell me a guy who's in here all of the time doesn't know what he wants?"

I squirmed under the look she shot me.

"What's going on with you two?"

"Nothing!" I exclaimed, wishing my voice didn't sound as guilty as I felt.

"Be careful, Faith. He isn't a one girl kind of guy, and I don't want to see you get hurt."

We stared at Kill, who removed his attention from the table of douchebags.

"It isn't like that," I said, walking over to him.

"Have you decided what you want yet?" I asked breathlessly.

He smiled widely at me, and I melted a little. "Yeah, but I'll settle for a patty melt, Kill style, for now," he said, pulling me closer to him.

The bar skanks bristled at the attention I received and I had to suppress the smirk.

"What exactly is *Kill style*?" I asked, letting my body press into him while ignoring the death glares.

I was testing my ability to handle the fan-girls, and the uneasy feeling in my stomach was showing me I wasn't handling it well at all. Kill whispered in my ear, making chills explode all over my body. My nipples hardened, and my inner thighs quivered as the hot air ghosted over my neck.

"If I told you, I would have to kill you, and what a waste that would be."

His lips turned up into a grin as a shiver ran through me. I wobbled away, talking to him over my shoulder. "Fine, have it your way, Killer, but I like to live on the wild side."

He laughed as I walked away, and I could feel the death glares climb to annihilate from Kill's table skanks.

"So, did you get his order, or were you to busy pissing off most of the girls in this place?" Ryan asked when I walked up to the bar.

I snickered, and told her Kill's order. She yelled over her shoulder toward the kitchen window.

"I could have done that," I said, as Jessie and Denise made their way over.

Ryan looked at me like I said something highly offensive. "Nobody gets to yell at Dax except me," she said, turning around slightly and telling him to hurry his ass up to prove her point.

"Got it," I replied, making Jessie and Denise giggle.

"Where are the guys?" Jessie asked.

"They'll be here later. Kill wanted to come in early and eat," I said, not wanting to get in the middle of Jessie's relationship.

"Didn't you cook dinner?" she asked suspiciously, like she had just caught me in a lie to keep Van out of trouble.

"I did, but you know how boys are; they're always hungry. Why don't you text Van and ask him when he will be here," I suggested.

"I'm not his keeper. Obviously he has something or someone better to do than come and hang out with me," she snarled.

Ryan opened her mouth to defend Van, but Jessie stomped away. "She seriously needs to get her head out of her ass. Van's head over heels in love with her. She's just looking for an excuse to push him away," Ryan said, as we watched Jessie walk around the bar with a fake smile on her face.

"I know, but she isn't going to listen to any of us. She has to get over her issues and be truthful to Van," I replied.

Dax yelled at Ryan, and asked if it was fast enough for her bossy ass. After they traded a couple more jabs, I finally got Kill's food.

Most of the table skanks had cleared since they couldn't seem to entice Kill. I sat Kill's food in front of him, and turned, but he snatched my hand, pulling me toward him.

"Stay for a while. The bar isn't busy, and I'm lonely," he said.

I made a point to look around the table at the girls still hanging around. It made me laugh he said he was alone when there were three girls hovering around ready to do anything to entertain him.

"Fine, but I get a bite," I countered, eyeing his plate.

Kill style was a patty melt on sourdough with avocado and lots of melted cheese, and it looked delicious.

"I wouldn't have it any other way," he replied, handing me half of the sandwich.

"Oh my, this is amazing," I moaned, taking a bite.

Kill laughed, and I felt the rumble of his body sink into my core. After polishing off the half the sandwich, I felt full and content.

"I don't think I've ever seen you eat that much; it was kind of was hot," he whispered into my shoulder.

I rolled my eyes, trying not to let him see how badly I wanted to attack him. Just then, the bell rang, and Jet walked through with Amy on his back. "Miss me motherfuckers?" he yelled, and the bar patrons clapped as he galloped to the table with Amy giggling on his back.

Van walked in hesitantly and spotted Jessie as she was refilling one of her tables. He stopped and D ran into him, since he was looking at his phone. D frowned at Van before making his way toward the table. Van kept looking at Jessie, waiting for a clue of how his night was going to go.

Jessie smiled at him, and after she finished refilling her table, she went over to him and kissed him lightly on the lips. Van pulled her back in, kissing her soundly while the bar cheered and whistled. When he let her go, he put his arm around her waist and walked her to the table with a smile on his face.

I drove home by myself since Kill had driven his car to the bar, and as silly as it was, I missed him.

Even with Ryan, Jess, and D warning me away from Kill, I had to admit, in the time I had been living with him, he hadn't done anything to confirm that their warnings should be heeded.

When we got home, I started to cramp from the impending civil war reenactment that would happen in my pants. I hunched over as I went upstairs, and put on my baggy sweatpants, and a tank top.

Everyone was in the living room when I came in. Kill's jaw was flexing with frustration. I quirked an eyebrow and he shrugged. I loved he was just as annoyed as I was that he wouldn't be able to hold me. I sat down next to him, as the boys argued about what to watch.

Jet ended up winning and put in the newest scary movie. D sat next to me, and I was uncomfortable by how close he was.

Kill moved his hand behind me and wormed his way under my tank top so we were touching skin to skin. I jumped when the murderer came out of the shadows and hacked his victim in two.

Kill laughed at my reaction, and I elbowed him in the side. He moved his hand out of my shirt and put it around my shoulders, pulling me into him.

"Come here Slick, I'll keep you safe," he whispered in my ear, so he wasn't disturbing everyone else.

D saw me reclining on Kill, and his eyes flashed with

anger as he got up from the couch. "I'm going to bed," he said, glaring at us on the couch.

"Are you scared? Do you want me to tuck you in?" Jet asked in a sing song voice.

I internally groaned. This was not the time to make fun of D. He flipped Jet off, before glancing at us one more time and stomping upstairs.

"Night D," I said, unsure if I was making it better or worse.

When the movie ended, Jet and Amy went upstairs, and Van and Jessie followed shortly after. I stayed reclined on Kill, as he tried to find something to watch.

"Are you ready for bed?" Kill asked when I started to doze off on him.

I nodded my head yes. He turned off the T.V, and carried me to bed. When he placed me down on the bed, we heard D's door open. Kill put his finger to his lips, signaling me to keep quiet. I nodded my head showing him I understood.

He walked out of my room and shut the door. I faintly heard him and D talk, but couldn't make out the words. After they were done, they went into their respective bedrooms, and I slowly let out the breath I was holding.

I turned on my music and waited for Kill. It seemed like forever before my door cracked open, and he crept in. I lifted the covers up, and shut my music down.

"You're awake?" he asked, as he pulled me to him and we got situated in our sleeping position.

"I don't know if I can sleep without you anymore," I admitted into the darkness.

"Good," he responded, and rubbed my back, lulling me to sleep with his gentle strokes.

# CHAPTER 30

My impending visit from aunt Flo moments away when I crawled out of bed. I made my way sluggishly into the bathroom to plug everything up, discovering I only had a couple of plugs left. Downstairs, Kill reclined on the couch looking as delicious as ever, and I wanted to throw something at his perfect head. He looked down at my night clothes.

"No run today Slick?" he asked.

I shook my head, walking to the refrigerator and pouring what was left of the chocolate milk and guzzling down the chocolaty goodness. I mentally added another gallon to my rapidly growing shopping list.

"Are you feeling alright?" he asked, getting up to get closer to me.

D came in, and although I didn't mind Kill knowing my monthly curse had returned, I wasn't ready to share with D.

"Yeah, I'm not feeling very good. I'm going to lounge around to see if I can kick this," I said, rinsing out my glass and putting it in the dishwasher.

"You don't have to practice with us today if you don't feel good," D said worriedly.

"I'll try; I don't want to let you guys down."

"Go lay back down, and I'll come up and check on you later," Kill said from behind me as he rubbed my shoulders with his strong hands.

I didn't move, letting his magic hands massage the knots out of my tense shoulders. D cleared his throat. I was barely able to open my eyes with the amazingness that was happening.

"Don't worry about it, we'll practice tomorrow," D responded, closing the refrigerator door, and walking past us.

When D had retreated out of the kitchen, Kill stopped rubbing my shoulders and pulled me into his chest, putting his chin on the top of my head.

"Why'd you stop?" I whined, sounding like a tired two

year old.

"Sorry. I thought I heard you snore, so I figured my unpaid labor was no longer required."

"I don't snore," I replied, elbowing him in the side.

"Come on, let's get you to bed."

Jet made his way downstairs, with Amy around his waist. They didn't seem to notice us, because they were too wrapped up in each other. Kill took my hand, and we went right by them as they made out against the banister.

Once we made it into my room, I couldn't hold back the laughter at Jet and Amy's love-a-thon.

"Ahh, there's my girl," Kill grinned. "I was worried about you. You didn't look so hot this morning," he said, getting comfortable on the bed.

"Yeah, sorry about that. I swear if you aren't rescuing me, I'm not feeling good. It is kind of annoying," I pouted as we got into bed.

"Enough. You need to get over this hang up you have about me rescuing you, and you've been feeling fine for the past couple weeks. It's hard on your body when you're constantly going as much as you do, and I don't even want to think about what it's going to be like when you start school, so give yourself a break. Hey I forgot to ask you, what happened last night with those guys anyway?" He went back to searching through the channels as if he didn't care about my answer, but the tick in his jaw gave him away.

"Nothing," I replied.

The glare he shot me told me he wasn't going to let my answer slide.

"He was just being a macho ass in front of his friends," I answered, snatching the remote, needing to do something with my hands.

"Why didn't you tell him off?" Kill asked, taking the remote back.

"He wasn't worth it," I responded, shrugging like it was inconsequential in the bigger scheme of life.

"You're worth it."

His words shot through me, sending energy straight to my shattered heart. We continued to watch T.V. as the Midol made its way into my system.

I got up, testing my body to see if I was ready to face the world. Kill stayed where he was, eyeing me and waiting to pull me back down if I showed any signs of pain. I rummaged through my closet and pulled out a pair of capri pants and a tank top.

"Where are you going?" he asked, still not moving from his position on my bed.

"To take a shower. I can't bum around all day," I responded, making him smile at my implication.

"Need any help?" he asked, his eyes went bright with mischief, and if my uterus wasn't purging itself like it was auditioning for the role of the bucket in Carrie, I might've taken him up on the offer.

"I got it," I said, walking to the bathroom. After I was showered, I emerged out of the bathroom feeling better.

Kill was still on the bed, the remote tucked under his chin, fast asleep. I studied him while he slept, and once again I was struck by his perfection. Ryan and Jessie's warnings were on repeat in my head.

My heart stuttered as I wondered what he was going to do when I relented to his charms. It was only a matter of time before I couldn't think of a reason to keep him at arm's length.

How fast would he walk away when I surrendered to him, and how would I live without a heart beating in my body? Because when he inevitably walked away, he would take it with him.

An evil plan hatched in my head, and I laughed under my breath, right before I jumped on the bed and let out my best warrior cry. He startled awake, trying to get his bearings. He blinked as I bent over him, our noses almost touching.

"Hey, sleepy head," I said, and because he looked so irresistible, I kissed him on the tip of his nose.

"Hey, that's quite a battle cry you have going on there," he said groggily. He pulled me down so I was laying on top of his chest.

"Thanks, I worked really hard on it," I said, breathing in his calming scent.

"I see you are feeling better."

"Yep, I'm ready for practice," I replied, pushing off of him, and helping him up.

"Let's do this."

After practicing my part, I was dismissed early with the instructions not to worry about dinner duty. Remembering I needed to renew my battle supplies, I figured this would be the best time to do it.

The boys were busy with practice, and I didn't want to bother them, so I text Kill to let him know I would be back shortly. Outside, I was relieved there wasn't anything waiting for me on my car today.

After stowing my newly acquired battle equipment in my car, I spotted a frozen yogurt shop at the end of the shopping center. It was a cool day, so I figured my chocolate milk would be ok while I went and got my yogurt fix.

I walked by a small Mexican restaurant, when I heard someone call out my name. His voice penetrated my daze, and I froze on the sidewalk. The restaurant had an outdoor patio, and it was full because of the nicer weather we were having.

Jason came toward me, and the only thing separating us was the low wrought iron fence surrounding the patio. My stomach churned as he stepped closer to me. My brain screamed for me to run, but I just stood there, unable to move.

He had a fake, charming smile on his face, and I had to swallow the bile rising up in my throat. Clarity finally snapped me into place. He was approaching me in front of witnesses; this could be my chance to finally nail him.

"Hey Babe, it's been a while. How have you been?" he asked when he reached me.

I needed to play this cool, so I could get the police on my side this time. "Jason, we can't be near each other. I have a restraining order on you," I said, wanting everyone to hear he was violating it in front of them.

He had the audacity to laugh like I had just told him the funniest joke he had ever heard. My stomach dropped to my feet from the evil smirk on his face.

"Faith, that was a misunderstanding. My dad explained everything to the police and had it dropped weeks ago. I love you. You'll always be mine. I have to go out of state for awhile."

His eyes went hard when he mentioned his trip. "We'll talk when I get back. I forgive you."

My hands went limp, my yogurt dropped to the ground, splattering my legs with sticky coolness, but I didn't care. I had nothing to protect me anymore. Jason was able to take away my sense of security in seconds.

"Are you ok?" Jason asked, reaching for me.

His movement snapped me out of my shocked state, and I turned around and ran to my car. My legs were shaking uncontrollably, but miraculously kept up until I slid into my car.

Jason called after me, but not for one second did I consider stopping. My ears buzzed, and I tried my hardest not to pass out.

On my way home, I became more frantic. I couldn't think of any other solution except to leave immediately, and get as many miles in between me and Jason as possible. I almost convinced myself to keep driving, and leave everything, but somehow I ended up in front of the house.

Jumping out of my car I ran inside. I didn't stop running until I was at my closet pulling everything off the hangers and throwing it on the floor so I could stuff it in bags.

I didn't hear Kill come in; the buzzing in my ears drowned out all noise except the panic running through me. Kill tried to get my attention, and when I didn't respond, he grabbed me from behind, pinning my arms to my side.

I screamed, picturing Jason behind me, finally able to finish the job. I struggled, whispering Jason's name, unable to make noise around the lump lodged in my throat. Kill removed his arms immediately and stepped away from me like I had burned him.

I turned around, ready to fight for my life. When I saw Kill standing in front of me, all the fight left me, and I sagged to the ground. He stepped toward me seething; his chest was rising and falling quickly, and his jaw twitched.

"So this is it? I knew you would go back to him," he sneered, running his hands through his hair, not taking his disgust-filled eyes off me.

# The End.

# SNEAK PEEK

Faith and Kill's journey is just beginning. Please know, not only do I believe in happily ever afters, so do my characters. As an apology for the sudden cut off, here's the first chapter to the next installment of The JackholeS series.

# Surviving Faith
## Kill

I knew Faith wasn't going to leave me for Jason, but the panic running through me refused to let me think straight.

"This is it?" My words were harsh when they flew out of my mouth, and I didn't miss when she flinched from my cruelty, her bright red face draining of color. My lack of support hurt her, just as much as it hurt me. I felt like my body was ripping in two.

"You're an idiot. I'm not going back to him, I'm running from him, and fuck you for the vote of confidence you have in me, asshole!" She dug her finger into my chest.

Her words were the final blow and my body sagged with relief. I couldn't act rationally when I was around her. I had all the confidence in the world in her. It was me who wasn't strong enough to handle her getting hurt. She'd been through too much to run back to her controlling abusive ex.

We both didn't deserve her.

"Why are you running?" Even though I felt I wasn't worthy, didn't mean I was going to let her go.

"Because, asshole, he had the restraining order revoked...." Her voice caught and my vision blurred with red. I was expecting a show down with her ex soon enough. I was relying on the restraining order to give me some time to think of a plan.

"He did *what?*" I felt the veins in my neck throb. I promised to protect her, and wasn't going to lose her.

"The restraining order... His dad had it removed, and all I could think when I found out was getting as far away from him as possible!" I'm not sure she noticed, but when she mentioned leaving, she stepped closer, until our toes touched.

"So what, you were just going to grab everything and run? Not tell anyone?" *Not tell me?*

"Yes, that was my plan before you interrupted me." She was still close. My fear of her leaving abated. Her actions showed me she was almost as far gone as I was.

"You aren't running away from him. If you do, you'll be doing it your whole life." I clenched my fists to my side, so I wouldn't pull her toward me. We both needed to calm down before we touched.

"What am I supposed to do, Kill? Please, give me advice, since you seem to know everything."

"Fight back. You don't seem to have a problem doing that with me," I answered, exasperated. I couldn't understand how someone who fought with me over everything laid down and let others walk over her.

"That's because I trust you!"

I opened my mouth, but what she just screamed in my face registered before I could get a word out. She trusted me. I'd been waiting months for those magical words, and I finally got them.

Before she could continue her rant, I roughly mashed my lips to hers. She threw her arms around my neck, holding on for dear life. Not expecting her to submit so easily, I groaned at her reaction. Reaching down, I grabbed on to her magnificent ass, hauling her up so she could wrap her legs around my waist. I sucked her bottom lip into my mouth as my raging erection brushed against her center.

The taste of my Faith exploded into me when I plunged my tongue into her mouth. I carried her toward the bed, and we tumbled onto the blankets, our mouths never parting, melded together in the passion we were finally giving into.

"Fuck, please don't make me stop," I hissed as I made my way down her neck, sucking hard on her sensitive skin. Instead of answering, she pulled my head back and bit my bottom lip. I pushed into her, wanting her to know what she

**411**

did to me.

"I don't care if a high school band marches through here, I need you," I told her. I refused to be denied this time. The cat and mouse game we'd been playing since we met was over. I wasn't sure who caught who, but I was done keeping my distance. I placed the seam of my jeans into her heat, making her gasp at the contact.

"You like that?" I growled, rocking into her again, making her shudder.

Her legs wrapped tighter around me. She was close to losing control, frantically clawing at my back to get more friction. I came back to her mouth, needing another taste, letting my tongue slide in to explore. She sucked on it with need.

"Fuck, don't do that. You already have me so close to the edge. You're going to make me embarrass myself." She giggled and rocked up into me with her lush curves. I have never had a girl giggle while I was on top of her. "That's it."

Faith let out a startled breath when I took her nipple in my mouth through her t-shirt, making me almost explode in my pants. The moment I first saw her I wanted her. Now that I've had her, she was in my blood, pumping through my heart and claiming me completely.

I nipped her perky nipple and her hips skyrocketed off the bed, making me chuckle when she held onto my head to keep me from leaving the greedy peak. "I can't have one jealous of the other," I explained, moving to her other nipple, giving it the same attention.

Tasting her through her clothes was not enough. I needed her, and I needed her now. I would take it slow the next time, but at this moment I needed to drive into her, making her mine.

"Do you have any condoms?" I asked as I ground into her.

I felt some of her desire evaporate. Shit, I don't know how I would be able to pull myself off her if she denied me. I wouldn't force myself on her, and as much as it would hurt, I would walk away and stay patient. My dick wept at the thought of not being able to thrust into her.

"What's wrong? Did I push you too fast?" I went to move off her, but she pulled me back. God, she felt like heaven. We were breathing heavily, and she shook her head as she tried to find her voice.

I tried to apologize, but she put her finger to my lips. As I bit the pad of her finger, she inhaled sharply, making my dick jump in my pants

"We can't have sex," she finally said. Every awful scenario I could think of ran through my head. I went to move again, but she latched her legs around me. I was losing control quickly, and having her so close was making it hard to think. "Once a month, I have an affair with Mr. Tampon. It lasts about a week, and it started today."

I laughed at her description, while my body cried. Fuck. There was no way I was going to last a *minute* when we finally got past all the obstacles in our way. She was opening up to me, and I wasn't going to ruin it. Dropping my forehead to hers, we stared at each other.

"Of course you would be on your period. I think the world's against us." I rolled off her, afraid I was crushing her, but bringing her with me so we wouldn't be separated.

"Where are the guys?" she asked. Alarm covered her face when she thought about how loud she'd been. If it wasn't for her period, I would have had her screaming my name in seconds; I didn't care who the fuck heard her. She was mine, and people needed to know. Especially, her douche box ex-boyfriend.

I reminded myself to keep it slow. Faith was skittish and she needed to acclimate herself to our relationship slowly. "Jet, Amy, Van, and Jessie went to see a movie, and D had a business meeting. Don't worry, nobody heard you screaming my name in ecstasy."

"I did not scream your name... yet." Her voice was husky with desire and it shot straight to my dick. Adding the 'yet' at the end showed me just how perfect she was for me.

"No? Well, then, I'll have to try harder," I told her, hitching one of her legs across my thighs. I noticed her rubbing them together and I knew exactly what she was doing. If I was going to walk around with blue balls she was going to suffer too.

"Sorry, you're going to have to suffer like me."

"You're evil," she pouted.

"Sorry, Slick. I've had a hard-on every time you're near me. You're not getting off that easy," I shot back as she laughed at my word choice.

"Really?" she asked curiously, propping up on her elbow to look at me.

"What?" I was having a hard time following her questions with all my blood being diverted to my pants.

"I turn you on?" she asked her green eyes wide.

Seriously? Did she not realize how hung up on her I was? I grabbed her chin so she couldn't avoid me when I answered her.

"Yes, you turn me on all the time. I'm afraid the band thinks I have a thing for them since I seem to be walking around with a hard dick all day."

She giggled, and I cursed her period. "What about you? Do I turn you on?" I asked, not letting her chin go. I wanted to see how much she was willing to admit.

"You do," she stated truthfully. I couldn't stop the cocky smirk from forming on my face.

I kissed her lightly, wanting to let her know how much she meant to me. She wasn't ready to hear it, so I showed her with my actions. She moaned into my mouth, and I took the opportunity to slip my tongue inside. I was ruined for anyone else as soon as our lips connected.

This kiss was more exploratory, getting to know each other's likes. Claiming each other's pleasure. I wanted to take it slow, but she undid my resolve when she bit my bottom lip.

Our kiss became more passionate, and she yanked at the bottom of my shirt to get to my skin. She ran her fingers over my back before latching on to my shoulders. I crashed into her, pressing my body against her, both of us grinding into each other like teenagers.

Her nipples dug into my chest. I reached under her shirt, and pinched the heated tips. She bucked under me and kissed me with abandon. I held my breath as her hands traveled down my back, reaching the waistband of my jeans.

414

When she hesitated, I realized we weren't going to get much further. I put my forehead on hers and cursed the piece of cotton residing in the one place on earth I craved. My erection dug in between her thighs and I ground my teeth together to get myself under control.

"This week's going to be fucking torture."

My eyes snapped open when she laughed. Yeah, I was definitely going to make her pay. "You think this is funny, do you?" I asked, stroking my hands up her sides, stopping when I reached her ribs. She tensed, guessing my intention.

"No, please don't," she pleaded, still laughing.

"I'm going to make this agony for you, too. You're going to feel my pain," I whispered.

Instead of tickling her, I ran my hands under her breasts, stroking them through her bra. Fuck, I had to be careful. I was trying make her crazy from lust but I was doing a fucking good job getting myself worked up. I leaned down and bit one of the peaks, unable to stop myself.

When she latched on to my hair and arched into me, it was all I could take. I moved so I wasn't touching her.

When she came out of her haze, I was already channel surfing, propped up on the headboard. My dick was so hard it hurt, but I needed to get a handle on myself if I was going to make it through the week. The game of torture had begun.

"You're an ass," she grumbled. God, she was fucking adorable.

She wrapped her arms around herself and pouted. Shit, I wasn't going to make it a week. She wouldn't budge when I tried to pull her toward me.

"Ahh, come on, Slick, don't be mad at me. I just wanted you to get a taste of what I'm going through." I shot her an innocent look, and her resolve crumbled right in front of my eyes. She was mine. I just had to wait for her to admit it.

"See, isn't that better?" I asked when she snuggled up to me. With her next to me, I felt like I was unstoppable. I didn't know how I was going to do it, but I would get her life completely out of her ex's clutches and into mine.

I pulled her closer as my desire to dive into her calmed. At least it did until she took my nipple firmly in her teeth and sucked on it. I was going to be permanently hard if she kept this up.

"It's war, you know that, right?" I told her through clenched teeth, my hands buried in her long brown hair.

When she settled into me, I asked the one thing I knew would keep me from rolling over and dry humping her. "So, what happened today?"

With a deep breath, she told me the story of running into her ex at a restaurant. My body seethed, and fear crept through me. I knew the asshole was unhinged, and his dad was high up, but to have the order removed was terrifying. I tugged her tighter to me as images of him hurting her assaulted me.

Faith was different. She was *it* for me. I thought I had feelings for Melissa, but now I realized it was just guilt because I couldn't protect her from her ex. When I met Melissa I wanted to help her get away from her boyfriend. I didn't love her; it was just an overwhelming sense of compassion that pushed me to help her.

I wouldn't feel guilt if Jason got his hands on Faith. I wouldn't feel anything because without her, there would be no life for me.

As soon as she finished her story, she jumped up and flew downstairs. Terror rushed through me as I ran to catch her. I caught up with her just when she unlocked her trunk and pulled out a gallon of chocolate milk.

My panic subsided from the relief on her face when she realized it was still cold. Fuck, she was perfect. While I helped her gather the rest of her groceries, I caught movement out of the corner of my eye.

When my head snapped to full attention, the figure was gone.

"What is it?" Faith questioned as we made it into the house.

"When was the last time you talked to Trent?" I tried to keep cool. If it wasn't for the fact I had just broken down her defenses, I would have been running after the fucker. I wasn't sure it was him, but it made me edgy.

The way Trent stared at her, through his black rimmed glasses, when he didn't think anyone was looking made my blood boil. Of course men would be attracted to her, but there was something different in Trent's eyes. His gaze was similar to the look her ex gave her the night I served him the restraining order. My Faith seemed to attract the crazies, and I was going to take it upon myself to protect her from them.

"Ummm, the last time I saw him was when he came into the bar. He tried to call me a couple of times, but I haven't answered the phone. Why?" She walked into the kitchen to put the groceries away.

"I thought I saw him walking down the street."

"Huh, he doesn't even live around here. It was probably just someone who looked like him," she said, shrugging it off.

"Yeah," I replied, trying to shake the bad feeling I had away.

The rest of the day, we employed war tactics, torturing one another when we found the opportunity. Taking my opportunity when she bent down to get into the refrigerator, I leaned over and sucked on the back of her neck, making her moan quietly.

I was pretty smug, thinking she wouldn't get her revenge because everyone came home while she was cooking dinner.

She was patient though, and after dinner was cleaned up we were on the couch watching T.V. She leaned over pretending to get something, and brushed her hand across my half-hard dick. I had to readjust myself on the couch to hide my erection. She was going to kill me.

Feeling excited when I snuck into her room, I wondered if I was going to get any sleep tonight. I knew we didn't have all of our issues resolved, but with every touch I was breaking down her defenses.

When I pulled her to my side, I grabbed her chin and lifted her lips to mine. All of the touching we'd been doing had driven me crazy. I couldn't wait a second longer to taste her.

The kiss started off gentle, but when she melted into me and pushed her fingers into my hair, I lost it. Growling, I bit her bottom lip before sucking it into my mouth as I yanked her closer.

When my bare hands skimmed under her shirt, she lost

control. She moved so she was straddling me, fisting her hands in my hair and plunging her tongue into my mouth, lost in the passion. She drove me crazy as she shamelessly rubbed herself against me.

Wrapping my arms around her, I flipped us over, needing to take control before I came in my pants. I pressed my bulge into her heat, wanting to be as close to heaven as I could.

I kissed down her face until I reached her neck. Sucking on it, I grazed my teeth over the sensitive area that drove her insane. She moaned loudly and tensed.

"What's wrong?" I asked at her mood shift.

"The boys."

"Fuck them. I can't control myself when I'm with you, and any resolve was removed when I had my first taste of you. When your affair with Mr. Tampon is over, I'm going to drag you up here and do what I've been wanting to since the moment I saw you. I don't care if you scream loud enough for the whole neighborhood to hear." I held back telling her she was mine. It hurt to keep myself from claiming her even if it was with my words.

"Deal," she replied, making my cock throb.

Moving off her, I pulled her to my side. I decided to let her get used to this before taking it further. Her situation gave her week to get used to being with me. She was quiet as we lay in the dark. I could hear her mind whirling, and I needed to get to her before she closed me out.

"What are you thinking, Slick?" I ran my finger over her pebbled nipple, afraid she was going to push me back into friend territory again.

"That I'm sick of fighting this thing between us," she admitted, throwing me for a complete loop.

"About fucking time," I told her as my chest puffed out. I kissed her with all the passion she unlocked with her confession.

"Kill, you realize this thing with Jason isn't over. I'm sure he has something planned."

She was trying to give me an out. What she didn't understand was I couldn't leave if I wanted to. Although I hadn't earned all of her trust, I refused to let her go, and I *wouldn't* let her get hurt. Jason would have to be dealt with. What she needed to realize was we were invincible when we were together.

"Faith, I've been with you since the moment I saw you, I'm not going anywhere. We will take care of Jason when the time comes. Now that I have you, I'm not letting you go."

Calm washed over her at my words, but I knew she wanted to argue. So, I stopped any further discussion by rolling on top of her and kissing her into submission.

# FROM THE AUTHOR:

I hope you enjoyed the first part of the JackholeS Series. I would love to hear from you. You can follow me on,
Facebook: **Joy Eileen**
Twitter: **@heyitsmejoy**
Email me at: **Joy@itsjoysworld.com**
I would greatly appreciate it if you could take the time to review Breaking Faith.

**Goodreads Breaking Faith**

**Amazon**

If you would like to get the latest news on Faith and Kill or my other projects please sign up for my newsletter.
**Joy Eileen's Newsletter**

# ACKNOWLEDGEMENTS

To acknowledge everyone who has helped me would be a book in itself. I want to thank everyone who listened to me yammer on about Faith and the JackholeS. Especially my clients who were stuck naked on my table with no escape.

Thank you to....

Lilo Abernathy for pushing me to pull this book out of the "drawer."

Ella Emerson for being the bestest friend ever.

Rebecca Fisher for scouring my first manuscript way too many times.

Andrea for printing it and changing the color of the page to pen.

Kristie for being the first person to actually read it.

Kira for polishing it all up and letting me freak out on her weekly.

Misty Buttercup for listening to me vent, and all the painful Skype calls.

Every one of my beta readers. Dayna, Maari, Melony, Alondra and everyone else I'm forgetting. I love you guys.

Kristen for my beautiful cover...Thank you so much.

Tracie Roe for the last edit.

And all of my new author friends. Finding the indie author community was like finding the greatest blanket fort, and I'm so grateful I'm home.

And to my Family. Thank you for understanding my need to hide in the writers cave, and supporting me when I needed it. You four boys are my rockstars.

And last but not least. Everyone who took the time to read the first story of Faith and Kill. Thank you for your time, I hope you enjoyed it.

# ABOUT THE AUTHOR

Joy Eileen is a born bibliophile who becomes deeply engaged with her characters, and has devoured more books than she would like to admit. She becomes obsessed with happily-ever-afters, and will read any genre that fulfills that requirement. Evading the library is something she has been known to do, because after befriending the characters returning them would be a heartbreaking event. Books are held hostage on her bookshelf, and any author that makes her ugly cry becomes her sworn enemy. Nicholas Sparks is one of the many on the list of villains.

As a massage therapist, most of Joy's stories come to her while working. With the sound of classical music, and snoring from a half covered hostage, characters are created. The victim (massage patient) has no idea that while their body is being manipulated, Joy has traveled into distant lands creating landscapes and inhabitants as she goes. Her patients should be wary as sometimes they are pulled into her stories and turned into characters. Hero or Foe? Well, that depends on how they tip.

If you or anyone you know is in a domestic violence situation please seek help.
The National Domestic Violence Hotline.
1-800-799-7233 | 1-800-787-3224 (TTY)

23641585R00258

Made in the USA
San Bernardino, CA
25 August 2015